CROSS-COUNTRY

Books By Herbert Kastle

ONE THING ON MY MIND

KOPTIC COURT

BACHELOR SUMMER

CAMERA

COUNTDOWN TO MURDER

THE WORLD THEY WANTED

THE REASSEMBLED MAN

HOT PROWL

THE MOVIE MAKER

MIAMI GOLDEN BOY

MILLIONAIRES

ELLIE

CROSS-COUNTRY

CROSS-COUNTRY

A NOVEL BY
Herbert Kastle

DELACORTE PRESS / NEW YORK

Designed by Ann Spinelli

Library of Congress Cataloging in Publication Data

Kastle, Herbert D
Cross-country.

I. Title.
PZ4.K195Cr [PS3561.A7]   813'.5'4   74-13066
ISBN: 0-440-03383-7

For Paul, Eddy, Marilyn and Arthur
...and especially Anny.

For the bourgeois, the world is fundamentally an orderly place, with a disturbing element of the irrational, the terrifying, which his preoccupation with the present usually permits him to ignore. For the Outsider, the world is not rational, not orderly.

THE OUTSIDER, by Colin Wilson

Children begin by loving their parents; as they grow older they judge them; sometimes they forgive them.

THE PICTURE OF DORIAN GRAY, by Oscar Wilde

CROSS-
COUNTRY

Prologue

She hadn't always been a cleaning lady, though some of her customers acted as if she had. She wanted to say to them that no one was *born* to vacuuming and dusting and washing other people's places. With most, however, she just did her work and counted her pay and tried not to compare or envy because envy was a sin and she didn't want to be more of a sinner than she was. But Lord, how she had to fight envying the young and pretty ones their looks, their nice homes, their softness and sweetness in life.

The big apartment house on Seventy-seventh Street held two of her ladies. One was on the twelfth floor and fat and forty and talky and jumpy like a woman without a man, though she had a man. If you could call the little old butterball that. Cloris didn't envy her. What good was a nice place and nice clothes and nice car and vacations without a real man?

The one on the second floor was a new customer, brought to Cloris by the one on the twelfth floor. That one she envied more than *any* of her ladies, and she had just about all she could handle, working two a day, six days a week. That one was *beautiful*, and class. And had money, you could tell by the furniture and the clothes. And by some jewelry she thought she'd hid real smart but hadn't because Cloris was always curious about new customers and looked around. In the bedroom, in the pocket of a fur coat, wrapped in a scarf, was a long box marked *Tiffany & Co*. Diamond earrings and a diamond necklace. Cloris tried them on; like she tried out the water bed; like she tried on some of the beautiful hats.

That one *had* to have more than one man!

Cloris had held onto *three* men, all at the same time, for a short while when she was eighteen. Then there'd been trouble. That was back in Memphis when Ike had thought he was her one and only.

She sighed, getting out of the elevator after her one-floor ride. It was all dead and finished. She had an apartment to clean. The pretty one's.

She had the extra key the doorman gave her on instructions from her customer. She unlocked apartment 2-F and went inside and put down her big rattan bag and closed the door. She started toward the kitchen, then something made her stop.

A *smell?*

She sniffed. Well, maybe . . . but she'd *seen* something for a split second; a subliminal stop light.

She began to look around the living room; then her eyes came to the bedroom doorway. She was off to the left now, having almost reached the kitchen, and couldn't see the bed or anything but one wall.

She gasped. She put a hand to her mouth. *A smear on the wall.*

"Dear Jesus," she said, and shook her head. *Not* blood. But it was brownish-red like dried blood.

Her heart was slamming her ribs and she felt faint and she moved very slowly back toward the hall door, not looking at the bedroom, telling herself she had nothing to be afraid of, yet smelling the strange smell and remembering the way the red-brown stuff was clotted on the wall and the thin lines trickling down from the clot . . .

She was at the hall door, her back to the apartment, when she asked herself what she thought she was doing. She couldn't just walk out and forget the job. And what had she seen anyway? A stain on the wall. She was *here* for stains and dirt and whatever else the rich, beautiful lady didn't want to bother with. So she'd wash it clean.

She took a breath and turned and started walking toward the bedroom.

Then she stopped.

The water bed. It had arms tied to the high brass posts up front. They dangled there, red-stumped, no shoulders.

The shoulders were down with the pretty girl lying in blood on that water bed.

Cloris sat down on the floor.

She began crying.

Softly first, then louder, then screaming until there was banging on the door and she screamed for them to come in because there were legs tied to the posts at the bottom of the bed and one hanging off and the pretty face turned into the red and the walls and curtains and window shades and even the ceiling had clumps and trickles and red and brown and it was just like the butcher shop back home when she was a child and someone took her out back where they did their own killing and the chickens and the pigs and the blood and she ran home and she wanted to run home now because of the blood and the smell, the smell was like that butcher shop, too, the fresh meat smell . . .

When someone touched her shoulder, she vomited and fainted.

1: | Monday p.m. and Tuesday a.m.

He had left his apartment-house garage and stopped at Croece's Gas Station where his long patronage and generous tips assured him a full tank of gas and the information that once he got to Pennsylvania the situation would be "real good." He headed for the Holland Tunnel and Jersey and the way west. And stopped at Brady's for a last pot of their delicate stew and a half bottle of their not-so-delicate Burgundy. And then remembered the club—Bantam Rooster, was it?—and drove into the Village, looking for it. And found the Bantam *Royal*.

That time with Judy . . .

He didn't want to think of Judy. One of the reasons, perhaps the strongest single one, he was leaving New York. Vacation, yes . . . but more than that. He *hated* this city! He hated his lifetime in this city! And Judy was the last episode of that lifetime.

He found a parking place up the street from the corner building with the red neon rooster, and took his topcoat and overnight bag from the seat. Greenwich Village was no place to leave valuables exposed. As he carried them to the trunk of the Jaguar, he heard footsteps and concentrated on placing coat and bag inside, quickly, along with his larger luggage. Only after slamming the trunk lid did he turn to look. He caught a glimpse of a girl, just her back, disappearing into the catercorner-set club entrance.

He looked around and hesitated and wondered at his reluctance to move, to either get back in his car and leave the city, or walk down the street and enter the club. He hovered, caught in an emotional aspic, unable to break free . . . until he saw someone approaching, a large man, a hulking shape, and even though it wasn't quite eight and there was no reason to believe the man was dangerous, he hurried to the corner. After all, this *was* Fun City, and the fun started early.

Inside, past the blue-suited man who extracted "a two-dollar admission fee," he found less fun than advertised by an outside sign, SWINGING TOPLESS CHICKS!, and a small lobby full of glossy photographs, the chicks in various stages of undress. There was a dimness that defied even his night-adjusted vision, and he would have stumbled into a small, round table in the room jammed full of tables if a tall girl in leotards and spike heels hadn't said, "This way, sir," and waved a pencil flashlight. She guided him between the tables to one directly in front of a stage on which a redhead with very fat boobs, and a stomach to match, was executing a desultory Go-Go under blue and red spotlights.

He ordered a double Scotch on the rocks, remembering that the strength of drinks in these places was about half what they should be, and watched the dancer. Her breasts were bare, as advertised. She looked at him and smiled and moved a bit faster. He glanced around, and realized he was the only customer seated at a table. The bar held a middle-aged couple, turned to watch the dancer, and a girl hiked up on a stool, speaking earnestly to the bartender.

The "swinging topless chick" finished her dance and trotted over to a back curtain. "Dianne, dammit, I've gone two over already!"

The piped music resumed, blasting rock. Dianne didn't appear. The dancer shouted, "That makes three you pick up on me!" and muttered imprecations and began to dance, more desultory than ever.

His drink came. He had to pay for it right then—three dollars. He tipped a dollar, though the whole show wasn't worth that much, in order to keep the waitress, not bad-looking, around for a moment's talk. She moved her body a good distance back from him as she bent to hear what he was saying over the loud music . . . and he wondered how many times she'd been grabbed.

"Not much doing, is there?" he asked.

"It's not even eight. We don't get going till maybe ten, eleven. Come around then."

He'd been around then. It had been busier, noisier, and the dancers had put more of themselves into their acts . . . but they'd left inside of an hour because Judy hadn't liked it.

Had to stop thinking of Judy. Had to watch the fat boobs. And maybe the next dancer would be better. And maybe then he'd leave; maybe then he'd be free of the strange reluctance to start his trip.

"Excuse me, can I ask you something?"

A soft voice, English-accented, and he turned to its owner. His eyes were better adjusted to the dimness now, and he could make out details. Not that it took much light to know that this was a very pretty girl. He appraised her professionally, even as he nodded and gestured at a chair.

She was shabby mod in ankle-length brown suede skirt and open leather jacket. Good face, pixie-cut blonde hair a shade too yellow, heavy breasts swinging free under a knit blouse of charcoal brown as she moved to the chair and sat down. Her legs looked nice enough when the high slit in her skirt opened, and her bottom looked trim enough, and she said, "You wouldn't happen to be traveling west, would you?"

His mouth almost sagged open. "E.S.P.?" he asked.

"My name is Lois. See what I left at the bar?" She pointed.

He didn't see, and she said, "A bedroll-pack. On the floor near the stool. I'm hitching out of New York tonight, or tomorrow, or whenever I can get a lift. Once on the road, the main highways, it'll be an easy number. But what a bummer getting out of this city!"

"What makes you think *I'm* traveling?"

"I passed you on the street. You were putting a bag and coat in the boot of your car, and I saw other luggage. And hon, take a tip. Don't leave a car like that and good leather like that out on *this* street too long."

"That takes care of the E.S.P." He smiled and she smiled and he introduced himself and wondered about taking a stranger into his car, pretty though she was. He finished his drink, stalling.

She leaned closer. "I'm not a whiz at it, but I can drive. I can help out a little with finances." She smiled wryly. "*Very* little. Thought I'd hit a friend here for a loan, but no go. Everyone's got the tights."

He nodded slowly, still undecided.

She stood up. "Let me get my things before someone hooks 'em."

She walked between the tables to the bar and hiked herself onto the stool to say something to the bartender and that high slit opened and her leg was strong; not too slender but beautifully shaped and very exciting in a calf-high boot. She got off the stool and bent for her bedroll, and that bottom was very nice indeed.

When she returned, he'd made up his mind. "All right. For a while, at least."

She smiled, standing beside him, not touching him but

very close, close enough for him to smell violets. Not an expensive smell, but that smile, that stance, promised much. "Sure," she said. "We have to be compatible. Give me half a minute." And she went off into the back where the washrooms were.

He decided on another double, and when it came took it down fast, and discovered that the bartender became generous on refills. Quite a drink, and he gasped a little and lit a cigarette . . . and saw that a new girl was on stage, high-breasted and smooth-hipped and flat-bellied with long black hair falling to her waist. He began to enjoy himself. He began to think that the blonde, Lois, might be a portent of good things.

The waitress set another double in front of him. His head was spinning, what with the wine at Brady's, and he chuckled and said, "Didn't order it."

"On the house," she said, and went to another table, where three men were crowding themselves back as far from the stage as they could get. Elderly gentlemen. Neatly dressed in a hick manner. Out-of-towners both covetous and afraid of big-city fleshpots.

He raised his glass and sipped, and wished he'd thought to ask for water on the side. But the second sip was smoother and the third smoother still and he had another cigarette and applauded loudly for the dancer and she gave him a shake of the breasts before going into her next number.

He finished the drink. And saw the blonde coming toward him. She picked up her pack and said, "Had enough yet?"

He said, "Yes," being careful not to blur the "s," and stood up. And swayed and steadied himself on the table. She came around and took his arm and said, "Like Saturday night back in Sydney."

He was embarrassed but accepted her steadying arm and said, "Be better once I get outside."

"Don't worry. Told you I can drive, if I have to."

And she might have to, he thought as they came out and turned up the street. Because it was a rocky, rocky road; he hadn't been this bombed in years. "Just sneaked up on me," he muttered. "Little wine and three Scotches . . . make that six, 'cause doubles . . ." And he remembered now the big brandy while packing. And all this hesitating and drinking was because he knew he wouldn't be coming back and after a lifetime in one city it wasn't easy . . .

They were at the car. She asked for his keys. He gave them to her, and the next thing he knew he was in the back seat, lying down. She got behind the wheel and said, "The Holland Tunnel, right? Then the Jersey Turnpike?"

His eyes were closed and he muttered yes and going-to-California and sorry. She said, "Just sack out, hon. You'll be driving in an hour."

He drifted off. But he didn't hear the engine start for quite a while, and before then the Jaguar rocked as if she was moving around, and it bothered him. It bothered him so much that he sat up quite suddenly as they were going through the tunnel, forcing his eyes to open and his mind to clear. There was a man driving. Lois sat beside him. She turned and said, "Don't get mad. This is John."

The man turned his head briefly. He had a beard and a mustache and long black hair. He looked young. "Hi, Evan."

They were coming out of the tunnel. There were gas stations and diners and taverns up ahead. Evan sucked air as hard as he could and leaned forward and put his hands on the back of the driver's seat. "Please stop at that diner up ahead." His head spun and he shook it and the bearded youth said, "But we just got going."

Evan put his hands on the youth's shoulders. Lois said, "Good idea. I could use something to eat."

Evan said, "You don't sound nearly as English now."

"Australian. You're getting used to me." She tried a smile.

Evan was angry and frightened, and relieved when the bearded youth drove off the road at the diner.

The youth said, "She always pulls the Aussie bit with strangers."

Lois said, "Not strangers, Johnnie-boy. New and interesting men."

Evan didn't bother answering their words or smiles. He was opening the door.

They all got out. He was still unsteady, but adrenalin was in his blood now and it fought the alcohol.

John walked by him. Evan grabbed his arm. "My keys, please." The bearded youth seemed to hesitate; then he handed them over, saying, "Yeah, sure. Hey, you're not mad, are you?"

He went back to the car and locked all four doors. Without looking at them, he walked to the diner.

He took a booth. They joined him, sitting together on the other side. Lois began to speak, and Evan said, "Not until I have some coffee."

Three cups and a beef sandwich later, he raised his eyes and fixed them on John. The youth fidgeted a while; then spoke.

"You think it was wrong for her to ring me into the hitch."

Evan looked at Lois. She said, "Okay. Maybe it *was* wrong. I'm sorry, honest."

John said he was going to get some cigarettes, and went to a machine near the door. He was tall and thin, perhaps six-two and no more than a hundred fifty pounds. Gaunt, but his hands were big, strong-looking, the wrists revealing bulging tendons and veins moving up under the sleeves of his jacket.

He came back and offered the cigarettes around. Lois took one and so did Evan, and John stood to light them both. He wore blue denims, faded, washed out, the way the kids liked them, but no tears in either Levis or metal-buttoned jacket.

"I'm sorry too," he said, sitting down. "It was a dumb thing to do. Lois and I met just a few days ago, see, and it's rough for a girl to hitch alone, dangerous, so she wanted . . ." He spread his hands. "A fucking dumb thing to do."

Evan said, "I don't care for obscenity. If you're asking a stranger for a favor, you should be more careful of your language."

John laughed. He had a high-pitched laugh that ended on an intake. It was a very young laugh, but Evan was no longer sure that the label "youth" fit him. He might be in his late twenties, perhaps thirty, hard to tell with all that hair.

"I didn't think anyone considered . . . *that* word, an obscenity anymore. I mean . . ." He waved his hands, which Evan took for an apology. "Well, I'm sorry about the way we did it and I'd sure like to stay on the hitch and . . . how about it?"

"You know what they say about picking up hitchhikers," Evan said.

"What do you mean?"

"How do I know you won't rob me, kill me?"

"Oh, man!" John glanced at Lois. She shook her head and muttered, "Hey, that's far out."

"How do you know I won't rob *you*, kill *you?*" He looked at Lois. "Rape you?"

She giggled. "A girl has to *resist* before it's rape."

John spoke quickly, as if to prevent her from saying more. "Look, we said we were sorry. We didn't *do* anything. We're not criminals. She's going to a friend in New Mexico, and I'm heading for L.A. and the old homestead. At least the old man." He tried a smile. Evan didn't respond. John spread his hands earnestly. "You don't know how tough it is for a guy to get a hitch out of New York. She was just doing me a favor, and I was doing her one by keeping her company on the road. When you said to stop we stopped, correct?"

Evan was looking at Lois. She was smiling at him. He made up his mind. "All right," he said, and picked up the check and walked to the cashier.

His head was quite clear now and he drove considerably over the speed limit. John was in back with the two bedroll-type packs; Lois in front beside Evan. They'd wowed over the Jaguar, and Lois had asked the price, and they'd wowed over the ten thousand dollars. A man who paid ten thousand for a car was a prime candidate for robbery, wasn't he? But he'd enjoyed telling them anyway.

John had stretched out and seemed to be asleep. Lois sat with head back, legs crossed, her skirt open to mid-thigh. The skirt was dirty, but in the way of good suede maintained a look of quality. Her legs were bare and brown. He asked why she'd left Australia.

"So many reasons, don't know where to start. Well, first there was Mitchel, my loving spouse. He had sexual problems. With me, that is, and nobody else. Then there was dear Daddy." Her laugh was brief. "Unreal, man. And there was the way I was living. Shithouse, as we said back home. And . . ." She shrugged. "No chance to do what I wanted to do. So came here, and got a green card, and now I've got my first papers."

He was glancing at her legs, her breasts, her sweet, smooth profile. A very pretty girl. A very desirable girl. And he hadn't had a girl in almost a month. The excitement began building . . . and so did a parallel worry about the man in the back seat. They didn't act as if they'd known each other only a few days. Inconsistencies . . .

"How long ago did you leave home?"

"Two years, this July. The day after my twenty-first birthday. For a present, Mitchel bent my front teeth."

"You don't look twenty-one, *now*."

"Clean living, man." She turned a cocky, mocking smile on him. "Where *you* from?"

"Manhattan."

"You own some sort of business, right?"

"No. I'm in an ad agency."

"You rich?"

He smiled.

"You look rich. Your clothes. I don't usually like suits and square stuff, but yours look great. You on vacation?"

"Sabbatical. A month's leave to travel and relax. Want to see something of the country, close up."

"I wouldn't mind seeing a bit of country, but not right now."

"Then why are you hitching west?"

"Going to Albuquerque, to a friend." She paused. "Met him in Los Angeles, when I first flew in from Sydney. Nice guy. Wrote him a few months ago from New York, and he said to come on out and visit, and . . ." She shrugged. "Why not? I'm tired of what I'm doing."

"Which is?"

She reached for the radio. He waited for an answer, but it didn't come. She fiddled with the dial and found rock music.

"I think your friend is sleeping."

"Nothing wakes him. For months we had a place on Ninth Avenue with the trucks and . . ." She stopped abruptly, and busied herself lowering the volume.

So John's story of their having met "a few days ago" was a lie. He glanced at her. She leaned back and closed her eyes. "Dead tired," she murmured.

Why would they lie about how long they'd known each other?

What difference would it make to him, or to any other person giving them a ride?

It was only nine-thirty, but traffic was thin this Monday night, almost all of it interstate trucking. He maintained an even sixty-five miles per hour, and glanced into the rearview mirror. The shape stretched out on the back seat remained motionless.

They would lie about the girl being close to the boy if

they wanted him to feel the girl was a possible make, thereby improving their chances of getting the ride. She'd flirt for the same reason. That wasn't too threatening.

They would also lie if they wanted to obscure their true backgrounds, their true identities, and that might mean they were planning something he would report to the police. *Very* threatening.

Now that he'd caught the lie, they might decide against doing anything . . . or they might do it anyway, and eliminate any possibility of his reporting it to the police.

He cleared his throat. "Anyone awake to give me a cigarette?"

No one responded.

He reached under his seat and touched the cold metal and turned it so that he grasped it correctly and straightened and jammed it under his left thigh. He drove, and watched the rear-view and the back seat.

His passengers slept . . . or seemed to sleep.

It wasn't until one-thirty in the morning that Lois rubbed her face and said, "Unreal! I just zonked out." She yawned and stretched and asked where they were.

"Pennsylvania. Feel better now?"

"Yes." She looked out the window and said, "Empty here." She glanced in the back, then turned the radio up. She moved head and hands to the music; her fingers did little snake dances. "You were saying you're in an ad agency. What do you do there?"

"Copy chief. Handle a group of writers."

"Bet you make better than twenty, twenty-five thousand."

He made seventy thousand, not counting expense-account cream and stock-option dividends. Would they be impressed by that figure; enough to gamble on his carrying sufficient cash to make a robbery worthwhile?

"I earn seventy thousand dollars a year."

She forgot the music. "You're putting me on!"

"If money is your goal, and you work directly toward money, you can make lots of it. It's a trick, like ringing the bell in a carnival test of strength."

She was quiet, looking at him. Then she said, "I'd never believe anyone, just off the bat this way. Y'know—big talk. But I'll bet you're telling the truth. You married?"

"I was, once."

"How old are you? I like older men."

"Forty-one." He was forty-nine, and proud of his physical condition, his youthful appearance.

"You look younger. You look, say, thirty-five."

"You deserve a kiss for that."

"If I deserve it, I want it." She leaned over and put her face in front of his. He kissed her, watching both the road and the rear-view. Her mouth opened; her tongue darted past his lips; her hand drifted lightly to his thigh. He slowed, using his right hand to caress her crossed legs. She moved her hand upward. He slowed even more. She reached his crotch, pressed firmly, intensified her kiss. He sighed, responding, feeling her fingers trace his response through his trousers . . . and at the same time shifted his eyes to look into the rear-view. She pulled down his zipper, reached into his fly, grasped his now-rigid penis.

His right hand stroked her bare thighs. She uncrossed her legs, and he went to the joining, the naked, moist joining. She said, her whisper louder, "Oh, baby, *yeah*." At that, the shape in the rear-view rose swiftly, something long and wicked gleaming in one hand.

Evan twisted the wheel hard right, slamming on the brakes at the same time. The four-wheel disks grabbed and held; the Jag skidded onto a dirt shoulder and came to a jarring, stalling halt.

He was wearing his over-the-shoulder harness belt. Neither of his passengers wore theirs. Lois was thrown into the windshield, and cried out and slumped down. John came up and over the seat back, his voice a thin wail: "*Jeeeee*sus!" He slammed both hands flat against the windshield, and a knife fell from the right. Evan pulled the snub-nosed Smith & Wesson .38 from under his thigh, and whipped it into the side of John's head. The bearded man fell forward between the two front seats, legs stretching into the back. Evan cocked the hammer and jammed the muzzle into John's ear. John lifted his head. Evan shoved it back down with that muzzle in the ear.

"Ow! Don't . . ."

Evan freed himself of safety belts and opened the door, his right arm extended to keep the gun close to John's head. The hirsute face turned toward him; the high-pitched voice strained for shocked incredulity. "What's the scoop, man?"

"Get out the other side. Take her with you."

"Let me explain . . ."

"*Move!*"

Evan waited until John had half-carried, half-shoved Lois out the passenger-side door, then reached to the floor and found the knife. He backed out of the car. A truck came roaring up behind him. In the sudden glare of headlights, sidelights and multiple taillights, he saw Lois's face rising above the Jag's roof line. Dark wetness ran from her nose. He also saw that the knife he was holding was about three inches of haft and eight inches of blade. He tucked it carefully under his belt, and came around the front of the car.

"My nose," Lois whimpered, sagging against John. "It's bleeding."

John held her upright with his right arm. He rubbed the side of his head with his left. "C'mon, man, we don't have any bread. What do you want to rob *us* for?"

That didn't deserve an answer. "Both of you, walk." He waved the gun at trees and bushes beyond the shoulder.

"What about our packs?" John asked.

"You won't need them."

"Sure we'll need them. It's all we've got."

"*Walk!*"

John helped Lois take a few steps. She turned her face to Evan. "I didn't know he was going to try anything. We were making out, right, baby? Don't tie me in with *his* caper."

"Thanks," John said. "Besides, I didn't *try* anything. I was just going to cut a piece off that cheese we have. I lean forward to ask if anyone wants some, and the car stops, and I'm thrown up front."

"I forgot about the cheese." She looked at Evan. "That explains it, hon. I don't blame you for thinking what you did, but I got to get to a doctor. My nose . . ."

Evan aimed the gun at John's belly. "If you don't walk . . ."

John dragged Lois forward. She began to cry. "Why are we going in the woods? I don't want to go in the woods. *Please*, Evan."

"Straight ahead," Evan said, walking some six feet behind them. Only then did he take time to zipper up his fly.

It was a thin copse, and after twelve or fifteen feet he saw it was going to open up into a field. He told them to sit down, their backs to him.

"Oh, God," John whispered. "You're not . . . ?"

Evan jumped forward and shoved him, and both John and the girl fell. John rolled over immediately, looking up at him. "I was only going to take some bread! I wouldn't have *used* the knife! You can turn us in to the cops. I'll admit . . ."

"I wasn't part of it," Lois wept, face down. "I swear! We were making out, remember, and I wanted . . ."

Evan bent and aimed the gun directly at John's head.

"For the love of . . ."

Lois twisted around, staring, mouth opening for a scream.

Evan pulled the trigger. The click was louder than John's strangled "*No!*"

Lois's mouth stayed open. Evan turned and walked back

to the Jaguar. He reached through the open door to the glove compartment, took out the box of shells and loaded the empty five-shot revolver. By the time he finished, he heard them coming. He drew the knife from his belt and threw it across the highway; then he opened the back door and got inside. He shoved a bedroll off the seat, sliding across to sit directly behind the driver's position.

They came out into the open, and stopped. He called, "John, you drive. Lois, back here with me." As they came forward again, he pointed the gun through the open door and fired past them. Lois turned as if to run. John grabbed her arm. Evan said, "Just a demonstration."

They pulled back onto the highway, and now John was the one whose eyes kept flickering to the rear-view. Evan sat relaxed. Lois sat as far from him as she could, dabbing her nose with what looked like a print bandana. She sniffled, huddling in the corner. He shoved the two packs toward her with his feet. "I'd like some of that cheese."

She looked at him, and at John's eyes in the mirror. "I don't know where it is."

"It's nowhere," John muttered.

Evan nodded, holding the gun in both hands, rubbing the metal with his fingers. "Now just say it. You were going to kill me, weren't you?"

They both spoke at once: "No . . . man, never . . . *kill?*"

"Why not? Money and credit cards and this car."

"I'd never let him kill!" Lois said.

"You'd let him steal?"

"We didn't talk about it. I mean, he said maybe a soft touch, yeah, but you have to be bonkers . . . crazy, man, to think about *killing!* I'm not like that!"

"But you, John?"

The tall man drove silently.

Evan began to ask, again, and John said, "For a car? A car I'd have to dump? Who could hang onto a stolen Jag? And who could use stolen credit cards for more than a few weeks . . . and not at all if it led to a corpse. Man, I've *been* in stir. Two months, but that was enough to make me know I'd *die* if I had to spend real time there. Even a year . . ."

"You'd get more than a year for armed robbery, and you were going to rob me."

"I wasn't sure. I wouldn't've known until the last second."

"You were coming up behind me with that knife."

"But maybe I'd have stopped. I didn't think you were watching, with Lois and all."

"You've done this before, so why all the hesitation?"

"Not with me, he hasn't!" Lois said.

"Not with anyone. Only a few rip-offs. It was just . . . being broke after losing my temp job at the post office, and everything so lousy the past few months. *She* didn't help, staying out nights, trying to split."

"I *told* you it was a temporary thing. I told you and told you, but you just wouldn't listen. Remember last week, when I said I was going to meet this guy in Albuquerque? You just kept talking about Los Angeles and showing me where your folks lived and getting enough money to rent a house in Hollywood Hills . . ."

"All right. He's not interested. We'll talk when he dumps us." The eyes flickered to Evan. "You're not planning on the cops, are you?"

Evan didn't answer.

"You can't prove anything. It's our word against yours. If you press charges, you'll have to stick around here and we'll tell what you did in the woods and Lois'll say it all started when you forced yourself on her."

Evan looked at Lois. She said, "Well, we'd have to say *some*thing. Just let us go, hon, please."

Evan said, "How is your nose?"

She touched it, and made a sighing sound. "It's not too bad, now."

He put the gun in his jacket pocket. "Let me see."

She hesitated, then moved across the seat to him. When

he raised his hand, she flinched. He cupped her face and moved it to catch some light and with his other hand felt the bridge and then the sides of her nose. She inhaled sharply. He said, "Just bruised. But if it looks bad tomorrow, we'll see a doctor."

"Tomorrow?" John muttered.

Evan pulled Lois against his shoulder. She went, but rigidly. After a while, she relaxed and began to cry. He stroked her head, bent and kissed her tear-wet cheek, felt the excitement rise again. "Easy, easy," he murmured, and looked into John's eyes in the mirror. He grinned at those eyes, and they snapped away.

It was after four when John said, "There's an open gas station ahead. We're almost empty. Should I stop?"

Lois seemed to be asleep, but her nipples were up. Evan had his hand inside her blouse, kneading those full tits. No special drive in him at the moment, but a promise for later. Oh, yes, later! He wondered if John could see. He didn't think so, but he wouldn't have minded.

"Yes," he said. "I'd also like to use the rest room."

"Me too. Teeth are floating. Or is that too obscene for you?"

Evan ignored it. They pulled off the highway onto a service road, and then into a large, fluorescent-lighted gas station. Three of the four rows of pumps were blocked off. John pulled up to the open row. "Hi-test, right?"

"If you can get it." He shook Lois. "We're stopping. Want to get out?"

She nodded sleepily, then put her hands to her blouse and looked at him. She did up the buttons, and got out and stood beside the car, drawing her leather jacket close about her. The attendant came over. As John talked to him, Evan leaned over the front seat and removed the keys from the ignition. The large, copper key from Judy's apartment was still on the ring. He fingered it and tested himself and it all felt good.

John got out and walked toward the building and the

signs at the side indicating the rest rooms. Lois waited for Evan, and walked beside him. "Cold for May," she said. "Hope it gets warmer."

"It will. Later tonight."

She smiled, but it was a nervous smile. That scene in the woods had changed things. He kept looking at her. She turned away from his eyes, his hard bright eyes, and went into the ladies' room. He walked a few steps further and entered the men's room. John was just backing from the urinal. "Two pounds lighter. Make that two quarts." Evan said, "Clever," and went into the booth. He locked the door behind him. When he came out, John was drying his hands on a roller towel beside the sink. Evan waited. John stepped away from the sink with exaggerated haste. Evan washed, watching him in the wall mirror.

"We going to be watching each other all the time?" John asked.

"I don't know about you."

"But *you're* going to be watching?"

"For as long as we're together. Which won't be long."

"You told Lois you'd take her to see a doctor tomorrow."

"That's right."

"I get it. Lois, not me."

Evan turned and waved politely at the door.

"Don't count on her leaving without me."

"I promise not to count on anything, ever."

John stared at him. Evan waved at the door again, not so politely.

"Listen, Evan, I'm sorry. I mean, if we could start over again, I give you my word . . ."

"And that's your bond."

"I'll do most of the driving. I'll sleep in the car if you don't want to stake me to a motel room. I mean, you can call the shots any way you please."

"Me and Lois?"

John smiled quickly, but not quickly enough to cover a tightness of expression. "That's up to her, correct?"

"Is it?"

"Man, you think we got to be your *slaves*? We could split right now, and nothing you could do about it. You couldn't play heavy with that gun . . ."

Evan chuckled. "Couldn't I? What's to stop me?"

"The guy at the pumps . . ."

"Why don't you go to the car and *see* what happens instead of standing here and talking?"

"If we could just start over, that's all. It's a long drive to L.A. I could really help you. Lois too. Company, and all. We're broke, but we could provide services . . ."

"That kind of obscenity I like."

"*Christ!*" John turned abruptly and walked out. Evan followed.

Lois was in the back seat. The attendant was trying to talk to her through the open driver's window. She nodded coldly, and he straightened when Evan came up. He was a balding, sharp-faced man of perhaps thirty. "Nice weather," he said, sounding guilty. Evan gave him his credit card and said, "John, you drive." The attendant walked to the island office. Evan got in back with Lois. John lit a cigarette and stood looking out at the highway.

"Creep," Lois said. "All the creeps with their make-out shit."

"Who?"

"That gas jockey, of course. Who'd you think I meant?" She snuggled up to him.

"Perhaps John."

"Well, yeah, him too!" She glanced at him. "But he'll be cool now, baby. We could work it out. You're not going to dump him?"

He shrugged. The attendant brought John the card. Evan said, "Here," and rolled down the window. He signed, gave John the keys, and they were on their way.

Lois snuggled again. Evan's hand went back inside her blouse. She kissed his chin, his cheek, his lips. He began to feel a loss of tension, a return of warmth. "What will you do in L.A.?" she asked.

"Play tourist. I'll play tourist at Grand Canyon first."
He watched the road for signs.

"I've never seen Grand Canyon. Think I'd like it?"

"Yes, but you're stopping at Albuquerque, aren't you?"

"Well, I'm loose about that. Nothing definite." She
groaned softly as he rolled her nipple. Her hand went to
his thigh; moved up and down, up and down. It didn't
dare as far as it had earlier.

"You know people in L.A.?" she asked.

"I've been there, on business. I've been to most major
cities, on business. But I never took the time to really *see*
them. Just hotel suites, meetings, clients, a few parties. Fly
in and fly out."

"You know anyone in movies, TV?"

"I've made a few friends over the years."

"I took the Universal tour when I was in L.A. Bet you
never had to take a tour."

"No. Are you interested in acting?"

"How'd you guess?" She began to straighten, but he
pulled her back with his hand on her breast. "I did modeling, dancing, acting. If I'd had a SAG card—Screen Actors Guild—I might have been able to make it. But no
green card to work in the States at that time, and so no
SAG card. But now, if I got a chance, I'd grab it!" Her
snuggle became more active; her hand moved higher on
his thigh.

He'd heard this kind of thing from many girls, and used
it to his own advantage on occasion. "If you decide to go
on to Los Angeles, we might speak to a few people."

"Really?" She twisted her head to look up at him. Forgotten was the tender nose, the scene in the woods, residual loyalty to John. "I'm really good, hon. Had a dramatics coach who said I was ready for *any* part. And
made my living at dancing right up until a few weeks ago
when . . ."

The sign came up, and Evan interrupted. "Take the next
exit, John. We'll stop for the night."

Lois began to speak again. He touched her mouth with his free hand and massaged her tit with his other and murmured, "Later." She subsided like a good little girl, but her eyes glittered and her lips moved slightly, phrasing arguments and sales pitches. And he didn't care. Not about what she did, and not about what John did. She was mattress stuffing, nothing more. And John would soon be gone.

Another sign indicated they had passed into the sliver of West Virginia that lay between Pennsylvania and Ohio. He kissed her, switching his caress to the left breast, the other piece of warm meat. He took her hand and moved it up his thigh to his crotch. She squeezed and stroked, whispering, "Can't wait, baby!"

John's eyes were in the rear-view. When they met his, they flashed away. Evan caught a glimpse of a down mouth, a drawn expression.

He liked that.

They swung off the highway at much too high a speed. The tires screamed and the Jag rocked as they came around the service road onto a two-lane highway. A motel sign winked through the darkness. "Beddy-bye time," John said, trying to sound cynical and cool, and managing to sound unhappy.

Evan liked that too.

He liked everything that was happening tonight.

And this was only the first night of his trip. And there were all the other days and nights to come.

How *lucky* he'd been to meet these two!

2: | Tuesday a.m.

He wasn't getting any younger, that was for sure, but he was certainly getting *bigger*, in the gut that is. Time was running out for Detective Sergeant Edmund Roersch, and while he couldn't stop it, he might be able to make its passage more pleasant . . . *if* he solved this case, got the right publicity, and made lieutenant. Then his retirement pay wouldn't give him the cold sweats when he thought of it, as he was doing now, lying awake in the big oak bed, alone despite Ruthie's being available. She was a sweet young piece, soft-spoken and ladylike for a hooker, and always willing to pay off in trade. A hooker and a cop in the same apartment house, on the same floor, and that's why she was always quick to spread for him. One of the department's side benefits . . . and Christ how he wished he could find a benefit that paid off in cold cash!

Ass, even the youngest and juiciest, wasn't much of an attraction for him anymore. He missed Helen. After thirty-one years of marriage, he'd thought he wanted nothing so much as to escape her cheerful chatter, her family and their get-togethers, her boundless lovingness, and her amazing enthusiasm in bed. Then they'd called him at the station. Helen was dead of a massive coronary, and he was alone at age fifty-six. Suddenly, completely alone, because he had no family of his own in New York, and there was no closeness with Helen's family, and they'd had no children. It was the last, the having no children, that people thought really hurt him now . . . but it didn't. He'd never missed having children, though he hadn't said so when Helen mourned aloud. He'd nodded, as he'd nodded at so many of the things she'd said as they were eating or watching television or driving in the car. Nodded and barely listened, thinking of this case or that, this horror or that, content to be free of the "children" who beat and stabbed and robbed and killed in the homes and on the streets of Manhattan; of the children who shot themselves full of heroin, or sniffed cocaine, and paid for it with others' cash, and blood; of the children who hated their parents for having brought them into this worst of all possible worlds.

Well, he was depressed tonight. The truth was, Helen would have made a good mother, and he might have managed to avoid too many mistakes himself.

He put on the lamp and got up and padded to the dresser. He searched the top, where he always put his wallet, watch, keys, gun and cigarettes, for the pack of Kents, and then remembered he'd left them in the car, deliberately, so he couldn't smoke over his limit—five a day; at least that was his goal.

He went into the next room, not throwing the wall switch, not wanting to see the deterioration of Helen's pride and joy—her super-clean living-dining room area. He hadn't used a cleaning girl since the second month after Helen's death, and that was five months ago. He dusted and vacuumed occasionally, though he couldn't remember the last time. He just didn't give a shit about the apartment.

He didn't give a shit about most things anymore. A good TV show, a few Scotches and cigarettes in Glen's Bar, his Sundays and Mondays off—though they'd called him in on the Keel case and he'd lost his Monday— Ruthie's fat white ass bending over the bed once in a while, once in a *long* while. And a lieutenant's pension so he could settle down outside the city.

There was one other thing, but this was in the category of dream, not plan . . . and a relatively new dream at that; since Helen's death: to score somehow; to make a big piece of change; to cut himself into something beyond the normal take from gamblers and whores and pimps and pushers, which had dried up anyhow since he'd been assigned to Manhattan West Homicide.

Edmund Roersch had never been adverse to a small piece of the pie, and had been on a pad or two in his time. But until recently he had believed in *limits*.

A cop who pocketed a few hundred a month for the wife and kids and aging mother, okay. People wanted to gamble. People wanted to boff whores. People wanted to smoke a little pot and sniff a little coke. Who could stop them? Prohibition hadn't worked with booze, and nothing worked with gambling, prostitution and drugs. Why shouldn't a cop take a little from the fat-cat Mafia, the slick pimps and pushers?

He hadn't discussed this with Helen, and she hadn't known about his small-time rake-offs in the past. But he'd joined her, outstripped her, in condemning those cops who forgot the limits; who ended up with hundreds of thousands in payoff money. Because then they'd stopped being cops who did their jobs, cops who didn't shirk danger when it came their way, and who kept the department's dirty linen within the department. Because they'd become racketeers, blackmailers, bad guys, without time or desire to conduct the department's business.

Now the distinction had blurred, because he dreamed of such a big haul himself. Not over a long period of time; a one-shot thing, in fast and out clean.

Now he was without Helen, and without limits.

He had close to twenty thousand in the bank, which the family men at the station would have admired, but which he knew wouldn't change that approaching retirement much. A hundred grand, two hundred grand; *then* there'd be deep-sea fishing in the Florida Keys and first-class travel and a taste of what the East-Siders had.

Of course, it was all hypothetical; there were no such opportunities on Homicide.

Meanwhile, there was the Keel murder to deal with. From sweet dream to stinking reality. What a lousy way to die. Tied naked to a bed and carved up like butcher's meat. No wounds to vital organs, so she might well have seen her arms cut off, and maybe known the legs were going too. A lake of blood sopping over the sheets, held by the plastic liner of her water bed. The eyes open, bulging; the face twisted, mouth screaming silently. And Helen used to lecture him on having more personal faith, a more positive approach to life. There was little on which to base such faith and positive thinking in *his* line of work.

He walked to the piano in his pajama bottoms; a broad man, big but not tall, big and gone to seed. He felt his flesh jiggle, and it upset him, reminded him of age and deterioration. And of death too. He took a cigar from the box and stuck it in his mouth and chewed it. But sweet Jesus, how he wanted a cigarette! He went to the couch and sat down, groaning and catching himself at it. And thought it was an old man's habit, *kvetching*, as Weir would say.

Bending to drop the cigar on the coffee table, he felt his gut bulging over the waistband of his pajamas.

Well fuck it! He could still take half the punks on the

streets with his bare hands, with all their judo and karate and kung fu and assorted crap! He could still put a man down with one shot to the head or body! He was still a tough cop!

He'd jumped to his feet in his anger, his self-hatred, and felt his flesh jiggle again . . . and knew it was all talk. Without a gun, he'd be lost in a real fight. Past the first few moments, he'd be winded and finished. It was deadline time, stroke-of-midnight time; he was going over the hill, and no way to stop it. He dreaded his next physical.

Let's catch a murderer. That was a game he played, and played better now than ever before. His score had climbed, rather than declined, over the years. Fewer personal distractions . . . and it was a way to forget Helen and jiggling flesh and age and death. It was better than booze and TV for losing oneself. And it was his best shot, his *only* shot, at lieutenant.

He went to the dinette and put on the ceiling light and opened his zipper case. And saw the long butt in the ashtray. He smiled like a child at Christmas-time, and went to the kitchen and mixed himself a Scotch. He returned and sipped and looked at the grisly photos of the twenty-five-year-old ad-agency receptionist who was a sometime model and actress; at the coroner's preliminary report, the responding radio-car team's reports, everyone's reports, including his own. And kept the promise of that half-a-cigarette in his mind.

Judith Keel had left her job at Grayson & Burns, Advertising, at five-thirty p.m., Friday evening. She was found in her second-floor, Seventy-seventh Street apartment at ten a.m., Monday morning, by the woman who cleaned for her once weekly. The woman had still been in a state of shock and under sedation at eight p.m., when Roersch had asked to question her. He hoped to get at that later today.

An autopsy report was expected sometime this afternoon, or evening, or perhaps tomorrow morning, considering the coroner's work load in Fun City. A preliminary examination indicated she'd bled to death, though there was always the possibility she'd been dead *before* the butchering. He sincerely hoped so, but because of the limbs being tied to the four posts of the brass bed, he felt he knew the kind of murder this was. He was more interested in whether she'd had sexual relations before or after death than in the condition of heart, liver, kidneys and other organs near and dear to forensic medicine. He was hoping there were no signs of sperm in or about her sex organs, or buttocks. It would fit in with the way he categorized this kind of murder, and murderer. That didn't mean he wouldn't categorize anew, if consenting sex, rape or necrophilia was indicated.

Her purse was open, and empty, as was a jewelry box. Drawers were open, the contents scattered about. But this was the most common of all false trails, used by those with personal motives to confuse police investigation. And it worked often enough.

The murder weapon, or weapons, was missing . . . either a large knife, or a saw of some sort, or both. It wasn't that easy to cut through arms and legs, even at the joints.

Neighbors in the victim's apartment house had been questioned yesterday. She was a pretty girl with a limited, or very private, social life. No reports of parties, or troops of men; no complaints to management by immediate neighbors of noise, either before the weekend of the murder, or during it. Which indicated she'd been gagged as well as tied. Any of several soiled towels in the bathroom hamper could have been used; or wadded toilet paper, facial tissues, the killer's tie or handkerchief; so many possibilities that Roersch stopped thinking of it.

As for the time of death, he didn't really need the coroner's guesses. She'd been seen in a local delicatessen at about ten-thirty Sunday night. She'd said hello to a neighbor near the elevators half an hour later. So she'd died between eleven p.m. Sunday and ten a.m. Monday. Good enough for the present.

Her employer and co-workers would be interviewed today; he'd do some of that himself. He'd also visit the apartment and talk to whoever was around, especially the regular doorman who hadn't been available yesterday. He hoped the killer was someone in her home or office. Or a regular date. Someone she knew. That way he'd have a fighting chance. Otherwise, it'd be rough. Used to be they solved nine out of ten murders in New York. Now it was *five* out of ten, and he wondered if even those bleak figures weren't doctored for public consumption. The backlog of unsolved homicides at Manhattan West was depressing, even for old cops who didn't depress easily.

He took the cigarette from the ashtray and lit it, careful not to consume more than was absolutely necessary to get it burning. He inhaled deeply, concentrating on expected pleasure. Somehow, the pleasure didn't develop. The smoke was harsh, and he was sorry he hadn't saved some of the Scotch to smooth it out. He finished it down to his fingers, nodding sadly. Always that way. You wait for something, look forward to something, and it turns out nothing.

A few times that way with Ruthie . . . but maybe those were the times he'd gone to her not with desire but because he hadn't known how else to fill an empty night. When he *had* wanted her, she'd given considerable pleasure.

He wouldn't lump her in with the disappointments. No . . . not that small, dark girl with the generous figure. He was leaning back, eyes half-closed, not really wanting her but knowing he would, soon. Too tired tonight. But another night . . . young and dark and beautiful and full of forgetfulness, full of life to infuse into someone not quite alive anymore.

It was four-thirty when he went back to bed.

Not quite alive, and not quite able to sleep. So he thought of Judith Keel. No signs of forcible entry on her front door. One of her two bedroom windows, leading to a fire escape, showed recent chips and dents, but just *how* recent was the question. No signs of a struggle . . . though her earlobes were partly torn.

She was pierced for earrings, and the holes had been distended, causing some bleeding. This could be unconnected with the crime—women damaged their own earlobes that way when removing tight or difficult earrings—or it could have been part of the robbery, done either before or shortly after the murder. Otherwise, no bruises on the head, torso or severed limbs. There were, of course, the rope marks where she was tied, but the rope was standard clothesline, so forget it, Dick Tracy.

No little black book; not even the personal telephone directory that *everyone* kept. No listing of names, addresses and phone numbers of any kind. Which could be important. Who would take such listings, except someone whose name was in them?

No needle marks on limbs or torso, and nothing that would qualify as drugs on the premises. So no junkie angle indicated. In Fun City, you always had to check out the junkie angle.

No Negro connections as yet—dates, visitors, whatever —and that was something else you checked, and fuck *The New York Times.*

"No nothing," he sighed, and put out his arm, reaching for Helen. He pulled over the spare pillow, *her* pillow, and hugged it . . . and thought of whoever had killed the Keel girl; thought of him without outrage, without anger, but with *hunger.* To get him. To make lieutenant and retire fast and leave this apartment fast. Otherwise . . . what?

His eyes opened and he stared into a darkness far deeper than the darkness of his bedroom. He was frightened.

"Where are you?" he whispered. "*Where,* motherfucker?"

It was simpler than he'd thought it would be. John

parked in front of the motel office. Evan asked for the ignition keys, left the car and walked inside.

Neither John nor Lois followed. The clock above the desk read twenty to five. A young man with a carefully arranged and obviously sprayed hairdo sat at a switchboard, reading a back issue of *Playboy*.

The clerk came over, placing the magazine face-down on the counter. Evan asked for two rooms, and made sure they wouldn't adjoin by saying one had to be ground floor, the other top floor. He registered for Mr. and Mrs. E. Bley, and John Bley. While the clerk got the keys, he flipped through the magazine.

He returned to the car and instructed John to drive to the end of the long, two-story building. When they stopped, the three got out. Evan removed his small suitcase from the trunk, and turned to where John and Lois now waited, each with a pack. He walked to John and handed him a key. "Upstairs and two from the end, according to the clerk." John looked at Lois. She took Evan's hand. John lifted his pack, went to the metal staircase and began to climb it. "Happy Valentine's Day," he said.

"Funny man," Lois said.

"I'd be funnier if I said thanks."

Evan resisted Lois's tug on his hand. He stood still, watching John reach the open second-floor landing and walk to a point almost directly above them. John used his key, and disappeared. Only then did Evan walk with Lois under the second-floor overhang to a door six from the end.

"Hey!" Lois said when they entered the room. It was large and cheerful, with two double beds. There was a dressing room with sink and mirror at the far end, and a door leading to the bathroom. The colors were pastel pink and blue.

Lois went to the nearest bed as Evan placed his suitcase on the folding stand. She tossed her pack on the floor, lay back and stretched. "I could sack out here for a week!

Luxury, baby!" After which she jumped up and ran to the color TV.

"It's five a.m.," Evan said, opening the case and finding his toilet kit. "No shows . . ."

But he was wrong. She'd tuned in an old movie. "Robert Young!" she squealed.

He looked. "Robert Taylor."

"Yeah, one of the biggies." She threw herself backward onto the bed, knees up, hugging herself. He saw tanned thighs and a black juncture, and remembered the last time with Judy. Lois smiled at him, holding the pose. He turned away, taking out underwear for the morning's change.

"Want to shower?" she asked.

"In a moment."

"Should I wait?"

"Go ahead. I'll join you."

She bounced off the bed and ran to him. She grabbed him around the waist and almost picked him up off the floor. "What a *great* place to make it! Except it's kind of cold. Where's the heat?"

"You're very strong," he said.

"Athletics. I'll tell you about it some day. I was a winner, baby. I could be again, in anything I tried . . . with a little help."

He knew what was coming, and kissed her on the head and disengaged himself. No show-biz talk *tonight!* He went to the dressing room and the thermostat and put it up to seventy-five. When he turned, she was slipping out of her skirt, her side to him. Her bottom swelled nicely. Then her blouse came off, and he saw her pride and joy. She kicked off her shoes, pushing those breasts as far out as a deep breath could manage, posing for him while trying to appear unaffected.

She was a surprisingly *big* girl without her clothing . . . and it wasn't just the ass and tits. Broad, sloping shoulders, heavily freckled down to mid-back. A narrow waist. Rounded belly. Flaring hips. Firm, thick thighs and bulging calves. Her arms, while soft-looking in repose, were round and full, and he remembered their strength of a moment ago. "Very nice," he murmured.

"I've heard better," she giggled.

"You're beautiful. Were you a dancer?"

"You mean my legs." She got up on her toes to slim them out. "I danced, but that's not why they're fat."

"They're far from fat."

"Well, thick then." She went flat-footed and frowned at herself in the dresser mirror. "Athletics back in Australia. I was fourth-rated sprinter, nationwide, in school. If I'd listened to my father, I'd've been in the Olympics, I reckon. But I wasn't happy at it. I wanted to act. Always wanted to act, hon."

Her speech had slipped. Her "h's" were dropping like flies, and the cockney-style Australian poured forth. She realized it, too, and laughed. "Man, I sound like the rear end of a kangaroo, don't I? Always that way when I talk about home." But she was back in control again. "Well, into the drink." She came toward him, shaking her hips and jiggling her breasts. "One thing I know," she said, dropping her gaze to his fly.

"What's that?"

She brushed past him, making all moving parts move dramatically. "You forgive me." Her laughter pealed, and she went into the bathroom and closed the door. He heard her continuing laughter, until running water drowned it out.

He went to the closet and undressed there. He brought his soiled underthings to the suitcase and placed them in the zipper flap. He slipped into his bathrobe, returned to the closet, and removed the small pistol from his jacket pocket. After a moment's thought, he went to the lamp table between the two beds, and placed the gun in the drawer behind the Gideon Bible. He lay down, and practiced opening the drawer and grasping the gun.

On the way to the bathroom, he noticed several picture postcards lying on the dresser—glamorized views of the motel. He sat down and took the ballpoint pen from its holder.

Dear Mom:
In Ohio now, on my way to California. Didn't want to upset you, but I might as well prepare you now—I don't believe I'll be coming back to New York. I'll send for my things, and if you want to visit . . .

Were they in Ohio, or still in West Virginia?

What difference would that make to Mom? Anywhere away from Brooklyn she called "out-of-town." New Jersey and the dark side of the moon were equally remote to her.

He tore up the card and looked at the bathroom. What the hell was he waiting for?

Lois was just getting out of the bathtub-shower combination, streaming wet. She grabbed a towel off the rack and began rubbing her hair. "Slowpoke," she said. "Left it running for you."

He took off his bathrobe and hung it on the door hook, trying to keep his back to her as much as possible. He turned quickly to the partly open shower door.

"Bingo!" she exclaimed. "Does that thing get *bigger?*"

He stepped into the stream of water. It was too hot for him and he fumbled with the faucets. "Let's hope so," he said, and slid the door shut.

He heard her laughter. A moment later the door opened a bit and she looked in. "I'm not sure we should hope so much. You got a small girl here, *that* way. Turn around, huh?"

"I'll be out in a minute."

But she took his arm and pulled.

As he turned to face her, and as she shook her head laughing, and as he told himself he had nothing to hide, had in fact something to be proud of, he remembered things.

Judy saying, "Christ, it *hurts!*" and disengaging, rolling

away from him, angry at him, hating him he'd felt, especially the last few times.

And his mother and the neighbor woman who owned the candy store, coming into the bathroom as he was lowering himself into the tub, thirteen-year-old Marvin Bleywitz; whispering to each other as he stared at them in shock, and the woman laughing, and his mother smiling; and he'd screamed at them to get out, get out and let him alone, and when they were gone he'd cried, ashamed of the thing between his legs, the thing they'd looked at, afraid it was wrong somehow, ugly and funny somehow, evil and dirty somehow. And that was because of something else, something that happened months before, when his mother had struck him, beat him with her fists, screaming at him because he'd done something, and raised her skirt, shrieking about him hurting her, killing her, and he'd seen the bloody thing . . .

Oh God the bloody thing that he'd hated and tried to forget and never could forget. The bloody thing that had followed Marvin Bleywitz, and later Evan Bley.

"Don't get mad," Lois said, and drew back and closed the shower door.

He heard her leave the bathroom. He used a washcloth and scrubbed himself. He washed for a long time. He forgot the stupid past and ran the water cold and jumped out, invigorated. He toweled himself briskly and left his bathrobe hanging on the door and went into the bedroom. Lois lay on the bed, watching television. She was nude. He put his hand on his penis and stroked himself. She looked up, watched a moment, then drew up her knees and clasped them to her and whispered, "Stick that thing in me. Fast."

He went to the bed and lay down beside her, not on her, intending to play a little, to make her do what he liked best before sticking her. But voices from the television caused him to look there, and it was another old movie, perhaps as old as the late Twenties, and it gripped him suddenly, hurting him with old things, dead things, finished things that had no right to parade around as if alive. He watched the woman in bobbed hair and long dress and painted lips, pretty and pitiful in the way of dead things; watched her walk to the man and say, "I'm not that kind of girl, Vernon!" Watched him show shame for thinking he might spend time in her presence, in her room with the door closed, though all they were going to do was eat dinner off a room-service cart.

"Baby," Lois said, her hand coming to his erection. "I'm ready."

The man on the television screen, as alive as men on the daily newscasts, yet probably dead, went to the door and opened it and returned and said, "I'm sorry, Margaret." The man and woman looked at each other; then she smiled and sat down.

It was totally ridiculous in terms of anything true and real in this day, perhaps in that day too.

It hurt him, because he wished such things *were* true and real.

He sat up. "Five in the morning," he said, and turned the damned thing off. "Five in the morning and that crap!"

She was looking at him. Her hand was still on him, but she was holding a limp thing, a dead thing. He made himself smile, and took her in his arms. He kissed her, and stroked her full thighs, her rounded belly, her fat tits. She sighed and pulled, and he moved back toward desire.

"Wow," she finally said, and raised her head to look at it. "Maybe ten inches! You ever measure it?"

"Every man measures it. Not quite nine."

"And thick as my arm! And it isn't really hard yet!"

"Make it hard." He put his hand behind her head, pushing.

She bent to his belly. Her tongue went into his navel and licked and moved down. She grasped his testicles lightly and licked his glans lightly. He groaned. "*Suck* it, for Chrissake."

She took him in her mouth, and he was almost there. She sucked with surprising skill, with professional technique, stroking his shaft, her tongue flickering, probing his urethra. He felt fire, fire, and jerked his hips upward, ramming it into her throat. She tried to draw back, gagging. He grabbed her head with one hand, pulled her hand from his testicles with the other. He pushed down with all his strength, feeling her mouth slobber against his crotch, hearing her trying to scream.

Good! Good! Ram! Kill the bitch with it! He was blazing with lust, the best feeling in years, perhaps the best in all his life. Her fingers tore at his belly. He barely felt it. *Ram! Ram! Fucking cunt! Fucking big-tit whore! Ram!*

Her strangled scream mounted; she closed her teeth, telegraphing the awful threat. He let go immediately; released her head and dropped his hips.

She sat up, shaking her head, coughing.

"Sorry," he panted. "Carried away."

She swallowed and rubbed her throat and glared at him. "What sort of fucking freak . . ."

He couldn't be bothered handling her anger now; couldn't talk, couldn't reason now. He grabbed her, and she said, "You bastard, *no!*" He threw her on her back. He said, "Beautiful girl, beautiful girl, carried me away," and kissed her mouth and kissed her breasts and grabbed her bottom and grabbed himself and found the notch and pushed.

Anger was still on her face, but her cunt was sopping. He kept pushing, and her face began to change. He got the glans in, and she moaned, "Ah, *baby.*" He shoved it in, bit by bit, though she was right, she was a small girl, and it hurt her and it hurt him, but the hurt was good.

In the beginning, Judy had cried out, "More, more!" even as she winced. And now Lois cried out, "More, the whole fucking cock, you bastard!" and winced. And he was half in and she was moaning obscenities, begging him to fuck her, stick her, bust her cunt wide open, "Spunk, baby, spunk!" And hearing her he knew it was right to fuck; right and good and a pleasure.

She spasmed under him, her voice a quavering sigh. "I spunked." And looked up. "Easy. Please, baby, *easy*. It hurts."

He shoved her legs up and over his shoulders, bending her knees to her head, straining her body, pounding her body. And her twisted face, half pain and half ecstasy, made it right again. He *rammed!* He closed his eyes and saw things, bloody things, and spurted his hatred, his blood, his rage into her.

She went to the bathroom without a word.

He went to the other bed and took off the pillowcase and cleaned himself. When she returned, he was almost asleep.

She lay down beside him.

"Sorry," he murmured. "Too rough, I know."

She remained silent.

He rolled over on his side, his back to her . . . but he was waiting. He knew he would want her again. He'd hurt her and satisfied her and he would want it all again. And more.

"Evan?"

He grunted.

"Are you always so rough?"

"No. Told you . . . carried away. You're terrific."

Her hand touched his head, stroked his hair. She snuggled up to him.

"Next time I'll be gentle," he said.

She giggled. "Not *too* gentle, baby!"

He turned and she came into his arms.

She fell asleep that way. He couldn't. Not ever. Always had to withdraw, be apart, be alone in sleep. But he waited before getting free and sliding to the edge of the bed.

He was beginning to doze when he realized he was on the wrong side. He couldn't reach the night stand and his gun.

He got up and walked around the footboard. Lois was too close to the edge, and he didn't want to risk waking her. He lay down in the second bed, touched the drawer, fell deeply asleep.

John slept uneasily. He dreamed. He saw Lois dead, under Evan. He awoke and had a cigarette; then dressed except for his shoes and went out on the landing. The Jag was still there. No great triumph. They wouldn't lose their fucking and sleeping to ditch him tonight.

Tomorrow, probably. But tomorrow would be a whole different ball game.

He went back to his room and got the grav knife from his pack. Not a monster like his Puma, but still functional.

He touched the button, and the four-inch blade slid out and locked in place. He wondered where Evan kept that gun.

He closed the knife, put it in his pocket, went out and down the metal stairs, padding softly, feeling the cold through his thickly calloused feet. He went directly to Evan's door, for the second time that night.

Bet Evan thought waiting until he'd gone to his room would keep him from knowing their room number. But he had come right out after closing the door on Evan and Lois; had heard their footsteps and stepped to the edge of the overhang and looked down. And counted doors.

He could open this lock in half a minute. And be inside and on the sonofabitch in two seconds. If he wanted to.

And he'd wanted to, earlier, when he'd come down and listened at their door and heard the squeaking, the groaning and moaning.

His girl! Their first night out of New York, she was shacking the guy who'd put them down!

He was hungry, thirsty.

There were machines in the motel office; he'd seen them when Evan had registered. He walked along the concrete path and looked up at the sky, growing light in the east.

The office door was locked. He took the knife from his jeans and flicked out the blade. He worked on the lock, prying, holding the miniscule fraction won, prying, holding, the way he'd learned to take doors and windows and anything else with a bolt or turn lock, learned from Billy Boy when they were ripping off apartments in Miami, way back when the road had seemed fun, when they'd ripped off that fourth and last place in Surfside. They'd been busted by a black-and-white; his first bust.

That had led to two great months and the first and second and last times he'd ever sucked cock. Fucking nigger bastard! He could still feel the other one shoving his head down, twisting his arm up behind his back; and looking across the tank cell at Billy Boy, who was turning away, having made his own deal somewhere else. No help there. No help anywhere, as some men watched and the two black bastards worked him over.

He had to suck the big one, Brown, while the smaller one played with his asshole, waiting for the mouth too. He could still taste it, and smell it; the vomit gagging his throat as Brown held him for the smaller one, and he did it again, swallowing because that's what they said to do and they had the muscle and Brown had the thick-bladed knife and held it and talked slowly about never getting out of here except in the white-pine box the county provided. Then afterward, trying to escape the second round, and then the third round, when they'd both taken turns going up his ass. Then being transferred to the second-floor cell where it was harder for them to get at him and where there wasn't anyone tough enough to overcome his resistance.

Four days later he'd gone before the judge and received a suspended and left sunny Florida forever.

The door clicked open. He opened it a bit more, held it, opened it, held it, until sure that no bell, no buzzer, no alarm would sound. Then he went to the soft-drink machine and the candy machine and didn't bother considering how to rip them off. He bought a Coke and a nut bar. He ate and drank, standing there, and finished and closed the door behind him.

On the way back, he tried the doors of the Jag. The rear right, the one Lois had used, was unlocked. He laughed to himself. Mr. Smartass, guarding his keys! He could jump the wires and be a hundred miles away, maybe two hundred, before they started their wake-up fuck.

But he closed the door and went up the staircase to his room. If he took the Jag, he'd take everything else—money and credit cards and that cheating cunt. Take it and use it as long as he could. If he went for anything, he'd go for it *all*. No more stupid small-time moves. Or emotional moves. He'd risked his neck on peanuts too many times. The next time, if there ever was a next time, it would have to be worth it.

He put the knife under his pillow, blade open, for the comfort of it. And thought again of Evan and that scene in the woods and downstairs with Lois. And wasn't as angry as he'd been before.

The guy had been jumped, correct? He had a right to fight back. So he'd taken Round One. Besides, whatever his plans, he'd paid for the motel rooms.

But Lois, the dirty, two-timing bitch! He'd really dug her, and she knew it. He'd given her all he'd had, while he'd had it. And if she'd played straight he might have gone back to part-time work at the post office, at least until there was enough to give them some security on the road. Like if a ride petered out and they were sweating for another, they could've made it by bus. And if she gave her sugar-daddy in Albuquerque a miss, they could've set themselves up in L.A. This way, they barely had enough to *eat* on, if the rip-offs and handouts didn't develop. This way it was always desperate time.

He closed his eyes and told himself to sleep. Tomorrow and tomorrow and tomorrow, as they learned in school . . . and he always paid the douchebags back.

3: | Tuesday p.m.

Grayson & Burns had the eighth to eleventh floors of the block-square, mile-high, mostly glass building on Fifth and Fifty-second, and from the moment he left the elevator and entered the lush waiting room—like an exhibit at the Brooklyn Botanical Gardens, it was so heavy with green things seemingly growing out of the floor—Roersch didn't like it. Because he felt old and fat and poor and badly dressed. Because the men and women in the waiting room, halls and offices were young or well preserved, and if not rich looked stylishly trim and *In*. Even those with gray in their hair, even the one man he saw who was totally bald, looked crisp and athletic and involved in joyous living. Roersch felt that he alone knew age and loss and occasional despair.

That one bald man was just lowering his fit body into a

chair behind a long desk in a stadium-sized office. Even his
scalp glowed with health and expensive suntan.

"I won't ask what this is all about, Sergeant. It's obviously in reference to Judith Keel."

Roersch crossed his legs, knowing his gray suit needed
cleaning, pressing, incinerating. He looked at the dark-
wood box on the desk, hoping it didn't hold cigars.

"Cigarette?" Morgan Burns asked.

"Yes, thanks."

They were long, brown, unfiltered Nat Shermans, and
Roersch felt a stab of guilt even as he leaned forward to
accept Burns's proffered light. "Gave them up myself,"
Burns said. "I admire anyone who has the courage to
ignore the Surgeon General and all that televised clamor
about life-and-breath, heart attacks, you know."

Roersch also knew the difference between admiration
and sly jokes. He nodded slowly, and dragged smoke deep
into his lungs. Some people felt all cops were shmucks.
There were times he felt that way himself.

The phone rang. Burns excused himself and swiveled to
face the windows. Roersch suddenly wanted to cough. He
controlled it. Burns spoke softly of "billings," "story
boards," and "presentations." Roersch stabbed the cigarette out in the ashtray, and put the butt in his pocket for
later. He looked around the office. Paintings, not prints,
on the walls, and to the side of the desk, standing on what
looked like a log of solid aged briar, a statue. It was
smooth black stone, a boy running, naked, the penis and
testicles exposed. More than exposed, highlighted, so that
you couldn't help looking right *there*.

He found himself thinking of the departmental lecture
on "Emerging Sexual Splinter Groups." Of course, that
might not be it. Helen had taken him to museums, and
they were full of such things. Still, he wondered if the rich,
successful, athletic Mr. Morgan Burns was coming out of
a closet.

Not important . . . except that it started a train of
thought. So far, his thinking on the Keel murder had been

totally male-directed—a man as murderer. And not just because the hacking of arms and legs required a certain amount of strength, but also because of the sexual nature of such crimes. Criminal history had very few women monsters of that sort. It had plenty of men, headlined by Gilles de Rais who'd butchered perhaps eight hundred boys, along through the overpublicized Jack the Ripper, Herman Mudgett of Chicago who claimed twenty-seven assorted victims, the German carver-cannibal Haarmann who also claimed twenty-seven, good old Charlie Stark-weather, and the Texas horrors—the Hinley, Brooks, Corll murders. In the Texas horrors, as in the de Rais murders, the victims were all males; the killers were homosexually driven, as were several of the others in at least some of their murders. And with lesbians also coming out of their closets . . .

Burns had turned, phone still in hand, and caught Roersch's eyes on the statue. He covered the mouthpiece. "By a newcomer, Depinder. Fine piece of work, isn't it?"

"Well hung, yes."

Burns put back his head and laughed. "Mr. Depinder prefers them that way." He swiveled around again and continued talking into the phone.

Roersch looked at the statue, and then at a painting on the wall to the right of the desk. Ancient Greek scene, like the white figures on blue background vases and dishes Helen had called Wedgwood. More color here, but the same style—white columns in the background, bright blue sky, and two nude women with pale flesh tones, arms around each other's waists, the smaller with her head on the larger's shoulder. Nothing definite, as in the statue of the nude boy. No one really *doing* anything . . . and yet it made him think things, feel things.

Roersch noticed the way the hand of the larger woman rested low on the hip of the smaller woman, splayed out over that hip, reaching for, touching, the pale bulge of buttock.

He remembered a porno film, years ago, before they

showed them in movie houses all over the city; a film at some lodge meeting his radio-car partner, Will Overton, had taken him to, trying to make him join up. Three women, going at each other.

And he remembered more of the research he'd done on famous murderers in his eager-beaver days as a novice detective, when he dreamed of solving case after case and becoming a lieutenant in a year, a captain in two, and a chief before retirement.

He turned from the painting. All he had left of *that* fantasy period was a backlog of information—and part of that information concerned the Countess Bathory who, in the late sixteenth century, had butchered hundreds of girls taken from the surrounding Hungarian countryside. Some said as many as six hundred, before even *her* power, her connections to the royal court, her castle and private retinue of soldier-servants, gave way to public pressure and a determined royal investigator. Such an operation wasn't possible in today's world, given the loss of personal power. But the *emotions* that drove such a lesbian bitch were bound to exist in some women today. Emotions that could be expressed in a *single* murder, say Judith Keel's, as well as in dozens or hundreds . . .

Well, there were always freak murders. No sense going overboard on the idea. No indication that Judith Keel was a les, or a bi.

But had she formed a relationship with one?

Burns turned to face him. "Well, Sergeant?"

"I know Miss Keel was a receptionist. I'd like to know exactly what she did, and where, and with whom."

"I can direct you to her immediate superior, Harold Cosset." He reached for the phone.

"Is there anything *you* can tell me? Not just business. Private life, in the office and out."

Burns was shaking his head, looking at the statue, smiling. He picked up the phone. Roersch sighed. He was glad he was approaching retirement. He was too old-fashioned to change his gut reactions.

He went from the eighth floor to the eleventh. The girl at the desk was about twenty, and stacked. She made him touch his thinning hair in an abortive combing gesture. He saw he didn't have anything like that kind of an effect on her. She seemed surprised he was there at all.

"Can I help you?"

"Mr. Burns called Mr. Cosset. I'm Detective Sergeant Roersch." He took out his wallet and showed his gold badge.

"What is this in reference to, sir?"

"Just call Mr. Cosset, *will* you?" His voice made her start, and reach for the phone. "Please," he added, turning away.

Another botanical gardens. Fucking faggot shit!

He caught himself. He wasn't being fair, or logical. This place was a hell of a lot nicer than any of the six precinct houses he'd experienced. It was the girl. It was her beauty, and her casual rejection of him as belonging here.

The girl said, "Mr. Cosset will see you now. Down the hall and to your left."

He said thanks and walked by her, looking straight ahead. She said, "Mr. Roersch, no one called *me* to say you had an appointment with Mr. Cosset. I just didn't know what you wanted. It's my job to know what people want with our executives."

He stopped. "Thank goodness. I thought I'd lost my sex appeal."

He was surprised at how hard she laughed. He smiled and said, "Sorry," and went through a door. And told himself he had to be less sensitive, less on the prod.

Cosset was about thirty; small and crisp and to the point. "Judy was the receptionist on this floor. The girl you just saw was her alternate, and now is the regular. I'm the personnel manager, so I handle them. Judy also did some modeling, right here in the shop. She talked about acting experience, but I never checked it out. No reason to. Her job wasn't important, and she didn't come to my attention too often. I mean, her attendance record was average, and she didn't have problems with other members of the staff."

Roersch nodded, looked at Cosset, nodded again. Cosset said, "Have I left anything out?"

"Well, you might not want to discuss her personal life."

"I'd be perfectly willing to, if it would help find whoever did that ugly thing to her. Those pictures in the *News*, God! But I didn't date her, if that's what you mean." He paused. "I tried. Half the men in G&B tried. Practically no one made it."

"Who did?"

Cosset waved his hands. "This kind of talk could mislead . . ."

"I'm just checking over the ground. If I feel a lack of cooperation, I'll have to send plainclothesmen around, asking everyone everything you can think of, including who liked her, disliked her, dated her, lunched with her, visited her, the works. *Detailed* interviews. I'd rather not interfere with your routine . . ."

Cosset said, "Thanks," dryly. "The only person I know who was close to her—he left with her sometimes; dated her, I think—he's on an extended vacation."

Roersch took out his little dime-store notebook for the first time today. "Name?"

"It doesn't mean he . . ."

Roersch simply looked at him.

"Yes, of course, you would know that." He shook a cigarette from a pack and lit it; then remembered to offer the pack to Roersch.

"No, thanks."

"Evan Bley, our copy chief. He's more than that, really, though Mr. Burns keeps the title of Creative Director."

Roersch got the spelling of the last name. And the address. And the name and address of the person Bley had listed as next of kin, his mother, Kate Bleywitz. And everything else, such as age, marital status, physical description, that Cosset had in his personal file.

"How can he be reached?"

"I don't know. I don't think anyone knows, including Evan, though you might check the writers on the ninth floor. I asked him myself, and he said he was just going to get in his car and drive west, all the way to California."

"When did he leave?"

"Friday was his last day of work. He'll be back in a month—four weeks, exactly."

"How can an important member of your staff disappear for a whole month without leaving an address, a phone number, the name of someone who can reach him? What if something he's worked on . . . what if he's *needed*?"

"He hadn't had a vacation in two years and wanted to avoid just such interruptions. If we don't know where he is, we can't bother him."

"He's almost fifty. His mother must be in her seventies, or older. What if anything happened to her?"

"So maybe *she* knows where to reach him."

Roersch smiled at the sharp tone. "Thank you. What sort of car does he drive?"

"You're not going to trace him, hunt him down, are you? He'll be upset if he thinks I . . ."

"Mr. Cosset," Roersch said.

"A green Jaguar sedan."

Roersch made notes, and decided to check out a few of the writers, especially the man taking Bley's place.

Roersch was getting hungry, he was far off his turf, and he didn't want to spend heavy for a meal. He still had restaurants where the tip was all he paid. The buck he saved today might be spent in Key West a few years from now.

Later, he'd go to the victim's apartment house; then to the cleaning woman; then to the mother's place in Brooklyn. And on, bird-dogging whatever leads developed.

He asked Cosset if he could use his phone. The man said certainly, and left the office. He called the desk and asked what was in on Keel. Miraculously, the autopsy report. It showed this was going to be one bitch of a case. No sexual assault; no indication of sex activity at all.

Except for the dismemberment, Roersch thought. Some freaks came in their pants while cutting a throat, or hacking off arms and legs.

Cosset had left his cigarettes on the desk. Roersch fought the good fight, and lost. When no one was around to remind him he was killing himself, it tasted pretty damned good.

Cosset returned. Roersch stood up, waved the cigarette, thanked him. "Did she have any close girlfriends?"

"Not that I know of. She usually lunched alone at her desk, except when some new man was trying to make the grade by buying her meals. That never lasted, since she wouldn't date them."

"Far as you know."

"Exactly. What went on outside—especially if the man was married—no one would be likely to know. For a pretty girl, she was remarkably aloof, and alone."

"Any reason for that married-man remark?"

"Married-man . . . ? No, *Jesus*, that's what I meant when I said I could be misunderstood! I was just commenting generally. I haven't any specific case in mind, or even a suspicion!"

Roersch chuckled and held out his hand. The small man looked at it, and shook it.

Bley's assistant was big, blond, and talkative about everything but essentials. He made references to Serpico, with a knowing grin, and said his cousin was on the force in Boston. "Bright guy, but no pull, no rabbis to hold his hand, dig?"

Roersch asked questions. He learned that Bley was "a fantastic adman, but remote, almost unfriendly when it comes to socializing." Judith Keel was "too good a girl to be true."

"I agree with you," Roersch said, nodding.

"I have a theory." Hearty chuckle. "You wouldn't be interested."

"Go on."

"Judy either hated men, or she was covering. I doubt she hated men. Just not the type. So she was covering. What would you say to the hypothesis she was a hooker, with this job as a contact for modeling jobs, maybe TV acting shots? She wore expensive clothing, had some good jewelry—a diamond necklace and matching earrings—and that apartment wasn't furnished in Monkey Ward. That brass-frame water bed alone—seven, eight hundred."

"You're an observant man. We could use you."

"The way I'm going here, I might take you up on that." Roersch smiled briefly.

"Of course, it all depends on how big a piece of the *pad* you get me." He said the word "pad" as if he'd just coined it, and gave it the big, hearty chuckle.

Roersch said, "When did you see this water bed, the other furnishings?"

"Pardon?"

"When did you see her apartment?"

"Oh, come *on* now, Sergeant!" He shook his head, chuckling again.

Roersch waited, looking at him. The chuckle grew thin, and died.

"I wasn't trying to *hide* that I'd been to Judy's apartment. No one had to *trap* me."

Roersch kept waiting, looking at him.

"Once, just once, she had a little gathering. It was a career thing, for a few of our top art men and writers, so she could promote herself as a possibility for ads and commercials. Evan and I were there, along with several other men. And our dates."

"Evan Bley was with a date?"

"*I* was with a date. Evan was with Judy."

Roersch nodded, watching the man's discomfort. "This theory of yours makes sense. She was earning about a hundred a week here; take-home pay about eighty. You say she had expensive clothing, diamonds and good furniture. So it's either a private income, or men." He paused. "Or one man."

"I didn't say *lots* of diamonds. Just that necklace and earring set."

Roersch went on, as if the blond man hadn't spoken. "One man, with a good income, say Mr. Bley."

"There's nothing wrong with buying a girl gifts. It doesn't mean . . ."

"Perhaps another man, also well off?" He smiled, inviting confidences.

"Not that I know of. And as for Evan and Judy . . . I don't think they were really heavy . . . I mean serious." He shrugged. "You know, just a bit of fun. They showed very little in the office."

"Naturally."

"Afraid I've run out of time. Got a client meeting in ten minutes."

Roersch stood up. "You've been very helpful."

"I don't see how. I was just talking. That hooking idea . . . the more I consider it, the more unlikely it seems."

"Yes, far more likely that one-man theory of yours."

"*Mine?*"

"Well, you led into it."

"No way a man like Evan would do such a thing! He has the world by the nuts! I never said . . . you assumed incorrectly . . ."

"Evan Bley is the only man here, that we know of, who dated her. He has the money to buy the nice things she owned. He left this office on Friday for a month's vacation, and no one knows where he is. Those are facts, not assumptions."

"But if you go on from there to assume he had reasons, motive, because he bought her things . . ." He faltered.

Roersch put out his hand. "Thanks for your help, Mr. . . . ?"

"McKenney. Didn't I introduce myself?"

"No. I just walked in and started talking."

"It's Vince McKenney. I'm here all the time."

"Where I can find you if I need you, right?"

"Sure, right. But why would you want to find me? I never had anything to do with Judy. Ask anyone . . ."

Roersch laughed. "Cop's sense of humor, Mr. McKenney."

When he was halfway out the door, he turned. McKenney was rubbing his face.

"But if Miss Keel was seeing another man, and Bley had this big investment and felt he was being two-timed . . ."

"That's one *hell* of an 'If,' " McKenney said.

"Yes. It's also one hell of a motive. And there are going to be one hell of a lot of cops around here in the next day or two. So if you know anything about other men, and about the laws on obstruction of justice and withholding evidence . . ."

"I know Evan wouldn't do such a thing. No matter what the provocation." He paused. "But he *did* think she was seeing someone else. He had her followed. By a private detective."

This was Break One. "How do you know?"

"That cousin I mentioned. He isn't a cop in Boston anymore. He works for the Congrove Agency here in Manhattan. I'd mentioned it around the shop, and one day Evan asked me about him."

"When?"

"Two, maybe three months ago. When I saw my cousin —we don't socialize, but he drops in occasionally—when I saw him a month ago, he let it slip."

Roersch sat down again. He got the cousin's name; the agency address and telephone number.

Then McKenney said, "She wasn't seeing another man. At least, she wasn't caught with another man during the surveillance."

Break One was reduced.

Roersch drove crosstown and downtown to King's Deli, where he ate heavily and drank two Dr. Brown's Cel-Rays and smoked the remainder of his Nat Sherman. And kidded the thin Puerto Rican bus boy, who smiled just enough to make a show and not at all with his eyes. Well, he was a *Negrito*, and who ever heard of a black liking a cop, at least in this town? Yet the kid showed good stuff; was a fast worker, clean-looking, spoke pretty good English. Sometimes Roersch wanted to say that he knew how rough it was and to keep trying, keep working, and stay off the shit, for God's sake, and you'll make it, get a good job and money and escape the hell-holes. But how could he? He barely believed it himself.

He leafed through his little book, and wondered whether Evan Bley had hated Judith Keel enough to kill her. A quick blaze of anger after an argument . . .

But the butcher job . . . it didn't fit in with quick anger; didn't fit in with anything he knew about Bley. It fit in more with Gilles de Rais and Countess Bathory and mass murderers.

He left a quarter on the table and walked out, giving the thank-you nod to Abe and his sister behind the counter. He crossed Ninth Avenue and turned left toward the station. He was anxious to read the reports. He was impatient to get back out for his bird-dogging. He wanted to start this thing moving, get more of a picture.

There were possibilities here.

Lois came awake slowly, eyes opening and staring sightlessly. She stretched and sighed, one hand between her legs, touching, rubbing. It was always this way in the morning, and the itch, the hunger, was rarely satisfied by whatever might happen during the day.

Then she remembered where she was, and with whom, and she withdrew her hand quickly and looked for Evan.

He was gone!

She sat up, and turned her head, and saw him in the other bed.

Why?

What had she said and done *this* time?

But her mind cleared and she knew this had been no Lois Chandler special. No LEAVE ME ALONE, MOTHER-FUCKER!

Like the time before she'd met John, when she'd worked at the Garden of Allah Massage Palace, the small guy with the beard had offered her a sharp furnished apartment and fifty a week just so he could visit weekday afternoons. But the first time he tried to make it with her, she blew the whole thing with one of her real fits, her disgust and hatred exploding all over the place. Man, he'd *scrambled* for his pants and the door!

Funny thing. She could whack them off all night at the Palace, and even use her mouth if there was a little turn-on, but fucking was something else again. She never knew how she would feel, until they took off their clothes. Then maybe one out of five got to her.

She wished it were different, but it wasn't.

She wished she'd never roomed with Clothilde back in Sydney, but she had.

Evan was turning over, his eyes opening. "What time is it?"

"Who knows?" She jumped off her bed and into his. "Who cares?" She nuzzled his neck and kissed his cheek and said, "Like sandpaper, baby." She put her hand under the blanket and on his cock. The monster was up. "Surprise!" she cried, and kissed his mouth and stroked his shaft; and whether he was in the mood or just had to piss made no difference now. His hands grabbed her ass, and he kissed her breasts, and he fingered her box, and she didn't have to act, she was hot for it.

She wanted to suck it, just a little, but she was afraid. What if he went the same route as last night?

She bent and licked it, quickly. He moaned. She said, "Put your hands behind your head, Frankenstein." He obeyed. She gave it about ten seconds of sucking, and then climbed on and rode him. His hands were rough, jamming her down on it, but this time she was with it, all the way, and he slid in easy, and even his pinching, his pulling her tits, his cracking her ass a few good ones, was okay.

She came fast.

She wanted to go on the same way until *he* came, but he turned her over, never getting out, and got a little rougher. It was the way he shoved her legs up and back; felt like her spine was going to break. Luckily, he came faster than yesterday.

He held her a few minutes, kissing her face. They looked at each other. He said, "What about Albuquerque?"

"Never heard of it."

They laughed together, and she went to the bathroom and took a long, hot shower. He was sleeping again when she came out, but woke as she began dressing.

"Hurry," she called. "It's three in the afternoon! I'm dying of hunger!"

He went into the bathroom and the shower ran. She finished dressing and looked in the mirror. She struck a few poses, recited a few lines from scripts she'd studied in acting school, nodded and pointed her finger at her image and said, "You *can* make it. Sure you can. And fuck them all laughing and saying it's a sucker game and it never happens. How else do they get all those actors, all those actresses? Answer me that, fuckheads?"

She heard a laugh, and whirled, and Evan was standing in the bathroom doorway, toweling his head. For a moment her face burned . . . and she was afraid the rage was coming. But he said, "You're not bad," and nodded.

She glowed. "I told you that, didn't I?" She ran to him and hugged his bathrobe-covered body. "Will you help me?" she whispered, knowing it was the wrong thing to say—too soon and too flat out—and yet unable to help herself. "Will you give me a chance at acting for some important people? An agent? You know."

"Maybe," he said, and he sounded stiff, cold.

She stepped back, not looking at him. "I'm going out for a while." She went to the door.

He said, "That's why you're here with me, isn't it?"

She turned angrily. "How can you say that? You know I'm madly in love with you. Have been for the many years we've known each other."

He stared. "You've got quite a temper."

"Yes." She began gaining control.

"But you're right, of course. I was being stupid."

"So was I. And I'm sorry, hon. Promise you'll always forgive me when I act like a nut?"

"If you'll promise to always wake me up as you did this morning."

"It's a deal." She went out into a sunny afternoon, a warm afternoon, and said, "*Yay!*" and jumped into the air like the cheerleaders at the school meets, when she'd run her guts out with her father standing behind the railing, his face straining as she passed him on her way to the finish line.

"Was he *that* good?"

John was sitting in the car, behind the wheel, sipping coffee from a paper container.

She walked over to the open window, and took the container from his hand. She sipped and made a face. "How can you drink it without sugar?"

He took it back from her. "I'm used to bitter things."

"Heavy, man, heavy." She turned to look around. There was a truck parked near the road, and that was it. Theirs was the last car here. "Where'd you get the coffee?"

"The office. It's complimentary. Free, that is."

"I know what complimentary means, you mother."

"Sure you do. Like with Evan. Complimentary Lois."

She smiled into his face. "Not really. It's a swap. He's got plenty to exchange. More than you'll ever have."

"Yeah, in the wallet."

She kept smiling. "I was thinking of somewhere else, little boy."

He flushed, and his hand drew back as if to belt her. "Don't," she said. "Remember the last time you tried to muscle me?"

"I remember. And I think you should remember I had something to lose then. Now . . ."

"Now you'd end up the same way as then. Only more so. Because Evan would put your ass on the road so fast . . ."

Something made a crumpling sound and she saw his right hand moving in his lap and then it rose and she ducked and the newspaper hit her bent head. He began to draw back his left hand, with the container of coffee, but thought better of it and raised it to his mouth and stared straight ahead.

"Lucky for you that was *paper*," she said, but she wasn't mad; she was sorry for him.

She began to turn toward the office, to get some coffee of her own, when the paper, barely wadded, flapped open and she saw it was yesterday's *New York Daily News*. And open to Page Four. And there was the picture of Judy and the headline about the "Slaughter-House Slaying."

She kicked it away. It caught a breeze and the pages separated and went drifting across the parking area.

She wanted to keep going, but had to turn to him. He was looking at her. She suddenly felt he knew, and she had to say something to make sure he didn't . . . because he *couldn't!*

"You got morbid taste, Johnnie, carrying that story around with you."

"What story?" he asked, voice very quiet.

"You know."

"You mean about your friend getting killed?"

Her throat seemed to narrow and she had to force the words through it. "What're you talking about, man?"

"Judith Keel."

She was going to bluff it through, when she suddenly remembered that cold night, maybe late February, when she'd thought she'd seen him ducking into a doorway after work. She and Judy had come out of the club and the bastard had been waiting . . .

"You followed me!" she shrieked, and lunged at the car. "You bastard! You had no right! You rotten . . ."

She was clawing at the window, trying to reach through and rip his face. The rage was sweeping her away and she barely understood what he was saying.

". . . and you opening the cab door for her like a nigger maid . . ."

"Bastard! Bastard! You had no right!"

She couldn't get at him. He had the door locked and had rolled the window almost all the way up and was glaring at her. She cursed him . . . and then realized Evan might hear. She took several deep breaths and fought for sweet reason, and said, "What right did you have to follow me? Did I ever follow you? Did I ever try to stop you from having a few drinks with a friend? So what right . . ."

"*Friend*," he sneered, and she had to choke back her screams of rage.

She shook her head and said, "You're sick."

It put him on the defensive. "I only did it once. I was sure you were seeing some guy those nights you stayed out late. But it was a dressy bitch with a prissy mouth, a real square who looked at you like at a pet skunk. If that was your *friend*, you're welcome to her. Only . . ." He paused. "She's dead, isn't she?"

They exchanged a look, and she waited him out.

He said, "You didn't even read that story. Just looked down at the paper for a second. But you knew . . ."

"Big deal. I heard about it on the radio back in New York. And how come you're carrying that paper around? How come you knew who she was, just from following me one time?"

Again they looked at each other. This time he waited *her* out, and she sighed and leaned against the car and said, "Listen, I got the shakes when I heard about her. I mean, what if they hassled her friends? My background's not *that* great when it comes to cops, dancing at topless joints and all. And being Australian. Maybe they'd just ship me back as an undesirable. So I was scared."

He rolled the window down. "Yeah, me too. I wanted to know who she was that night I followed you to her place. I got a cab when you did. I asked the doorman about her. And then . . . well, I called her a few times, saying I'd make trouble, saying I'd tell her friends, her family . . ."

"Tell them *what?*" She had to control fresh anger.

He shrugged. "You know. I wasn't sure, but I wanted to scare the bitch. And what if she'd told someone and maybe called the police? What if they traced me and thought I'd killed her? I'm what they call a *vagrant*, correct? The cops would've loved to put me through the wringer!"

She nodded understandingly. "I hope they catch the retard who did it," she said.

"And put him away for life."

She began to say something, and he began to say something, and they laughed a little because they'd both been saying that Evan didn't have to know.

She walked away. She was sort of glad it was out in the open with John. But what a drag, his following her and phoning Judy! Unbelievable, man!

She entered the office. There was a fat old guy behind the desk, like the ones that used to come to the Palace, only poorer-looking. "Do you have coffee for the customers?" she asked.

"For the pretty ones, yes." He grinned, his eyes going over her, tits to toes.

"May I have some, please?"

He went to a percolator on the back shelf and poured into a paper cup.

"Cream and sugar," she said.

"Sweets for the sweet," he said, and brought it to her, eyes straight on her chest, that grin a mile wide.

"Jesus," she said, taking the cup.

His smile faded a bit. "Now, now, never take the Lord's name in vain."

"Kiss my ass."

His face went pale.

She sipped and put the container down. "Coffee stinks too," she said, and turned to the door.

"What room are you in?" he called, voice shaking. "If you're not registered here . . ."

She was smiling, opening the door, when the girl came out of the back, about eighteen and dark and built small, with a cute face and big eyes. "Everything all right, Dad?"

Lois said, "Everything's fine, isn't it, Daddy?"

The old prick turned and stomped through the back door. The girl looked after him, and then at Lois.

Lois smiled. The girl finally answered the smile, worriedly. "He's touchy, sometimes," she said.

"They all are. Just don't take too much crap from him."

The girl blinked, began to nod, stopped.

Lois said, "Stay cool now," and went out.

Evan was walking toward the Jag, carrying his suitcase and her pack.

John drove again. She and Evan sat in back. John put on the radio, rock music, real loud. Evan said, "Turn it down a bit, or better still, find softer music."

"The generation gap," John said, and fiddled with the dial.

"The intelligence gap," Evan said, and Lois was surprised at how mad he'd gotten. "The taste gap."

John shrugged, and turned the dial. An announcer was speaking of Watergate. "Loud or soft," Evan said, "*any* music is preferable to *that*. I'm on vacation. I refuse to listen to the garbage, the horror, that passes for news in our times."

John said, "Yes, master," and turned the radio off.

Evan nodded and smiled, and John grinned into the rearview, and they hit each other with their phony cool.

Lois sighed and leaned into the corner, closing her eyes.

If there was going to be a war, she didn't want to see it. She just hoped it ended fast, with John getting the boot before he could try anything dangerous. Last night was one thing, *before* she'd known what Evan could do for her, and make her feel. Now it was another thing entirely, and no way would she let John make waves.

This was the Hollywood special, and she was the prize passenger!

4: | Tuesday p.m. and Wednesday a.m.

They ate dinner at a restaurant outside of Indianapolis, a large, red-leather, pub-style steak house with soft lights and flickering candles. It was eleven o'clock and Evan was exhausted; he had driven for the past four hours. Flashing his eyes back and forth from road to mirror, and keeping himself ready for some sort of move from the rear seat, where John had reclined, had drained him of all energy.

As it turned out, John had slept those four hours, and Lois, moving to the front seat, had slept too . . . so they were talky, chipper, cheerful.

Evan had a growing headache. "We did well," he said, looking at the table and the remains of three steak dinners.

Lois excused herself to go to the bathroom. John leaned back in his seat, yawning and stretching. "We sure did. Man, that was one great meal! Nothing like beef, no matter what the vegetarians say. My mother was a vegetarian for a while. She tried everything to stay young. Actresses. They refuse to admit they're human."

"*Are* they?"

John laughed. "Bet Lois'll be that way in a few years." Then, quickly, "Not that she's a bad chick. I mean . . ." He shrugged. "Hell, it's okay with me whatever she does. We had our go." A pause. "Like I said, wish I could start this hitch all over again."

Evan recognized the conciliatory tone, the renewed peace offer. But John was lucky to be in the car *this* long. He'd thought to put him out soon after leaving the motel.

"What was your mother like?" he asked.

"I told you, an actress. She had supporting roles in a few big flicks, and the lead in a small bomb. Carla Carlson, she called herself. Ever hear of her?"

"The name isn't familiar."

"That was her hangup. People not knowing her name. My father bankrolled movies once in a while as an investment. That's how mother got her one lead role. Father was in real estate and construction; put together deals that led to shopping centers and industrial complexes."

Evan sipped tepid coffee, nodding, wondering where he was and what he was listening to. Out of town; the dark side of the moon. Rona Barrett rejects. He lit a cigarette.

"Know what the holiest night of the year was at our home? Not Christmas Eve or Easter sunrise. Academy Awards night. Jesus, you had to sit so quiet, or else you went to bed. No loud breathing allowed. And the way she cried at those stupid acceptance speeches. You have no idea . . . I still can't watch the fucking thing without a gut-ache."

"Is she alive?"

"*She* thinks so. And yours?"

Evan said, "Yes, a simple old woman," thinking he could really mean it now. But his headache was worse.

"Are you going home to her?" he asked, because he was *running* from his.

John paused. "Well, it's more going home to a *town*, L.A. And I'll see my father . . ." He shrugged. "She lives in Frisco now. If I go up there, later, I'll see her. If I decide to." He rubbed his face, as if *he* had a headache now.

Lois returned, threading her way through the tables, getting looks from two bus boys changing settings for tomorrow's lunch.

"Thought you fell in," John said.

"I feel sick."

"That's because of your strict diet."

"Ha, ha." She'd eaten a truly enormous dinner.

Back at the car, Evan told John to drive.

"Hope we stop soon," Lois said. "I got these cramps."

"Then why stop at all," John said, "if it means what it usually means?"

"Not *that*! I just have a stomachache."

Evan got in back. Lois began to follow. Evan said, "I'd like to stretch out and sleep."

She said, "That's cool," and got in beside John.

John said, "You can both sack out. I'd drive all the way to L.A., the way I feel now."

Lois looked back at Evan, forlornly. He lay down, using her pack for a pillow, and closed his eyes. He gave himself to the sway, the rushing sound, the flicker of light across his eyelids. But he kept his hand on his pocket and the hardness of metal.

He half-slept, and heard them talking. Lois was saying she felt better. There was the sound of a match scratching, and movement, and then she whispered, "No way!"

He didn't bother looking. His head ached and he had to sleep.

They stopped once, for gas and Lois's trip to the toilet. John stayed in the car, and Evan moved only enough to hold out his credit card and sign the slip. Then sway and rush and flicker put him back under.

Later, he heard John whispering intensely. "What difference can it make to you? I'm not asking for anything but your *hand.*"

She whispered too. "No!"

"I know your plans. So okay, I accept them. This can't change anything, except to get me off the hook."

"Use your *own* hand, mother!"

John's voice rose a bit. "That's the squarest thing . . ."

"*Shhh!* What's wrong with you? What if he woke up?"

"You once said you dug group scenes."

"This isn't grouping; this is sneaking."

"Bet he wouldn't mind. Bet he'd dig it."

The car slowed, weaved a bit, and Lois's whisper grew sharper. "Let *go!* I *won't!*"

She looked back at Evan, just as he opened his eyes. "Go on," he said. "Help him."

She gasped. "Hon? You awake?"

"It's all right with me."

"Well, gee, I wouldn't . . . do you really mean it?"

"If it's not something you dislike doing."

John kept his eyes straight ahead; drove slowly and steadily.

"I don't dislike . . ." She shrugged. "You *sure?*"

"I don't mind. Go on."

John looked at her. She turned to him. He reached out and took her hand. Evan sat up slowly, quietly, so as not to intrude. John had his fly open. He drew her hand to it, pushed it inside. She turned her face from Evan, not looking at either of them, and manipulated John inside his trousers.

"Take it out," John whispered.

"I can do it this way." Her voice was choked, shaky; she was worried.

Evan said, "Why not make him comfortable?"

The car slowed even more. John glanced down as she drew out his penis. Evan leaned forward. It looked stubby;

thick and short. It was uncircumcised. Lois jerked it up and down, face turned to the dashboard. John sighed, shifting weight. "C'mon now," he muttered.

Evan leaned over the seat and touched Lois's head. "You can do better than that."

She turned to him. Their eyes met, and locked. She began stroking John with some feeling, some instinct for *his* feelings. John said, "Baby, yeah!"

Evan drew Lois's head to him. They kissed. Her tongue came into his mouth. He turned his eyes so as to watch her hand. She was stroking sweetly now. He drew away and pushed down on her head. She went down as he pushed, and stopped when he let up. So he pushed all the way, and she took John in her mouth.

The car went to the side of the road, bucked and stalled. John leaned back, eyes closing. And Lois stopped; raised her head and looked at Evan. He was leaning over the seat, breathing hard. "Suck him," he said. "For me."

She went back down. With hand and bobbing head, she brought John to orgasm; then opened the window and spat. She wiped her mouth with her bandana, and slumped in her seat. John zippered his fly and started the car. He drove back onto the road without a word.

Evan was shaking with excitement. "Come back here." She looked at him.

He reached out and stroked her head, her face; dropped his hand and caressed her breast. "Please," he said.

She squirmed between the seats, and he dragged her back violently and his hand grasped her bottom and his hand went to the slit in her skirt and found the moist juncture; the very moist juncture. They kissed and he fingered her and she writhed. He glanced at the rear-view mirror and saw John's eyes flickering there. He opened his belt and trousers and dragged down trousers and underwear. He drew Lois's skirt up around her waist and placed her on his lap, her back to him, and fitted her onto his penis.

"Oh Jesus," she said, and leaned all the way forward,

her head coming to rest on the top of the front seat. John turned briefly to look at her. "Jesus, Jesus," she said, rotating her bottom. Evan humped under her and she squirmed, bucked, ground, gasped, "Sock it, baby . . . sock it!"

John turned his head again and brushed her lips with his. She grabbed him by the hair; held him and kissed him. The car swerved, tires shrieking.

Everything stopped while John righted the car, and pulled to the side of the road. Then it continued.

In the blackness, with sudden explosions of light and sound from passing vehicles, Evan grasped the pliant waist and squeezed the firm breasts and rammed up, faster, harder. And watched John and Lois kissing, straining at each other's mouths, reaching for each other's bodies.

And it was good. It was a loss of one-to-one and forsaking-all-others and fearful possession in copulation. It was the forbidden three instead of the Biblical two. His violence was gone, except for the violence of lusty thrusts and strong clutches of flesh and explosive obscenities.

He groaned deeply and orgasmed.

She said, "Don't stop! Little . . . while."

He was drained now, but had enough left to bring her to her conclusion. Immediately afterward, she slumped forward. His penis was still inside her. He felt their juices dampening his thighs, and that too was good.

John drove onto the highway. Lois leaned back against Evan. He stroked her belly, held her hand. John said, "Well, you'll save on motel rooms."

Lois laughed. John joined her. Evan looked into the rear-view and saw the eyes there and began to laugh too.

They laughed for quite a while. When Evan's penis slipped out of Lois, she shrieked laughter, and he felt it was the funniest thing that had ever happened to him. She turned to kiss him, and said, "Are we all in-laws or what?" and Evan laughed until tears ran from his eyes.

Later, after Lois had cleaned him and herself with her bandana, he asked John for a cigarette. It was passed back to him with a "Sure thing," and he said, "Thank you," and their hands touched.

It wasn't until they stopped at a service station that he thought to check his jacket pocket. The pistol was gone.

He managed to remain behind, instructing the attendant, while John and Lois went to the rest rooms; then he searched the car thoroughly, and didn't find it.

While he'd slept. At the previous gas stop. While Lois had gone to the bathroom and John had smoked in the front seat and he'd slept until asked for his credit card. John could have taken the gun.

Or Lois. While fire had fogged his brain. While he'd fucked with pants down and jacket on. Her hand could have reached back into his pocket and taken the gun. And handed it to John.

He walked toward the bathroom. He shook with rage.

He was afraid too, but rage was stronger.

It had been so good and they had ruined it.

He could return to the car and drive away and leave them here with nothing.

But he kept walking. It was a contest, a game, and he always won at games. One way or another, he always won. Without joy, without satisfaction, most of the time . . . and this had promised both joy and satisfaction, and they had robbed him of the promise.

John came out of the bathroom. "Hey . . ." he began, and Evan went by with the rage bubbling inside him.

In the bathroom, he washed his face with cold water, over and over, and lectured himself about control, poker-faced control, and the game being far from over.

John or Lois or both.

He'd find out soon enough.

He returned to the car. They were both inside; Lois in front, John in back.

"Thought you'd want to drive a while," John said.

He signed for the gas and got behind the wheel.

"What time is it?" Lois asked.

"Two o'clock," John said.

"Where are we?"

"Illinois. Past a town called Effingham."

Evan took his Triptik map from the side pocket, locating Interstate 70 and Effingham.

"We're making some time," John said, leaning back and crossing his legs. "Should be in St. Louis by four, four-thirty, right, Evan?"

"Maybe sooner," Evan said. He put the map away, hooked up his harness, closed his window, and drove onto the highway.

He picked up speed rapidly. When he hit ninety, Lois said, "In a hurry, hon?" trying to sound playful.

"Yes," he said, and pressed the pedal all the way to the floorboards.

The Jaguar surged over a hundred ten. He risked a glance into the rear-view. John's legs were coming uncrossed.

"Hey, that's pressing your luck, isn't it?"

Evan kept the pedal floored. The car was beginning to shudder as the needle crept over a hundred twenty.

"Evan!" Lois said. "You're scaring me!"

He'd never had it up this high, and wondered about his front-wheel alignment. The shudder was severe now.

"Jesus, you'll kill us!" John shouted, mouth almost at Evan's ear.

"Where's my gun?" he asked, beginning to fight the wheel. But he kept the accelerator all the way down, and the speedometer needle kept moving, toward a hundred thirty now.

"Man . . . slow down . . . here's your gun, dammit!" The .38 was pressed to his head.

"Put it on the seat beside me."

"You slow down or I'll . . . !"

"You'll fire? And *parachute* to safety?" He laughed. They were moving at a hundred thirty-five. Two trucks were passed so quickly they seemed to be going *backwards*.

"I didn't know anything about that!" Lois shouted, bracing herself against the dashboard. "Please, Evan, don't stop like before!"

A curve was coming up, gradual enough but on a decline. He wondered how the car would take it.

There was a sudden implosion of air; a sudden eruption of howling sound. John had opened the rear left window. Evan couldn't take his eyes from the road. They were entering the turn, and the Jaguar was accelerating in the decline, its left shocks hitting bottom, its tires screaming. The shudder threatened to tear the wheel from his hands.

"Look back here!" John was screaming at him. "Just look!"

But the turn seemed endless, and the car became terribly light, almost weightless on its right side. In a second, that side would lift from the road and they would go out of control and what would be left wouldn't fill a cigar box.

He was sorry he'd pushed it this far, and yet strangely calm. He was also strangely satisfied, because they hadn't won the game.

"I'm throwing it out!" John screamed.

The turn ended and the Jag righted, held the road again, and he glanced into the mirror where John held the gun by the barrel, waving it, drawing it back when he saw Evan's eyes on him. He threw the .38 into the night.

At least he *appeared* to have done so.

Evan said to Lois, "Get the gun from him."

"But he threw it away!" She was sobbing, staring at the highway racing into their headlight beams.

"Don't try to fool me," he said, his arms and shoulders and neck aching from strain. And taillights rushed toward them in both lanes of what was now a two-lane highway. He centered the Jag in the left lane, flashing his brights.

"Oh God," Lois said, and put her head down and covered her face.

John said, "I *swear*!" and fell back and curled into fetal position.

It was too late, though now he was convinced the gun was indeed gone from the car. Too late to do more than let up on the gas, and poise his foot over the brake pedal. To step down would destroy them as surely as hitting the vehicle they were overtaking. To step down would spin them out of control and into a flaming wreck. He kept flashing his brights, but both sets of taillights remained in their lanes, blocking him.

He said, "Here we go," and just *touched* the brake and heard the shriek of rubber. He saw that the vehicle in the left lane was a car and that it was some distance ahead of the vehicle in the right lane, which was a van. He pressed down a little harder on the brake, and was by the van, and turned the wheel, controlling the urge to *twist* it. The Jag screamed into the right lane, barely missing the rear of the car in the left lane.

Their speed had dropped below ninety. In a moment it was at seventy, as he kept tapping the brakes. At sixty the car he'd passed came abreast of him and a voice shouted, "Crazy bastard!"

He continued to slow, and then the van was passing, a face turned whitely to stare at him. And then he was stopping at the side, releasing his harness at the same time.

John was out before he was.

Lois said, "Let him off at a station . . ."

He was out, his knees shaking. John was moving around the back of the car, looking back at him. Evan followed slowly, the shaking moving up his spine to his head. He was trembling all over.

John had stopped and turned, deep in shadows. Evan moved toward him. John said, "I took it when you were sleeping at the gas station, after we ate. I was going to dump it, for all our sakes. I didn't have the chance . . ."

"You were going to use it. On me."

"Maybe I kept it longer than I should have. To make a point. Like you're not the only one who can score, understand?"

Evan was within striking range now. John's hands came up. Evan's hands moved out, moved around, the fingers ready for gouging, chopping, punching.

"Karate?" John asked, and backed another step.

It was jukarte, a combination of judo and karate, with elements of Chinese boxing or kung fu thrown in for good measure. Two years and seventeen hundred dollars in private lessons and *randori* combat had led him to a brown belt, at which point he'd stopped.

Maybe he shouldn't have. Maybe a black belt and arms-combat training could have handled what he was facing. For John had drawn something from his jeans, and it grew into a knife with a quiet *snick*.

They looked at each other. He hadn't won the game after all. It was just beginning.

Lois cried, "For Chrissake, *enough!*"

John held the knife out low; swung it blade-up in a slow half-circle.

Evan was afraid. Because he knew he had to play out the game.

He began to move.

John threw the knife away. "It was just to put you down, to even the score."

Evan was almost on him.

"I don't want to fight," John said, "Evan . . ."

It was his name that stopped him. His name said brokenly, appended to that surrender.

It reminded him of another name said brokenly, appended to *many* surrenders.

"I don't want you to see Miss Kravitz," Evan Bley when he was Marvin Bleywitz had begged. "Mom, please . . ." Sometimes she would accept his surrender, his broken sounding of her name, her title. Sometimes she would stay execution of the threat to see his teacher—Miss Kravitz or Mr. Darben or Miss Denny. And sometimes she wouldn't; would march him to school the next morning to ask *how come* her Marvin made only a B in English when he was a *natural* A student and had scored *so high* in the intelligence test in fourth grade. And sometimes his mother would send *a little gift*—not always at Christmas—of stockings to a woman teacher, of socks to a man, and the humiliation would be compounded, though she always managed to make them accept the gifts. Then he would never know whether his increased grade was due to his efforts, or the gift; or his *decreased* grade, or his unchanged grade . . .

"I don't want to fight Seymour," Marvin would beg, "Mom . . ." And for a while she had allowed him his escape hatch. But then she had learned of the bullying—standard in the Brooklyn school system—as she learned of almost everything that happened to him, by going down into the street and seeking out his friends, his schoolmates, and *questioning* them with her red smile, her generous handouts of nickels and dimes, her gifts, her bribes . . .

He'd been taken by the hand, and no surrender, no broken sounding of her name, her title, had stopped her. She had made him go up to the bigger boy and, watching from a doorway down the street, had made him fight. Without changing his frightened inability in any way, she had *forced* him on dire threat of "spankings," and they were beatings of maniacal intensity, to attack Seymour. It ended three times in humiliating defeat. Compounded when he got home because she punished him, screamed he was like his father, weak, worthless, a failure, a coward, she had to change him, save him . . . and her slaps and punches and screams that were also blows, rained down on him and he begged, he wept, he fell . . .

Everyone had known. Seymour had known. And the fourth and last time he had been forced to attack—a useless, trembling flurry of blows, unaimed, symbolic, hysterical—Seymour had pushed him off and made a disgusted, go-away gesture and left. "You see?" his mother had gloated. "You won. Now I'll buy you a malted." He hated malteds. Too rich, but that was why she wanted him to drink them. To get big, to get fat. And he choked down his rich, sickly-sweet reward and ate a pretzel stick with it because, "You like pretzels, don't you?" and was at last allowed to go home with her, to withdraw to his room, to sit at his desk and lose himself in a book, a story, a life full of triumphs. He would be a writer, he thought. Because a writer could create triumphant worlds, safe worlds, worlds where only what *he* wanted to happen would happen.

"A teacher is a steady, *safe* job," his mother had said. He was older and he had been in the Air Corps and he rejected her advice . . . and he became a teacher. "I don't want to be a teacher," he'd thought, the day before switching from a Creative Writing major to a Secondary Ed major, "Mom . . ." He still lived at home, had to in order to make the G.I. Bill carry him through his Master's Degree. The only sensible thing to do, wasn't it? She was in the next room . . . but she was also *inside* him, and she didn't accept his surrender. He became an English teacher at Sewanhaka High School, Floral Park, Long Island. And learned it was hell to be in school, no matter *what* side of the desk he was on, because it was a constant reminder of childhood, of surrenders and broken sayings of her name, her title.

And hearing John's surrender, his broken saying of *his* name—"I don't want to fight, Evan . . ."—he felt an ache of recognition, of compassion. He went back to the car and got inside. He started the engine, and Lois said, "I really didn't know about the gun."

He nodded, racing the engine, feeling the shudder, the raggedness. It would need a tuneup, soon.

Lois was looking out her window. "Are you leaving him here? I wouldn't blame you, hon, but it's so late and this is a nowhere spot."

He kept racing the engine.

It was a while before John came up on his side, standing back near the open rear window. "Can I have my pack?"

"If you want it."

"I got some sort of choice?"

Evan hooked up his safety belt. Lois moved beside him, and he glanced at her. She was frantically searching for *her* belt.

John opened the back door. Evan swung around. They looked at each other, as they had over the knife. And again John said just the right thing. "I've got no one."

Evan said, "Get in," and drove onto the highway.

So here they were, John thought, stretched out on the back seat, eyes closed, making out he was asleep, because what else was there to do? He didn't know what to say anymore . . . not to Evan and not to Lois. He'd had his chance to do and say it all; first with the gun, and then with the knife. Using the gun at that speed would have been suicide. Using the knife? Well, he just hadn't wanted to, that's all.

He'd really meant to get rid of the gun right after taking it from Evan's pocket. But he'd also wanted to even things out and start fresh, as an equal.

Lois? Shit, she was over and done with.

That's the way it always was with him. First a chick meant ass, and then she began to mean company and friendship, and finally she meant love and wildness and holding on no matter what. Later, he wondered why he'd bothered.

Guess he was sick.

He sure was sick of what he was! Sick of the last ten years . . . almost eleven, since he'd left home six months after his parents' divorce.

That six months! Worse than his whole nineteen years of life up till then! And yet, some people, looking in from the outside, might have thought he'd had a good deal. After all, he hadn't gone to school, or worked. He'd had his own place, out back of the big house, and could've used Dad's pool and tennis court. He had his old Volks, and the Honda, and all the friends who brought their cycles over for tuning and minor repairs because that's what he did, worked on cycles and read and lived on about ten bucks a week that Dad gave him.

It was all cool in school, and if he'd gone along—been *able* to have gone along—with the studies and grades and career, he'd still be in L.A., maybe in a house of his own like Chrissie, now Christopher the lawyer, who'd caught a bit of shit from big-brother John toward the end of things.

But he'd faltered badly in his senior year, though it had been a real hassle to study from the very beginning. Even in Plummer Grade, the private grammar school he'd gone to, there'd been problems. Mostly fighting.

He couldn't be sure of the very first fight, but he could remember lots of them going way back. And kids didn't fight at Plummer; no reason to. He'd managed to *make* reasons, though it hadn't seemed so at the time.

The Goodman kid. They'd been playing soccer and there'd been an argument about a body block. And suddenly he'd gone wild, begun hitting the kid with everything he had, and there'd been blood and Mr. Windom holding him and, later, a suggestion that his mother seek professional assistance. Which meant a shrink.

She'd resisted that, until a few weeks later and another fight, only this time the kid was bigger and better than he was, and *he'd* done the bleeding. Still, everyone said he'd thrown a fit for nothing, so it was off to Dr. Mendices.

Good old Aaron Mendices. Those long nothing hours sitting and talking, making things up so that it wouldn't end, because he'd sort of liked the two hours a week: they were a change, they were peaceful, and where else could a kid say what he wanted to, without interruption, for hours at a time?

But Mendices had played dirty. He'd said little to John and much to Mr. and Mrs. Fredericks. And what he said to the parents was that the boy was unable to cope with school and home, and that something was obviously very wrong at home, and that the violence was his way of escaping problems still very much hidden in his young mind.

How he got *that* from the bullshit, John never figured out. All he talked about to Mendices, as he remembered, was wanting to be a farmer and live alone and read only what he wanted to read instead of the junk they handed out in school.

He could have told Mendices lots of straight stuff, if he'd wanted to. Like Mom fucking that actor in the study when Dad was out on the patio with the other guests. John saw her get it bent over the *Louis Quinze* desk with her evening gown up over her head and that young mick bastard grunting over her ass; watched from the closet where he'd fled when he heard them coming, since he was supposed to be in his room upstairs. And she never wondered why the TV was on, and never even turned it off; just said, "Hurry, darling!" and moaned and groaned while twelve-year-old Johnnie suffered hatred and shame and rage in the closet.

And there was Dad and that woman down the block, Liza Something, who was married to the big guy who'd had a stroke and couldn't walk and, now that he thought of it, probably couldn't fuck either. John had played sick one afternoon and a teacher drove him home and he let himself in the house quietly so as not to have to hassle with Mom . . . but Mom was out and Dad and Liza Something were in one of the three guest bedrooms, getting it on fast and furious, if *sounds* were any indication. He didn't see that one, just listened at the door and heard the whole thing. It didn't bug him as badly as with Mom. In fact, he'd gone to that room in the middle of the night and jacked off thinking of the big-titted Liza Something getting it right there in the same bed.

And the time Dad had broken down the master bedroom door. What would silken-voiced Mendices have said about *that*?

The first John had known of it was Chrissie shaking his shoulder and crying and saying, "Johnnie, wake up! They're fighting! Make them stop!"

He'd left Chrissie in the bedroom and gone down the second-floor hall, and there they were, screaming at each other in the big foyer at the bottom of the stairs. Mom was saying something about getting more love from a "one night stand" than in all the fourteen years of her marriage, and Dad was shouting, "Now it comes out! Now you admit whoring all over town!" and she kept telling him about this guy and that.

She must have seen something coming, because she stopped talking in mid-sentence about a famous singer being mad for her, and turned and ran up the stairs. Dad came after her, but slowly. He was talking to himself. What John heard was a word new to him. "Douchebag," Dad said. "Dirty, filthy douchebag." Over and over. And his fists clenched and unclenched. And he began to move faster, and by the time he reached the top of the stairs he was running. And his face was so different, John wanted to scream in fear. A purple face with wild eyes and gaping mouth. A madman's face. A killer's face.

By the time Dad reached the bedroom door, Mom had locked herself inside. He pounded on it a few times, and she screamed, "Go away! I'll never let you in here again!" At that, Dad had stopped and stood still a moment, almost smiling. Then he stepped back, the purple threatening to burst his face apart, and began kicking under the knob.

Wood splintered; the lock gave; the door sagged open. His mother began crying, begging his father to get hold of himself, saying she'd lied about all the men just to make him jealous.

His father rushed into the room.

There were blows, screams, curses—and then a frantic high-pitched barking as Mom's little poodle, Denise, got out of the closed-off dressing room area where she slept. As the barking continued, the other sounds stopped. So maybe the worst was over. No one could help liking that eight-pound, gutsy mouse of a dog!

Then Mom said, "Don't hurt her . . . Bryant, *no!*"

There was an awful dog scream, and Denise came *flying* out the door to land on the carpeted floor. Her belly was caved in and her head moved and her legs moved but she couldn't move off her side. Dad came after her, his right shoe red at the toe . . . and he kicked again, sending the toy poodle against the wall. And again, sending her to the landing near the stairs. And again, a running kick this time, like at the start of a football game, to spin her into the air and down to the foyer.

Dad turned to Mom, and she stumbled backward, out of Johnnie's sight, saying, "Please, Bryant, I'll never again . . ."

"Instead of *you*," Dad said, looking down and extending his right foot. And the toe of his shoe had bits of intestines and bits of brains mixed with the blood. "Because I wouldn't spend a *minute* in jail for a douchebag." When he turned to the staircase, he was smiling. He looked at the raw meat he'd made as he walked down, and as he walked past it, and he still smiled. The minute he went out of the foyer, Johnnie vomited.

The next morning, Denise was gone and the Chinese maid was working on the blood and vomit stains outside the two bedrooms. He asked for his mother. "Vacation," the maid said, eyes on the carpeting.

The "vacation" lasted three weeks. Dad never mentioned Mom once, and neither of the boys dared ask.

When Mom came home, she was changed.

She was a *slave*; a cowed, terrified slave.

About five years later, when she informed John she was going to Mexico for a divorce, she said that the only reason she'd come back home after Dad kicked Denise to death was because he'd sent "a gangster" to San Diego, where she was staying with friends, to threaten her life. "And, of course, I wanted to be with my children." But when discussing the divorce a few days later, she was forced to admit she'd granted custody of Chrissie, then fifteen and a half, to his father. As for John, "You're old enough to do what you want, but I'll be on the road a good deal . . ." So she'd simply handed them over to Dad. Which wasn't too bad, since Dad was happy now, courting a young brunette he'd met during a business deal, and hinting he would marry her as soon as the divorce was finalized.

That's when John had asked if he could move into the little cottage attached to the garage. His father had smiled and poked him playfully on the shoulder. "A make-out pad, right, Johnnie?" He'd gone along with the deception, seeing how pleased his father was to get him out of the house. But as for his making out, he was a nowhere guy with the girls at that time.

Then he was in the cottage, with some old furniture Dad dug up, and spent his nineteenth birthday drinking Gallo Burgundy with a kid named Burton who was seventeen and kissed his foot. Burton came from Hollywood, Cherokee Avenue, and didn't have two dimes to rub together. But he had his cycle and he knew how to ride it and together they ripped around.

It all looked cool to those who knew him. But Jesus he couldn't make his head come together, he had nightmares about drowning in mud, he wanted to kill every bastard who looked sideways at him, he couldn't sleep without wine, lots of it, and he couldn't even *talk* to a girl because he had no patience with the fucking games you had to play. In fact, that was the whole thing, the games people had to play to study and work and succeed. It all broke down for him that summer. It all flew apart and he saw people as ants, scurrying around, lugging things twice their own size. He couldn't figure out *why*, not to say *how*, to join them and become normal. His friends went back to school, or had to go to work, except for Burton, who talked of ripping off supermarkets and gas stations, but was scared of his own shadow unless John was there to back him up. Except with broads. Burton was big on broads, and sometimes he got one to come over and ball John without the game, without the bullshit. And so he got his rocks off about once a week and Burton slept over a lot and sat around a lot and tried to learn about engines.

John knew he wouldn't go back to UCLA. How could he play the student game? He didn't even know how to walk into a class anymore. He'd trip and fall. He'd laugh and cry. He'd hit someone. And how could he sit there and listen to the shit? He didn't know that kind of English anymore. It *wasn't* English. It was something called College. It was something for game-players. He couldn't speak it, or understand it.

Later, he'd understood he was very close to being insane. Later, he'd remembered the inability to get up until two or three in the afternoon as a drifting into death. And that fucking hot sun and the sounds of Chrissie and Dad and his new wife and their guests playing tennis or splashing around in the pool.

Burton disappeared over the Labor Day weekend. John couldn't make himself wake up and even when he did he couldn't make himself leave the cottage. He knew he could go nowhere, do nothing, had to stay put until things came together again. If he was forced back to school, he would end up dead or in jail or in a hospital.

He waited and watched and listened, and heard his father coming to the garage for the Mercedes. He walked out and confronted him, straining every ounce of his being to speak Parent. "Hey, Dad, how's the weekend going?"

His father said fine, and "You don't look well, Johnnie."

It was an opening, and he said it was all part of worrying about going back to UCLA. And then, as his father frowned, he said, "I want to coast a while, re-evaluate my goals, just until next semester." Bryant Fredericks nodded slowly, and asked what sort of job he had in mind. He said he wasn't sure, wasn't really planning on working, hoped he could count on the ten bucks a week and time for thought. When his father began to argue, he added, "I'm kind of, well, *confused*. I've been thinking maybe I should go back to analysis." At which point his father said not to be hasty and to try that period of coasting.

That was the worst; it seemed to get a little better afterward. He was able to reach a point by Christmas where he could sell his Honda and pack everything of value into the Volks and leave in the middle of the night without telling anyone.

He'd driven to Frisco, and looked up Mom. She wasn't around, but some cigar-chewing guy was and he let John sack out on the couch for three days; then Mom came in for time off from her road show in Spokane. She was all lovey-mother for a day, but it began to wear thin as night approached and she and the cigar-chewer began looking at each other. So he said, hey, he had to split, on his way to New York to try Columbia U., and his mother had given him fifty bucks and off he'd gone. But not far. Just to Haight Ashbury and a night in a park and then a contact and then a month-long high on stuff he'd never tried before—all sorts of stuff. By then his bread was gone, and most of the new friends had disappeared, along with a groupie chick who'd given him her snatch on and off. So he sold the Volks and hit the road.

That was ten years ago. And here he was on his way back to L.A. for the first time since then. And at least one thing was different: he wouldn't mind a little luxury for a change. He was tired of hitching, brawling, lock-ups, rip-offs, and cop-out chicks like Lois. He wanted the sun, the ocean . . .

He wanted some *peace*, dammit!

5: | Wednesday a.m.

He had fallen dead asleep at eleven, unable to keep his eyes open for the late news, but now he was wide awake and his bedside clock read a few minutes to three.

That's the way it had been lately. Fall asleep all right, but up in the middle of the night with the nothingness pressing in on him. Tonight, however, there was something to think of. He'd had a long Tuesday on the Keel case.

But he didn't *want* to think of it. He wanted something pleasurable.

A Scotch? A cigarette?

Roersch put on the radio instead and fiddled with the dial. Rock music. Jesus, nothing but rock music! Didn't anyone but freaks stay up late anymore?

He cut to the short-wave band. He fiddled with the dial, and heard blurry voices, and tuned them into clear voices.

"Give me the gossip about Ann and Finley some other time," a man's voice said, irritably. "Where've you been for two weeks?"

"Vacation," a woman answered. "We drove up to Loon Lake on the spur of the moment. No chance to call because Dave was always around."

"C'mon now, Cindy! No chance at *all?* Two whole weeks? What sort of bull . . ."

"If you're going to be that way, Barry, I'm hanging up!"

Hanging up? Didn't short-wave radio hams say "signing off" or something like it?

"I'm sorry. But you've been, well, *tight* with me lately."

"I'm a married woman. If it wasn't for Dave worrying about my driving home late from the night shift and putting in the car-phone, we'd *never* get a chance to talk."

Car-phone—like the patrol-car radios—actually a short-wave radio transmitter. And the response from the home phone obviously went through a transmitter too. Listening in was like a phone tap.

"We can talk at my place," Barry said.

She snorted. "At your place it's into bed and slam-bam-thank-you-ma'am. *This* is the only way we talk."

"So I'll thank him for the phone next time we go bowling! Now come over and we'll have a drink . . ."

"No thanks. I think we've had it."

"Don't say that! I love you."

Roersch turned off the set. He wondered how many people realized car-phones were radio phones, radio *shows* for whoever happened to tune them in on a short-wave band.

He went to the kitchen and had a fast Scotch. And lit a cigarette. He'd bought a box of Nat Shermans, liking the all-tobacco, quality smoke, despite the buck-ten price. Something else he could afford once in a while if he made lieutenant; could afford regularly if he found a way to score big. And a way had presented itself to him. Not a plan yet; just a hunch, a sensing of what might develop.

He put that firmly out of mind; but he'd been turned off relaxation and sleep, and onto Judith Keel.

He got his little notebook and zipper case of reports from the dresser and sat at the kitchen table, the overhead fixture casting too bright a light on the glossy eight-by-ten official photos and sheafs of paper. He'd always preferred working at home—*thinking* at home, that is. Or anywhere out of the station. Too much shit going on at the station. Collars and filling out reports and kissing ass and bullshit about the pad and politics and sports and women. Lately, there'd been a lot of talk about cracking down on the fags because of the runaway-boy problem, the murders in Texas and the porno operation in Los Angeles and the Greenwich Village pads where juveniles were taken in by older men. Roersch felt it was a temporary swing of the pendulum; it would blow over; it had better, or the hard-liners like Captain Deverney and Inspector Blakely and their kind would have a free hand, at least for a while. That meant broken heads and more people who didn't deserve it getting hurt than the criminal few who did.

Besides, as he'd said to Deverney—with a smile, of course; always a smile for the captains—"What about the runaway girls and the men who take *them* in?"

The captain had given the unbeatable answer. "Hell, Eddy, you're not comparing that and *fags?* We try to get the girls back, sure, but at least when they're with men, it's *normal!*"

Yeah, as normal as Deverney fucking a sixteen-year-old runaway hooker for three months, on the promise she wouldn't be jailed or sent back to her folks. And then trying to pass her on to one of his buddies. The kid had cut and run, and Deverney had smacked his lips over her "nice, tight ass" until he got himself another. He always had some young girl on the hook; pure blackmail, Roersch felt, and a lot worse than the pad the Knapp Commission was so hot about.

But he wasn't the Knapp Commission, or any sort of reformer, and no use wasting steam on Standard Operating Procedure. He went through the photos, the reports, his notebook.

It had been a bad day, from one point of view, and a good one from another.

In terms of the people he'd been able to interview, and what he'd gotten from them, very little, very bad. In terms of growing realization, hunches, pretty good.

The doorman at Judith Keel's house was an elderly spook, nice guy really, no love for the badge, of course, but no need to send for Jones or another black detective to break down barriers. He'd talked freely, though what he had to say was nothing. Miss Keel had very few men friends, even fewer women friends, stayed to herself. He didn't recognize the name Evan Bley, but then again he wouldn't have to. He didn't announce visitors; just opened doors, hailed cabs, was window dressing. The inside door-lock mechanism operated on a buzzer. The visitor spoke into a phone-box, identified himself to the tenant, and was admitted when the tenant pressed a button. Sometimes the doorman recognized callers who came often, but rarely by name. And Roersch had no photograph of Bley. He'd get one later today, but he already knew Bley had visited Judith Keel.

Bley's mother hadn't been home. Roersch had phoned three times. No use going to Brooklyn until he could be sure she'd be there. He could have one of his men see her, but it was something he wanted to do himself, something he felt would be important, interesting, revealing about Bley.

McKenney's cousin, the private detective who'd tailed Keel for Bley, was no longer employed by the Congrove Agency. They had a home address and phone number, but a call had gotten Roersch a recording: "The number you have dialed is no longer in operation. Please make sure you are dialing the correct number . . ." He had Jones working on it.

The cleaning woman lived on Tenth Avenue in a tenement that made Roersch sigh. She was still sick over what she'd discovered.

She'd begun working for Miss Keel five weeks ago. "Miss Keel said her other cleaning woman just stopped coming." She knew nothing about Miss Keel, except that "the apartment was always messy Monday mornings." She couldn't be sure about seeing a personal telephone directory on the phone table in the bedroom, but she *thought* she had . . . or maybe that was because everyone else had them.

She shook her head when Roersch asked if she'd ever found a man in the apartment, or if one had ever called while she was there. She said she was instructed not to answer the phone, and no man ever came, except last week a delivery man with a package. No, she didn't notice the return address. Then she said, "She had a girlfriend over the last time I cleaned there."

Roersch asked for a name, a description. She didn't remember any name, because Miss Keel had already gone to work, as usual, and the girl was getting dressed in the bedroom. "She just said 'Bye' or maybe something else, and walked out. A blonde girl. Maybe some people would say cheap-looking. But she didn't *do* anything, *say* anything."

Yes, Miss Keel had photographs on her dresser. An older man and woman in one; a man alone in the other. (Roersch made a note. They'd found only the parents' photograph.)

Judith Keel had a father and mother in Rye, New York, this information taken off her employment card in Harold Cosset's office. They hadn't had to be informed; the father had seen the story in the newspapers. They had already identified the body; it would be released to them in another day or two, what was left of it.

The Bureau of Criminal Identification at Headquarters had five sets of clear prints, two sets of smudged, all taken from Keel's apartment. It would be a while, maybe forever, before any matching was done. And that only if the owners of the prints also owned criminal records in New York. Latent Prints would send sets to the nationwide FBI file in Washington, and there too they'd try to make a match.

The autopsy report was nothing. Full of nothings. No sex. No drugs. No bruises, except on the severed limbs, where they'd been tied at wrists and ankles. But indications of a "fair amount of alcohol in the deceased." That wording indicated they'd had little to go on.

He shrugged. He had little faith in the so-called science of criminology. Prints, okay. Sometimes. Though unlike movies and TV shows, it almost always took a full set, *ten* fingers, to get a positive identification and to hold up as courtroom evidence. And there were so many surfaces prints wouldn't hold to, or would aviate from—evaporate in short order. Guns almost *never* took prints. So solving a case was putting primary information together and bird-dogging and leaning on your informants and adding it all up and getting lucky. Especially getting lucky.

And staying with it. Nine out of ten homicides that were solved had one cop who stayed with it, whatever his reasons.

He would stay with this one.

Getting lucky? Most often it was a professional police informant who knew something. Less likely was a witness who had seen something. In this case, maybe another butcher-style killing, where he could place his suspect. And best of all was the killer blowing it, confessing in some way, not necessarily to the police. Say Bley, with a friend, a drinking companion, a girl, talking and letting things slip and that person getting in touch with the police.

Since Roersch was assigned the case, he would get the information. And he would make the collar. And get the publicity. And if it was Bley, he might get something better than publicity and a promotion. Not what Deverney settled for with his runaway kids . . .

Fantasy. Daydreams. Bullshit. First put the pieces together.

Nothing much to put together, yet. Evan Bley had played with Judith Keel. They were both single, so no pressure there. But he'd spent on her, maybe heavy, and more important he'd had her followed by a private detective. All right, the cousin said the eye had found nothing. Let's see what the eye himself had to say. Bley might have hushed him with a payoff; might have given him enough for a vacation from work.

Bley and Keel. Bley jealous enough to have her followed. Keel killed between eleven p.m. Sunday and ten a.m. Monday, and Bley on vacation since Friday five p.m. and heading for Los Angeles.

A good beginning. He'd worked with less, and made out.

He wanted another Scotch, another cigarette.

What he really wanted, he realized with surprise, was a piece of ass.

He went to the bedroom and dialed Ruthie's number. It rang about ten times before her voice, thick with sleep, irritable and drawn out, said, "Hello?"

"It's Eddy Roersch."

"Who?"

"Detective Roersch."

"Oh, hi, what time is it?"

"Can you come down the hall?"

Someone spoke in the background, and she replied, hand muffling the phone. Then she said, "Gee, no, I'm, uh, busy."

"Tell him he's used up his twenty bucks."

"*Fifty* for the night," she said, angry. "Sometimes a hundred." He chuckled. She said, "Anyway, it's not that. It's my kid."

"You have a kid?"

"Didn't I ever tell you? Four years old. She lives with her grandmother. Say hello to my friend Eddy, Jen."

He groaned and the child's voice said, "Hello. It's still dark here."

He said, "Yeah, here too. Tell your mother goodnight."

But Ruthie was back on the phone. "Listen, come over for breakfast."

"At three-thirty in the morning?"

She laughed. "Before you go to work."

"Maybe, but don't wait for me."

"I make the greatest coffee. Even Jen likes it."

"Yeah, we'll see." He hung up and lay down and wondered at Ruthie having a kid. Nice world. What happened when the kid got a little older?

He closed his eyes. Big day coming up. Put this thing together. Where was Bley now? What was he doing? Probably sleeping like a baby.

They crossed the St. Louis city line at a few minutes to five, and stopped at an all-night gas station where Evan got directions to the Parkside Inn Motel. John awoke and hunched over the back seat. Lois stayed asleep, mouth open, snoring slightly. Evan thanked the attendant and got back in the car, but he didn't need the map the man had marked for him. He was beginning to remember this town, and it wasn't a pleasant sensation.

He hadn't been to St. Louis since December of 1968, a month before flying to Mexico for his divorce. Before then, during the six months he'd courted Merri, he had come here for two extended visits, taking her back home as his bride at the end of the second visit.

During their one year one week of marriage, they'd visited her family together three times. Then he'd come for her, that Christmas of 1968; come in rage and pain, determined to kill the brother-in-law. After dealing with the situation, he'd left her there, for good, returning to New York with enough evidence of infidelity, stupidity, insanity and just plain avarice to destroy any hopes she'd had of alimony.

Lucky she'd signed the agreement his lawyer had drawn up, the total severance with no obligations, financial or otherwise, on either part. Lucky she hadn't tried to fight it, because even though he'd had everything on his side, his leaving town without attacking her had been a miracle. He remembered clearly that last night, trying to drink himself under, and realizing it wasn't going to work, that he had to leave right that moment.

He turned onto Lindburg Avenue, knowing where he was and making himself smile, telling himself he had triumphed, if not in the way he'd preferred to; telling himself he *hadn't* lost that game, had *never* lost a game, never would even in death . . . because he would pick his own time, his own way. And smiled more naturally, feeling he was further from death than ever before, stronger and more secure and growing happier. But the motels and shopping centers and theaters and side-roads became more and more familiar, and his smile wouldn't stay, and he *felt* St. Louis, the flat, dismal, small-minded trap that had almost caught him once, almost drained his life away.

He drove more quickly, risking a ticket, wanting to get into a room, away from the look and smell of this place. A feeling that had lasted more than six years.

"Oh, Merri, if we were playing now!"

"Who's Merri?" John asked.

He'd spoken aloud. "My ex-wife. She lives here in St. Louis."

John said, "You got any kids?" His voice was quiet and diffident.

"No. The only thing I was spared."

"Kids might have helped."

Evan didn't answer, because nothing would have helped.

And yet, he'd loved her as he'd never loved anyone before or since.

Judy? A re-enactment of Merri. And before Judy, other

dingies, as Vince called them. Always the same kind. Always the sexy little girls with the fucked-up minds. Always the crazies, the pretties, the children with the lush bodies.

His insanity . . . but it would change, it had to change.

It wouldn't change with Lois. He glanced at her. She'd closed her mouth and curled tighter, breasts bulging over an arm.

"You going to visit her?" John asked.

He laughed.

"How long're we staying?"

"You're sure now *you're* staying?"

John leaned back. "I'm hoping," he said, and smiled into the rear-view.

Evan nodded. "Long enough to catch up on our sleep. Maybe take a little sentimental journey . . ." he made a laughing sound . . . "before we leave. An hour or two driving around town."

"It's a nice town," John said quietly. "I spent a few months here some years ago. Met a chick and she was okay. Nice times going to Forest Park and the zoo and the museum and some rock joints. Rough over in East St. Louis with the race scene and all, but otherwise an easy town."

Evan marveled at that. An easy town! Could he face spending time in this city?

He hadn't dared risk it when they were pitching a subdivision of Anheuser-Busch last year and Burns had wanted him to head up the presentation in St. Louis. He'd said the campaign was all wrong, and fought having it presented, and Burns had gone himself.

Another win for Bley, though inadvertent. Busch Bavarian hadn't fallen to them. They hadn't even landed the experimental low-calorie beer that was supposed to compete with Gablinger's. He'd come out smelling like a rose, though he'd had to walk softly around Burns's delicate ego. Still, Burns had come through with a heavier-than-expected year-end stock bonus.

How would Burns react if he called from Los Angeles to say he wasn't coming back? There were some good agencies on the West Coast. A new agency; a new life. He'd lose his piece of the action, and probably wouldn't be able to match the overall money . . . but he didn't really need that much money. Just a month ago, his accountant had conservatively estimated his estate at six hundred thousand dollars, and since he owned no property beside the condominium apartment, most of that was easily converted into cash.

Who was he saving it for? No children; his mother too old to need money; an ex-wife he wouldn't leave a pair of old socks. He could go on an extended vacation—take a full year—without even denting his capital. He was sick of work, sick of the past, sick of New York which framed the past. He'd dreamed of living in the sunshine . . . Why not do just that, in Los Angeles? Lie on his back and read . . .

Still, he'd probably look for a partnership. Clovis-Royal in L.A. was struggling along with about eighteen million in billing, but developing a rep for creative ads on the style of the old Doyle Dane. He knew Ray Clovis from the rough days at Bates. More importantly, Clovis knew *him*, and what he could do. Good chance of a deal there. And if they ever sent him to St. Louis, he'd come laughing all the way!

And yet, pulling into the motel parking lot, remembering his last stay—tracking down Merri, the anguish, the tearing of his mind and heart—he knew he was going to rent only *one* room; bring John in with him and Lois. Not because he wanted orgies, but because he wanted *people;* people close around him tonight. John had said, "I have no one." Neither did Evan Bley. Except for his hitchhikers.

He parked and shut the lights and shook Lois's shoulder. He said he would register and be back for them. He walked across the blacktop, past the almost-solid lines of cars, most with rental company plates, and remembered that it had always been crowded at the Parkside Inn. In the past, he had felt comfortable with the business-like bustle, the dressy ambiance of the huge motel with its two clubs, three restaurants and large convention auditorium. And despite its popularity with the transient business community, its three hundred rooms generally assured that accommodations would be available. Also attractive had been the proximity to Merri's folks' home . . . something he hadn't considered until now.

But he didn't know if they still lived on the shabby hillside road some twenty minutes away. He didn't know if Merri herself still lived in St. Louis. Besides, there was nothing to fear about a *motel!*

This was a *room* to him, nothing more; a brief resting place. They would leave after breakfast. He'd forget the sentimental journey . . .

An acid test, actually. As was staying here. To prove he'd lost the old pain and fear, the old ways. Another game, and he didn't back away from games.

He walked inside. He moved briskly along the corridor, remembering the right-hand turn and the broadening out as he passed the closed Lanai Room. Then he was entering the blue-carpeted lobby and approaching the desk.

He got a suite, signing in for Mr. and Mrs. R. Bley and son. He started back to the car.

A few minutes, a few hours, and he'd be over his St. Looey blues.

As it turned out, it took considerably more time than that.

He was awake at seven-thirty, Lois sleeping beside him, John on the couch-bed in the sitting room through the archway. He was looking at the phone, remembering the calls, the never-ending calls, trying to run Merri down that last visit. He was remembering love . . . and wondering where she was tonight, with whom she was tonight. He was more than remembering anguish at her being with Phillip, her brother-in-law, or another of the many men she'd *loved.* (She never had affairs, she insisted, after being confronted with his knowledge. It was always *love,* no matter how short-lived.) He was frightened at his residual pain, remembering what such pain had led to with Judy.

He turned to Lois and began caressing her bottom, her sides, her breasts. She stirred and murmured, "Get off it, huh?" He turned her head and kissed her lips. He needed her, right now.

She came awake on the instant, jerking away and twisting to face him and balling her fists. "Goddamn can't you leave me be for even . . ." Then her eyes cleared and she looked at him and said, "Hon? What is it?"

He reached for her. She came to him, and repeated, "What is it?"

"I want you."

"All right." She offered her lips, her body. Both were too tight, too tense, and he worked on her, and she began to relax. But again she asked, "What is it?"

He said, "Memories," to get her off the subject. He continued to work on her, opening up her legs. He was gentle, gentle, kissing much and murmuring her name . . . and she grabbed his penis and said, "*Gimme!*"

He was turned off, but he fought it and stroked her and murmured, "Sweetly, nicely," remembering the words from somewhere, said just that way, sweetly, nicely, and tried to fix onto *where* he'd heard them, *who* had said them, certainly not his mother, with her *drive,* slaps, bloody . . .

He turned away abruptly, rolling over with his back to her.

"Hey, you blow my mind! First it's one thing, then, bam, another!"

He wanted to scream, "Shut the hell up!" Instead, he said, "Easy. You'll wake John."

"Well, don't you want that? Isn't that why we're all in the same room?"

He didn't answer. He was still remembering sweetly,

nicely . . . and then it was there. His Aunt Rose, when he was young, very young, and spending a day . . . No. *Many* days, that time Mom had cut her foot at the beach and couldn't get out of bed and Rose had taken him home with her for days and days. Before going to bed, she'd asked for a kiss, as Mom did, and he'd hugged her hard and pressed his lips to hers hard and turned away. She'd stopped him, that small, soft, childish-looking woman with no children of her own; held him, laughing, saying, "Marvie-boy, is that the way you kiss? That's not the way. Here, sweetly, nicely," and she'd kissed him, stroking his face, his head, and it had been sweetly, nicely, and he'd pulled away, angry, upset, afraid, and run to the room and the cot and hid himself from the ache she gave him, the ache that was worse once he was home with Mom.

He was crying. He didn't know it until Lois said, shocked, "I didn't mean anything. It can't be *me?*"

He shook his head, and stopped the foolishness. He was vulnerable, too vulnerable tonight. He turned to her and said, "*Gimme.*" She went down on him and he slammed her, and disliked her, and she hugged him afterward and said, "You're the fucking best!"

A compliment. Sweetly, nicely was for lucky little boys. And he hadn't been lucky and it was too late and forget it, Marvie-boy.

But he didn't. When she murmured about calling John in and really making "the night move," he said he was too tired and tomorrow maybe, the next night maybe, they had plenty of time.

He fell asleep. Later, with sunshine filtering through the draped windows, he was awake and the bloody thing was back. He remembered it. For a moment. He could have brought it into consciousness, held to it, relived it, known it, had done with it . . . but he shook in fear, in revulsion, and told himself it was a vague dream. And it slipped away.

He slept again, badly. He dreamed of Judy.

6: | Wednesday a.m. and p.m.

At eight o'clock Roersch was on his way down the hall, zipper case under his arm. He'd just decided to skip the one-flight ride and take the stairs, when he made yet another decision. He turned and went back past his own door to the end of the hall and rang the bell of apartment 2-J. A child's voice squealed excitedly and short-span footsteps pounded and the door opened.

He looked down. Ruthie's kid was small and plump with dark hair cut shoulder length and a big-cheeked smiling face. And a big rear pushing out her short skirt. He bent and patted the rear as Ruthie came into the kitchen archway. "Like mother like daughter," he said. He took the hand the child put in his and nodded at whatever she was saying and walked into the kitchen.

Ruthie wore a Chinese kind of thing, a short, wrap-around robe of bright yellow with black dragons on it, and those big-heeled shoes—maybe six or seven inches high, klunkers, they called them—and nothing else that he could see. When she bent over to open the oven, he found he wanted the kid out of there.

Ruthie straightened and saw the way he was looking at her. "Jen, show Eddy your new dolly, huh?"

The kid ran into the next room. Ruthie came to the table where he was sitting and put an arm around his shoulders and kissed his cheek. "How are you, you old pig?" He had his hand up under her robe, stroking that smooth ass, and she sighed and murmured, "She goes home at three. Can you be around?"

He looked at her in surprise. Always it was *he* who did the asking, and while she gave in with little fight—at least lately; at the beginning she'd been kind of sullen—she'd never come on this way. And now that he thought of it, who was she wearing the big-heeled shoes for?

"You having problems?" he asked, moving his hand between her legs.

She glanced at the bedroom door and pulled his hand away. "What makes you think that?"

"Some pimp moving into your operation? Some vice cop pushing for too much on the pad?"

She turned away, angry. "I'm fine. Just 'cause I act nice . . ."

The kid was back, holding up a doll almost as big as she was, and he had to admire it and then the kid insisted he *talk* to it. He said, "Hello, Mary," which was the name the kid had given her. "How are you? Can I come see you at five-thirty or six instead of three, or do you have a trick coming in?"

When he looked at Ruthie, she was laughing. "I don't know about Mary," she said, "but I'm taking the day off. Five-thirty or six would be fine."

He nodded, and smiled when he saw she was taking hot

corn muffins from the oven. The kid said, "Mommy makes the *best* muffs."

He said, "Right."

The kid grabbed one off the plate and screamed and dropped it because it burned her fingers. Ruthie ran to her, but he picked her up and held her on his lap and said, "The doctor knows how to make better." He was going to put butter on the stricken fingers, but instead he kissed them and wet them with his saliva and the child quieted and looked at him with tears running down her cheeks.

He remembered Helen and her hunger for a child. He kissed her fingers again, then put the child back in her chair.

Ruthie moved around, bringing eggs and bacon and coffee. He didn't look at her, embarrassed, wondering at himself, but he knew she was looking at him. And when she sat down, and when they were eating, her hand came under the table to his thigh and patted it and rested there a moment.

He ate quickly. He had to get to work. She had no business touching him that way.

He was at the station at nine-forty, and talking to Hawly in his office five minutes later. Hawly had the Keel reports in front of him. He was sorting the mound of paper expertly: the goddamn Form DD-5's, the duplicates and triplicates that had driven Roersch nuts until he made the deal with Chauger. Now he simply signed the papers. A murder case required so many reports it could effectively stop you from doing any real thinking. But Bill Hawly was a natural scholar, a test-taker and paper-filer. He'd make captain for sure. He'd been a fine traffic cop, a fine desk sergeant, and he was a great administrator. He'd never solved a homicide case, yet was a lieutenant at Manhattan West Homicide. Roersch had solved nine, and assisted in at least twenty more.

He tried not to think of that . . . then did, turning it to the problem at hand.

He'd solved *ten*, if he was right about Bley and Keel.

Yet he'd never make lieutenant . . . he knew that now.

And didn't care now. Because he was still going to retire first-class. And *live* first-class. Thanks to Bley.

Two people, and two people only, would know who had killed Judith Keel—Edmund Roersch, and Evan Bley. And Bley would be most grateful for Roersch's keeping the story so exclusive!

The decision made, he concentrated on Hawly; on responding in such a way as to block all movement toward the logical suspect.

"In what direction are you moving, Eddy?"

"Toward retirement, Bill."

Hawly smiled carefully. "These reports indicate *no* set direction. Unless you're going to update them this morning?"

He wasn't going to update them, ever. He'd feed Chauger a little shit now and then to make it appear the case file was growing. He'd do the real updating in his mind, until he was ready for the collar . . . or the payoff. "Not this morning, Bill. Might have more by tomorrow, or Friday."

"This Bley, Evan, bachelor . . ." he was reading from Chauger's tech-type report, signed by Eddy Roersch . . . "are you following through?"

"Nothing to follow through on, Bill. A little circumstantial, but nowhere near enough to set wheels turning. I've got a hunch, a sad one, that we've drawn a vagrant, a psycho who just happened to gain entrance. You know how rough *that* is."

"Are you aware," Hawly muttered, flipping paper, "that there are several similar cases, here and on the East Side?"

"Not really similar, Bill."

"Two that I'm aware of. Young women. Bodies mutilated."

"Not mutilated in the same way. But I'm aware, Bill. I'm putting it together. I'll follow through on Bley, though he's not the type. Too much money, heavy career, a lifetime spent working and rising through the ranks. He's just a weak 'maybe' on the Keel case. A 'no' on the others."

Hawly leaned back in his chair. "Is this going to go into the unsolved file? *Is* it, Eddy?" He sounded like a coach at half-time.

Roersch shook his head. "Not if it's up to me. I'll do my best."

"And you're the best we've got."

Roersch would have liked to say, "You're fucking-A right," but answered, "Thanks," and stood up.

Hawly said, "Put in a request for the files on these two cases." He pulled a large pad toward him. "Jane Austen . . ." He stopped, chuckled, and looked up with his big-kid look. Roersch knew another bad joke was coming; Hawly was famous for them. "Wonder whether it was pride or prejudice responsible for her death?" He chuckled again, and Roersch joined him and stopped chuckling when Hawly did. "And Corinne Bain. Here, take the sheet." He tore it from the pad.

Roersch stopped at Chauger's desk. The stocky young detective was working at his typewriter. Reports, naturally. "Yours or whose?" Roersch asked. Chauger grinned. "At five bucks per set, Sergeant, I'm thinking of quitting legwork."

"Not just yet. I want the folders, everything, on these two homicides. I think one, maybe both, are over at Manhattan East."

Chauger nodded, taking the sheet of paper. "Monday okay?"

"No."

Chauger nodded again.

Roersch checked for messages, then made a call to Mrs. Bleywitz.

"Who?" the high but far-from-weak voice shrilled.

"Detective Sergeant Roersch, Mrs. Bleywitz."

"*Who?* Wait. I'll turn up the aid." There was a whistling sound, and she said, "Is that better?"

"Much," he said.

"*What?*"

He began to shout. He explained that he needed some information about her son. That her son could help him.

"Naturally," she said. "It's the girl who worked at his office. I know. The television had it. But he's on vacation. Out of town."

He asked if he could come over and speak to her.

"Sure. Better that way. I don't hear so good on the phone."

On the way out, he remembered to ask Chauger if Jones had called in.

"*This* early? He's probably cooping in some Harlem cat house."

Roersch looked at him.

"Hey, just kidding, baby. I know he's the *poh*-leece."

"I don't think so, *baby*. I think you got some shit on the brain."

Chauger smiled, for the sergeant. Chauger shuffled his papers, like Hawly. Roersch walked out. He was getting edgy. He was picking up on things he'd never bothered with before. He used the siren to the Belt Parkway and all the way to the Brooklyn Battery Tunnel. Then he slowed down.

Kate Bleywitz lived on Eastern Parkway, half a block and across the street from the huge main-branch Brooklyn Public Library with its wide vista of Prospect Park and the War Memorial. Traffic was heavy in the memorial circular drive, and he had to inch up to two changes in the traffic light before being able to shoot onto the parkway and make his U-turn around to the apartment house entrance. The parking places were all taken, so he flipped down his sunshield with the department emblem and backed into the illegal corner spot.

The house had once been something special. This entire area had been upper class, but now it was part of Crown Heights, and the encroaching ghetto and rising crime had driven out the money and left a lot of old people and those who were willing to take a chance for a big old apartment at a reasonable rental.

Mrs. Bleywitz's place wasn't all that big—a studio setup, one long room combining living and bed room, and a small kitchen with a half-table and two chairs. It was gloomy, two windows facing onto a narrow courtyard, one window giving an angle view of the library, the park entrance, and a piece of the memorial. It was at this window that Kate Bleywitz stationed him, pointing out "how much you can see from the fifth floor, hah?"

He said yes. She adjusted her hearing aid.

She was old, maybe seventy-five, maybe more. She was thin, her blue dress hanging on her, falling too far between knees and ankles, giving her not so much a dated look as a second-hand look. Her hands trembled, the veins clear beneath the waxy, spotted skin. But her face was strong, sharp-featured, the eyes piercing despite thick, silver-framed glasses. Gray eyes. Quick eyes. And her mouth—it shocked him. Lipsticked bright red; a wide, mobile mouth that twitched in caustic humor. No, not humor; inner laughter, at the expense of the rest of the world. Inner rage . . .

"So you look more at the old lady than the view. Maybe you *like* old ladies?" The bright-red lips twitched.

"When I can't get young ladies." He chuckled.

She nodded but didn't smile. He felt he'd said something dirty. He got to work. "Do you know how I can get in touch with Evan, Mrs. Bleywitz?"

"*Marvin* is my son's name. He changed it for business, because who knows what people think about a Bleywitz, yes, Mr. Rodish?"

"Roersch."

"It isn't Jewish. Bleywitz is. So *Marvin* made himself Evan Bley. But to me he's Marvin. What did you ask?"

He didn't like her. She made everything an argument, a battle, a game she had to win. He wanted to ask her how the hell she knew he wasn't Jewish. But he didn't ask. Because she *would* know. That above all, she'd know.

And pumping her wasn't going to be easy. He'd have to find a weakness, or a way to make *her* motives work for him.

"How can I get in touch with Marvin?"

"Why do you want to get in touch?"

Before he could answer, she said, "Sit down. The couch is a bed but it's also a couch. And comfortable. A Castro convertible. The best. Marvin gave me the best." She laughed; it wasn't a cheerful thing. "That's a Jewish joke, Mr. Rodish."

He didn't correct her. She watched him a moment, and corrected herself. "*Roersch*," she said, the voice heavily mocking. "You know, I didn't ask to see your papers. They say never to let a man in the house without he shows his papers."

He showed her his badge.

"My, my, is it real gold?"

The twitching lips made his "no" unnecessary, but he said it anyway.

"Well, at least you have honor."

He waited out the twitching mouth.

She asked if he wanted a cup of coffee. He said no. Some fruit? No. Well, *she* would have coffee. She went to the kitchen.

He found he was sweating. Old bitch! He took out his cigarettes, and looked around. The furnishings were all reasonably new, and quite good. Lamps, tables, dresser, mirror, color TV, paintings. And photographs. All over, framed photographs.

"If you'll forgive an old lady, I don't like to smell smoke."

He put the pack back in his pocket. "Sorry."

"The television says to *say* we don't like it. For you as well as me. My Uncle Pincus, God rest his soul, died of cancer of the lungs. When I visited him at Kings County, he was a skeleton." She looked at him a moment. "You could lose a few pounds, but a skeleton you don't have to be."

He smiled. "I'm giving them up."

"So is Marvin. For at least ten years."

She went back to the kitchen. He went back to examining the photographs. An infant, a little boy in knickers and cap, a teen-age graduate in mortarboard, a pilot in the old Army Air Corps. And when he turned, on a dresser behind him, Mrs. Bleywitz and the teen-age graduate, Mrs. Bleywitz smiling out of a strong, young face; the same graduate but older, in college cap and gown; a man receiving a framed award; the man sitting in a Jaguar sedan.

"Marvin, my son," the shrill voice said.

He turned. She was carrying a cup, her hand trembling, but she carried it without looking at it, without worrying, a sure woman despite age and spastic tremors.

"*All* the pictures?"

"Who else would I have?" She sat down in the room's only armchair, and raised the cup to her lips. "He was my life." She sipped.

"No other children?"

"You maybe think *I* killed that girl?"

He made himself laugh.

"Not that I care what happened to her, to any of those *courvas*." She sipped again. "That's not a nice word. Whores."

"Why do you think Miss Keel was . . . that?"

The red lips twitched. "All of them. You find me one that isn't. All of them. His taste."

"Did he ever say anything about her? To make you think that?"

"You think maybe *he* killed her?"

"Mrs. Bleywitz, this is just a routine investigation . . ."

"Like on television. They always say routine. They always arrest the man. Columbo says routine all the time. He always arrests the man. But he's funnier than you."

He leaned back in the couch.

"Go on," she said, and sipped.

"Did he ever say anything?"

"Maybe he did. Would you have to bring him back if he said anything?"

Her eyes, peering over the rim of the cup, had changed. For the first time, they'd shown . . . *hope* was reading a look too fine . . . but they'd shown interest, for sure.

"Maybe. But not to accuse him. Only because he might be able to help us find the man who did it. He knew her well, was her friend . . ."

She cackled.

"He knew the people *she* knew. He's the one person who can fill us in on her friends, acquaintances . . ."

"The tramps she ran with."

"Did he ever say anything?"

"He wasn't the kind to tell his mother about *courvas*. But she was in the car—the new one. See in the picture? A beauty, that car. His taste *there* was good. In everything but women, good. She was in the car and I was downstairs and he had to let me meet her. Oh my, what a girl to meet a mother!" She drank deeply. "Later, he visited and he had something on his mind. I asked why he was troubled. He said it was nothing. I asked about the girl. He said it was nothing, but then he got up and he walked around and I asked again. He yelled at me. He said not to bother . . . no, not to *pry*. So I knew. He was sick about her. She was hurting him. I know my son. Even if he's Evan Bley and not my son anymore."

"I'm sure he thinks of you . . ."

The cup came down on an end table. The eyes fixed him. The lips didn't twitch; were pressed into a blood-red gash. He felt he had to say something.

"I never forgot *my* mother, or father. I'm sure Marvin . . ."

"He won't come back," she said.

"His vacation is up in a month. His job . . ."

"He doesn't need jobs. He's worth I don't know how much, maybe a *millionaire*. Maybe not that much. But he doesn't need jobs. He won't come back. He kept talking of

California. Of new lives. As if we can lose the old . . ."

Her head suddenly jerked; an emotional spastic reaction. She began to get up, then sank back and put her hands up to her face. Her voice shook, grew weak. "He was my life and he won't come back. Not because of her. No, he wouldn't dirty his hands on her. Because he . . ." She dropped her hands. "All I wanted was to be with him. Not even that. *Near* him . . . he should live in the city like he did and visit once in a while and talk on the phone."

"He'll be back."

"Never. He wants to forget me, this city, everything."

"Well then, I'll have to bring him back. We need him."

"Can you *force* him?"

That look again.

"Maybe. If I had a reason."

"What can I tell you?"

"You never heard him talk about the girl, besides what you said?"

"Never."

"He never threatened her, said he loved her . . ."

"Never!" It was almost a scream. "What he felt was what men feel for *courvas*. What he felt for that wife, the same. The same, maybe she was *worse!*"

"He's married?"

"Divorced. Never really married. Not in *shool* . . . temple. Just some out-of-town *shkutz* married them. A piece of paper. Then he found out what I knew from the moment I saw her. She was a *courva*. So he divorced her. But he was angry. He was crazy, that time. He could have done things . . ." She stopped, and Roersch realized he was leaning forward, transfixed.

"Go on," he said.

"That's over. He's divorced."

"Do you remember his ex-wife's name—maiden name?"

"I never knew it. Her first name—Merri. In St. Louis someplace she lived. I hope to God she's dead and burning now!"

Her venom was filling the room. He pushed through it. "She's alive, isn't she?"

"I said I hope not. I don't know. She was alive to be divorced, that's all I know." She stood up. "I don't feel good." She was very pale, shaking badly. She looked at Roersch. "You're sitting on my bed."

He jumped up, and moved aside as she shuffled forward. He said, "Could I have a recent picture of Evan . . . Marvin?"

"No. These are all I have. His agency has pictures—those awards he won. Ask them. He was in the newspapers, the *Times*, the advertising page. He has pictures at his apartment." She sank down on the couch. "Goodbye, Mr. Roersch."

He didn't go. "If I could examine his apartment, find something to prove to my superiors that he could be of help to us, a material witness . . ."

"Columbo had a material witness," she said, her eyes clearing. "Perry Mason had a material witness. You can bring him back, even put him in jail to protect him?"

"Well, not jail . . ."

"But you *could*?"

"If I was able to give a reason."

"How could you find him?"

He would normally have fluffed that off, given a vague answer like, "We have our methods . . ." but the gray eyes, cleared now and sharp and *desperate*, were on him. And that mind was on him, too.

"We know he's driving to Los Angeles. There are several routes he could take . . ."

"He belongs to the club—that A.A. thing."

"Auto Club? A.A.A.?"

"Yes. He gets maps from them. They could tell you?"

He nodded. "And even if they didn't, there's the quickest way to go, the old Route 66, and a northern route, and we could use the LETS system—the Law Enforcement Teletype . . ."

"Even so, you might not find him. Not driving."

"Then we'd certainly find him in Los Angeles. That car of his—it's unusual enough. And we'll get his license plate number. And we might learn who his friends are in L.A. And he might call his office . . ."

"Even so, even so," she muttered, the eyes dimming again.

He gave her the clincher. "If I could look through his apartment, I'm sure I'd find something to tell me where he's going to be staying—reservations at motels, and at his final destination in L.A. People always make notes. Unless his cleaning lady went into his drawers . . ."

"He never has a cleaning lady. He never lets anyone go into his place, touch his things." She got up. "You can do it. I give my permission. Look in his apartment."

"I need *his* permission, or a warrant . . . if I do it that way."

"Get a warrant. I give my permission. I'm his mother."

"I need more than that, to do it *legally*, by court order." He paused, hoping she'd catch on. "I can do it another way, not strictly legal."

"Do it. How many times I have to say it? I'm his mother!"

He shook his head. She hadn't caught on. "Anyone over twenty-one becomes legally responsible. A legal adult retains full power of self-determination."

"And a mother means nothing." She said it flatly.

He hesitated, wondering how best to ask her. There were two ways she could help him. If the management at Bley's apartment house knew her as his mother and would let her in, or if she had a key.

"I have some keys," she said. "I'll give them to you. Three keys it takes to get into that house. Foolishness. Who bothers rich people? It's poor people who live with the *shvartzes*."

He nodded solemnly. She went to the dresser. He waited as she searched a drawer. When she turned, he stepped around the couch. She gave him a key ring with three keys on it, each with a small tag. The tabs were labeled in heavy black ink—FRONT DOOR, TOP LOCK, BOTTOM LOCK— in deference to Mrs. Bleywitz's failing sight. She also handed him a card with an address and apartment number printed on the back; the front was Bley's business card.

"Make him come back," she said, and she was begging. He nodded. "I'll return these soon, Mrs. Bleywitz."

She shrugged. "No rush. He gave them to me before he left, to water the plants." She pointed to the kitchen. "So now I got two plants." She went to the couch and lay down.

He said thanks and goodbye and left. His hopes for Bley as the killer had gone up, way up. With a mother like that—and she was old now; imagine what she'd been when she'd had full strength—with a mother like that, hating women would come naturally.

And with a mother like that, being vulnerable, being a patsy, would also come naturally.

He drove to Manhattan, using the bridge off Flatbush Avenue this time because he was hungry and wanted to go to the Italian place on Eleventh Street in the Village. Mario was too talkative but he remembered Roersch and was always good for a bowl of minestrone and a plate of veal parmigiana and linguini with clam sauce. Fattening, yeah, but he'd start dieting later. First he'd take Mrs. Bleywitz's son Marvin to the cleaners.

If Bley was the killer. *If* he could make a case that would crack the man. If he could keep Hawly and anyone else at Manhattan West Homicide from making the same case.

Which reminded him. He walked to the phone booth down the street from Mario's and called the station. Jones was there, and said he'd located Nicholas McKenney, the private eye.

"He's a junkie, Sergeant. He got so scared when I flashed the badge, he almost shit his pants. He's got the eyes and the face and the shakes. And the needle marks.

That's why he lost his job at the Congrove Agency. Out too much."

"What did he say about the tail on Judith Keel?"

"Did the job himself. He was on her for two weeks, and she was clean. She saw no other men, and saw Bley three times during that period. But I think he's lying, Sergeant. Maybe not about the surveillance, but about something."

"What makes you think that?"

"Well, here's this way-out junkie. I mean, shot all to hell. And he's out of work. Yet he had a decent pad and he didn't look like he was hurting for junk or food or anything. And at the Congrove Agency, they said he was into them for two weeks' advance salary when he left, and he owed a few people he worked with, but he paid them all off. So I got an idea."

Roersch said, "Damn!" under his breath. And thought: *Bley paid him to say Keel was clean in his report, so as not to have a motive for murder on file at the agency.* "What's your idea, Willis?"

"Two ideas. He took money from Bley to do a job on her, and junkie-style didn't do it. Or, same style, he did it. He did the Judith Keel murder, on contract."

"*That* kind of job? On contract? Cutting off arms and legs? You'd better forget . . ."

"To make it look like a psycho, Sergeant. And remember, he's a mainliner. I stripped his arm myself. A heavy mainliner. They can jump any way at *all*. He could even have done it on his own, turning on for the chick while tailing her."

"No sex, Willis."

"So she resisted. So he went the psycho route for real. So he did well robbing her, enough to pay off his debts and coast for a while."

Roersch sighed.

Jones said, "Yeah, no indication of any of this in his

report for the agency. No other evidence, hard or soft. But it's a few lines for *my* report, right?"

Roersch chuckled into the phone. He was sorry now he'd farmed the private eye out to Jones. He hadn't thought anything like this would develop. A lesson. He had to do *everything* himself from now on. Bley was his pigeon. "Yeah, Willis. But hold it until I see you about four o'clock."

"I don't know if I'll be around. Hawly wants me on the Colitz case. You know, the real estate dude who got mugged."

"He died?"

"Last night. And I still got work to do on Marshal for Hawly."

"I thought we closed Marshal out?"

"An anonymous phone call. Woman said she saw the whole thing and named a man. It smells like a personal revenge thing, but we got to check it."

"Okay. Don't bother writing a report. I'll think it over, see McKenney myself, and handle the paperwork."

"Hey, thanks, Sergeant!"

He jotted down the private eye's new address and went into Mario's. He got the big greeting, the latest on children and grandchildren, then the angry line about black and Puerto Rican crime in the streets of Greenwich Village. Nothing about *la cosa nostra*; that was big business, of course.

He ate and nodded and blocked out the man's voice. He was still on top of things. He'd see this Nicholas McKenney himself. He didn't believe Bley would farm out a murder to a junkie. He was too smart a man for such a dumb play. He was too public a figure, too moneyed a figure, to leave himself open like that. No, it had to be something else.

But say McKenney had done it on his own, a nut thing on the spur of the moment. He'd still say—be *glad* to say when led to it—that he'd done it for Bley. And that would nail Bley as killer by proxy. And the pressure would still be on and it would all still work. Because Bley had troubles. Bley had that mother and Bley had Keel tailed and Bley was a natural patsy . . .

Shit, he was solving problems before they developed! Jones and his detective-story crap! It was almost never that complicated.

Bley was solid in motive and solid in access to the victim and solid in timing . . .

He decided he was thinking too much. No need to *make* it be Bley. It would become Bley, naturally, because Bley was the natural suspect. And when he confronted him with the evidence, Bley would revert to type, to Momma's-boy, and fold and pay and be scared out of his pants and never again hurt a living thing. And that was a hell of a lot better than putting him in jail, right? That was rehabilitation, and a life saved for society and everything they said prison was supposed to do that everyone knew prison *couldn't* do.

He stopped it there and began listening to Mario. He agreed that the police force should be doubled, tripled, whatever Mario wanted. He bought a bottle of Chianti and insisted the old man join him. He figured he'd check in at the station, then go home and enjoy Ruthie, then see the private eye. Tonight, late, when there was less traffic at Bley's East Side address, he'd go there and see how to handle whatever security existed. Having a key might not be enough.

He raised his glass. "*Skoal*, Mario."

The old man rolled his eyes at the ceiling. "How many times I got to teach you? *Salud, paisan!*"

7: | Wednesday p.m.

Evan drove past the house, U-turned, and drove past once again. He went to the bottom of the road and made his turn in the gas station and went back up the road, past the frame houses. The only thing this road had was its incline, refreshing for plains-flat St. Louis. Otherwise, it was sad.

He reached number 137. He was afraid. He pulled to the other side and looked at the one-story house; a cottage, really. It was a different color. It used to be gray with black shutters. Now it was dirty white with green shutters. Equally sad.

His heart pounded. The memories; the life with Merri.

He cut the ignition. He *wouldn't* back away. Why shouldn't he drop in? Ask about her? Her mother hadn't liked him, but she'd approved of the marriage. She'd approved of the money, the position, her daughter's landing money and position. She'd taken the Jew along with it. Merri hadn't. Merri had taken her brother-in-law and three other men. All in one year. Four men in fifty-three weeks.

He opened the door and got out. He was wearing his suit, and mod Cardin or not, he was sorry he hadn't changed into his suede or his tie-dyes. Merri had liked suedes, tie-dyes, Levis, unusual clothing. She'd had him grow a mustache, which he'd shaved off just before the flight to Mexico and the divorce. What was it her sister had said, laughing, that first visit after the marriage? "Merri grows mustaches on all her men." He'd thought it a joke. It turned out to be true. After she bedded a man, she got him to grow a mustache, dress mod, dance rock. And when he fit her image of perfect lover, she dumped him for someone else. Half the men in St. Louis must have mustaches by now.

He tried to smile at that, but there was a Pinto in the driveway, and if the Colters still lived here it could be Merri's.

He crossed the road. A dog began barking inside the house as he walked along the blacktop driveway. Merri had loved animals. She'd missed having a dog in his apartment, but a no-pet clause was in the condominium purchase papers. He wouldn't have minded a dog, though he'd never had one. Mom said they spread germs. Mom said there was enough "dirt" to clean as it was. Mom wanted no competition.

He was at the door. He didn't remember a name plate, but looked for one, hoping it would say anything but Colter. The dog inside was going crazy. He didn't find a -name or get the chance to knock, because the door opened a crack. He began to speak, then stopped. He recognized the eyes, the broad little nose, the mouth with the sensual lips and slightly protruding teeth.

The door opened wide. He looked at her. She was older, a little heavier, and her drab housedress did nothing for her. But she was still Merri, still beautiful enough to choke his throat. He said, "I was passing through and thought I'd see how you are." He was proud of how casual his voice sounded.

She shook her head slowly, in disbelief. "My God." The dog behind her was medium-sized and white, jumping up and jumping back and barking hysterically. She turned to it. "Shobie, *stop!*" The dog slunk to a table and under it. She smiled. "I got at least one male well trained."

"Probably beat it every day."

"Twice a day. Males like that. Not doing it was my mistake with *you.*"

"No, your mistake with me was *having* more than one male."

"Well, I've got only one now."

"You're married?"

She grinned the wild grin he remembered so well, her overbite giving her a slightly mad look. She turned and waved him in. Her ass was still classic. Her body was still good, if plumper than he'd ever seen it. She was about thirty now.

He came inside and shut the door. The place was shabbier, poorer than he remembered it. Perhaps the same furniture, with a few additions, and grown older.

"Shitsville, right, baby?"

"Your husband could do better, yes."

"Which one? I've had two since you."

He looked to see if she was joking. He couldn't tell from her smile. "And you're married now?"

"You've asked that twice, Evvie. Interested in another shot?"

He answered her smile. "Once was enough, thank you."

She waved him to a couch and asked if he wanted a drink.

"Won't be here that long."

"I'm surprised you came around at all. Six years, right, since we've seen each other?"

He nodded. "And I'm surprised you let me in."

She shrugged. "Bygones. I guess you feel the same."

He didn't, but nodded.

"Was it you who did that to Phil?" she asked.

"Did what?"

"He was beaten up by a couple of hoods. Robbery, or mugging, the police called it. The day after you left here that last time. I always thought you had it done, because of finding out about us."

He made a surprised face. "Was he hurt badly?" (He'd received the note at a post office box, as arranged, and learned that dear brother-in-law was in St. Louis Jewish Hospital—nice touch—with multiple fractures of both legs and one arm, plus total loss of front teeth, two broken ribs, and internal injuries not yet determined.)

"He was in a wheelchair for almost a year." She watched him carefully, and he felt he was going to smile, and he did.

"You did it, didn't you, Evvie?"

He put back his head and laughed. Because he'd been so afraid, and was now so relieved. All this fear of seeing her. All this fear of St. Louis. It was too damned funny.

She smiled a little. "C'mon now, admit it. After all these years, what harm could it do?"

"You'd put me in jail today, if you could."

Her smile remained, but she nodded. "You bet, baby. Or let's say I'd love to know something that *could* put you in jail. I'd make you part with some of your loot, you cheap sonof . . ."

He leaned forward, his laughter gone, a wave of red rage sweeping over him.

She said, "Same old nut." He leaned back, the rage receding. She stood up. "Nice seeing you and all that. I've got to get dressed."

"Fucking your father-in-law today?"

"Did that the last marriage out. Real kick."

She turned to the door, swaying; her old whorey walk.

That ass rolled beautifully. He couldn't help remembering how he'd held it; how he'd made love to her, told her he'd loved her . . .

She was looking back at him. "Five hundred and you can have it." She grinned.

"My mother always said you were a *courva.*"

"You know what you can do with that old kike."

He reached her in two long steps and grabbed her by the forearms and slammed her up against the wall. She said, "Shobie, *sic!*"

The dog came out from under the table, snarling. He said, "One hundred."

She laughed, and moved against him. The dog was still snarling, coming closer. She said, "*Shobie!*" The dog slunk back under the table. "If I ever find a man like Shobie, especially with a few bucks, I'm faithful for life."

"Yes, *his* life. And I'd give him six months, tops."

She was rubbing against him now, the wild smile back, the eyes flashing, putting her face up to his. He was responding, and it was insane, and he wanted her this one time, this last time, wanted her so badly he felt he would spend in his pants.

"You lasted a year, baby," she murmured. "If I'd played it smart, you'd have lasted forever." She kissed him, and his hands left her forearms and went around her and stroked her body.

"Why didn't you?" he asked into her neck, inhaling her odor, and it was the same, a non-deodorized odor, yet sweet, exciting.

She was fumbling with his fly. "You know me. Mercurial Merri."

"Hey," he said. "That's real English."

She giggled. "Number Three was a high school teacher. I always wanted to fuck a high school teacher, and this one was pretty good and swept me off my feet. I loved the poor jerk . . ."

"You love them all."

She pulled back a moment, looked into his eyes, nodded. "Never balled a man I didn't love." She suddenly grinned. "I must admit I wonder at this great big heart of mine sometimes." The grin died. "But it *seems* it's going to last forever, at the beginning."

"Like old Evvie."

"You were my big mistake. You had it all. I'm not sorry about any of the others, but I'm sorry about you."

Which alone was worth the hundred. Which alone was worth the trip to St. Louis.

"You going to pay me that two hundred now?" she murmured, getting him out of his pants.

"One hundred. After we finish." He could barely speak the words as her hand, her tiny hand, stroked him.

"Too big for me," she murmured. "Always too big, but how I loved suffering with you!" She slid down, kneeling, took him in her mouth. She worked a moment, and he said, "God!" and she drew back.

"I'll take that one-fifty," she said, and the bargaining was over. She had that look that meant she'd made her stand.

He didn't have his checkbook. It was in the glove compartment of the car. He told her. She said, "I can wait a minute. Get it."

He took out his wallet. He had three hundred in cash. But that was for emergencies, and it was a long way to Los Angeles. He said, "Be right back." She smiled. He went out, and got the checkbook, and began to close the door of the Jag, and looked at the door of the house. It was open, and she was stepping outside to look around. Then she stepped back and slowly stripped off the housedress. He could see her wild grin from here. He could see her firm boobs, her rounded belly, that thick thatch of black hair that she seemed to cultivate like a garden, was proud of. And finally she turned, looking over her shoulder in a pose reminiscent of the old Betty Grable pin-up that had decorated World War II barracks. Except that

Grable had never had half Merri's ass—bulging suddenly from her upper thighs and swelling even further, further, then dimpling and tucking back in at her waist.

He wanted her more than anything in the world.

And he never got what he wanted. Mom had taught him that. But he won, got what other people wanted—money and honor and things.

He slid back in the car and closed the door. He started the engine, or tried to. It sputtered and died. By the time it caught, Merri had whirled around and gestured at him—*stop!* He turned the wheel hard left and came across the road into her driveway. She called, "Evvie! One hundred!"

He waved and backed out . . . and the car stalled. She bent for her dress; was pulling it on when he got started again. He gentled the gas pedal as he shifted into reverse. She came running out, belting the housedress. "Okay! For nothing! For *us.*"

He backed farther and leaned out the window. He wanted, he wanted, and he said, "I'm on my way to Los Angeles. Things to do. I'll stop on the way back." And there would be no way back.

She ran to the road, calling, "Wait . . . maybe I'll go with . . ."

He roared down the hill. He looked into his rear-view. She was standing there, his Merri, his little *courva.* He'd won. That was the important thing.

When he got to the motel, he picked up the extra key at the desk, in case Lois and John were out.

He unlocked the door, but it opened only a few inches and hit the chain. He called, "Lois? John?"

There was no answer, no movement, for a moment; then John said, "Who is it?"

"What's the matter with you? Open up."

Footsteps padded; the chain was removed; the door opened. John stared at him, bleary-eyed . . . and now he smelled the sticky-sweet odor of pot. He came inside and quickly closed the door. "Where's Lois?"

John waved at the bedroom. He walked there, and she was on her side, sleeping. He looked at John. John said, "No, she wouldn't. I wanted to, but she wouldn't. Is it important?"

He shrugged. "Get ready. I'm starved."

"We thought you'd split. Did you? And change your mind?"

Evan walked to the sleeper couch and the coffee table in front of it and picked up the sheet of motel stationery. "Didn't you see this?"

John came over and took it and rubbed his eyes and read aloud, mumbling, "Be back soon. Get packed and ready. Evan."

He dropped the paper and hurried to the bathroom. "Just a minute," he said, and went inside.

Evan stared after him. Had the man been *crying*? Probably a jag, from the pot.

He went to the bedroom and shook Lois awake. She fought him with sweeping arms, then sat up, then jumped to her knees and grabbed him and hugged him. "Evan! I knew you wouldn't! I knew!" She kissed him so hard he drew back, protesting.

She ran around, getting her things together. He lit a cigarette and sat on the edge of the bed. Quite a greeting. He felt strange. Different.

Almost happy.

8: | Wednesday p.m.

She hoped Evan would take them to eat someplace else; someplace away from this super-square motel. And that's how it shaped up as they went to the car and put their packs inside.

But the car wouldn't start. So back they went to the room, and he called the local Auto Club and they arranged to have the Jag towed to a nearby garage for a tuneup and wheel alignment.

She and John sat around while Evan called from the bedroom, and now she was so hungry she had to drink two glasses of water to get rid of the ache in her guts. John was still a little dopey from his second joint and sat beside her on the couch, eyes half-closed.

Evan came in and said they had to wait for the garage men. And that the Jag wouldn't be ready until tomorrow noon. He was going to get his suitcases and they should get their packs "because there's no sense *courting* robbery."

Back to the car they went, and got their things, and back to the room again. And now Evan decided to change, and went into the bedroom and closed the door. John dropped onto the couch. She said, "Christ, it's almost three and still no food!" John said, "Funny, I'm not that hungry anymore." She said, "You mean you couldn't go for fried eggs and bacon and sausages and pancakes?" He held up his hand. "Funny, I'm dying of hunger now."

Evan came out of the bedroom again.

"Wow," she said, looking him over.

He asked if she liked his outfit.

"Yeah!"

John said, "Welcome to the hippie freak community," and they all laughed, but no way would anyone call Evan *that*. He was *In*, but it was rich and it was *right*. She went over and took his arm and felt she'd have to fight off a mob of teeny-boppers to hold onto *this* stud. She wanted to go out and be seen with him.

"Maybe we'll go dancing," she said. "You said you do rock."

He nodded. "Later this evening." He paused. "We might not come back here before then. Wouldn't you and John like to change?"

She looked at John and John looked at her. Evan said, "Don't you have anything else to wear?"

"Not anything *better*," John said.

"Need a few more things," she muttered, ashamed now. Before it hadn't seemed to matter. "Left most of my clothes with a friend. She's holding them to send me when I settle someplace."

John said, "I got a few more pairs of pants and shirts and stuff, too, with the same friend. Woman who runs the house where we stayed. You can't lug around a wardrobe when you're hitching."

"Well, perhaps we'll pick up an outfit or two . . ."

"Really?" Lois interrupted excitedly. *"Today?"*

He nodded. "Right after we eat."

She grabbed him and kissed him, and there was a knock at the door, and it was the guy from the garage. Evan gave him the keys, then went back to the phone and arranged for a rental car.

And, at long last, they went to *eat!*

It was at the motel coffee shop, full of dressy squares. The hostess gave her and John the quick look, but when Evan said, "A booth, please," the bitch led the way.

Evan encouraged them to eat as much as they wanted: "You've earned it with that long wait." He seemed happier than before, and she thought that things were really going to jell now. Even John would have a good go and it would be fun until L.A., when John would split. Then it would be more fun, more *important*, just she and Evan.

They ordered and she put her arm through his and leaned against his shoulder and smiled into his face, feeling he would take care of her forever, she would love him more and more, it was the greatest break of her whole life!

And Jesus, how *handsome* he looked now that he was *really* dressed, in a way she could relate to, in a *young* way.

His outfit was really something—brown suede boots, and a skin-tight pair of flare-bottomed, blue suede tie-dyes that must've cost a *fortune*, and a puffy, ruffled shirt of pale red, and a short leather jacket with a few metal studs placed around the pockets and bottom edging.

He gave their order to the waitress, and Lois listened to his voice as if hearing it for the first time. Soft and not too deep. But strong. The voice and the *look* he gave you —straight out from dark brown eyes; *that* was strong, too.

She hugged his arm again, and he gave her a smile, and she felt his strength like a warm blanket on a cold night. It came from *inside* him—drive and purpose. It was the total man, *her* man, her Evan.

They ate like pigs. They kept the waitress hopping with

coffee refills and second orders of toast and sausages. Evan quit first and she quit second and John cleaned up the table.

Evan asked for a cigarette. John said he was out, and Evan went to the machine near the cash register. She watched him with pride.

John said, "Don't play it so heavy. You'll scare him off."

"No play, baby. The real thing."

"Sure, sure. Give it at least a week before . . ."

But Evan was almost at the booth.

They smoked. Evan talked about a big shopping center nearby and some small stores downtown and she described the kind of outfit she'd like to get. John was quiet, maybe a little tight, and she hoped Evan would give the go-ahead for a real group scene tonight. John needed something to keep him cool, and there was nothing like balling to drain *that* man of the tights.

As if he'd been reading her mind, Evan said, "And we might find a girl for our silent friend here."

John said, "I'll take all the help I can get."

Lois said, "We'll use Evan as bait," then saw from John's funny smile that it was the wrong thing to say, though Evan laughed and looked pleased. Besides, now she *was* playing, acting . . . because she didn't want another girl around. Not that she would let herself slip in front of Evan, but there was no point in complicating things.

She could keep them *both* happy, all by herself, the week or two on the road to L.A. After that it was Normalsville forever.

There was a blue Chevy four-door parked at the lobby entrance. Evan went to the desk and signed some papers and got the keys, and they were on their way, Evan driving and she beside him and John slouched low in back. Evan took them to a big shopping center just down Lindburg Boulevard, a *monster* place really, and a salesman at a store called Famous Barr said it was the biggest shopping center in the States. She tried on a few dresses and pant suits, but she wanted something *special*, something to match Evan's outfit, and for that she needed a hip shop, a head shop with a clothing sideline, and there wasn't any such shop in the center. Evan said he knew some places in the Forest Park area, and they decided to drive there. But first, John picked out a pair of brushed denim baggies and a gray shirt with epaulets.

"Pay you back in L.A.," he said, "when I get some bread."

Evan nodded.

John looked at a pair of multi-color suede high-heeled shoes, a real groove, while Evan used his credit card . . . but put them down when Evan returned. Evan said, "Try them on." John shook his head. Evan said, "Hurry. They close early in this town." John put them on and they looked good and Evan paid for them, too.

Back in the car, John was real quiet. Evan glanced at him in the mirror and said, "Satisfied with the items?" John mumbled, "Yeah," and then, a little louder, but not much, "Thanks a lot. I mean it . . . I'll pay you back."

Lois felt she had to say something to get rid of an uncomfortable silence that filled the car. "So will I, baby, tonight." And she gave him a wicked grin and a little pat on the leg. "For *both* your hitchhikers."

Evan said, "Now that's the kind of prompt repayment I like."

But John said, "I pay my own debts. Never walked away from a loan in my life."

And that was that. He was still uptight, and quieter than ever afterward, when he should have been happy as hell. She couldn't figure him out!

Their next stop was a small shop on a broad avenue named Lindell. It was called Mod-Maid and Lois kept trying on outfit after outfit, and the excitement kept building, like Christmas-time . . . a Christmas she'd never had before. Not because she counted on getting everything she wanted, but because it was the *beginning* of getting everything. And not just from Evan; on her own, too.

The salesgirl was tall and dark and on the heavy side, but still pretty. She spoke with a hick twang, almost like the Beverly Hillbillies, and kept looking at Evan, who stood near the windows and talked to John.

Evan looked over every time Lois came out of the little dressing booth wearing a new outfit. He'd nod or shrug or shake his head, and she agreed with him most of the time, and put aside the clothing they both dug for final selection later.

It was almost six and the shop closed at six-thirty and there were no other customers, no other people there, except for the short, fat manager or owner who smiled a lot and kept his eyes respectfully away from her. She was willing to bet he'd be going for feels and make-out if Evan and John weren't there.

After a while, she narrowed it down to two outfits. She called Evan over to the dressing room and asked what he thought of the skirt and blouse she was wearing. He smiled and nodded . . . and she quickly slipped out of the skirt. He drew the curtain closed, or *almost* closed, looking in through a half-inch as she changed. She smiled to herself at the way his eyes got hot, because she was wearing a pair of black panties from Frederick's of Hollywood, real stripper stuff with just an inch-wide band around the waist and not much more covering the crotch and running up between the cheeks.

He liked the second combo she put on—a long velvety dress, tight green-and-red floral design on an *alive* gray background, and a wild satin jacket, black with silver threading, wide lapels and flared at the hips. Together, a real kick-in-the-head! He said, "I opt for that." She said, "You got it," and pulled off the dress. He glanced back into the shop, where the others had been playing at not watching him watch her. "How about these to finish it off?" she said, and pulled down the Frederick's panties and put on another pair, pale pink lacy stuff you could see right through. He wet his lips. "Keep it up and it'll be an early evening." She laughed, and he went back to John.

The salesgirl came over, opening the curtain a little, asking if she wanted to try on any of the other size eights. Lois was taking off the lacy panties and said no, she'd decided. The girl said that was fine and could she have the rejects still in the booth. Lois began to say she'd bring them out, but the girl leaned in and picked them up off the floor, brushing Lois's body with her arms, her head, then backing out and going away.

When she came out, she wore the foxy new outfit with the Frederick's panties underneath, and that thin strip of silky material rubbed her crotch as she walked, made her randy. She looked at Evan and popped her lips at him and was happy, so happy she could even have sung *Waltzing Matilda* the way Dad always made her do as a kid. Then she saw herself in the full-length mirror, right down to her feet, and realized her old boots didn't work with this outfit.

Evan and John were back near the window, and so was the salesgirl. Now she was looking at, and talking to, John. Lois waved her over. "You carry shoes?"

Beverly Hillbilly said, "Nao . . . but they's a place two doors down the street got *great* shoes—klunkers and boots. Ah'd go with klunkers if ah was you."

How the hell had she ever got a job as a salesgirl? Made Lois feel like Einstein!

Evan went to the register with the girl, and Lois turned away, wondering if he'd get mad at the bill. No cheap stuff this—she'd totaled the price tags. A hundred and sixty dollars. She went over to John. "I'm wearing these," she said. "How about changing into your new stuff?"

"You mean right here?"

"Sure. Let the hillbilly get a look at you."

He glanced at the salesgirl, who was bending over the counter to point something out to her boss. She showed one hell of a ripe bumper, and Lois turned from it and waited out John's long stare.

"Why not," he finally said, and went to Evan and got the keys to the car and went out. Evan came over to her, saying they'd have to wait a few minutes while the owner phoned for credit clearance on his American Express card. She said, "Could we walk down the street, hon? These shoes just don't match this outfit. Hate to ask . . ."

He said all right.

The shoe store was closing. The young salesman said sorry, and Evan was ready to walk out, but she said *gee* and *please* and gave him the soft smile and clinched it by hiking her dress up above her knees as she sat down in the chair and put a leg up on the footstool. He said, "Well, if you'll make a quick selection . . ."

She found the shoes she wanted right away. She had the salesman sweating with those Frederick's panties and then sweated a bit herself when he said the price was forty-eight dollars. She glanced at Evan. He just took out his wallet and handed over another credit card. There was no phone call on this one, maybe because it was under a hundred dollars, and maybe because the salesman was in a hurry to split.

Back at the Mod-Maid, John was leaning against the counter, looking longer and leaner than ever in his baggies and high heels, but looking good, too. His denim jacket went with the new outfit.

The girl was laughing at whatever he was saying, then she went into the back of the store.

"I asked her out for dinner and dancing," John said as they came up to him. He handed Evan his American Express card and a slip. "You suggested it, in a way."

"No sweat," Evan said.

Beverly Hillbilly came out about five minutes later, wearing an imitation leather outfit: shiny black mini-wetsuit—matching micro-skirt and blouse-jacket—and black boots with spike heels. She hitched a long-strapped bag over her shoulder, and said, "Awl raidy!" Yeah, for a ten-dollar trick!

Lois took Evan's arm, and the hillbilly, whose name was Alma-Jean, took John's arm, and the owner or manager came to the desk. He said, "Have fun!" and Lois glanced back to catch a look like a sweaty jock.

She wished they could have latched onto a *quieter* type for John. She didn't look forward to going out as much now.

She and Evan were in the front seat of the rented Chevy, Alma-Jean and John in the back. Alma-Jean leaned forward and touched Lois's arm. "Ah know a *rail* nahce place for dancin'." Lois said it was up to Evan. He said they'd eat dinner first at a place he remembered for its great steaks. He stopped and asked directions at a gas station.

Alma-Jean said to Lois, "Ah've eaten at Reuben's. *Rail* good food." She smiled . . . and Lois told herself she was *not* getting any sort of signal.

But at Reuben's, after they'd had a good meal and lots of wine, she excused herself to go to the john, and Alma-Jean said, "Me, too!"

She closed the door of the booth, but Alma-Jean kept talking from the sinks about leaving St. Louis for *Nyew York* or another city where people weren't "so *squaire*. If you don' git married and raise *bayabies*, they think yore *queer* or something. If you know what Ah mean?"

Lois tried to pee quietly. Funny, because almost always *she'd* been the one pushing; now she was the one *getting* pushed. Except, she told herself as she came out of the booth, she was probably imagining the whole thing.

Alma-Jean was using a styling brush on her straight black hair. Lois washed her hands and brushed her own hair. Alma-Jean pursed her lips admiringly. "Pretty hair, honey." She reached out and touched it lightly. "Yore built real well, too." Lois remembered the business in the dressing room. "John says you all going to *Los Angeles.*

Ah wouldn't mind taggin' along. Might be we'd have a *bawl.*"

Lois turned on her and said, sharply, "Is that the way you *really* talk? Like a funny TV show?"

Alma-Jean blinked. "What's that, honey?"

"You heard me, honey. How long do we get the hillbilly routine?"

Alma-Jean's face changed; began to come apart. She said, voice trembling, "That's not nahce! Ah've . . . *I've* been here . . . only fahve weeks." She turned away, hands going to her face. "That's *mean!*" She began to cry. "Mah town's *small . . . Want* to learn . . ." She cried harder.

Lois took the big girl by the shoulders, turned her around and drew her close. She stroked the bowed, shaking head and murmured, "Easy, baby, I had too much to drink," and patted the fat bumper. Alma-Jean stopped crying and snuggled and kissed her cheek and said, "Ah ain't mad, honey." Lois stepped away as two women entered the washroom. She waited as Alma-Jean repaired her eye makeup. Well, she'd had to find out.

Now Lois knew she was in trouble. Now she wanted a last taste of that sweet, sweet fruit. And trying to sneak it could be dangerous.

Back at the table, Evan had ordered a *third* bottle of wine. And by the time they finished that he was saying they should go back to the suite before going to the rock club. And she was afraid and turned to John and said, "But we want to dance, right, John?" He looked at Alma-Jean. Alma-Jean leaned into him and his hands went under the table and Alma-Jean closed her eyes, nuzzling his neck and sighing.

When they came into the suite, Alma-Jean said, "What a great big *baid!* Bet we'd *all* fit!" She ran through the archway and threw herself on it, face down.

John and Evan looked at each other. John said, "Can we pick them?" Evan said, "Can we *ever?*" And they laughed together like two kids, two little boys getting high.

In the bedroom, Alma-Jean had rolled over, that micro-mini up to her belly button, her dumb white panties dark at the crotch, and was looking at Lois, looking and waiting. And the damned fools laughed, the goddamn assholes laughed and took off their jackets. Next would come their pants.

She marched to the couch and sat down. She couldn't stop the party and she couldn't stop whatever would happen, but she could work a drunk act. And if Evan and John kept drinking, got real stoned, the con would go unnoticed.

"What's the hurry?" she asked. "Haste makes waste, right? I want something to drink."

"More wine coming up," Evan said, going to the phone.

"I'd like Scotch," Lois said. "And a joint. John, roll us all some joints."

John looked at Evan.

Evan nodded, already on the phone, ordering a bottle of Johnny Walker. John went into the bedroom and there was lots of laughing. When he came out, he had his plastic bag and Zig-Zag papers and Alma-Jean said, "A rail *bawl!*" and hugged him and looked at Lois.

Lois went to the TV, which had a radio section on the UHF dial, and found rock music and began to dance. She held out her arms to Evan and he hung up the phone and danced with her. And surprise, he could move, knew steps, routines, was a lot better than John and most dudes. Which helped her lose herself in the beat.

The booze came. They drank and smoked joints and she nursed her Scotch and saw Alma-Jean doing the same. She made sure Evan and John had fresh drinks, again and again. And John danced with Alma-Jean. And it became a party, a pretty good party, even though two of the guests weren't wanted.

After a while, she allowed herself to watch those long, round legs, those rolling hips, those big boobs bouncing under the blouse-jacket, the whole hot package bumping and grinding away to Led Zeppelin. Another few drinks, and she'd maneuver the party to the bedroom.

Roersch didn't leave Ruthie's place until nine-thirty, which surprised him and delighted her. Not that they'd had that much action. The action had come at six-thirty, after a drink and a smoke and a little TV. It had gone well. Better than *well* and different from all the other times. Slower, with more humor, more affection, holding her and playing with her and laughing with her.

He finally grabbed her big ass and humped her down into the soft mattress and called her a "fucking great whore" and came harder than he had in years. It weakened him, and he lay panting on her, and then rolled off and kept panting. That was why it took a few minutes for him to realize she'd turned away. When he raised himself to see her face, she buried it in the pillow. When he rolled her over, she shouted, "You don't have to remind me!"

He explained it was something said in passion, something he said to *all* women, even his wife, right before coming. A kick of his.

"But they *weren't*," she said, sitting up.

"Yeah? Who's to tell? You make a straight-out deal for money. Others make their deals for meals and presents and husbands. Every woman whores. At least every woman who's got enough on the ball to *make* a deal."

She thought a moment, then shrugged and lay back down. She turned when he tugged her, and came into his arms. They lay face to face, body to body, and he stroked her, explored her curves, her softness, her fullness, her beauty . . . really, Jesus, she was one beautiful woman!

He told her so. Then he told her he was hungry.

She was also one beautiful cook. She'd prepared something she called *quiche Lorraine*, a pie-thing with custard and cheese and onion and bacon, all in a flaky crust. Except for the one slice Ruthie had, he ate the whole thing himself, along with a full quart of beer, and finished with a cup of her strong, black coffee, and sat there, empty of desire and full of food, enjoying a Nat Sherman cigarette. They talked. He told her about working on the Judith Keel murder, but not too much. She said she sometimes worried about ending up that way herself, taking strange men into her home or going to hotel rooms with them. He felt uncomfortable, and changed the subject to Jen. He asked about the father.

"A guy named Roger. Thought I loved him, and thought I'd get him to marry me, and was wrong on both counts." She smiled slightly. "Instead, he got me into hooking. I was waiting on tables then, and when my belly got too big he carried me a while. Then he showed me how I could pay him back, fast, and do better for myself too."

"Does he visit Jen?"

"Haven't heard from him in three years. He doesn't know he's her father. And it makes no difference anyway. Never think of him. But I'm not sorry I took out the coil that time. Jen's the best thing in my life."

He left a few minutes later, and she walked him to the door. He bent to kiss her, and she touched his face and said, "Thanks for listening to the whore cry in her beer."

He said, "Cut it out," brusquely.

"Well, I *am* a whore, and it's okay from now on if you want to call me that when we ball."

"You're also something else. A lot of things."

"Like what?"

"You're a lady. You're a mother." He got out the door with: "And the best piece of ass in Manhattan."

Which left her laughing.

He was at his apartment, putting the key in the lock, when he glanced back. She was in her doorway, watching him. He nodded, and went inside.

Enough bullshit. Enough crap with whores . . .

That made him feel rotten, so he got to work, dialing the private eye's new number. Still no answer—he'd tried phoning twice before leaving the station. Maybe Jones had scared Mr. Nick McKenney, cousin of Bley's assistant, out of answering, or even out of that apartment. What this called for was a stake-out . . . but he couldn't use normal procedure anymore. Had to handle everything personally, if he was to keep the pigeon for himself.

No doubt about it. He was going to lose a lot of time, a lot of sleep, maybe even a lot of important information, working alone this way. And he'd have to manipulate the reports so as to hide the fact that he *was* working alone. A sergeant heading up a case used several detectives . . .

Again, he was thinking, worrying, too much.

He decided to drive over to McKenney's right now.

He was almost out the door before he remembered he'd put away his service revolver and handcuffs before going to Ruthie's. He went to his dresser, but left the .38 lying there. Instead, he opened the top drawer and got his off-duty weapon. It was a tiny .25-caliber automatic with all the stopping power of a kid's squirrel gun; he used it only for personal protection, to flash like a badge in case any of Fun City's fun citizens pushed him. After all, he was involved now in law enforcement only to the extent of completing the case against Bley.

He left the handcuffs on the dresser with the .38. What did he need cuffs for? The only man he'd use them on was driving to Los Angeles.

9: Wednesday p.m. and Thursday a.m.

Nick McKenney now lived in a converted brownstone on Thirty-fourth Street. It was not the best of neighborhoods, but far from the worst. The lobby was small and clean with a row of mailboxes and a white-on-black plastic sign that read, "Ring Bell Over Mailbox For Admittance." He found McKenney's box and pressed the button. No answer. He pressed again, and again, then found the mailbox with "Keeler-Super" and pressed that. A tinny electronic voice spoke: "Yes, who is it?" He glanced around, and saw the grill on the other wall. He stepped over and said, "Police."

"You're kidding. Who *is* this? You playing games, Rick?"

"Sergeant Roersch, Homicide."

"We get all kinds of nuts . . ."

"You want me to break down your door?" That got the

desired results. Keeler, a tall, cadaverous man of perhaps sixty, cracked the door a moment later, looked at Roersch's badge and stepped aside.

"You got a tenant here, Nick McKenney?"

"Front back. One–C."

"I'd like to check if he's in."

He didn't wait for an answer, but brushed by the super. Keeler said, "Want me along?"

"That's right." He spotted the door down the hall, and also spotted the crack of light at the bottom. The light went *out* a second later, which made him smile. The ex-cop's reflexes were far too slow.

Roersch knocked. "McKenney, open up, I saw the light go off."

No answer . . . but movement inside the apartment, *away* from the front and the door. Roersch turned, and bumped into the super. "His windows . . . where do they open?"

"An alley between the two houses on your left . . ."

Roersch had already begun running.

"And one on the courtyard in back. Follow the alley . . ."

Roersch was outside, down the stone steps, turning left. He was cursing. Why the hell was the jerk complicating things? He hadn't been busted by Jones, so why run? Could the junkie have done the butcher job?

He was panting, blaming it on all that screwing and eating, as he turned into the alley. Halfway down the alley, he thought he saw a shape darting back toward the courtyard. He drew his .25 from the hip holster, came another step forward, and stopped. He crouched, leveled his gun with both hands, and shouted, "Halt! Halt or . . ."

He wouldn't have fired. Not at that dim shape. And how could he justify killing McKenney when he'd come here on a routine check?

But he never finished his warning. He caught a blur of motion on his left, and turned his head to catch the full weight of a man coming down from the window ledge.

He'd overrun his quarry. They went down together. Hands were straining at his automatic, and he was on his side, cheek scraping the pavement, trying to get his left arm around the man who was pressing him down.

He got hold of something, a belt maybe, and pulled. The man came off him and scrambled to his knees. Roersch clubbed at his head with the gun. He heard a wail, and struck again, and again, and the shape flattened out. Roersch got to his feet and backed off and leveled the gun.

"Are you all right?" the super called from the street. "Do you want I should call for help?"

Roersch gasped, "No. Go back. Open his door."

"If you say so."

"I say so." His eyes were adjusting, and he saw the man struggle to his knees, head down like an Arab praying, rocking that way too.

"McKenney. Get up now, slowly. Walk back to the street."

The man stayed on his knees, rocking.

"I've got a gun on you," Roersch said, and waited a moment, giving him time. "No more warnings. Get up slow and walk slow, to the street, then to your apartment. Move fast and you're dead."

It was bullshit. Unless he jumped him again, tried for the gun again, tried to run away . . .

Christ, a fucking junkie killer, and Bley and his hundreds of thousands down the drain!

"Why?" the man on the pavement asked, raising his head. "I didn't hurt her. She was dead when I got there. I sold the necklace, but I didn't kill her. Why persecute me?"

He wasn't getting up. But he was talking. Roersch wouldn't push him. They'd talk here a while.

"We're not trying to pin it on you. We think we know the man."

"Bley. That's the one. He had her tailed. He hated her

guts. He paid me not to write the report . . . the real report. My head's bleeding. I need to lie down."

"Do you want a doctor?"

The head came up. "No! You'd have to take me in! I'll die if you take me in! I can't face cold turkey now. I'll get the necklace back. I'll do anything to help you nail Bley."

"Can you stand up? We'll go inside and treat your head."

McKenney began to get up. Roersch raised the gun to keep it on the largest target area—chest and stomach— and pushed McKenney to the wall with his left hand. "Turn around, hands against the wall . . ." Roersch frisked him. "All right. Why'd you jump me?"

McKenney straightened and put out an arm to steady himself against the wall. "You stood there with the gun. In another minute you'd have turned your head and seen me. I was almost out the window. I couldn't go back in, and if I just dropped down you'd have shot me. I was a cop; I *know*! If someone drops out a window in an alley and you have a gun and you turn around . . . I shot a kid once. Lucky I didn't kill him. He turned out to be someone who lived in the place. That's how I left the force . . . I was only on coke then . . . my head's killing me . . ." He gagged, bent over, vomited heavily.

Roersch waited, turning his nose from the stink. *This* was what Bley's money would get him out of: the dryness of throat and the guns and the panic and the stink . . . and someday, maybe, the bullet from the dark and the Inspector's Funeral.

McKenney finished. "I can walk now. I'm turning, okay?"

"Okay."

"I'm walking to the street now, okay?"

"Just go on, slowly, and I'll follow. Don't worry. We'll talk."

"But cold turkey . . . you won't do *that* to me?" He began to walk, and to cry.

They came into the street, and sure enough there was the super and about five other people, one a woman. Roersch brought the gun in close to his side, hiding it, but the woman turned away and covered her face, as if seeing something terrible. When they went up the steps to the lighted lobby, Roersch realized what she'd seen. McKenney's face was crisscrossed by tiny rivulets of blood.

Roersch followed him to the rear apartment, where the door stood open. The super followed, calling, "How about an ambulance?"

Roersch said, "It's all taken care of. Thanks. You're a good citizen." Roersch closed the door on him. He just hoped that neither the good citizen nor his neighbors would do any phoning on their own. What he *didn't* want was a pack of radio cars responding to an Assist Patrolman.

They stood in a darkened kitchen. "Lights," Roersch said, his gun pressing McKenney's back.

McKenney moved and the lights came on. Roersch turned him to the wall and spread-eagled him and did another frisk, now that he was able to see what he was doing. He came up with a good-sized switchblade knife, taped under the stocking above the left ankle. "What's this for?"

"I didn't use it, did I?"

Roersch put it in his pocket. It was too small for what had been done to the Keel girl, but he'd get someone at the lab to check it for bloodstains. He'd tag it "owner unknown."

He should call an ambulance. He should book McKenney for flight and resisting and assaulting. On any other case, he'd have done all these things.

But he wasn't working for the New York City Police Department now. He had to accept that, and act accordingly. No use getting torn between what he would do as an officer and what he was doing as a private party. He was a private party here . . . in officer's disguise.

"Sit down. You want a drink?"

"There's some juice in the fridge."

It was grapefruit juice, unsweetened, icy cold, and Roersch took a glass from the drainboard and poured it full for McKenney, then took a long gulp from the bottle. "All right," he said, leaning back against the refrigerator, the gun in his right hand but hanging limp. "Go to the sink and wash up."

McKenney did just that, wincing and groaning as he bathed his head.

Roersch took another drink. McKenney dried himself with the dish towel, returned to the table and finished his juice.

"Your cousin told me about you," Roersch said. "I have sympathy for a fellow officer, even an *ex*-officer. I'm inclined to look for ways to help you."

McKenney watched him, waiting for the trap or the angle.

When Roersch remained silent, McKenney said, "There's not much left from the necklace. About eighty dollars. I paid three months' rent in advance and bought . . . what I needed. But maybe I can raise five hundred, if you give me a week."

Roersch began to shake his head.

"All right. I'll try something tomorrow, the latest Friday."

The fucking pad. "I don't need it," Roersch said. "I need a promotion." Promotion from poor cop to rich civilian. "Help me get it, and you don't get booked."

"Jesus, thank you," McKenney murmured. He crossed himself and finished his grapefruit juice. "I didn't tell that spook everything."

"You mean Detective Jones?"

"Oh, he's a friend of yours?" A quick laugh, a nervous shake of the head. "I didn't mean anything. Just a way of speaking. Bad upbringing. Some of my best friends . . . Didn't tell him . . . well, would *you?*"

"No, I wouldn't've. If I'd stolen a necklace from a girl's apartment, with the girl lying there butchered in her bed. If I'd been casing the girl long after finishing my surveillance, long after being fired from the job. If maybe I'd killed her myself."

"As Christ is my witness, I *didn't!*"

"If I'd seen who *had* killed her, and not reported it."

"I *did* see him! I figured . . . well, I'd make sure . . . I'd wait . . ."

"And shake him down when you got hold of him."

McKenney waved his hands. He wore a dingy white shirt and unpressed tan trousers. His junkie's pallor was accentuated by a scraggly day's growth of beard. He kept scratching his neck and fidgeting. He cleared his throat, raspingly, and asked for more juice. Roersch poured what was left into the glass and put the empty bottle on the drainboard.

McKenney drank, hand trembling worse than Mrs. Bleywitz's. "Listen, what difference does it make what *I* did? It was all nothing; all scrounging for a buck. It's what *Bley* did, last Sunday, when I was watching him. I swear it! I swear I never touched that girl . . ."

Roersch held up his hand; a teacher with an over-anxious pupil. "Tell me what happened, the *way* it happened, and you'll be all right. Fuck around with me, and you're booked."

McKenney nodded. "You got a cigarette?"

Roersch hated to part with one of his treasured Nat Shermans, but he removed a long cigarette and brought it to McKenney. He stepped back to the refrigerator, envying the junkie his first deep, shuddering drag. Hell, why should a junkie worry about smoking? They never lived long enough to die of lung cancer.

McKenney began to talk. "Congrove is a big agency. They try to keep the client from dealing with the operative on his case by channeling everything through the front office. But Bley insisted on getting my name and phone number and working out a routine with me before I started the surveillance."

"Which was when?"

"It's in my notebook . . . but roughly, end of February."

"Where's the notebook?"

"In the top drawer there." He pointed at a row of drawers beside the sink.

Roersch opened the drawer and came out with a dimestore, pocket-sized notebook much like his own. He moved back to the refrigerator, and tossed the book on the table. "Now tell me the essentials, day by day, until the murder."

McKenney said, "If that's what you want." He opened the notebook, and his head shook slightly, and he'd developed a facial twitch, a tic at the right side of his mouth. He fumbled with the pages. "Here. February twenty-sixth. Monday. I was to start the surveillance at her place of employment, that ad agency Vince and Bley work for. I was to be there at four-thirty to make sure I got on her by five, the time she left work. I was to stay on her until two a.m., what they call a full leisure-time cover. Same every day through Friday, unless she called in sick or failed to show for work. But she showed up every day that first week. It changed on the weekend. Bley was taking her someplace—Vermont, I think he said—so the tail was off for Saturday and Sunday. He was spending most weekends with her at that time. He was suspicious of her just weekday evenings."

He used a shaky finger to run down a page. "Monday was nothing. She came right home. She traveled by Fifth Avenue bus to her place on Seventy-seventh off Third, and I was able to use the company car. I was able to use it almost all the time. She stayed home that Monday, unless she left after two a.m." He turned the page. "On Tuesday . . ."

"You're assuming she was alone. You couldn't run a check on what was going on in her apartment, could you?"

"That was part of what Bley talked over with me before the surveillance began. He doubled on me. I'd phone in if she stayed put past eleven o'clock and seemed to be alone, and he'd call her to say he was thinking of dropping up. If she didn't block it, he'd either come over, or back out some way. During the two weeks I was on her, she never blocked him those evenings she seemed to be alone."

"Did he ask for day-by-day reports? Did you report when you called him?"

"Company policy was a weekly report, and he didn't seem rushed. But the surveillance was accurate, so far as *any* of them are. On Tuesday she went home. Then at six-thirty . . ."

"Let's go back to Monday. That's a good-sized apartment house. Maybe a hundred units; two hundred or more tenants; people in and out all the time. Didn't you have any specific individuals to watch for? Didn't he give you any names, descriptions, information on other men?"

"That's right, forgot. Three men. All from the agency. An artist named Ronny Layden. Big wheel and part owner Morgan Burns." Roersch blinked. "And guess who— Cousin Vince. Bley supplied descriptions and photographs of Layden and Burns. Damned good photographs from the agency's publicity files."

"If you continue to forget things, I'm going to forget how you feel about cold turkey."

"But I really forgot! This surveillance has a million goddamn details. And none of them are important because Bley . . . Okay, I won't forget any more details. Tuesday she went out again about six-thirty and took a bus to Washington Square and met a friend, a girl, at a bar in the Village called Polaris. They talked a lot, and at one point the friend got hot and began to walk out. Keel went after her and they came back to the table and spent another half hour there. Then they went down the street to a restaurant and ate dinner. Keel took a cab home, alone, at nine-thirty. No further action."

"Describe the friend," Roersch said, thinking of the blonde the cleaning lady had seen.

"Good-looking and young, maybe twenty, twenty-one. They made quite a team, and got some action from men in the bar. They turned it off as fast as it came. Shorter than Keel, long hair, reddish-brown, I guess, with some of that frosting they spray on the front. Showy chick."

Roersch nodded, knowing it could have been a wig, also knowing it could have been one of a million other women.

"Wednesday she went to a movie directly from work. She sat alone. It was a lousy art film about Italian Jews under Mussolini. I could care less."

"Skip the reviews."

"She went home about eight-fifteen. I usually parked about twenty feet from the entrance, on the other side of the street, an illegal spot but since I was always in the car . . . But it was taken. I had to park a block away, and walk up and down. Cold, too. Anyway, I almost ran into Vince; had to cross the street fast."

He sucked smoke, and looked at his cigarette as if wishing it was something he could stick in his arm. "Vince never got past the lobby. I watched through the outer doors. He talked into the box and went to the inside door and shook it. Then he went out and got into his Firebird and drove away, taking the corner like a crazy kid. I figured little cousin was crossing his boss. Bley was his boss, right?"

"But blood's thicker than water. You wouldn't have put it in the report for Bley to see, would you?"

"Never considered it. Besides, as it turned out, I didn't have to. Bley didn't want me to write a straight report. He wanted a whitewash. Guess why."

Roersch decided to have a cigarette, and lit up. He inhaled, but not as deeply as McKenney. He'd read an article that said some of the bad effects of smoking could be avoided by *half* inhalations.

McKenney said, "Don't you get it? He didn't want his

motive there for the cops to find, when he made his move." He smiled, waiting for approval.

Roersch said, "You were short of money."

"What's that got to do . . . ?"

"With a habit like yours, you're always short of money. Now tell me about Cousin Vince."

McKenney looked at his fast-diminishing cigarette. "You'll see it makes no difference. I figured to hit Vince for a small loan. I owed him nothing. He was always so goddamn superior with his college education and his big jobs, putting me down even when I was on the force. But I wasn't sure I had enough to squeeze him, even for peanuts. What I did was call him the next morning and explain about the surveillance and tell a little white lie. I said I'd been on Keel for a *month*. He came apart so fast I was ashamed for him. The big executive! He offered me two hundred, which I jacked up to five with no trouble. I swore I'd keep it out of the report; that no one would know he'd been making Keel." He dragged on his cigarette, which was getting down to the fingers. He knew how to hold it; an old pot smoker's expertise with roaches. "Met him in the men's room on the ninth floor and got my check and was able to resume the surveillance on Keel with hardly a ten-minute wait."

"Did your cousin *admit* an affair with Keel?"

"He said he'd met her one night outside a theater—pure coincidence—and they went to dinner, and then to her place. He said she invited him in for a nightcap and that was all. I said it was a *long* nightcap. He said yes, they'd talked, she was an *intelligent* girl. He said he met her once again, because she was upset about something and wanted his advice. They went to dinner and again to her place for a drink and they talked two, three hours. Both these times had to be in late January or February, since he assumed I knew about them, and I'd told him I was on Keel a month. As for the time he didn't get past the lobby, the time I'd *really* seen him . . ." He began to check his notebook.

"Wednesday, February twenty-eighth," Roersch muttered, thinking how that notebook could complicate things if Hawly ever got his hands on it.

"Right. Wednesday, the twenty-eighth. He said that time he was drinking and found himself in her neighborhood and decided to talk to her about *his* problems, which were probably full balls and a stiff prick." He tried a man-to-man grin.

Roersch didn't hide his distaste. McKenney said, "You're going to bust me. I can feel it." He waited for Roersch to say something. Roersch said nothing. He was fighting *not* to visualize Nick in Judith Keel's apartment, because she might *not* have been dead when he took that necklace, and might very well have been dead when he walked out her door. The cop in him was struggling to overcome the private citizen. If the cop won, the run for the money, Bley's money, would fall apart.

McKenney went back to his notebook, hands trembling worse than ever. "Vince said those were the only three times he'd ever met the girl outside the office—two, really, since she wouldn't let him in the third time. He said he never balled her, and that she wanted to talk about Bley the second time he saw her. She was afraid of Bley. He'd acted crazy a few times. Vince said the reason he was giving me the money was to avoid any conflict in the office."

He turned a page. "Thursday, Morgan Burns came to the lobby and was admitted. He was up there only ten minutes. No other action.

"Friday, her girlfriend—the one she'd met Tuesday—came over about eleven and stayed. She was still there, unless I happened to miss her, when I left at two."

Roersch shifted weight, leaning more heavily against the refrigerator. "Unless you happened to miss her?"

"Well, you know . . ."

"You're telling me something, Nick. Five to two a.m. is a long tour. Nine hours. You mainlined occasionally, didn't you? In the car, I mean?"

"Why should I? I've got a home."

"Nine hours away from that home. Five days a week. You mainlined. You nodded off. You dozed. Some surveillance."

"Friday," McKenney said, voice weak, "I spotted no one. I was on the ball. I was supposed to write up my report and bring it in Saturday morning. But Bley called me at home. He came over and we talked. I gave him what I had . . ."

"Including Vince, right?"

"Well, I had to give him something solid . . . I saw he wanted to know . . . I saw . . ."

"You saw a chance to make more money."

"I wasn't sure, but I figured . . . Well, I'd give him the straight story . . . what I'd seen. Ethical, right?"

Roersch came to the table and sat down. He rested the gun on the table, aimed directly at McKenney's chest. "The ethics of a junkie blackmailer. You padded the report for Bley, didn't you? Brought in *more* men, or heavied the action on Morgan Burns and your cousin. Because you saw a hurt man, an angry man, a man who could be made to do something to that girl. You'd already figured the angle of his not wanting a written report; saw a big payoff for a whitewash." He leaned forward. "What you did, Nick, was help kill that girl."

McKenney shook his head. His voice trembled. "Jesus, that's way out. I didn't pad Vince and Burns."

"Then you added someone. And Nick, I'm going to speak to Bley soon, *so don't bull me!* Tell me *everything,* or you'll be cold turkey for sure!"

"All right. I added another guy. I said she'd come in with him and he'd stayed at least six hours, probably the night. I used one of the nights she hadn't gone out, when Bley hadn't come over after doubling by phone. I had to make up a description, so I made him an older type, because she seemed to go for older men—Bley and Burns; and Vince isn't all that young. I said he was distinguished, big . . ."

"How did Bley react?"

"He said he knew the man. Said it was her uncle and all perfectly innocent. But he was walking around like a tiger, pacing, trying to smile and sweating and saying all perfectly innocent. Maybe I was wrong making up the guy . . . but I never touched her! It was Bley! He was half-crazy, ready to kill . . ."

"So they went away for the weekend. The man half-crazy, the man ready to kill, took her to Vermont and brought her back without a scratch."

McKenney wet his lips. "I'm not finished yet."

"I think you are. I think you've confessed, Nick. You've admitted you've blackmailed and stolen and been at the scene of a murder. Might as well go all the way."

McKenney bent to his notebook. "It's all here," he whispered. "I was just playing for money. I wouldn't *kill* for money. I was a cop . . ."

"How about for a juicy piece of ass? Maybe a juicier kick with a naked chick begging for mercy and you carving her up?"

McKenney shook his head. "It's all here."

Roersch leaned back. "How much did Bley give you for the whitewash?"

"Two hundred. He said there'd be another two hundred next week . . . termination of the surveillance. I didn't argue, but I knew I'd get a lot more." He fumbled with the notebook. "If I'd known what was coming, I'd never have touched it. I made about two thousand, total, but I wish I'd never . . . I wish I'd never smoked pot with that bitch Nancy and then the coke she called happy dust and said was so *great* for bed and then the needle. It happened so easy." He looked up. "Can't you understand that? I'm not a goddamn *junkie*. I'm a cop who got *caught*. What if it happened to you?"

"I'm really crying for you, Nick." He kept his cold gaze on the blinking, poached-egg eyes across the table. "I'm all broken up."

Down went the graying-blond head. "Next Monday," he muttered.

"Louder!"

He started, said, "Next Monday. She went shopping before going home. Some young guy tried to pick her up at a Gristedes Market. She brushed him off. He pushed a little—a good-looking guy who couldn't believe such a cold brush-off. She *yelled* at him, and the manager came over, and the guy looked like he'd been hit in the head. He apologized and left. She looked upset, and didn't check out her groceries, and went to her apartment. At six-thirty, the agency wheel, Morgan Burns, and the artist, Ronny Layden, drove up and the two went inside. They stayed a long time." He looked up. "They had to be Keel's visitors, right?"

Roersch nodded slightly.

"I figured they had a group thing, an orgy thing. It's a logical assumption, isn't it?"

"For a degenerate mind, yes. Why couldn't they all be friends?" But he remembered Burns's superior smile, his rejection of any possibility he knew *anything* about Judith Keel, in or out of the office.

Why would a man act like a homosexual and proud of it if he *wasn't?* Or did it take a truly degenerate mind to figure that threesome of Burns, Layden and Keel?

Maybe there were areas of the homosexual mind he didn't understand. He'd have to see Burns again, and this Ronny Layden, and Vince McKenney.

"Just how long is a long time?" he asked. "How long did they stay?"

"They were there when I left. And I didn't leave at two. I wanted something good for Bley, and this was better than what I'd made up." He paused. "I had a fix. I made it weak. I didn't nod off. I didn't sleep. It was easy to see if anyone came out that late. No traffic. No one around. Not even the doorman, who went off at one. I stayed till five. Then I felt I was going to conk out and went home.

They stayed all night, right? Why would just friends stay all night? No reason except a group thing."

"Get on to Tuesday."

"Nothing. She went home and stayed there and I spotted no one and gave Bley a call at eleven like we'd arranged and . . ." He coughed and cleared his throat. "Could I have some water?"

"Finish your story and you can have all the water you want. You were a cop. You know how nice we treat junkies, don't you?"

"Yes." A very weak word. "Bley called her, and again she said to come over, and this time because I'd told him about the older guy being there one night when she said Bley could come over . . ." He cleared his throat again, a dry, rasping sound that made Roersch wince inside. "This time Bley came over and stayed an hour. After that, nothing."

"You stayed until two a.m.?"

McKenney nodded weakly.

Roersch said, "It doesn't figure. You'd already arranged your shakedown. You probably knew you'd be leaving the agency. You couldn't hold a job for long . . ."

"I stayed till two, that night. But afterward, I began cutting hours. Still, not important. You'll see. Could I have another cigarette?"

Roersch said, "Bad for your health," and felt pretty goddamn mean. He'd never been this mean as a cop.

"Wednesday was a repeat of Monday," McKenney said. "Burns and Layden came over, earlier this time, about five-thirty. They were still there when I left, which was about eleven. I figured Keel was a hard-core swinger . . ."

"And that you'd like a little of the action yourself. Which was why you kept tabs on her afterward."

McKenney shook his head.

"Nick, I've seen pictures of the girl. A Grade-A beauty. Unless you're telling me you're queer . . ."

"I'm telling you I'm sick."

"That could explain the butcher job."

"You know what I mean. I wished I *could've* felt horny. I'd have tried a squeeze for a different kind of payoff. She'd have come across, too, if she was as afraid of Bley as Vince said she was."

"What did Vince say?"

"That time she met him because she wanted to talk, she said Bley was acting crazy. She said Bley had cut open her water bed, and belted her around, and threatened worse if she ever had another man in the bed he'd bought for her. Things like that." He shifted in his chair. "So if she was afraid of Bley and I could tell Bley about other men, she'd have come across for me. I knew that. But I couldn't *feel* anything. It wasn't in me. It *isn't* in me. Maybe when I kick the habit . . ." He didn't finish, and he didn't look up. He turned a page in his notebook.

"Thursday she went to Grand Central. I rode the train with her to Rye. She was picked up by an older man and woman and I couldn't get a cab fast enough. I waited in the station until after ten; then I went back to the city."

Her parents, Roersch thought . . . and realized he hadn't seen a report on Mr. and Mrs. Keel. They must have given a statement when they came to identify the body. Who had taken it? Had Chauger typed it? Why wasn't it in the folder?

If they knew about Bley—about his cutting the water bed and hitting her and threatening her—they'd apply pressure. That would be rough to handle.

But if they'd known, they'd have raised enough of a fuss to reach Hawly and Hawly would have reached him. Also, the newspapers had interviewed them, and he'd read nothing beyond their grief, their statements about Judith being a good girl, the usual stuff . . . even in the *Daily News*, and their Page Four was as good as most official reports.

"She didn't come to work on Friday, but I made her place at five o'clock, figuring to stick around a few hours. She came out of the house at six and took a cab to a restaurant called the San Marino on Fifty-third. I was hungry, and it was the last day of the surveillance, so I figured what the hell and went in after her. Morgan Burns was waiting at the bar, and they went to a table. I got a table, too. Best meal I've had in New York. And interesting bit of action. Burns gave her an envelope—plain white business kind. She checked inside, and smiled and put it in her purse. It looked like a pad-type operation. If it wasn't a payoff, what was it?"

Roersch said, "Who knows? Who knows *anything* from your fucked-up report? You've admitted to two fixes on the job, and I'll bet there were more. You've admitted to cutting hours the second week. You called Bley three times when she stayed at home, and who watched the shop while you found a phone?" McKenney tried to say something, but Roersch continued, laying on the deep disgust. "Bley's doubling was the only check on Keel when she was in the apartment, supposedly alone, and that's a loophole a hundred guys could slip through. You had only three men to watch for, but anyone walking into that house could have made his way to her. You lied about a phony lover to heat up your pot. And who knows what else you lied about . . . to me. This isn't police work, it's *shit!*"

McKenney fumbled with his notebook. He shook his head slowly, again and again. "Burns took Keel home in his car. They sat a while near the entrance. I can't be sure, but they could have been making out. I know he kissed her. Then she went in, he drove away, and I went home. Bley called me about two-thirty, figuring *that* was when I'd get home. He said he was coming over. When he did, he looked pretty bad. Booze, I think, and judging by his eyes, no sleep. I gave him the week's action, and he started explaining things . . . walking around and rubbing his face and making with the easy smiles, only he was so steamed, so crazy mad, I figured Keel could get hers before morning. Then he said I was to do what we'd agreed at the last meeting—write a whitewash. She'd seen no men, gone with no men. He took out his checkbook, and I said my job was worth more than a lousy four hundred dollars, total. He said he'd raise it to four *now*, which made six. I said eight now, which made a grand. He looked at me. He was bending over my table in the other apartment, writing the check, and he put his hand on his hip, brushing back his jacket. There was a gun in his belt. He was loaded for action, either me or her."

"We know he didn't kill you, or he'd be wearing a medal. Did he pay you?"

"After a while, looking at me, and that hand near his gun. Then he wrote the check for eight hundred. But I figured on more . . . after he did whatever he was going to do to that girl."

Roersch said, "Didn't you think to stop him from doing anything to the girl?" when what he was thinking was, "Don't you think Bley *knew* you'd try to shake him if he did anything?"

McKenney fiddled with his notebook.

"You didn't care. You say you're a cop, but you didn't care."

"How many cops care?"

Not a bad answer. Especially to a cop who was now a businessman out for a payday.

McKenney said, "When Bley left, I followed him . . . went out a window in case he was watching the door, and got my car, and tailed his Jaguar. He went home. After a while, I did, too, but I didn't sleep. I had to work out something . . . a way of *being* there when he punished Keel. And how could I do that if I was on the job for Congrove? So I knew I was going to blow the job, but I'd hold onto the two hundred a week as long as possible. On Monday, I was given a new assignment, tailing a teen-age girl who was screwing around with a married doctor. A rich bitch from Central Park West, one of those townhouses . . ."

"Unless *she* visited Keel, drop it."

"I didn't tail the kid properly; got onto Bley every night at five, though he usually worked later—six, six-thirty, sometimes seven and eight. Even weekends. From Vince, I learned they had meetings if an account was in trouble . . ."

"You tailed him from early March until last week?"

"I figured it could be worth a hundred thousand. I did some research on Bley, and he's *heavy*. His apartment alone—a condominium—seventy-five thousand when he bought in, and that was eight years ago. The current value . . . Jesus, he's worth two, three hundred thousand at least. I could've been halfway to China by now, *rich*, if he hadn't disappeared on me. And I'd've waited him out, if you hadn't landed on me."

"You mean you tailed him every day from the end of the surveillance? Give me the date."

McKenney searched his book. "Friday, March ninth." He looked up. "Almost every day. Rented cars to avoid being spotted. And used disguises—wigs and phony mustaches and funny hats. Because I was sure he'd punish her, fast. I didn't figure him for being as smart, as patient, as he was. He let everything cool down, including himself. He was waiting for his vacation, only I didn't know anything about a vacation until he disappeared Monday and I talked to Cousin Vince."

"Give me a quick rundown on Bley's activities from March ninth."

"He worked and he went to movies and he stayed in his apartment a lot and maybe broads visited him there, but not Keel. And he didn't go to her place or meet her, except once on the Friday after the surveillance ended." He checked the book. "March sixteenth. He was at her place for a little over three hours. That was it, until last Sunday, May thirteenth. He went to Brooklyn a few times; his mother . . ." He cleared his throat. "Listen, I've just *got* to have some water."

Roersch nodded. Nick said, surprised, "I can walk to the sink?" Roersch nodded again, the tough act no longer important. He was going to get it all now.

Nick hurried to the sink. Again, he put his head under the tap and bathed and drank. A sick man, a sad man, a dirty and dangerous man. His notebook could be destroyed easily enough, to keep anyone but Roersch from knowing about Bley. But Nick himself was more difficult to dispose of.

Nick returned to the table. "I was saying I was on Bley almost every day. I lost maybe three, when I was sick. I stayed tight on him weekends, when I figured he'd most likely see Keel. But he didn't, until last Sunday. And even then I didn't think he would, because he stayed in his apartment from Friday night until Sunday night. Then he drove to Keel's place and went inside. It was about eight-thirty." He paused. He fiddled with his notebook. He looked up. "This is the payoff. This is the important part. I'm giving you the whole case, the collar, your promotion. You've got to give *me* something. A guarantee."

Roersch leaned back and crossed his legs. "You want a lawyer to draw up a contract?"

"Just give me your word you won't book me."

"I give you my word," Roersch said flatly.

McKenney's tic became rhythmic. He put his hand to it. "*Swear* you won't book me."

"I swear."

"At least not tonight! Swear on Christ and Mother Mary you won't book me tonight!"

Roersch let the coldness slip away. "All right, Nick. I'm not Catholic, but I swear you won't be booked tonight."

McKenney would *run* tonight. Just a little more pressure and he'd be gone by daybreak. He'd run from charges of extortion, blackmail, robbery, leaving the scene of a murder. He'd run from becoming a suspect in that murder. He'd run from cold turkey. He'd keep running, and no one would catch him . . . because no one would be looking for him. Roersch would see to that.

"Keel came down alone about ten-fifteen. I hadn't seen Bley come out and I got shook up, wondered if I'd lost him; wondered if there was another way of getting in and out of the house, like a basement door on an alley, which I'd never bothered checking before because why should I? Now I realized I'd slipped not checking it out. And it was too late if he'd left. And maybe I should tail Keel? But I decided no.

"What I did was walk up to the doorman ᵕnd light a cigarette and offer him one and say nice night and stuff. And then ask how come a big house like that had no garage. He said it was built a long time ago and reconditioned two years ago and the older houses didn't have garages, didn't need them when there'd been plenty of parking space on the streets. I said I was interested in an apartment but worried about security in these old houses. I asked whether tenants or outsiders could get in or out by a basement door. He said no one could get in or out except by the front door. And then he said there were no vacancies, and he was looking at me a little tight, maybe thinking I was doing a case job myself. So I walked away.

"Keel came back about eleven, carrying a bundle of groceries, and went inside. Bley came out forty minutes later, on the button. He was rushing; almost running. Something had to have happened. I checked my watch and wrote it in my book, because this could mean my deal. Eleven-forty. I couldn't get in now, not the way I planned to, with the doorman on duty, and besides it was important to see if Bley tried to dump anything—his gun, another weapon, bloodstained articles of clothing; if I could pick up something like that, I'd have him cold. So I went with Bley, figuring to return to Keel after one and take the big chance, a check of the premises."

Roersch was listening intently now. He said, "And figuring the worst that could happen is you'd pull a robbery."

"The thought entered my mind . . . but I was riding a hunch, putting things together, and that was only a sideline. I forgot it . . . until later.

"Bley drove to his place and parked in the basement garage, but he didn't go into the house. You know where he lives? Northern edge of Sutton Place. There's a small

club about a block away, Grennoir's, it's called, and he
went there. I couldn't get too close. If he spotted me . . .
well, I took one quick walk past Grennoir's and looked
over their half-curtain and saw him at the bar, drinking. I
figured that was about all the risk I could afford, and went
back to my car. I still had plenty of time before one a.m.,
so I waited. But he was still there when I gave up.

"I was at Keel's house at one-ten. The doorman was
gone, and Sunday night is like a weekday night, work the
next day, so it was dead. I went to the lobby, but a young
guy came in and I didn't even have to use my card trick,
sliding back the lock. When he walked to the door, I just
stepped aside and fiddled with my own keys, as if slower
than him. When he opened the door, I said thanks and
walked in behind him. I got off the elevator at two, because the listing in the lobby said she was in 2-F. I found
the apartment and no one around."

He was speaking quickly now; he was into the climax of
his story, reliving the tension and excitement. He seemed
to have forgotten the threat Roersch represented. "If she
had a chain lock, okay, because I could handle most of
them with my pencil after carding the door lock. But if she
had a bolt, I'd have to make some noise, ramming it with
my shoulder . . ."

"Nick, we both know there's no door that can't be
opened. I have confidence in your ability. You got inside."

"With just the card. And I saw her right away. You
come into that living room with a clear shot at the bedroom . . ."

"I know the apartment."

"There she was. I almost forgot to close the door behind
me. I mean, it was the worst thing I've *ever* seen. A real
slaughter-house. Blood on the walls and floor and on her
and she was lying in a real pool of it. It was like someone
had *painted* the place in blood. I have a sensitive stomach,
and I almost barfed. The arms and legs were still tied to
the bed, the arms hanging there, one leg half off . . ."

"So you and your sensitive stomach went through the

place like a vacuum cleaner, taking the diamond earrings and necklace, other jewelry, cash . . ."

"Just the necklace. I found about thirty dollars and a few fake-stone rings; they looked good because of the gold settings, but later a friend who knows said they were worth about a hundred apiece, and I got twenty."

Roersch did a little fishing. "Why did you take the phone books, and the pictures?"

"Not me. I took what could bring money; nothing else. It must've been Bley."

"Was he carrying anything when he came out?"

"Maybe under his topcoat. It was a chilly night."

"Where did you find the necklace?"

McKenney hesitated; then muttered, "Around her neck."

"I see. That sensitive stomach of yours again."

"Whatever *I* did is nothing! You've got *Bley*! I've given him to you!"

Roersch stood up and stretched, the automatic firm in his hand. "If I believe you. But there's no way you can prove anything you've said."

McKenney began to protest. Roersch said, "No written report to the Congrove Agency. No corroborating witnesses. No way to place Bley in Keel's apartment at the time of the murder . . . and no way to pinpoint the murder. This even if I forget you broke into her apartment and stole valuables. This even if I forget you're a hungry junkie who'll do anything for a buck."

McKenney stared at him. "You swore on Christ and Mother Mary! You swore you wouldn't book me tonight!"

"It's no longer tonight." He flashed his wristwatch. "A few minutes past twelve."

McKenney jumped to his feet, fists clenched, face twisted in rage, eyes bulging.

Roersch thought for a moment he'd overplayed his hand and would have to kill him. Then McKenney sank down, covering his face with his hands.

"Another thing," Roersch said, "your worst mistake of all."

McKenney's hands dropped. He looked at Roersch with streaming eyes.

"You left Keel's place to follow Bley at eleven-forty. You didn't return until ten after one. That's an hour and a half. Do you know how many people could have gone into her apartment in that time? Do you know what a lawyer defending Bley would do with that time? You blew it, Nick." And yet he himself was satisfied that he had enough to break Bley. And he'd get more. He'd get so much that Bley would say *thank you* as he paid a quarter of a million and up for his life! "Wasn't her body still warm when you removed that necklace?"

"I . . . I think so."

"It certainly wasn't cold, because she'd been killed *recently*. It could have been as recent as ten minutes before you broke in, or an hour, or two. It could have been Bley, or someone who came in while you were tailing Bley." He sighed deeply. "Nick, Nick, you've made a solid case against only one person—yourself."

McKenney turned to the table and his book. He looked at it, as if to find answers there, proof there, escape there. Then he put his head down and closed his eyes.

Roersch walked to the table and took the edge of the notebook and tugged it from under McKenney's head. The man never moved. Roersch put the book in his pocket, looking down at the matted grayish-blond hair. He could see brown spots where blood had clotted. He could see the pallid neck; a hand trembling against the table. He could smell acrid, oniony sweat; the cold sweat of fear, of defeat. The side of the face turned upward was an old man's face.

Roersch walked to the door, slipping the safety back on his automatic, tucking it into his hip holster. He opened the door. McKenney raised his head dazedly. "Don't go anywhere," Roersch said. "We have to talk tomorrow." He left.

McKenney would sweat about a stake-out, but he'd run anyway. McKenney had no choice.

Roersch went back to the alley, and saw again what he'd taken to be the shadowy figure of a man. It still gave him a start, but he kept walking and came to the clothesline and the bathrobe moving in the mild breeze. He walked back to the street, satisfied all loose ends were tied up here. Cop or private citizen, he never left loose ends. That was why he had to check out portions of Nick's story. Not that it would change things. Learning what had been moving around in this alley hadn't changed things. The same went for learning what Burns and Vince Mc-Kenney and the artist had to do with Keel. The same went for running down any and all leads . . . tying up loose ends, while drawing the rope tighter around Bley.

He drove toward Sutton Place, listening to police calls. After a while, he switched to AM, searched the dial . . . and smiled a big, gray-toothed smile as he located *real* music, Sinatra singing *It Was A Very Good Year*. Past midnight and all those freak disk jockeys and their freak listeners, and Sinatra! It called for some sort of party.

He lit a Nat Sherman and took a three-quarters inhalation.

10: Wednesday p.m. and Thursday a.m.

Alma-Jean tossed her head around, mouth opening and eyes going all ways. John felt it coming, coming, and held back, and took a look at the other two. Lois had rolled onto her side, facing him and Alma-Jean. Evan had rolled over, up against her, and Lois shifted and used her hands between her legs . . . and then they both exhaled, made that sound and got that look, and he knew Evan was in her. He was screwing Alma-Jean and Evan was screwing Lois. And Lois was stroking his side, and Evan was reaching across to grab Alma-Jean's boobs. And Alma-Jean reached out and tried to get to Evan but couldn't make it and let her arm lie across Lois's side, and stroked her. John let go of Alma-Jean's right leg and stroked Lois's face, looking at her and saying, "You next. God, you next!" She gave him a wiggle of tongue, and he felt that was it, he was coming, and fought not to; closed his eyes and thought of bad things, that jail . . . Brown's cock up his ass . . . but somehow, with all *this* going on, it wasn't a turnoff. Still, he might have made it, held off and got another five minutes, if Lois hadn't dropped her hand from his side, put it on Alma-Jean's belly, moved it down to where he and Alma-Jean were joined, circled his tool with her thumb and forefinger . . . and *tightened* that ring so that he was fucking her hand and Alma-Jean's box at the same time.

No way he could resist that! No way, and he didn't want to, and he said, "God *damn!*" and collapsed.

Alma-Jean kissed him and giggled. Lois put her arms around the *both* of them and kissed everything that came close . . . and ended up kissing Alma-Jean's mouth. Alma-Jean twisted under him, turning to kiss back and hug back. And John thought, *Shit, here it comes,* and looked at Evan. Evan's eyes were closed and he was humping hard and Lois was showing signs of flipping out completely. No wonder, with that *huge* thing up her! And with Alma-Jean kissing and stroking and making little crying sounds.

He pulled Lois's head away from Alma-Jean and she opened her eyes, and he thought how *clear* her eyes looked when she'd been so drunk, even higher than he was, higher than any of them. But a moment later, he wasn't sure because his head was beginning to whirl again, now that the exertion of screwing was over. Couldn't be sure of anything, except Evan panting, gasping, saying something . . . and was that something *"Merri"*?

Lois rested her head on her arm and looked at Alma-Jean, who looked at her. Evan said, grunting as he worked, "Alma-Jean . . . you like . . . Lois?"

Alma-Jean nodded. "A rail *kick*, baby. Ah mean, Ah never *trahd* it before, but Ah'm *willin'*. Want to *see* it?"

Evan said, "Maybe."

Lois began to gasp and jump, and then she made a long,

groaning sound and went limp. John wasn't sure it was real; it had come so pat, so on cue, like she was freeing herself for Alma-Jean. But Evan took it straight. He pulled out and lay back and said, "*Whooo!*" John laughed, relieved that it was all cool, and he was able to give his own "Whooo!" letting himself go and feeling the booze and pot and loose, *unwound* feeling after a good lay.

Evan turned his head and said, "Hey, John, how're you doing, man?" which was *loverly* and not at all the old Evan. John said, "I'm all here, man, I'm light as smoke." And he was, he could've floated, and the room turned slowly, and the smell of cunt hung in the air like rich perfume. He said, "Who wants a drink?" Everyone said, "*Me!*" together, like cheering at a football game. He got up and kept his back to them and *ran* toward the door, because he was naked, man, and that thing was shriveled-small and he didn't want comparisons.

Lois said, "Dig the li'l ass," and Alma-Jean said, "Awl *white* and *nahce!*" and giggled her silly giggle. But except for staggering once and bumping the dresser, which made him get together, the pain clearing his head, he was out that door and out of sight and getting what was left of the whiskey. Which wasn't much; just enough for four drinks. He divided the ice equally, two cubes each with an extra for Evan.

When he returned to the bedroom, it was party-time again. Alma-Jean was on her hands and knees, spraddling Lois, who lay there with eyes closed, shaking her head and sounding drunker than ever. "Evan, no, you don' wan' tha', do you?"

Alma-Jean said, "*Shore* he does, honey! C'mon, let's give the *sweetie*-pah a show. Ah never trahd it an *whah* not? Ah mean, if'n you ain't *trahd* it, don' knock it, raht Evan?"

Evan was up on an elbow, watching and laughing and he said, "*Raht*, Alma-Jean. It'll give the boys a chance to rest. Rape her, Alma-Jean!" Which was one hell of an opening, and John wasn't too surprised at what followed. Lois kept shaking her head, but one knee came up, like by mistake or reflex or what, and it was right on target, between Alma-Jean's legs. Alma-Jean said, "*Oooh*," and spread a little more and pressed down on that knee and rubbed and she put a hand on one of Lois's tits and Lois shook her head, saying, "Stop her . . . all wrong."

Evan said, "Just relax. Let Alma-Jean do it." And he sank back down and John could see he was turning on again, that monster growing along his leg. Damn, he wished it wasn't so big. Made him feel . . .

"Refreshment time," he said, and came to Evan's side of the bed. Evan sat up and took a glass and John wasn't sure if he'd gotten the extra ice cube. Evan drank; and John saw Alma-Jean put her hand on Lois's box, her fingers into it, and Lois's face twist like it never had for *him*. He took a glass off the tray and drank half the booze down in two long swallows. He said, "Time for a drink, girls." They didn't hear him. Lois was shaking her head, muttering, "No, don' want . . ." And Evan was saying, "Go on, Alma-Jean, go on." He was getting stiff again, not laughing anymore, watching intently.

John put the tray on the lamp table and went around to the other side of the big bed and got in. Alma-Jean had lowered herself flat onto Lois and was kissing her face. Lois kept mumbling, "No, isn't right," but her body was moving. John tried to watch Evan's face, to see if it changed, to see if Evan tumbled to what Lois was playing at. The hitch depended on Evan and his staying happy. He'd stop Lois if he had to.

But he didn't have to . . . and that last drink had him spinning through space, and he saw Evan sink back down, out of sight behind the girls, who were twisting now, turning now . . . and the next thing he knew they were sixty-nining, and from the sounds, the gasps, they were making it, they were getting there.

He sat up and looked past them and Evan was flat on

his back, jacking off . . . or at least jacking it up. Because
it was a fantastic turn-on, watching a lezzie scene . . . if
you weren't involved with one of the lezzies. He felt a
tightness, an anger . . . but he also felt his dick hardening
and he rubbed it and wanted to get at her.

One of the girls, he didn't know who, made a high
yelling sound and the bed really *bounced*. Then Alma-Jean
got off Lois and rolled onto her back, so that he had to
slide closer to the edge of the bed. She spread her legs and
Lois got down there and went at it, alone, so it must've
been Lois who'd yelled, who'd come. Lois was all hands
and moving head. Lois was tuning that hillbilly freak,
playing her like a violin, making the moans, the little
screams, come louder, faster. Lois was a fury, and there
was no getting near her now, because she was lost in the
hillbilly's meat. The screams got goddamn loud. Evan
lifted himself up and stared.

John said, "Hey, Evan, they're bombed, correct?"

Evan said, "Put on the lights."

John gave Lois a sharp crack on the ass, and said,
"Time for the switch," but she didn't stop, not for a second. He went to the doorway, figuring the lights would
stop her, at least slow her down. He put them on, and saw
Alma-Jean half sitting up, mouth open, clutching Lois's
head with both hands. She was yelling, "Oh Gawd baby
Ah'm *dyin'* Lord Ah'm dyin' Jesus Gawd lover Jesus
Gawd . . ." She *bucked* like a bronco, once, twice, and
went down like a pin-stuck balloon.

Lois fell sideways, putting her head in the pillow beside
Evan. She rubbed her mouth there, and curled up and her
body heaved. John said, "Man, when she drinks . . ." but
Evan was looking at her and even though he was still
up—who could help it?—his look wasn't all turn-on, all
happy.

Alma-Jean was lying on her back, mouth open and
panting. Evan said, "You really liked that, didn't you?"
She didn't look at him and she didn't answer. John

crawled over him, in beside Lois, and said, "Switch time." He put his mouth to her ear and whispered, "Get that girl *working!*" Lois was, as he figured, not as drunk as she'd made out, because she raised herself and said, "Hey, Alma-Jean, it wasn't bad, but never again. What you want is a man, right?" She and Alma-Jean looked at each other, and Alma-Jean said, "*Sheeit!* Ah've *haid* a man! Ah want a *drink!*"

John said, "It's here." He got the glasses off the tray.

Lois put away her Scotch without lowering the glass. Alma-Jean sipped. Alma-Jean barely drank. Evan said, "Anyone want a cigarette?" and walked to the living room. John said, "Yeah, me," and followed him. At the door he looked back. Lois was bent close to Alma-Jean, whispering, and it wasn't lovey-dovey, man, it was like razor blades! She shook Alma-Jean's arm, and Alma-Jean shouted, "*Quit*-eet!" and jumped up and ran toward John. John looked into the living room. Evan had a smoke going and was entering the bathroom.

John shoved Alma-Jean back into the bedroom. He said, "Listen, you dumb . . ."

She screamed, "Ah'm *through* takin' shit from *awl* you! Ah'm *splittin'!*"

Lois came up behind her and said, "Baby, come back and let me explain the next act, okay?" Her left hand massaged Alma-Jean's boob and her other hand slid low on the fat belly and stroked and squeezed, and John turned away to let her do her thing.

They had to get out of this with Evan happy. Goddamn hillbilly! His foot twitched as he went to the couch and got his shorts and slipped them on.

He sat down and watched the bathroom door. He tried to hear Lois and Alma-Jean in the bedroom, but there was nothing from there. The toilet flushed and he crossed his legs and put a smile on his face. He felt like he was posing for Mother's Polaroid. She'd make him smile, then take so long focusing the picture the smile turned stiff and unnatural on his face.

It was stiff and unnatural now.

Lois and Alma-Jean came out of the bedroom. Alma-Jean went to the couch where her clothes were, but Lois said, "Just the boots, baby." Alma-Jean looked at her, sullen, then shrugged and began putting on the boots. Lois stepped into her klunkers, and when she stood up her legs were yay-long, and John forgot to worry about Evan. And looking at Alma-Jean, also standing up, at her big thighs dead-white against those shiny black boots, at her big sagging boobs, her *huge* ass, he felt his shorts tightening and said, "Who wants the honor?"

Alma-Jean made a face, and he suddenly wanted to *kick* that ass! Lois must've read him, because she said, "First Evan gets his, *alone*. Then we'll see." She came over on those six-inch klunkers and she was trim and tight and her boobs, while not as big as the hillbilly's, stuck out round and firm.

Evan came out of the bathroom. He looked tired. He straightened when he saw they were all looking at him, and sucked in his gut, and said, "Dressed for a formal dinner, ladies and gentlemen?" Which gave them all a laugh and loosened things up.

Lois got the music going, but Evan said he was hungry. "There's a barbecue place down Lindburg. As I recall, they close at midnight." He went to the couch where their clothing had been tossed before they'd gone to the bedroom, and picked out his things.

"Man, barbecued spare ribs!" Lois said.

"And chicken and beans!" John said.

"And cold beer," Evan said, sitting down to put on his stockings.

They all dressed, except for Alma-Jean. John paused to look at her. She just sat in the armchair, naked except for her boots, staring sullenly at Lois. "C'mon," he said.

"Ah'm not goin' *nowhere.* 'Cause you *said.*" She was speaking to Lois.

"I'll get the food," Evan said, finishing first and standing up. "We'll eat here and watch television. Maybe a little later, if the spirit is willing and the flesh strong . . ." He smiled at Alma-Jean. "Make that if *Alma-Jean* is willing."

She remained sullen, and continued looking at Lois.

Lois turned away, but John saw how her face whitened.

Evan said, "The girl's had too much to drink." He himself seemed steady now, if not quite sober. "Be back in about an hour with a wide selection of heartburn-producing agents." He went to the door.

"Ah'm not *hungry*," Alma-Jean said.

Evan turned and looked at her. He was no longer smiling. Then he went out.

Suddenly, John was worried. He'd gotten that same look himself, when he'd taken the gun.

Lois whirled on Alma-Jean, glaring. John went over to the naked hillbilly and said, "Don't be dumb. This could be a beautiful night. Don't spoil it."

"Ah don' wawnt to *spoil* it! Ah wawnt what she *said!*"

Lois stalked into the bedroom and slammed around. John sat down on the arm of the chair and murmured, "Baby, play it smart and whatever you want, whatever she said, will happen. Just like it did before. No problem. Just be patient." He put his arm around her shoulders.

She shook it away. "Ah don' *lahk* that! Ah figured . . . she *said* . . ."

He jumped up and swung as hard as he could . . . with closed fist to her ear. She slumped without a sound. He was shaking. He wanted, God how he wanted, to kick that dumb face all to hell!

"What do you think you're doing?" Lois shouted.

He turned. She was in the bedroom doorway. "Doing?" he said, and he began to gain control. "Doing! I'm taking care of the shit *you* started!"

"Me? Who the hell picked up this goddamn idiot!"

"And who the hell turned her on to freak street?"

"If it wasn't for you and Evan, we could've had our own scene. Now you're just begging for the cops. Hit her a few more times and we'll *all* end up in jail!"

"Well what the hell am I supposed to do? Let her sit there talking until Evan comes back? Let her tell him you promised her another les scene? Make him wonder . . ."

"She's *your* date, so get her out of here! Whatever I promised, I'm not delivering. She's too damned *low* to keep around!" She walked to the hall door. "I'm going to get some fresh air!"

Alma-Jean stirred, moaned, fluttered her eyes.

"Get her out before I come back or we'll *really* be in trouble!" Lois slammed the door behind her.

So there he was, alone with the bitch, and she was looking at him, and she was crying, and that big mouth was opening again. He clapped his hand over it. "You make any trouble, they'll have to sweep you up with a broom!"

Her eyes widened; the tears stopped running.

He said, "Are you going to dress and leave *quietly?*"

She nodded. He removed his hand from her mouth, but watched closely. She said, almost whispering, "Lois *promised* . . . Ah don' really *lahk* men. Ah'm *sorry*, Ah *try* . . ."

"Then you shouldn't have done the number with us. Now get dressed and take off."

She dressed quickly. She slung her bag over her shoulder, and tapped it. "Ah only got a dollar an' change. How'm I gonna get *home?*"

"How much does a cab cost anyway?"

"More'n *that*. Evan should pay. He's got heavy *braid*. You all gettin' some, why shouldn't *Ah?* Ah balled, din't Ah?"

"Not *him* you didn't. And you're not waiting around to ask him anyway."

"Rich *Jew*, raht? Why should *you* care if'n I get some?"

He sighed and took out his wallet and gave her two dollars.

"Yore *kiddin'!* Ah'm not gonna . . ."

He grabbed her arm and *hauled* her to the door and flung her outside. And watched to make sure she left. She didn't say anything until she'd walked about fifteen feet down the hall; then she turned, smiling a bad smile. "Ah'll *tell* him what Lois said she'd do. He'll *kick* yore asses. Ah *know* yore type. Yore *bums*, you and her, *moochin'* . . ."

He ran back inside and looked for the key and couldn't find it and didn't have time to find it. He got a matchbook from the coffee table and tore off the cover and ran back to the door. She was walking quickly, but looked back at him and nodded a *you'll-see* nod. He put the matchbook cover in the lock slot and pulled the door shut, without the *click*. Then he turned to Alma-Jean . . . or where she should have been had she stayed on the main corridor. She hadn't. There was a turn on the right, and other turns off that, and he didn't want to lose her. He broke into a run. He had to catch her and make sure she got in a cab and hauled herself out of here!

She'd head for the parking lot, to watch for Evan's rented car. He'd find her before she found Evan.

He was raging in the old way, so hot he felt *cold*, icy cold. Filthy lezzie fouling up the group scene and threatening to blow the hitch . . .

"Douchebag," he panted, coming out into the parking lot and stopping and turning and looking for her. A hundred cars at least, but not a living soul.

"C'mon," he whispered, beginning to walk, beginning to search. "C'mon, douchebag."

All he wanted was a minute alone with her here in the dark. *Just one lousy minute!*

One of the last houses on the uptown perimeter of Sutton Place was Bley's address. It was relatively new, for Sutton Place. It was relatively modest, for Sutton Place. That put it on a par with the best anywhere else, excepting upper Fifth and some of the newer condominiums there. It had a quiet blue canopy running from the street through a deep entryway, and on his first walk-by Roersch spotted the uniformed doorman sitting to the left of the glass doors, in front of the second set of glass doors, beyond which were the elevators.

He continued walking, crossing the street and heading back on the other side, fingering the keys Mrs. Bleywitz had given him, wondering if he could avoid identifying himself, so as not to leave tracks. Not that he expected anyone from the station to double him . . . but the safe way was the best way.

It was a nice night, the weather finally mild after a raw, rainy April and early May. In a neighborhood like this, with some trees and some space to the streets, with a trace of water in the air from the East River, and—most important of all—with good distance between itself and poverty and garbage and ghettos and hate and violence, it almost felt like spring back home.

But he'd visited Poughkeepsie not too long ago, and it wasn't home anymore, not only because of his parents' being dead and his sister moved to Detroit, but because of the change in country air, the cluttering and crowding that hadn't been part of his childhood of forty to fifty years ago.

A long time; a lifetime. The *world* had grown cluttered, crowded, dirty in that time. A man needed leisure and money to find clear skies and sweet air and safety and pleasure in such a world. Which brought him right back to Bley, his ticket out of New York to the good life.

He crossed the street when he was opposite Croydon Towers, the name on the blue canopy. He walked quickly, purposefully, and hoped his brown suit wouldn't look *too* out of place after rolling around in that alley . . . when it hadn't been all that good right off the Robert Hall rack.

He paused to shine his shoes by rubbing each in turn on the opposite pants leg, and used his pocket comb on his thinning grayish-brown hair, and straightened his tie. And knew it hadn't helped much.

Well, hell, he was a cop, not a goddamn *model!* He pulled open the door before the doorman could get it, and brushed by him without so much as a nod, and aimed a key at that inner door-lock.

He had it in, and was turning it, when the doorman— looked like a retired patrolman, red of face and with a fine-veined whiskey nose—said, "Excuse me, sir. You looking . . .?" He said, "I'm looking for no one," and went on to the elevators. One was waiting and he stepped inside and punched Six, and looked defiantly out at the lobby and the doorman, who was looking at him.

The elevator door closed. Roersch sighed, thinking he'd overplayed his hand. He shouldn't have risked antagonizing the man . . . who might just contact the local patrolman, or put in a call to the nearest precinct. Wouldn't *that* be fun! Still, he could handle whatever happened on the way out. He was a detective sergeant, not a burglar.

He felt more like a burglar as he reached the sixth floor and checked the card Mrs. Bleywitz had given him and found the apartment written there. He approached 6-G and looked around and used the two keys on the two locks. And stepped into darkness.

He was not a man who grew excited easily, grew anxious easily, but he was excited and anxious now.

He moved quickly, putting on lights in each room. It was a truly luxurious setup; only three rooms, but *what* rooms! Big, high-ceilinged, furnished better than anything Roersch had seen outside of Helen's *Better Homes & Gardens*. Soft lighting, good paintings, heavy dark-wood furniture; thick carpeting everywhere but in the bathrooms —there were two—and kitchen.

He ended in the kitchen, and began his search there. He checked all the cupboards, drawers, the broom closet. He even searched the space which held the foldout ironing board. He checked for knives, big knives, serrated knives. He found one that could have done the job, but it didn't look as if it had ever been used—part of a set of four hanging in a wooden holder on the wall. He took it down anyway, holding it by the blade end, and put it on the kitchen table. He went into the living room and turned slowly, examining everything—walls and floor and furniture. No photographs here. Nothing in the open deserving of notice. But a closet near the hall door, a long breakfront with bar equipment on top and solid wooden doors, and a circular, stool-like piece with brass handles on the curved side, these he would search.

He went to the stool-like piece first. Helen had called it, or something like it at Sloan's, a commode. He tugged the brass handles, and two doors opened to reveal a good-sized storage area inside. It was full of records, stacked in metal slots. He tried to remove the entire record holder, but it was fastened to the base of the commode. He took out a half-dozen records—all heavy classical, not a Mantovani or even a Fiedler among them. He leaned inside, peering behind the records, and saw something. He reached in, and came out with a large manila envelope.

He sat on the floor. The envelope had either fallen off the top of the tightly packed records, or it had been hidden. *Hidden*, he hoped, as he opened the clasp and the flap.

There were four Danish porno picture booklets and a stack of Polaroid photographs bound with a rubber band.

He sighed, disappointed, but went through the booklets anyway. Men hid these goodies; men didn't let them lie around for any visitor to see.

The first two were the usual thing—sixteen pages plus the covers, printed on both sides with color photos. *Porno Players I* had a plot: an older woman enters a house that has male whores, selects a white and a black, and does everything with them until they come all over her body. *Porno Players II* had three girls in lesbian scenes for half the book, then a switch to a teen-aged girl and a musclebound man in heterosexual acts. He put them aside, feeling some response, thinking if Bley had much more of this stuff around, he might just end up knocking at Ruthie's door again!

The third book had nothing on the cover but a whip. Inside was one of the most brutal exhibitions of sadism Roersch had ever seen, and he'd seen plenty of pornography during his brief tenure on the Vice Squad. Seen it, and appropriated some of the more reasonable stuff. A girl was bound, gagged, suspended from what looked like a gymnasium wall. She was beaten with whips and knotted scourges, burned by a fat man with a cigar, tickled by a black-booted dyke with a feather and spanked by the dyke with a heavy paddle. She was then hung from the ceiling in a sort of leather cradle, mouth still taped, wrists tied to ankles, her breasts pierced by long hat-pins, her buttocks dripping blood from a metal-tipped cane wielded by a young man in Edwardian costume. The finish had her lying on a mat, bleeding from her mouth, nose and many wounds, arms held wide by two nude women, legs held wide by two nude men, while the cigar-smoker and the Edwardian pissed on her.

It twisted his guts, despite his knowing that most of this material was faked. What wasn't fake was the sick catering to sick minds; the *need* some creeps had for this; the ideas it gave them.

The fourth book also had a whip on the cover. He wanted to throw it aside and get on with the Polaroids, but couldn't. A lifetime of thoroughness, of checking every possibility, made him flip through it. And lucky he did! This one had different models, a different setting—a barn with all its leather and iron—but much the same tortures. Where his luck came in was . . . this one been marked with red pen on two of the pages.

Those pages showed the female victim bound to an old wagon, painfully bent backward, face and crotch up, around a large wheel. No one was beating her, and she wasn't gagged as in all the other pictures. But she was being choked by an enormous penis shoved down her throat. Her eyes bulged, her face was agonized, and that penis distended her mouth to its utmost. The red pen had drawn a line and a cartoon balloon from that tortured mouth, and written, "I'm dying! Please . . . EVAN . . . I'm *strangling!*"

On the opposite page, the same scene, with the penis now all the way in to the genital hair and testicles. The girl's mouth was spilling sperm at the edges, her eyes were rolled back, a strong male hand was *tearing* at her blonde hair. And another cartoon balloon: "I deserve death! EVAN! Forgive me . . . *aaaaah!*"

Evan, in big red capital letters. *Evan*, playing at killing a woman with his penis.

He had settled for a knife.

Roersch replaced the first two booklets in the envelope, and put the two sadistic ones aside. He took the rubber band off the Polaroids, which had cardboard backs showing top and bottom. He turned the first one over.

Judith Keel, nude, lying in her water bed with its big, brass posts; a long-legged, high-breasted beauty, smiling at the camera.

He went on, looking at other nude shots of Keel, hoping Bley had taken a different kind of picture, a *last* picture, the night of the murder.

It was too much to expect. But there was one picture of Keel and Bley together, nude, and he had his penis in her mouth, and he was as big, maybe bigger, than the stud in the porno book. He was holding her head and pushing deep into her mouth, and she didn't look happy, was trying to shove him away with both hands. Roersch bent closer. The look on Bley's face showed more than sexual excitement; seemed cruel, sadistic . . .

He put the picture in his pocket, wondering who had taken it. Who would Bley trust . . . ?

Self-timer. He'd find a self-timer when he found Bley's photographic equipment. Except that people took their cameras along on vacation.

The last three Polaroids were, again, nudes . . . but not of Keel. They were of a blonde girl, not nearly as well proportioned as Keel . . . but looking at her, Roersch was instantly excited. "What a piece of ass," he murmured reverently.

She was simply that kind of woman. Her face—full-lipped, sloe-eyed, passionate without any phony lip-action or smiles or gaping, groaning mouth—struck out at him. And her ass—in each of the three poses she featured that ass—was a peeled peach, a ripe melon, a beckoning target for only one kind of arrow. She wasn't really beautiful; just sexy as hell, and desirous as hell. In one shot she was standing sideways, not having to bend in the slightest to make that rear stick out. In another she was bent over a piece of furniture—Roersch looked across the room at the breakfront, and nodded—a little black dress drawn up over her naked bottom with one small hand, her head turned and looking into the camera with solemnity, expectancy. In the last she was standing with her back to the camera, on high heels, looking over her shoulder, that big ass displayed and that small smile saying, "Take it!"

He wondered why Bley would bother with Keel, with *anyone*, when he had a girl like this.

And then he wondered if perhaps the blonde wasn't out of Bley's reach, out of anyone's reach; whether she wasn't another unsolved murder case. Which gave him a reason for taking one of the pictures . . . to check against photos of murder victims. He chose the one with the largest, clearest face portion—which also happened to be the one with the largest, clearest *ass* portion—and put it in his pocket along with the Keel-Bley photo.

He put the records back, the envelope with the two straight porno books behind the records, and closed the doors. He brought the sadism books to the kitchen and placed them beside the knife. He returned to the living room and went to the breakfront.

About every kind of booze he'd ever heard of, and a twelve-bottle rack of French wines. A corkscrew with a nude female torso as handle, and a stack of porno party napkins, but nothing that couldn't be found in any bachelor's apartment.

The closet was deep and long, with two large sliding doors. It held three winter dress coats, and all were of a quality to make Roersch envious. Plus a blue leather jacket with sheep's-wool lining, a suede half-coat with what looked like silver-mink collar, and no less than four skiing jackets.

One shelf held four wool ski hats, assorted skiing gloves and poles and other items, an electric hand-warmer among them. And, of course, a pair of skis, stacked flat. He went through all the coat pockets, and found nothing beside tissues and theater ticket stubs. On the floor were two pairs of ski boots and a pair of knee-high rubber fishing boots.

Roersch got a small chair from against the wall and brought it over and stood on it to see to the top shelf. This was a rich man's home and rich man's closet and he was going to strip the richness from that man.

It didn't make him feel all that good. It wasn't as if Bley had been *born* to the gold and silver. It wasn't as if he hadn't fought for it . . . and just thinking of that mother of his made him realize what a hell of a fight it had been, at what a cost these prizes had been won.

The top shelf held some cardboard boxes. Three of them were nothing: a purple vase, a cuckoo clock, a big silver bowl that may have cost a lot but had too much engraving, too many trimmings. Wedding gifts, maybe, that Bley wouldn't use or show. The fourth box was bigger than the others, and heavy, and Roersch couldn't get the sides up while it rested on the shelf. So he took it down, and opened it on the floor.

It was full of photographs, eight-by-tens on heavy paper. Five were framed and glass-covered; a thick stack was unframed. There was a large white album engraved in gold lettering, "Our Wedding," which accounted for much of the weight.

Three of the framed pictures were of the blonde with

the great ass, only now her ass didn't show. Head shots, and she was still sexy as hell. One was inscribed, "To Evvie, with all my love, Merri." The handwriting was a backward twelve-year-old's. The other two were wedding pictures: the blonde in a modern, knee-length wedding gown, holding a bouquet of roses; the blonde and Evan, she in her gown and he in a tux, both smiling. This time Bley's smile was real, was happy.

So this was Merri, Mrs. Bleywitz's *courva*. The old lady could be right.

The album had twenty-four pages, each with a shot of a wedding party that didn't include the groom's mother. There was a picture of Merri, Bley, a taller blonde who looked enough like Merri to be her sister, and a squat, curly-haired character who had one arm around the bride, the other around the could-be sister, and grinned at the camera. He wore his tux like an orangutan, but still looked more at home with the two blondes than Bley did.

Despite everything he knew and suspected about Bley, Roersch found himself feeling sorry for the man . . . the man in that wedding picture; the man so out of place with the blondes and the young ape. *Cheap*, as the cleaning lady had said about another blonde. Cheap, all of them . . . except Bley.

He turned the page. Bley and Merri with an older woman, a hard-faced, hard-eyed woman who wore a big wooden cross on the outside of her flashy evening gown. The photographer had posed her looking at the bride and groom. She didn't smile. She *stared*.

The same woman showed up in three more shots, and Roersch figured her for the mother of the bride. Who must have known her son-in-law was Jewish. Who had worn the biggest cross she could find, and worn it as blatantly as she could.

Cheap. As Ruthie the pro could never be. Cheap, the whole damned shebang. With Bley standing out like a distinguished sore thumb; a hopeful, pitiful, happy sap.

"His taste, in everything but women, good," Mrs. Bleywitz had said. Roersch agreed, and wished he could tell her whose fault it was.

He spent some time examining Bley in these and other photographs. Bley looked tall, maybe six feet, and slim and firm. In good shape. At least he had been, *then* . . . though just how long ago the pictures had been taken he couldn't tell. They weren't dated, and Mrs. Bleywitz hadn't given any dates. Bley had a serious face, even when he was smiling; the eyes, the smile itself, were serious. He had a high forehead, and a good head of dark, straight hair, worn rather long for a man his age, in his position. He also had a *mustache*.

Roersch took the Polaroid of Bley and Keel from his pocket. No mustache there. And the face a little older. But the hair still long. The body still firm, though beginning to soften at the gut; still younger looking than his age according to his employment record, forty-nine.

Roersch went through the loose photographs. Some from the wedding. Many of Bley and Merri on vacation at the beach—blowups of snapshots.

There was also a photograph of Bley and his mother, taken not too long ago, judging by Mrs. Bleywitz's appearance. It was another blowup, full-length shot of mother and son, Bley's arm around her shoulders, both smiling. Mrs. Bleywitz's smile seemed real enough. Her Marvin's was an exercise in muscle stretching. But that wasn't what shocked Roersch . . . because he *was* shocked, clear through. That red pen had been used again. And used in a way that made Roersch *certain* Bley was insane.

Mrs. Bleywitz wore a long print dress and a pill-box hat with veil. It must have been St. Valentine's Day, because the dutiful son had brought his mother a gift: she held a large, heart-shaped box of candy. The red pen had added another, smaller heart to the picture; a solid red heart which dripped blood onto the dress and puddled on the floor. A heart drawn directly over her crotch.

He put it aside.

He turned over several of the unframed wedding pictures, and each was stamped by the photographer—name and St. Louis address. He chose one of Bley and Merri frozen in a dance, a wedding waltz, faces laughing at the camera.

He put the photos and the album back in the box and returned it to the closet. He brought the two large photographs to the kitchen table. He found a glass in a cupboard and filled it with cold water and drank it down. But his mouth remained dry and he felt a little sick. He blamed it on that wrestling match in the alley with Nick McKenney. He was getting too old for such shit.

The bedroom had a huge dresser, a leather-topped desk with drawers, two lamp tables with a drawer each, and a wall-length closet with four sliding doors. Anything else didn't concern him, as anything else couldn't hide evidence.

He searched quickly now. He was almost finished with the dresser, was going through the right-hand bottom drawer, when he found a balled handkerchief under a pile of undershirts. He placed it on the dresser top and opened it carefully. A pair of pendant diamond earrings, the diamond in each about a carat. The handkerchief had several small brown stains. Both earrings had dried blood on the pins—the part that pierced the ear—and one had dried blood on the diamond. Roersch put the whole thing in his own handkerchief, and tucked it into his pocket. This just about did it, as far as he was concerned. This was probably enough to crack Bley. And Bley's leaving the necklace on the corpse didn't bother him. No reason for it to bother him. Bley had been scared off before he'd been able to take the necklace. He'd gotten the earrings and heard something or imagined something and run. Or he'd left it on her as some sort of symbol . . .

So it *did* bother him. So he'd get the answer from Bley himself, when the man confessed.

He moved to the desk, where he saw a legal-size yellow pad with lined pages. On the top page was a penciled list:

St. Louis—Merri? Drive around? Shake the past?

Grand Canyon—Bright Angel Lodge, 3 or 4 nights, need reservations this early? Make for 19th to 22nd. Mule trips start yet?

Los Angeles—2 nights at Bel Air Hotel—need reservations, make for 24th and 25th. Look for furnished apartment, Doheny, Robertson, other good streets.

There was a telephone number followed by the notation, "My A.A.A. rep., check with him on any changes, Triptik, etc.—Mr. Lowenthal."

There were two sentences heavily underlined: *"Don't back out! Pay her back!"*

And again; *"She deserves the worst! Don't back out!"*

Roersch tore off the page, folded it and put it in his pocket. He flipped through the rest of the pad, then bent to a waste basket beside the desk. It was empty except for a crumpled sheet of paper, which he smoothed out. It was a typed letter, undated, unsigned, unfinished:

Well, Judy, so we've come right down to it, haven't we? You admit I've been a bankroll for you, a source of gifts, nothing more. You admit you want to see other men . . . and we both know you've *already* been seeing them. But don't think you can get away with it! I'll never let you go until you pay back everything you took from me . . . gifts *and* money! I'll drive up with a moving van and have the bed, the rug, the desk, every piece of furniture taken out! I'll get the jewelry . . . and I've got canceled checks to the amount of almost three thousand dollars. If you try to stop me, I'll kill . . .

That was all. And Roersch was disturbed by its being left here; by the list and the earrings being left here. He was disturbed by Bley's stupidity, when Bley wasn't a stupid man, *couldn't* be a stupid man and have gone as far as he had.

But Bley was an *unbalanced* man.

A man could be insane and still succeed at his job. Hadn't Vince McKenney said of Bley, "A fantastic adman, but remote, almost unfriendly, when it comes to socializing"? A loner. A talented, hard-working psychopath. A classic type of killer, especially of women.

He had him!

Still, there was no hurry according to the timetable on Bley's pad. He could catch him by being at the Grand Canyon Saturday to Tuesday, or at the Bel Air Hotel next Thursday and Friday. His Sunday and Monday off would cover the Grand Canyon, and he'd work a trade with Jones or give Hawly a personal-problem story to get Thursday and Friday. It looked real good . . . *if* Bley followed the timetable.

He'd check Mr. Lowenthal at the A.A.A. to see if Bley had made any changes of plan. If not, if everything continued to look good, he'd keep on working a while longer to strengthen his case, and clear up a few loose ends, such as the characters Nick McKenney had seen visiting Judith Keel.

He folded the sheet of paper and put it in his pocket.

In the top-left drawer of the desk, he found a framed photograph of Bley, its glass broken, a jagged center section missing. Across the lower portion was written, "To Judy, with love, from one who takes love seriously, Evan."

The photograph the cleaning lady had seen on Keel's dresser. Almost certainly taken from her apartment the night of the murder, along with the earrings.

He examined the frame, looking for stains. Nothing obvious, though there was a darkening of wood at the base.

He'd assume it was blood. He'd present it as blood,

along with the actual dried blood on the earrings, to Bley, to break him. But he couldn't have it checked, couldn't have the earrings checked, because that would get the department after Bley.

He'd feed the lab Bley's kitchen knife, Nick McKenney's switchblade. They would lead to nothing, but it would fatten the file.

He had all he needed now to confront and break Bley. No real reason to go on searching.

Except, he told himself, curiosity.

He put the photograph on the floor near the doorway, so as not to forget it.

In the desk's middle-left drawer was a Moroccan-leather box. Inside were letters. A ribbon-tied bundle of eight were from Merri; a quick examination of dates and contents showed they were from before their marriage.

A long shot, but he tore the flap off one envelope for her name and return address. Might have to trace her; might have to get her help in finding and nailing Bley . . . if she was still alive.

There were other letters from other women, but none of the names meant anything to Roersch, and the dates were scattered over the last four years. Still, he copied down the four names in his notebook, to check against lists of murder victims. He *could* get lucky; he'd once hit a daily double at Yonkers; the odds were about the same.

Finally, there was a Christmas card from Judith Keel with a handwritten message on the inside flap:

> Let's hope the Holiday Season makes my Evan kinder to his Judy. Let's hope the dark suspicion, the anger and undeserved accusations, disappear forever. Because how can I love someone who says he'll kill me? (Ha, ha! Big joke!)

Not so big a joke, and all on Judy.

He put the card in his pocket. His jacket was beginning to bulge. He finished with the desk, and went to the closet.

The first thing he saw was more clothing than any one man had a right to own; the next thing, a flat, green leather attaché case with brass fittings.

He took the case out and emptied his pockets into it and put the framed photo of Bley and Keel into it. He carried it to the desk. It felt good in his hand; was a beautiful piece of luggage. He'd always wanted a case, a *good* one like this, but they cost as much as seventy to a hundred dollars.

Well, now he had one . . . though he'd had to steal it.

He laughed at himself. Taking a payoff from Bley was worse than stealing; was blackmail, extortion, dereliction of duty, and allowing a murderer—maybe a mass murderer—to escape unpunished. So no more shit and no more dumb feelings! Yet he still felt . . . uncomfortable.

The law had been his entire adult life. He had bent it occasionally in the way of a cop on the pad, in the way of a cop who forces a search without a warrant by getting some lame-brained suspect to agree, in the way of a cop grabbing a free meal. But he had never broken it this way before. The law had been his life, and that life was coming to an end.

Good thing too, he told himself, because that life was killing him! He wanted—*needed*—a little of the sweetness, the luxury, that only big money could bring. And he would get it!

The closet-rack held eight suits, every one of them a beauty, well spaced out the way such expensive clothing deserved. On the floor were six pairs of shoes and a pair of ankle-high boots, all on shoe-trees. On the single shelf were five dress hats. And Bley must have taken a considerable amount of clothing with him!

In a corner of the closet was a low metal filing cabinet with three deep drawers. He dragged it out, went through the drawers, found files under various product names— whiskies, coffees, cars, deodorants, a hundred other things, and all big brands. There were folders with typed ads, with scripts for TV ads, with clipped ads from newspapers and magazines. He played the obvious hunches, looking under K for Keel, M and Mc for McKenney, B for Burns, C for Colter—Merri's maiden name—and even under A for Austen and back to the B's for Bain, the names of the two murdered girls Hawly had thrown at him. But he found nothing, and shoved the file back into the closet.

He brought the chair over from the desk, opened the closet doors in the middle, and stood up to get a better view of the shelf. In addition to the hats, it held three boxes, two of which were instantly recognizable to Roersch: a flat box, empty, marked Smith & Wesson Firearms; a small box marked Remington .38 and half-full of revolver ammunition.

So Bley was armed. He wrote a reminder in his notebook to check Bley out for a pistol permit.

He took down the third box, a large cardboard container, and put it on the floor. It held an unusual phone; a handset and cradle on a black box; a phone without a dial. There was a cord and plug attached to the black box-base. Roersch saw the printed sheet stuck in a corner, and took it out. It was headlined "Mobile Telephone," and further down on the sheet was a section on installation in an automobile. The phone didn't look new, and he studied it a moment, thinking of the possibilities. If Bley had used it in his Jaguar and removed it only before leaving for Los Angeles; if he'd used it to call Judith Keel . . .

He took out his notebook and wrote a question: "How can I check on ham radio operators, short-wave and FM radio listeners, anyone who might have heard a man named Evan talking to a woman named Judy?"

Having the names of people who had overheard Bley quarrel with Keel, heard him threaten her, heard the prelude to murder, might be the extra pressure . . .

He scratched out the question. He didn't need those people. He could do as well *saying* he had them, *saying* they would testify. The pressure would be the same as if he'd wasted a week running them down.

He put the car-phone back in the closet. He went to the lamp table on the right side of the bed. It held a tan Princess Phone, and in the single drawer were the Manhattan telephone directories—white and yellow pages. No personal directory. They were scarce in this case. But Bley would have taken it on vacation, if it had addresses and phone numbers of people in St. Louis and Los Angeles.

The other table held far more interesting items, considering the picture Roersch was drawing of his murderer. There were three penis-type vibrators—small, medium, and ten-inch. There was a tube of vaginal jelly, a can of contraceptive foam and a package of "extension-tipped rubbers"—French ticklers. There were four lengths of clothesline, about a foot each . . . like those used on Keel, though shorter. But no way to match standard clothesline for use as evidence. There was a feather duster and several loose feathers. There was a box with something called Duo-Vibra-Balls, and a folder explaining that they were to be placed in the vagina "for super turn-on, him and her!" There was a page torn from the classified section of that garbage heap that passed for a newspaper, *Screw*, and several ads were checked, all for sex implements or pornography.

Roersch closed the drawer and walked around the room, picking up both pillows on the bed, tilting a painting to see if there might not be a wall safe . . . but thinking of something else all the while. How would he judge a man *not* suspected of a sex crime for owning the stuff in that drawer and in the commode? While he himself had no use for *Screw*, he knew a few of the younger cops who enjoyed it. While he himself felt that vibrators and sex-aids were not only unnecessary but kinky, maybe sick, he knew that other people found them helpful. As for the ropes and feathers, they *could* be innocent—more sex-aids. And when it came to straight porno, while he didn't seek it out, he'd certainly enjoyed lots of it.

But these weren't the possessions of an ordinary man. The ropes could have been used, or planned for use, on some unwilling female, another murder victim.

He went into the bathroom, green-tiled floor to ceiling, with both a sunken tub *and* a stall shower. He checked the medicine cabinet, and then the storage area under the sink, and finally a linen closet. Nothing.

He went back to the living room and the guest bathroom opposite the kitchen. Smaller, but still fully tiled and with a stall shower. Very little in the medicine cabinet, and a supply of toilet paper under the sink.

He went to the kitchen and took the knife and photographs and sadism booklets and placed them in the case. Then he went from room to room, shutting the lights. He ended up back in the living room, standing near the door.

He threw the wall switch, and stood in darkness. He closed his eyes for a minute, thinking, *feeling* the presence of the man who had lived here.

He stopped that. *Confusing. Allowed too many questions to creep in.* He wasn't playing that sort of game now. He was moving toward a specific goal, as quickly as possible.

He stepped out and closed the door. The Yale lock snapped shut, and he used the key to turn the upper lock. He walked to the elevators, where a couple was waiting. Man about forty, woman about thirty or very well preserved. Both dressed casually, but with style and money. He smiled and nodded, and received a brief nod in return from the man. He turned away a bit, and felt them looking at him.

Look at me next year, he thought. *I'll belong then.*

They rode down together. Roersch wanted to lean against the wall; he was dead tired. But he stood straight.

They reached the lobby, and he allowed them to leave first. The doorman was ready at the inner doors, and said, "Good evening, Mr., Mrs. Weiler." And then, as Roersch gave him a nod, "Evening, sir."

The doorman turned and got the outside doors. Roersch

walked close behind the couple, moving briskly until he reached the street.

Then he slowed. His ass was dragging. He felt a hundred, at least.

He reached his car, tossed the case on the seat, got behind the wheel.

He drove west, and then downtown. He felt something besides weariness, something he blamed on exhaustion.

He was depressed. With all he'd accomplished, he was depressed.

Dead tired. That's all. A good night's sleep, and he'd wake up singing. A good night's sleep, and he'd add up what he'd gotten today and know that he'd won. He'd forget the goddamn hair-splitting, nit-picking, unimportant questions.

Bley was the one, and nailing him for the payoff was all that mattered.

Allowing him to go on didn't matter? Allowing him to kill another cheap broad, maybe whoever got close to finding out about Keel? It didn't matter that he was some sort of Jack the Ripper, a My-son-the-madman, and might keep on killing the rest of his life?

This was the second time today he'd worried about that. Exhausted, because the day had been so long. Exhausted, and his guard down. Besides, the mass killing theory was just that, a theory. Keel was the only murder he was working on. And, as he'd decided while drinking Chianti at Mario's, Bley would be so shocked, so terrified at having been caught, he'd avoid swatting a fly, not to say hurting any human being! And it was valid as hell to save a man from the disaster of prison . . .

Was Bley *alone* in that car of his, traveling west? Was he looking for a girl, the type he liked, the *courva* type? Or had he found her; maybe a hooker . . . like Ruthie?

Exhausted, and the same old shit, and it wouldn't change anything. All the worrying in the world wouldn't stop him from getting that slice of the pie from Bley!

Roersch turned on the radio. Nothing but rock. He turned to the police band. And caught a 10:13—Assist Patrolman—and felt his blood quicken and leaned forward, foot tensing on the gas pedal, ready to move, waiting for the location.

It was on Amsterdam and 123rd, too far away.

And what was he thinking of anyway? He wasn't going on any shootouts! Not at his age, and *this* close to retiring with a bundle!

What the hell was *wrong* with him?

He picked up speed. He was angry at himself. He'd have a stiff Scotch and a Nat Sherman as soon as he walked in the door. He'd earned them!

He lit the Nat Sherman while yet some five minutes from home. He didn't enjoy it, but refused to admit it. He smoked determinedly, clearing his throat and watching the thin traffic and keeping his mind empty.

Later, after *three* stiff Scotches, he was in bed, almost asleep . . . and still he wondered whether Bley was alone; whether he hadn't found some girl; whether that girl was dead, or going to die.

And knew he'd have to check police reports along Bley's route, along *several* routes if necessary, to put his mind at rest.

Only then he slept . . . and not too well.

11: Thursday a.m. and p.m.

Evan was up before Lois, and when he walked into the sitting room John was breathing heavily, regularly, on the sleeper couch. He moved softly, not wanting to waken him, wanting to be alone for a while. He hadn't slept well, despite last night's heavy drinking and heavy sex. Maybe it was all that sharply spiced food—barbecued ribs and chicken and beans and potato salad and cold beer—more than enough for four, finished by the three of them. Not exactly conducive to a restful night. But still, he'd thought he would sleep later than *this*. It was only nine-thirty, and they hadn't gotten to bed until two.

He closed the bathroom door and ran the shower and examined himself in the mirror while the water grew hot. He looked old this morning. His stubble of beard was gray at the chin. Of course, he'd had gray facial hair since his mid-thirties, while the hair of his head was still dark brown.

He touched his sideburns. Beginning to gray there too, and rather rapidly the last year or so. He took off his bathrobe and stepped back against the tub to examine his middle. First he sucked it in and tensed up, and looked trim and muscular. Then he let go, exhaled and relaxed, and his stomach went out, gave him a pot-bellied look. He pushed it out even further, to see what the future would bring . . . and turned away from the reflection of an aging, graying, big-bellied man, a man who would be entering his fifties in September, a man moving toward death . . .

He adjusted the water and got into a shower much warmer than he usually liked. He needed warmth this morning. Not just because of the chill in the bathroom. There was a chill from within; a chill of complex components, not the least of which was the party last night.

He washed, returning again and again to his genitals, feeling *dirty* there. That low-bred girl! That swinish, ruttish, brutish girl! He used a washcloth on his hands, his face, his genitals, making his skin sting, and wished he had a stiff-bristled brush to rub even harder, to *scour* the filth away!

And yet, he hadn't done more than *touch* Alma-Jean; hadn't laid her; had merely shared a bed with her.

And shared a lover with her.

He used the washcloth once again.

He came out and toweled and began to feel cleaner, better. Alma-Jean was gone now. They'd leave here as soon as the Jaguar was ready, and never come back. And more than that, he would never again allow himself to become involved in such . . . such *corruption!* He'd lay down the rules to John and Lois—no more strangers; no more filth. He just wasn't able to go along with *that* kind of group sex. Too set in his ways. Too old, probably . . .

He broke that thought off short. He was feeling better, stronger, *younger* by the minute. Lois believed he was in his thirties. Most women said his early forties. What men thought didn't concern him.

He got his razor and spread foam-lather onto his face and began to shave. With each stroke, his strength increased, a sort of reverse Samson. With more and more of his clean-shaven face revealed, he grew more and more aware of how lucky he was. He'd never lacked for young girls, had he? Nor for success and money. And now he'd gained the one thing he *had* lacked in New York—time, leisure time, to live and enjoy a young woman.

Lois was that woman. At least for as long as he wanted her. She wouldn't withdraw . . .

Another thought he had to break off short. It brought his hand to a halt and brought his eyes to a new view of the nearly clean face in the mirror.

Ugly.

"You'll be ugly all your life if you think dirty thoughts," his mother had said . . . and from twelve or thirteen, perhaps even before then, his true life, his *inner* life, had been nothing but one long dirty thought. He wanted *girls!* He wanted to do things to them, incredible things, things that if his mother knew, if she even suspected one *tenth* of what they were, would bring the whole world falling in on him.

And once she *had* known. Just once, she had seen a minute portion of his depravity, and it had led to the bloody thing . . .

The water ran in the sink and his hand held the razor and he brought it up toward his neck and he wanted to open it and take out the blade and slash, forget, escape . . .

He continued shaving. He finished and ran the cold water, no longer looking at his face; scooped up coldness and dashed it in his eyes to come awake from that horror, that nightmare . . . then looked in the mirror and saw the ugliness and remembered and stood frozen and let it come because it had to, finally, after the years of working and sexing and drinking and sleeping to forget. He was on the road now to a new life and he would beat this thing, this foolish childhood memory that he stopped even in nightmares, because the horror always awakened him before it could run its course.

He was at the very start of his sexuality, just come to puberty, and to masturbation. The dirty thoughts had begun to make him ugly—he was able to see the change in the mirror each morning before school—but he was powerless to stop the thoughts, the need to find relief from the thoughts. He was a small, plump boy at the time, not yet having begun the strong surge of growth that took place between fourteen and eighteen, that brought him to an inch shy of six feet, all gangly arms and legs, and even uglier than before. But he was ugly enough, he realized each morning in front of his dresser mirror, seeing the flapping ears, the puffy cheeks, the big effeminate eyes so out of place under the coarse, unmanageable hair. His nose wasn't even a nose; two upturned holes he equated with skeletons. He was *fat* with all the food his mother shoved down his throat, and *soft* from all his avoidance of competitive sports. He didn't *smell* right. He was sure of it, and suffered untold agonies standing in line or marching from the schoolyard into the building, waiting for the other children to notice. That they never did, that they blamed some other child for farting or failing to wash, was just a continuing streak of undeserved luck he was sure would run out the next minute, the next hour.

He hated himself, and he hated school, and he hated his home. He had no real friends, though he played with one boy for a while and then another, and his cousin came over occasionally, and less often his cousin's sister, and once they even slept together in his room with the folding cot pushed up against his bed for all three of them.

It was the Monday after the Saturday Cousins Morris and Rita had slept over that he was so oppressed by his increasing ugliness, so guilt-ridden by his filthy thoughts, so afraid of what he would become, that he swore a silent oath to change. And went to school, and looked back to see between Dorothy Morenstein's plump legs, and rubbed his stiffening penis, and thought of Saturday night and how he'd touched Cousin Rita's nine-year-old ass while she and Morris slept, how he'd pressed his stiff member up against her hairless little vagina, how he'd masturbated against her, twisting away at the last moment to come into his stocking. And went home and drank the milk and ate the cookies his mother insisted he have each day after school, and went to the bathroom, *dying* to jack off, remembering Dorothy Morenstein's fat thighs, remembering Cousin Rita's moist slit . . . and he forgot to lock the bathroom door.

His mother walked in. Just like that, with him sitting on the toilet, his already massive dong in his hand, jacking away and moaning "Dorothy" and moaning "Rita," switching back and forth in fantasy from fat thighs to moist slit . . . and coming.

His mother *screamed*. He leaped up, trying to hide the spurting shame, trying to claw his way back from her, closing his eyes not to see her red mouth open and screaming. Because she screamed again and again, ear-splitting, earth-shaking, world-ending. And there was no way of getting back from her, no way to tear the tile from the wall and the wall from the building.

She was on him. She struck his head, over and over, both arms flailing.

She stopped after only a few minutes. She stepped back and she said, her voice a hollowness in a million-mile cavern: "Look at you." The echoes of those words twisted him around, and he danced in agony, pushing the still-stiff penis into his underwear, tripping over his pants and falling against the tub.

"Look at the *filth*."

No more screaming. Much worse than screaming. And for the first time he began to cry, to beg: "Momma, I didn't mean . . ."

She was silent while he spoke, and what could he say?

He'd counted on her cutting him short, and she didn't. But after he stopped speaking, pressed between toilet and bathtub and dragging up his pants and crying, she said, "Here in the toilet is where you belong. Don't ever come out." She turned and went out and turned again and, looking at him with white face and glaring red mouth, closed the door slowly, shutting him in with the ugliest person, the filthiest person on God's earth. The person he most hated in all the world.

He stayed in the bathroom from three-thirty until five-thirty, sitting on the toilet and crying, crying all the time, but silently, afraid she would hear him and come back. After two hours, he was numb and cried by rote.

It was then she opened the door. "Come out here," she said, still white and terrible. "Come out, filth!" Her voice was rising again and the worst *wasn't* over and the damned were *never* released from hell and it would go on and on and he began to scream, "I'm sorry! I'm sorry!" and wasn't sorry, was insane, was going deep into hysteria. *"I'm sorry!"*

"You yell at *me!*" she shrieked, and her voice was bigger than his, bigger than almost anyone's, shook the walls and ceiling, shook his mind. "After *this?* After making me suffer and *bleed?*" And she drew up her dress and she had never done anything like that and she drew it above her waist and she tore at her pants and she tore at a white pad and it was bloody on the other side and *she* was bloody there, trickled blood even as he stood frozen, mouth open to scream *I'm sorry*, and he followed a thin trickle down her leg and he didn't understand and he was convulsed with disgust and horror and guilt, most of all guilt that he'd done this to his mother, that he'd driven her to *showing* this to him.

He sat down on the floor. He covered his head with his arms, blocking out the horror and the world. He didn't hear the door close.

He didn't know how long it was, but she touched his head and he started and he whispered, "I'm sorry," and he was. "Make better," he said, and cowered, his head pressing the rim of the toilet.

"All right, come and have dinner."

He didn't understand. He said, "Make better."

"Stop that! Come and have dinner!" A shout, a bellow, the usual thing when he asked for a few more minutes to read, to avoid dinner which meant stuffing of food he hated into a stomach that was ready to vomit it out. And this wasn't the usual; this was the end of the usual, his world, his life.

"Make better," he said.

She slapped him. He felt the slap, but it didn't hurt. How could anything hurt a monster like him? "Make better," he said.

She screamed, "Marvin, *stop!*" She'd called him Marvin and that was normalcy, and he finally looked at her face. She was frightened . . . but why? He wouldn't do the filthy thing anymore, make her bleed anymore. He said, "No more. Make better."

She waved her arms and stamped up and down, almost *jumping*, and then began slapping him again, furious slaps, which was also normalcy. But she screamed things which weren't part of his normalcy. Things about his father "denying" her, and Marvin being her life, and not meaning to show him, and he hadn't made her bleed, and he was a bad boy but she forgave him.

Years later, he understood. It was a brief understanding, because he couldn't face it. His mother and father had ceased being lovers. His mother's sexuality was blocked, twisted, directed at *him.*

But the child in the bathroom understood only that he was ugly and hateful, ugly and sinful.

She was still screaming things and slapping at his bent head when his father came in and dragged her into the kitchen. Then his father came back and knelt by him and said, "All right, what did you do?"

How could he tell him? Though now it was shame, not fear, that stopped him. He didn't fear his father, except as his father might cause his mother to scream and fight and hit. His father did that a lot. His father stayed away a lot, lately, and when he was there he made his mother scream; and then, when he left, his mother would find reasons— when you were as filthy as *he* was, there were *always* reasons—to scream at *him*, and hit.

They had never talked of it. *Never.* He felt his mother had forgotten it completely. Not even when she was screaming and hitting did she mention it, or come close to mentioning it. Of course, he jacked off again . . . but never when she was in the house. He tried to stop, wept and swore, but he couldn't help it; was tormented by the *things* he wanted to do to women.

And here he was in St. Louis. And he was forty-nine years old and he had a girl waiting, a beautiful girl who would do whatever he wanted, and he didn't have to jack off and there were other beautiful girls and no one thought he was dirty and no one thought he was ugly.

Until they moved away from him, rejected him, cheated him as Judy had done.

He used after-shave lotion and deodorant spray and put on his bathrobe. He stepped to the door. Those that had rejected him were gone from his life. Judy. Before Judy the others. Even that silly bitch, that low one-night stand, Alma-Jean. All of them, gone from his life.

Lois and John waited. They admired him. He *wasn't* ugly.

He went back to the mirror and recombed his hair and fiddled with the part. He smoothed out his eyebrows and tried a smile and made it smaller to show less teeth, to be cooler and more sophisticated. And combed his hair again.

The Jaguar was delivered at twelve-fifteen. They'd had breakfast in the coffee shop and were sitting around, the television going. John was exceptionally quiet. Lois was filing her nails and shooting glances at a rerun of *I Love Lucy*. Evan said, "About last night."

They both looked at him, but quick.

He tilted his head. "You expect maybe a world-shaking pronouncement?"

John got the joke and chuckled. "Well, that hillbilly was one big drag, and I feel sort of responsible. Never again."

Lois said, "Amen! I shouldn't drink at *all*, can't hold it, and I had a gallon. But that Alma-Jean, wow!"

Evan spoke quietly. "You didn't seem to mind her all that much. At least that I could see. And I could see quite a bit."

"Oh, well . . ." She was flushing. "I'll try anything, once."

"Exactly," Evan said. "We tried it once. It was fun. But as far as I'm concerned, no more. Bringing a stranger in that way is *out*, from now on."

"I'm with you all the way," John said.

Lois nodded.

"But I hope," John said, "that we'll make the material we've got go a little further." He was looking at Lois.

Evan also looked at her. "The lady has the deciding vote here."

Lois resumed her filing . . . but after a moment she looked up and they were both still watching her and she grinned a sly grin and sighed a mock sigh and said, "All in the line of duty."

At one o'clock Evan drove through the parking lot toward the exit, Lois beside him, John in back. The Jaguar was smooth and efficient again, a joy to handle. He glanced into the rear-view, and John was turned, looking out the window. Evan asked what was wrong.

"Nothing. Crowd of people over at the back . . ."

His voice was drowned out by a wail of sirens coming fast. Two police cars turned into the lot from Lindburg Boulevard, screaming by as Evan paused before exiting. An ambulance and a third police car were approaching. He pulled onto the road before they reached him. The noise was deafening, and he accelerated to get away from it.

"Room service strikes again," Lois said. She was still filing her nails.

John continued to look back.

Evan drove faster, and they left the sirens, the motel, and shortly afterward St. Louis, behind.

Roersch was up early, and at the station before eight. He sat at his desk in the five-desk room and went through his notebook and leaned back and thought things out and in the clear light of day it was simpler, much simpler. At eighty-forty Jones came in and said, "You need sleeping pills, Sergeant?"

"I need a little help," Roersch said, and took Nick Mc-Kenney's switchblade and Bley's big, serrated kitchen knife from his old plastic zipper case. He'd tagged them unknowns, in case they actually had anything on them. "Get these checked out for bloodstains. Don't bother with prints."

Jones was a big black man, twenty-eight years old, with a big plain face. He wore his hair a little bushier than last year, but last year his head had been practically shaven. He was a good detective and had a quality Roersch admired; he refused to be defensive about being a Negro cop in a town where black crime was getting worse all the time. But he didn't play movie-wise-guy either; he worked at his job and made some of the most prejudiced people in the world—white police officers, who had *reason* for their prejudice in their daily lives—respect and like him. Excepting the fuck-offs like Chauger and the unreachables like Captain Deverney.

Jones had opened the switchblade, and now turned his attention to the kitchen knife. "You don't really expect anything, do you, Sergeant? The switchblade's never been used, or else it's polished clean. The big one's brand new."

"In the joining of blade to handle . . ." Roersch began.

"You haven't been down to the lab lately, have you?"

Jones interrupted. "The only *joinings* they investigate is where their girlfriends' legs meet."

"What's the matter with you, Willis. Haven't you heard of the miracle of modern science? Don't you know anything about forensic medicine?"

"Sure," Jones said, putting the knives in a big envelope. "I take it all the time, when I'm constipated."

Roersch fought back laughter. "You may not make sergeant this year, Willis, but *Sanford and Son* for sure."

Jones said, "That's a promotion over *Amos and Andy*," and went out the door.

A good man, Roersch thought. He'd miss him, and maybe a few old friends, like Jimmy Weir, at other precincts.

He checked his watch. Almost nine. Deverney came in between nine and nine-thirty; no telling exactly when the plague would strike. Roersch decided to have a cup of coffee and some cheesecake at Abe's, then head for Grayson & Burns.

He bought a *Daily News* at the stand near the deli, and went through it as he ate, looking for murders—out-of-town murders. Nothing that fit. He handed it to Abe as he went out. "Make it a *Times*, maybe?" the short man said. "I'm an intellectual." Abe waved the paper at his bus boy. "Hey, Manuel, you want a *News*?" The slim youth said, "Nah. We don't like violence in the *barrio*."

Roersch walked out, laughing. The morning was bright and mild. And full of laughs. He felt the laughs would be coming much more often from now on. About time, too. It had been a grim seven months since Helen's death; not too many laughs in the year before then, either. Not too many since he'd become a cop, come to think of it. But a private citizen, one with money, could laugh at anything.

He was driving his car from his alley parking space when Chauger flagged him down on the sidewalk. "Got those files on the Austen and Bain murders, Sergeant."

"Okay. I'll read them when I get back."

"Another thing." Chauger smiled his smoothest smile. "You're overdue on qualification. You know, your guns."

Roersch was blocking the sidewalk with his Plymouth. Two kids, maybe fifteen, swaggered into the gutter to pass him and muttered to each other, and he read the "fucking pig" lip movements. He felt their hatred and sighed and said, "I was at the range only . . ." And nodded and drove away. Only six, six and a half months ago. And every New York policeman, from rookie patrolmen to silver-haired chiefs, had to qualify on the firing range twice a year; had to have their duty and off-duty guns checked out; had to attend the lectures that went with the checks.

He wondered if he could put it off until after he'd seen Bley, and then put it off until he left the force.

Chauger wouldn't have mentioned it unless Hawly or Deverney had mentioned it, so it might be tough.

He drove onto Fifth and turned uptown. He'd never enjoyed having to spend a full day at the pistol range, but he'd known it wasn't a *wasted* day, known that the best shots were those who fired their fifty free rounds and fifty of their own *at least* the required twice a year. Better shots used the range more often; once a month was a good idea. Statistics proved that the better shots survived more often in shootouts.

But he *had* survived. And Bley wouldn't get a chance to use his .38 because Roersch would have the advantage of complete surprise . . . would come up to him in Grand Canyon or L.A. and smile and *wham*, up against the wall, mother!

Shit, a day was precious now.

So the laughs had ended early and he was irritated and the irritation lasted as he went to the Grayson & Burns main reception desk on the eighth floor and asked for Ronny Layden in the art department. Another pretty girl protecting the employees, and he identified himself and leaned heavily on the girl with authority and manner and voice, and she led the way herself down a hallway of offices to a section of cubicles and stopped in a doorway. "Ronny, this police officer . . ."

Roersch said, "Thank you."

The girl walked off, looking back.

Roersch stepped into the cubicle. He'd start here because Burns was too smooth, too composed, to give anything away . . . if there *was* anything to be given away. This man, or boy, half-sitting, half-standing against a tall stool before an artist's easel, wouldn't be as difficult.

"Ronny Layden?"

The man-boy came to a full standing position. "Yes, I'm Ronny." His voice was low, soft. His entire manner was low-keyed, soft. He was small—no more than five-three, and slim and small-boned—and in his early twenties. He had a delicate face, his hair brown and reasonably short and very neat. He wore a gold turtleneck shirt and tight chino trousers . . . very tight around the crotch. He made Roersch think of that statue in Burns's office . . . which made the visits to Keel even more puzzling. And Layden was *frightened.*

Roersch came closer, opening his wallet to show his badge and I.D. He held it out longer than usual, allowing Layden to read and absorb. "Homicide," he said, "not Vice Squad."

Layden seemed to draw back, without actually moving. "What's that supposed to mean? I haven't done anything, in either area."

"You've been to a murdered girl's apartment, haven't you? You didn't come forward to offer your help, did you? And your *purpose* in that girl's apartment, with your employer . . ." He paused.

"Business," Layden said faintly. "Layouts . . ."

"Layouts," Roersch repeated heavily, and now he was playing the pig, the Deverney hard-liner, the beat-em-up-in-the-back-room stereotype. "C'mon!"

Layden *did* step back. "We . . . were friends. Miss Keel invited . . ."

"Don't make me take you in for questioning. You wouldn't like it. Such rough, *rough* men."

Layden looked at him and moved his lips and looked at the phone.

"Mr. Burns will be involved soon enough. First *you* tell me why you and Burns visited Miss Keel so many times."

"Twice. Well . . . three times, if you count . . ." He reached for the phone. "Mr. Burns will want . . ."

Roersch pulled the handcuffs from his belt. "Turn around." He spun the man against a cluttered desk-table, careful not to hurt him in any way. "Hands behind your back."

"But is this necessary?" Layden cried. "I have nothing to tell!"

Roersch drew the delicate wrists together, held them in one hand, touched them with the cuffs. "Sex, whatever the style, is no crime. Not to me. If that's what you're hiding, you're a fool. I want to know exactly why you and Burns spent at least two nights at Keel's apartment. I'll check your story with Burns. And if it's simply a ball, the three of you having fun . . ."

Layden giggled hysterically.

Roersch let him go, allowed him to turn, waited.

Layden looked past Roersch, and waved. "All cool, Glory. Little rehearsal before shooting . . ." He stopped as whoever had paused in the doorway went away. He spoke to Roersch, voice low, not looking at him. "You'll cost me my job. I didn't particularly want to go there. It's . . . sex in business. Do you understand?" He didn't appear hopeful Roersch would.

"I think so. The boss wanted the junior employee, and junior had to oblige."

"Yes. I didn't exactly . . . *suffer*." He giggled again, still upset but not quite as much. "First I tried to talk my way out of it, saying it was a bad idea as long as I worked for him. He countered rather adroitly by saying perhaps I *shouldn't* work for him. End of resistance."

"Why go to Miss Keel's place?"

"Morg—Mr. Burns, that is—has a permanent relationship. A marriage, so to speak." He finally looked at Roersch to see how he'd take it.

Roersch saw his chance to get it all. "Jesus, you're timid for a gay in the nineteen-seventies! Why don't you grow up?"

Which surprised and shocked Layden; which made him flush and say, defensively, "I come from a very strict home . . ." He took a deep breath. "Morg had some sort of deal with Judy. I'm not in on all the details, but he brought friends there once in a while, because it was *safe*. A hotel never is, for a man in his position. And if he'd rented another apartment, Gordie might have found out. Gordie's his wife.

"We went to Judy's place once, briefly, to make the arrangements . . ." He interrupted himself. "And to have a quickie. That grown up enough for you?"

Roersch smiled.

"Then we came back to spend the night, twice. Morg liked her water bed. Twists and turns with Morgan Burns." He leaned back against the table-desk, crossing his legs at the ankles. "Do you arrest me?"

It was Roersch's turn to look away. "What did Miss Keel do while you were in her bed those two nights?"

"Went down the hall to a friend."

"Man or woman?"

"Woman, according to the name I heard. Lizbeth."

Still finding other places for his eyes, Roersch said, "What's your opinion of Judith Keel?"

"I really don't have an opinion. I heard rumors about her and the top writer, Evan Bley, that's all." He moved back to his easel. "Are you going to speak to Morg about this?"

"I have to."

Layden hopped onto his high stool. "I'm a good artist. We'll find out if that counts for anything, won't we?" He looked grim.

Roersch said, "No problem. He'll respect my source of information, and I'll respect his right to privacy."

Layden looked up from the easel . . . and Roersch suddenly *saw* the man, the boy, with his pretty face, the features put together as sweetly as any woman's. And the figure tight, muscular, small, neat . . . pretty too, though not as any woman's. The bulge in the tight trousers . . .

He walked out, a hand raised in farewell. This was one time he was glad he wasn't younger, better-looking. And he was glad they'd stayed in their closets during his youth, his prime. It was a fucking wild thing to open your mind to all the possibilities in life! A fucking dangerous thing!

And how simple an explanation of the visit to Keel's place! Why hadn't he at least *considered* it? Why hadn't Nick McKenney?

Because they *weren't* open to all the possibilities; didn't understand what was happening to this world; hadn't fully accepted the third and fourth sexes of male and female homosexuals.

He wondered if Jones and some of the other good prospects on the force understood. They'd damned well better!

Burns kept him waiting ten minutes, the secretary saying he was "in conference." He used the time to close his eyes, to consider what remained before he could go after Bley. Not too much.

Layden said Keel had a friend in her apartment house, on the same floor if "went down the hall" could be taken literally. That didn't jibe with Jones's report and the reports of the responding radio-car officers. But it wasn't important, except as "Lizbeth" might know something to tighten the case against Bley.

The important thing now was to get Bley's route from the A.A.A. And get *to* him. And apply sufficient pressure by means of the actual evidence he had, plus what he could *present* as evidence—the car-phone for example—to crack him wide open. It didn't have to hold up in court. It simply had to *appear* that way to Bley; had to hold up so that he'd write a check for two hundred thousand, two hundred fifty thousand . . . he'd see just how much Bley could raise and convert to quick cash.

Burns said, "Having a little nap, Sergeant?"

Roersch opened his eyes. "Just trying to figure out why you lied to me. You said you knew nothing about Judith Keel, yet you visited her three times, spent two nights in her apartment with Ronny Layden, this during the short period of a surveillance on Keel's residence."

Burns's superior smile was dead and gone by the time Roersch finished. "Surveillance," Burns muttered.

"Do you want dates? Layden's story about using her place for your affair?"

Burns sagged. "That stupid little . . ."

"Mr. Layden was cooperative only because I *forced* him to be. I'd have taken him in, just as I'd have taken *you* in. For lying. For hiding what might be useful evidence. For making yourself suspect."

"What did Ronny say?"

Roersch told him. Burns nodded slowly. Roersch said, "You paid Miss Keel during your dinner at the San Marino restaurant. What for?"

"You never know when Big Brother is watching," Burns muttered. "I paid her for the use of her apartment."

"A standard arrangement?"

"Yes. Will any of this become public knowledge?"

"Not unless you're hiding something else. Something I'll turn up later."

"Nothing. I can't take publicity, Sergeant. I can be open with most of the people in the agency, and with *all* my friends. I was relatively open with you. But clients . . . Midwest cereal tycoons, beer barons, the *cigars* as my account execs call them . . ." He shook his head. "It would force me out of active participation in my own agency."

Roersch stood up. "I wouldn't want that, Mr. Burns. Not for you." He gave him a hard look. "Not for Ronny Layden."

"You surprise me."

Seemingly on his way out, Roersch took off on another tack. "What would you think of Evan Bley as our murderer, Mr. Burns? Just off the top of your head."

Burns was quiet a moment, then shrugged. "In for a penny," he muttered. "I think he could very well have done it. He terrorized Judy. Actually came at her with a knife one night; controlled himself and took it out on the water bed instead. Beat her several times, I believe, though she didn't quite say that. She was out ill one Friday, and wore dark glasses the following Monday, and I assumed from what she'd told me before that it was Evan. But I didn't have to assume she was terrified of him, nor did she have to tell me. That came through quite clearly when he phoned one evening while I was there . . . with someone, but not Ronny. She was sure he'd come over. She said he'd managed to get to her place within *minutes* after phoning; had done it several times in the past month. She rushed us out in an absolute panic. No one should be *that* afraid of a lover, no matter how much she's accepted from him, no matter how quickly she's back-pedaling."

"He gave her a lot, did he? And she was trying to break it off?"

"Gifts and considerable amounts of cash. She was a strange type. Perhaps not so strange for a heterosexual. She grew restless under the yoke of passion, of love."

"Not so strange for *any* sexual," Roersch said.

"Yes, sorry. I'm accustomed to making my little criticisms, scoring my little *touchés*. It's the way the *demimonde* compensates for slings and arrows."

Roersch didn't understand all the words, but got the point.

"She said that whenever a man began to care for her, began to try for a permanent relationship, including marriage, she felt claustrophobic, choked, wanted out. It happened that way with Bley, except that he didn't accept the dismissal. Is he a serious suspect?"

"Not too serious. It looks more and more like robbery

and freak sex by a stranger. By the way, Bley knows about your visits to Keel."

"No problem. Evan also knows *me*." He leaned back, peaked his fingers and sighed. "I'd hate to lose that good a writer, that creative an administrator, even if he did kill the girl. His last campaign—Drink Seven Great Coffees in One Cup of Baxter's Instant—secured a five-million-dollar account that was on its way out, and got us a crack at their decaffeinated. You must have seen it. He came up with the headline, created the visual of the jar with its different shadings of beans, wrote every last word of the TV campaign. A worker and a talent, that man."

"You haven't lost him yet," Roersch said.

"I think I have, whether or not he had anything to do with the murder. The way he assigned all the work in transit before he left . . . the way he said goodbye . . . I got the definite impression he was going to stay in Los Angeles. Besides, he was always willing to fly there on business; not so with Chicago, some other towns. I feel he's wanted out of New York for quite a while, and this is his way."

Roersch went to the door and opened it. "You made out with Keel in your car that night you took her to the San Marino restaurant."

Burns stared a moment, then exploded in laughter. "Made out! I believe I gave her a chaste kiss on the cheek by way of thanks for continuing to provide me with a shack joint."

"You paid her, didn't you? Wasn't that thanks enough?"

"Sergeant, it was a *gesture!*"

Roersch caught something; a flicker in the usually level glance. "The gesture included a little tit-feeling, ass-squeezing, cunt . . ."

"That's enough!"

"Yes, enough to make me know you're lying. You tried Judith Keel, didn't you? There was no man with you that night; no Ronny Layden or other lover." He came back into the room, sharking now, heavy now, moving in on a liar now . . . and hoping, praying this wasn't some sort of left-field break. "So it's bullshit about your not caring for women. Just like it was bullshit about your not knowing anything about Keel's private life. You fucked that girl, didn't you? And if Bley suspected it . . ."

Burns was flushing, blushing, as if caught in the filthiest of acts. "Close the door," he whispered. "Your voice . . ."

Roersch closed the door.

"Perhaps once or twice a year, I'll make it with a woman. To prove something to myself. It can't be the usual kind of woman. No randy bitch. It has to be . . . a highly selective woman. Judy was that kind. But you can't think I had any reason to harm her?"

Roersch came to the desk and leaned on it. "What if she was blackmailing you with threats to tell Bley? You said he was rough. You'd be afraid of him. And you said you valued his work . . ."

"Not enough to *kill!*" He was shaking his head and trying to laugh.

"How many times did you fuck her?"

"Can't you speak a little more . . ." He waved his hands. "Once. I don't recall exactly how long after that dinner at the San Marino . . . say a week to ten days. And that was the end. I didn't use her apartment afterward; didn't speak to her or approach her. I barely *saw* her, keeping away from the ninth-floor reception desk. It . . . embarrassed me."

"Why? Didn't it go off all right?"

"It went off beautifully, by her standards. And so did she. She said I was the first man who'd given her an orgasm in six months. So ego had its day. But . . . you have to understand something. For me, it's an *unnatural* act. Wallowing in . . ." He shook his head. "Suffice it to say I just didn't want to see her again. I suppose if you and Ronny Layden . . . well, *then* you'd understand."

Roersch did, and walked to the door. "I want a recent photo of Bley. Can you get it for me?"

"It'll be waiting for you at the main reception desk. Give me five, ten minutes."

Roersch opened the door.

"Is that it?" Burns asked.

"That's it," Roersch said, and went back to the waiting room and took the elevator to the ninth floor, the copy department. He walked past the receptionist, the girl he'd snapped at the other day, and waved and said, "*I'll* protect the executives from now on." She made a gesture of helplessness.

He strolled toward Vince McKenney's office. Everything was going along smoothly. He'd cleared up a few loose ends, without weakening the case against Bley. Actually strengthened it.

The typewriter was going; McKenney was hunched over it, jacket off, sleeves rolled up, biting his lip. Roersch said, "What's the idea, McKenney?"

McKenney turned, angry at the interruption; then he saw who it was. "What?" he said, voice weak.

"I spoke to Cousin Nick. Do you know what it means to impede the investigation of a criminal offense!" He came a step into the office. "No more of your shit! I've had nothing but lies around here! I want to know exactly what you had going with Keel, and where you were the night she was killed."

McKenney nodded quickly. "I had a one-night stand with her. I tried a few times afterward, but no go. And the one night was nothing. She's not . . . she wasn't a real woman."

Roersch didn't want that. An unnecessary complication. She was woman enough to have had a long affair with Bley and quickies with at least two other men.

"So you paid your cousin five hundred dollars for *nothing?*"

"To compensate for his changing the report, so Evan wouldn't know. I didn't want my job in peril. You can understand that, can't you?"

"I can also understand how you'd hate her for rejecting you."

"I can account for every minute of my time last Sunday! I was at my parents' home in Oyster Bay. We went sailing, my father and brother and I. We had a late dinner. I was tired, had a little too much to drink, and slept over. I didn't leave until seven-thirty, seven-forty, and drove directly to the office. I was here about nine. The receptionist wrote my arrival in our time book."

Roersch asked for the parents' address and phone number. McKenney gave it without hesitation. Roersch said, "You could have stopped at Keel's place first."

"And carved her up in five minutes and arrived here spotless?"

"You leave the timing to me. From Oyster Bay to this address wouldn't take an hour and a half."

"With Monday morning traffic? I was lucky . . ."

Roersch turned to leave.

"Sergeant, I'm telling the truth. I'm sorry I misled you before. I just hoped I could stay out of it, completely."

Roersch believed him. He'd make the call to McKenney's parents' home, but he expected no problem there. It continued to point to Bley. He doubted he'd get the murder weapon, and there weren't going to be any eyewitnesses . . . which would have blown his deal anyway. So all that was left was checking the A.A.A.

He went to the eighth-floor reception desk, where an eight-by-twelve manila envelope addressed to "Sgt. Roersch" was waiting for him. It held a large, glossy photograph of Bley, a publicity-type picture in suit and tie with dignified expression. On the back, someone had written, "Bley, Evan C., update file, January 15th."

He headed for the station, but he was hungry. He hated to hit Abe for more than two meals a week, but going anyplace else meant traveling out of his way and wasting time. So he walked into the deli at eleven-fifteen, and handed his sour-faced host a *Times*. "With apologies, intellectual."

Abe managed a small twitch of the lips. Roersch had a

sandwich and iced tea and was out before the noon-hour rush.

As soon as he walked into the station, he saw Chauger bending over his desk. The squat detective was reading the Keel file. "Solved it yet?" Roersch asked, and pushed past him and sat down.

Chauger said, "You're not working the staff very hard on this, except for our *poh*-leece."

"That's right. Where are the Austen and Bain files?"

Chauger tapped two folders tilted into the In box.

"Thanks. You must have typing to do. Or cooking or cleaning."

"Say, Eddy, you want to talk about Keel? I've got a few ideas."

Roersch felt something coming. No way to block it. He leaned back. "Shoot."

Chauger's voice dropped; he bent close. "The only suspect, so far, is Evan Bley. Man obviously has money. Lots of money. Enough to buy his way out of a collar if the situation developed correctly."

Roersch waited.

"Say Bley paid this private eye, McKenney, to whitewash the victim, Keel. Say he paid someone else to keep him out of it. And lived happily ever after."

Roersch continued to wait.

"What do you think, Eddy?"

"That you're better at typing, cooking, cleaning."

Chauger straightened. "You think of it, Eddy. You've got this case *very tight* under your vest."

"Haven't worn a vest in years."

"You need any help, just let me know." He sat down at his desk, his back to Roersch. Then he turned his head. "I could do a job for you, Sergeant. Just like the typing. I don't charge much, do I?" He began to type.

Roersch dialed the A.A.A., and asked for Mr. Lowenthal. The woman said, "A moment, please." While he waited, he looked at Chauger's back, Chauger's pink-white neck, Chauger's short brown hair. He kept himself tightly contained. Chauger knew nothing. Chauger was fishing. A smart bastard . . . but not smart enough. He knew less than Jones did. He'd made an educated guess, but he had no facts. Only Nick McKenney and Eddy Roersch had the facts. And Nick was long gone, if Roersch knew anything at all about people.

Still, something had to be done, and Roersch wasn't quite sure what. He was working on it as he said, "Marty."

Chauger turned, smiling easily. "Yes, Sergeant?"

"I'm going to let you slip under my vest and onto the Keel case. You'll assist Jones in checking out several leads."

"I've got six reports . . ."

"Tomorrow, *eight sharp*, I want you over at Latent Prints. We've no reports on the sets we picked up. Push them. Get their asses moving. I want you to see to it personally . . ."

Mr. Lowenthal came on the phone. Roersch held up his hand. "More to come."

The squat young detective said, "Yeah," and turned back to his typewriter. His fishing expedition had caught him a load of crap-work. He'd complain to Hawly, and Hawly would get him out of it, considering Chauger handled the sacred typing of the holy reports. And that would be the end of that . . . or would it? How to stop the damned thing *right now*?

Mr. Lowenthal said he couldn't give out information over the phone; he had to see identification and the like. Roersch said he'd be right over. Mr. Lowenthal said he wasn't sure he could remember Mr. Bley's exact route, though he *thought* it was to St. Louis via U.S. 70, and then 44 . . . Well, he'd think about it. If Bley had placed any reservations through the Auto Club, they'd definitely have a record of *that*, and it would help re-create his route.

Roersch thanked him and hung up. As he was passing

Chauger's desk, he made a sudden decision. "You know," he said, stopping, "it just hit me. Were you saying *I'm* working some sort of squeeze on a suspect?"

Chauger looked up, startled. He hadn't expected a head-on collision. "Eddy . . . you're kidding."

"I'm not. And if *you're* not, let's go into Hawly right now. Or the captain. Make a formal charge. Call the Knapp Commission. Because I've been around too long, my record is too good, to let it be spoiled by some punk typist, to take any sort of shit . . ."

"Hey, Sergeant, *easy.* I didn't mean . . . I was speaking *generally* . . ."

Roersch had allowed his voice to rise, and now he saw how to cap this thing. He hauled Chauger up out of his chair by the shirt-front. "You pad-hungry, lousy . . ."

Chauger tore free and jumped back, arms outstretched, face dead white. The uniformed sergeant at the reception counter across the room turned and stared. Hawly's door opened and the lieutenant looked out. Chauger said, "Jesus, you don't think I meant *you* were acting unethically? I swear . . ."

Roersch turned and stalked away, past Hawly and the desk sergeant, out of the room and out of the station. He got his car and screeched down the alley, in case anyone was watching from the john window or the front door. Only when he was several blocks away did he drop the mad act.

Chauger would think twice before he made another pitch . . . or a complaint. This *could* end it, though retirement immediately after the payoff was definitely out now, too risky; it could set that little fuck to sniffing around.

He reached for his cigarettes. He'd held off all day, but he needed one now.

He lit up, inhaled deeply, then inhaled again, moderately. He had too much to live for to blow it with cancer.

He also had too much to live for to blow it by being *careless.* This bit with Chauger . . . might be for the best.

He'd forgotten everything but nailing Bley; forgotten he himself could be nailed.

Had to be careful. Look around. Make sure he covered his action. With Bley as well as Chauger.

Bley might decide to bluff it out; say, "Take me in," and threaten to expose the shakedown attempt. What then?

It just didn't worry Roersch, despite his trying to set it up as a danger, so as to be considered, then handled as he'd handled Chauger. Because Bley could be squeezed in more than one area.

The cartoon dialogue he'd written into the porno books. Those nude pictures of his ex-wife; of himself with Keel. And most important of all, that Valentine's Day picture of his mother with the bloody heart.

Bley wouldn't be able to face revelation of such things —few men could!—even if he could face trial for murder. Even if he was *innocent* of murder. Which he wasn't.

The worst that could happen was that he'd have to let Bley walk away without paying. The very worst, and highly unlikely. No *danger* from his pigeon.

So what had changed?

Only the possibility of quick retirement.

Quick retirement would have been stupid, even without Chauger. Would have caused talk; left him wide open to speculation . . . and then someone might have reviewed the case and asked questions.

All right. Another year.

Damn, damn! He wanted out so badly!

Maybe not a full year. He'd gradually grow sick, have dizzy spells, go to the doctor a lot, complain of weakness, con the medics.

Easy enough. Especially with his near-perfect record. And so an early medical retirement, or at the worst a desk-job at Headquarters until his doctor said he had to get away from the job, the city, the strain.

He stabbed out the cigarette. Okay. A year. And out.

He should thank Chauger. He was still going to get his payoff, but now he'd keep it.

12: | Thursday p.m.

He was coming at her again, the big, ruddy face all twisted, coming at her and crying and his pants open and his thing coming at her and it was night. He'd reached her and his face coming down and she'd screamed, "It's *me*. It's Lo-lo! *Daddy* . . ." He was on her and it made no difference that she was a little girl, *his* little girl, only fifteen; she screamed for her mother while knowing there could be no help from Mum, never any help from Mum. But her screams must have been heard and the neighbors had called for help and the police were at the neighbors' door and came for Dad and Lois said it: "He raped me, his own daughter. I want a doctor." An officer covered her with a blanket and sat her in a chair and she didn't like the way he looked at her; and he touched her nose with a towel and she felt the blood then. There were two broken ribs also and she found out when they drove her to hospital and Dad following in an ambulance, strapped into a jacket, ranting about criminals and degenerates and a law-abiding man being forgotten in this God-forsaken nation.

She was in the hospital three days and hated it. Because the night nurse brought in a day nurse and they looked at her and turned their backs and whispered and she heard "own father" and she was an exhibit. What she hated even more was the young doctor and an older doctor and later two more doctors coming in and all four examining her and asking her what happened, "Let's have the details, did you find yourself responding, enjoying it?" *Enjoying it!* And the young doctor looking at her breasts like Dad and the older doctor pressing her stomach and she jerking away because THEY MADE HER SICK THE WHOLE DAMNED CREW THEY MADE HER WANT TO PUKE AND SHE DIDN'T WANT THEM WITH THEIR THINGS HIDDEN IN THEIR PANTS THE FILTHY PIGS SPUNKING INTO WOMEN THE DIRTY . . . THE . . .

"Wake up," Evan was saying, shaking her, and she scrambled back from him and she was up against a door. She was in the car and it was dark and they'd been driving all day and she'd been sleeping, dreaming. John was bent over the seat, looking at her. He said, "You're okay now, Lois. You see us, don't you? You're okay now?" He'd gone through this before with her and the first time he'd tried to comfort her with his stiff prick right after she woke up and she'd tried to kill him. So always afterward, he was very careful to make sure she was fully awake.

She smiled for them. "Wow, what a nightmare." She'd never told John about Dad. It was the sickest, the dirtiest.

It had cost Dad two years of his life, and even now he had to report once a month for what he called "discussion" but it was a combination of parole and mental examination. He'd never get off the hook. But Mum still had to live with him, and knowing Dad he was still getting a snootful down at the King's Inn once in a while and coming back to give her his red thing and spunking and laying it on with those big hands and she whimpering and hating it.

"Christ, I'd like a drink!" she said, and looked out the window. Nothing to see; darkness and countryside and lights from other cars. "What time is it?"

"Almost nine," Evan said.

"Where are we?"

"Between El Reno and Clinton."

"That's Oklahoma," John said.

"Last big town," Evan said, "was Oklahoma City."

They seemed pleased with all this, and she said, "I guess we're making good time."

They both said yes and Evan said they might even make Amarillo tonight. It meant nothing to her, but she said, "Wow." She had to go to the bathroom. "Could we stop somewhere?"

Evan said they'd stop for gas, and he hoped they could combine that with a stop for dinner at a roadside inn. John said they shouldn't waste too much time eating because it was a *fantastic* night, so clear and mild, and he was looking forward to driving to Amarillo, or right through till morning if Evan wanted him to. And they grinned and nodded and John leaned over the seat as Evan talked about the "tach" and "redlining" and they looked so fucking chummy she wanted to ask if maybe they hadn't worked a little sixty-nine while she'd been sleeping. But it wasn't so much irritation with *them*, as with the dream. Why the hell did she have to have it? She *hated* it, so why did it come back over and over again?

She stretched, and leaned closer to Evan which meant closer to both of them, and said, "Show me too," like a little girl. They both laughed and John stroked her head and Evan squeezed her thigh and they looked at her and at each other, and she knew what was shaping up for later tonight. She would have a martini, maybe two, since that was the drink that hit her the hardest, because for one moment she'd been ready to belt them both and scream, LEAVE ME ALONE!

Life was never simple. Everything going along okay, and then something fucks you up. Something baby, always something waiting offstage . . . an Alma-Jean or a night-mare. What would it be next time?

She snuggled up to Evan and said, "Back, boy," to John and laid her head on Evan's shoulder and closed her eyes as if to nap . . . but no way would she let herself sleep again! "Gotta go potty," she murmured into Evan's ear.

He said another fifteen minutes, at the most.

She let the hum and movement of the car drift into her brain. She didn't sleep, but she couldn't help remembering Dad's next great number—getting her married.

It began after Dad got out of the mental hospital; maybe five, six months after. During the two years he'd been away, she'd managed to enjoy life a little. She'd grad-uated from high school at seventeen, and high school hadn't been half-bad with Dad gone and no more Satur-days and Sundays running her guts out on backroads and training, training all the time so he could have the Gurny name in the Olympics, his big dream, and he always blamed Mum for "trapping" him into marriage and ending his own "promising track career at its peak." Lois had concentrated on dramatics those two years, and after high school, she went out and tried modeling, dancing, acting. She got a few low-paying modeling jobs, bikini stuff, be-cause one thing she had over most chicks was a good body. And she attended an acting school two nights a week, was just beginning to get into it, when Dad got out of hospital. Knowing what he thought of show biz, she decided to drop her dream . . . for a while. Until she could leave home and be on her own.

Dad was back at the insurance company and God only knows what he told them about his stay in hospital be-cause he had his old job and he was doing okay as he always did in his job. Mum thought his two years had changed him completely because at first he didn't touch a drop, not even a beer, and he didn't raise his hand, not even his voice. But Lois wasn't fooled. She saw the mad-ness waiting in his small, wild, pale-blue eyes. She saw the clenched teeth, the muscles lumping in his jaw. Still, she tried to keep up the contacts with at least a few of the people she'd met while modeling. Especially Clothilde Hudson, who was an older woman, maybe forty, but stylish and up on everything, just what Lois would have loved Mum to be; a career woman, a theatrical agent, not dependent on any damned man. She had an apartment on Military Road, Dover Heights, with a beautiful view of the ocean, and she'd furnished it like nothing Lois had ever seen before—groovy and rich and full of surprises. Like the little alcove with the beaded drape separating it from the living room, and a bed with a leopard skin spread; and she kept it for close friends who wanted to stay over. She'd had Lois over for dinner, twice, and they'd talked about acting. Clothilde said she might even represent Lois after they'd known each other a while longer, even though she handled only "established talent." That was the night Lois suddenly blurted out what had happened with Dad. She'd never talked about it with anyone, but Clothilde had been so warm, so understanding, and it just happened. Clothilde had come to the chair where she was sitting and raised her up and held her in her arms . . . and said something Lois hadn't understood fully; not *then*.

"It's over. You survived and you learned something most women don't learn about the nature of this society, its bestial animal nature, until their lives are already spent and it's too late for *real* love. Love that comes not because genetics say so it must be, but because *you* say so it *will* be."

When Dad brought Mitchel Chandler home, Lois was surprised. Mitchel wasn't the beer-swilling square, all sports and business she expected from Dad. He was tall and he was built nice and he had a mustache and his hair wasn't all that short. He liked dancing and movies and travel, and he liked Lois.

It wasn't bad, seeing him twice a week. The first few times they ate dinner in the house and sat in the parlor and talked or watched the telly. Their fourth date he took her out to dinner . . . and he changed, went on the make.

But not too much. He was sort of shy. Only at the very end, just before she went inside, did it happen. Standing near the door in the darkness, he felt her boobs and sighed and kissed her with open mouth.

Still, nothing she couldn't take, or handle. And Dad kept insisting she be home by midnight, no matter how much he liked Mitchel who was "an up and coming Tri-Mutual executive and no doubt about it." So there were movies and dinners and dancing and a little making out. She got so she almost liked it when he put his hand inside her bra and rolled her nipples.

When Mitchel took her hand one night at a restaurant and told her he'd discussed marriage with her father, and that he had an apartment all picked out and she wouldn't have to work, she realized something great had happened, sneaked up on her as it were. She could have marriage and a career . . . and be free of Dad!

They had the wedding at home, and the minister was Mitchel's cousin. Everyone understood they couldn't have a big affair, what with Dad having been in hospital two years and money that tight. And Lois didn't care. She had Mum's old wedding gown, made over, and Mitchel looked *distinguished* in his tails and boiled shirt, and it was a great party afterward. They danced in the kitchen with the table taken away and everyone applauding as they waltzed.

They had a nice little apartment, not like Clothilde's and not in the best part of town, but not that far from the ocean and Military Road that she couldn't walk it in half an hour.

It was away from Dad. It was freedom and adulthood . . . at least so she thought.

Maybe that's the way it would have been, had she been able to play her part in bed. Mitchel thought he was getting a wife, and Lois thought she was getting freedom, and it turned out they were both wrong.

She begged off that first night, saying she was tired. He was upset, but said okay. He said okay the next two nights also, but then he tried to force her. She cried and fought him, and he went crazy, almost like Dad, and slapped her around and dressed and stomped out. And didn't come home until three that morning. He was drunk and he said he'd had himself a piece and to hell with her.

She called Clothilde the next day.

"Hon," she said to Evan, "I'm really *hurting* for a bathroom."

At the very next exit, he turned off to a gas station. Across the road was a steak house and he said, "See? Good luck's going to be with us from now on."

John said, "Lois, wait a minute and I'll walk with . . ."

But she wasn't walking, she was *running*, all the way to the bathroom. It had come over her suddenly, a weakness and lack of control. She couldn't seem to stop, and finally she began to retch.

She kept going from the toilet to the sink and washing her face and rinsing her mouth and hoping it would go away. She'd had this before. Bad times turned her insides rotten. Thinking of Dad and Mitchel. Of Clothilde. Of her hopes falling apart when she got to L.A., and the same in New York.

Now at last she had another chance, and the dream and the memories and last night with Alma-Jean frightened her. What if she blew it?

"Don't get sick," she pleaded with her image in the mirror.

A woman and little girl came in. The woman tried not to react, but the little girl said, "*Stinky* in here!"

Lois went out, embarrassed. And before she and Evan and John could be seated in the restaurant, she had to go again.

They both looked worried when she returned. Evan said, "You might as well admit it, you're ill."

"Well, maybe it'll go away. I know you want to make Amarillo."

John said, "You look like a ghost. Is it that diarrhea and throwing up?"

She nodded.

John turned to Evan. "Might as well forget Amarillo. She's had this five, six times before. It runs her into the ground for twenty-four to forty-eight hours. Once it went on three days. First I thought it was a virus, but I never caught it."

Evan said, "Have you checked with a doctor?" John said, "She wouldn't go even when we had the money." Evan said, "It might be something that needs attention." And he felt her head. And John said she'd been able to hold down lemon juice and hot water. And Evan called the waiter.

She was with friends. Evan cared for her. And John . . . well, he cared too, because of the past. She drank the lemon juice and water, and began to feel better, and was tempted to say she'd try and go on. But she remembered how it came back every few hours.

They were directed to a motel down the road. There were no suites, so they got two rooms. Evan helped her into the one he and she were sharing, and John followed with the luggage. She was weak and they helped her undress, and she was cold and Evan helped her into his bathrobe, and then she was under the covers, sliding into nothingness.

She roused long enough to look up at them and say, "Sorry folks, no performance tonight. Your tickets are good tomorrow."

She smiled at their smiles. Her audience. Her friends. And one friend would split and the other friend would become her lover, her forever-and-ever. And then the movies. Starring Lois Chandler.

Everything had meaning; God was there. All the suffering had a purpose; to bring her to this man at this time. All the sins were forgiven; to make her life fresh and new.

Today is the first day of the rest of your life.

Starring Lois Chandler.

13: Friday a.m.

Roersch didn't have to use the Law Enforcement Teletype Service to check on parallel sex murders along Bley's route. The *Daily News* featured the St. Louis motel killing on Page Four of its Friday morning edition, which came out late Thursday night. It stopped him dead as he was walking toward his car, flipping through the tabloid and tilting it toward the neon tubing which ran across the top of the long window on Glen's Bar.

He moved up against the window and said "Jesus" softly and skimmed the story and rolled the paper and stuck it in his jacket pocket. And stood there, thinking this was what he'd wanted and now that it had happened this was what he'd feared. Bley had killed before and would kill again. And he was going to let him go.

He went back into Glen's. The bald ex-fighter said, "You forget something, Eddy?"

"Yeah."

"What?"

"I forget."

Which was his game with Glen, buying a drink and earning another with what Glen considered superior wit. Which was enough to crack Glen up. Glen had won thirty-six middleweight fights and lost fifty and retained most of his marbles and was just dopey enough to keep the customers laughing without turning them away.

Roersch sat at the bar and sipped the Scotch Glen poured him and nodded at the pug's talk of Mets and Jets and no decent white fighters. And wondered why he'd ever thought he liked this place. Losers ran it and losers came here. The old neighborhood and the old used-up people.

He reached for the paper, touched it, left it in his pocket. First his drink.

He finished it and paid for another, his fourth of the evening, and thought of calling Ruthie again. He'd wanted to see her tonight; had called at six and she'd said she had a trick at eight and wasn't sure if it was a few hours or a full night. A regular, she said. A wealthy Philadelphian who "dated" her when he came in on business.

It had bothered him. Only because he felt a little down, tired, long day and Chauger . . . he told himself. Anyway, he got it free, was no John, so what the hell was he crying about?

He went to the phone booth and closed the door. The fan didn't work; the booth smelled of spilled booze and cigarettes; the walls were covered with names and numbers and scribbles. No obscenities in Glen's Bar. Too middle-aged. Too tired a place for raunch.

Ruthie answered, voice low. "Hello?"

"It's Eddy again. Your trick leave?"

"Sorry." Whisper. "All night. Can't talk."

"Yeah, 'bye."

The line clicked.

"Go back to sucking and fucking," he said, and heard

his bitter, bitter voice and raised an eyebrow at himself and hung up.

At the bar, Roersch took out his newspaper. But he didn't read. He let his eyes slip out of focus and told himself to go home.

Home. Where the hell *was* home?

Used to be LaGrange, not far from Poughkeepsie. Beautiful farm country; corn fields and apple orchards and stock farms. Sweet land. They'd had a farm life though his father was a mechanic in Hopewell Junction, another small town in the LaGrange-Wappingers-Fishkill-Poughkeepsie area. *Big* area; big open hunk of country in New York's Dutchess County. Mother and father and sister Ceil and Eddy in a big old house not far from where they later built the Taconic Parkway. Back then it was all farms and in summer grazing cattle and swimming in the little pond they later made Hillside Lake with bulldozers and vacationists from the city. But then just the pond and the grazing cattle and the corn and the apple orchards. Great summers, with old Cole Bradford and Chick Sawyer and the other kids, he forgot their names. Old Cole and old Eddy were a team. Baseball at the level Bahank field and swimming at the pond and sometimes Lake Walton and fishing in a dozen streams and goofing around and talking about girls and not getting much. But Mary Straub, boy! She'd liked him and lying there near the stream where he'd caught trout with his father's good split-bamboo pole and their arms around each other and forgetting to be afraid and her thick cotton pants sliding down her hard thighs and strong legs and how she sucked in her breath when he entered her. And how she said, "Eddy, no," and helped and she was a year older than him and good at it and they did it three times that day and he sweated out her period. All that summer they met and all that summer they did it and at the end of summer he loved her, wanted to marry her. She didn't laugh when he mumbled it; she just said, "We'll see," and two years later she was married down in Putnam Corners to a typewriter repairman and he never saw her again.

But it was sweet. And winters were almost as good as summers, with the frozen pond for ice-skating and snow for sledding and sometimes the blizzards that all the adults talked about and acted as if they hated, but everyone loved blizzards. The rolling land was leveled out pure white and no school and no work and the snowball fights and Ceil crying because he hit her in the face and old Cole saying, "Hey, Eddy, no fair with *girls!*" Cole and Ceil had a year, maybe a little longer, of being sweet on each other. Cole was really hit hard when Ceil started going with the older guy from Poughkeepsie, but he got over it. Life was too sweet for kids back in LaGrange for them to do the crazy things kids did now when they hurt over a boy or a girl. Spring was maybe the nicest time of all, because you could smell it and taste it and know summer would come and school would end. And autumn was so damned *pretty* that even with school starting again you couldn't help jumping out of bed in the morning and laughing and kidding Ceil and showing up for football practice. Eddy had been second string and could've been varsity but he just didn't care enough to stay late and come early and give up his weekends. He loved to sleep late Saturdays and when Mom finally let up on early Sunday services he slept late then too. And Jesus those breakfasts she used to make with the sausage fresh from Kraut Schermer's meathouse. Or slabs of pink ham and five, six eggs and those heavy brown pancakes and yellow corn bread and the milk in metal pitchers. They had the best food in the world and all they wanted because it was all around them!

Sweet land and sweet days. And the sweet days had come to an end like the sudden slam of a door. His mother had died when he was eighteen and Ceil and her husband had moved away and his father had died when Eddy was twenty-one and working for the sheriff's office through Paul Bennet, *Mister* Bennet who was the local state rep and a buddy of Dad's. He helped Eddy get the job in the sheriff's office, but Eddy wanted something better than hick deputy and was reading up on New York City Police and State Troopers. Mister Bennet had a friend, a captain over in the old Fourth Precinct in New York, and said he'd write him and to be patient and they'd see what could be done.

Eddy bowled Fridays with Cole, and that was about all they saw of each other since Cole had got married at twenty and worked for a plumbing supply outfit clear over the river in Monroe.

On one of those Fridays, something happened that changed his life. In the next alley was a group of four city people, two men and two women. One of the women kept putting the ball in the gutter, and the faces she made and the way she threw up her hands and looked around finally got Eddy. He laughed, louder than he meant to, and she looked his way. He stopped laughing fast, but she put her hands on her hips and said, "I'd like to see you play tennis! I'd like to see who'd be laughing then!"

At that time who played tennis but rich kids, and who knew rich kids in LaGrange and Poughkeepsie, certainly not Eddy Roersch. So it was a crack about his class, his place in society, he knew that right off, and it made him go pale with anger and he had to control his voice as he said, "All right, Miss. When do we play?" determined to get a racket and get some lessons and fight like hell to show this city bitch what he was.

She stared at him. The guy with her said, "Helen, forget it," and seemed worried. Later, Helen told him he'd looked ready to kill, his big hands clenched and his big jaw clenched and his head tilted forward as if he were ready to charge.

She half-turned away; then faced him again and said, "I get it. Tennis. But I didn't mean it *that* way. It's just that I'm an absolute *clown* at every sport but tennis. Even tennis . . ." She smiled.

She wasn't all that pretty. Not pretty as Mary Straub. She was a small woman . . . strange, he'd never thought of her as a *girl*, even then when she was only twenty, nine months younger than him. She was on the plump side and her hair was short and brown and she had a *mature* look, a serious and grown-up look. But her smile was radiant— very wide and full of small white teeth and a deep dimple in her left cheek. It changed her; made her cute, if not beautiful. He smiled back and said, "I laughed, so I'm the one who's sorry."

She met him the next day, Saturday. She had her brother's Plymouth, a beauty, and she let him drive it. The brother was the guy who had seemed worried in the bowling alley, so she wasn't there with a boyfriend. She wanted to see the countryside and he drove her to LaGrange and they got out and walked and he even took her to the stream where he'd first laid Mary Straub. She went back to the city on Monday, but she gave him her address.

It was eleven months later that Mister Bennet told him to go to New York City and see his friend at the Fourth Precinct. Eddy was packed that night, and on the train the next morning with two suitcases and a big trunk borrowed from his landlady. He had everything he owned, including his two hundred and eighty dollars in savings. And he was a rookie patrolman operating out of the Fourth within three months; they didn't have extended Police Academy courses and college courses thirty-three years ago; and he'd been a cop that long, that damned long . . .

He ordered another Scotch and Glen said, "Past your bedtime, Eddy, or are you off tomorrow?"

"No, got Sunday and Monday off for a while. More Scotch and less ice this time."

"Yeah, sure," Glen muttered, and he was insulted because he always gave the regulars more than he had to.

Roersch hadn't looked up Helen right away. He'd been on the force almost a year before he'd dropped her a card. She answered and they met at the Paramount in Times

Square and saw a show and went out for dinner. He was lonely and she was lonely and they began to date. He still wasn't sure he loved her. He hadn't been sure of love, of what it was, since Mary Straub.

Six months later, she brought up the subject of marriage in that straight-out way of hers. "There's a man who wants to marry me. I can't put him off forever, and I want a home and family. I'd prefer you, Eddy. I'm in love with you. I have to know what you feel."

He told her he wasn't sure. She said, "Thank you for being honest. Would you take me home now?"

On the bus, he told her a cop didn't make that much money, had late tours of duty regularly, could get hurt, even killed. She said, "I understand, Eddy. You don't have to give reasons."

At her door, he asked if he could see her again. She said, "It would make me unhappy. I don't like being unhappy, Eddy." She kissed him and went inside.

He didn't see her for two months. Then he came to her home and took her for a walk and asked if she would marry him. She said, "Are you sure?" He said yes, though he wasn't; had decided he was hurting her, and that she was the best woman he would ever know . . . but that still didn't mean love.

It had never changed, though he'd never cared more for any other woman, never had more than a one-night stand with some piece, never fallen or had a real affair like his old friend at the Fourth, Jimmy Weir, now a lieutenant at Patrol Boro Manhattan North. Jimmy had fallen in love at forty-five with a young chick and blown his marriage and married the chick, and she left him inside of a year. But Jimmy always said the six months before he'd married her and the six months after were the only happy days he'd ever known.

Maybe that was a clue to what was wrong with *him*, Roersch thought. He'd had so many happy days as a kid in LaGrange, maybe he'd used up his quota. Maybe that was why he couldn't love like Weir, like Helen, like in the movies; *heavy* love. Maybe that was why despite thirty-one years together and all Helen had done to try to make him happy, their apartment had never felt like home to him.

So where *was* home?

Back forty years in LaGrange.

Go home, Eddy. Get a time machine and go home.

He checked his watch. Almost one. He'd be a tired bull tomorrow.

And yet, he didn't want to go back to the apartment . . . with Ruthie and her trick down the hall.

No, he didn't want to go back to the apartment.

He focused on Page Four of the *Daily News*. The story was headlined:

NUDE, MUTILATED AND DUMPED IN GARBAGE

The sub-head and story more than paid off the sensational headline, along with a teletype photo of a blanket-covered body being handed into an ambulance. "Sex, alcohol and evisceration bring attractive brunette to her last ride," the picture caption read.

Body of Girl Found in Motel Garbage Bin
Causes Fears of St. Louis Jack the Ripper

St. Louis, Mo., May 17

Dressed only in black leather boots, the body of an attractive young brunette was discovered at noon today by garbage collectors emptying a large metal bin behind the parking lot of the Wayside Inn Motel. Roy Veeks, who saw the body tumble into his truck when the bin was tilted by automatic lever, said, "First I thought it was an animal, a sheep maybe, or a hog. Because it was like a butcher shop, her stomach open and everything hanging out."

The girl, unidentified several hours after discovery, was described as in her early twenties, about five feet five, dark hair and eyes, "plump and pretty" according to coroner's assistant Harold Cohen. Mr. Cohen stated that her death was "horrible, among the worst I've seen in five years on the job." The victim had been stabbed repeatedly in the chest and neck, and her stomach opened "laterally, from right hip up toward left breast." Her intestines had been pulled out and draped around the victim's neck and shoulders.

The coroner estimated the time of death as between nine and twelve hours before the body was discovered, or midnight to three a.m. It was also established that the victim had experienced sexual union shortly before death, and that she had consumed considerable amounts of alcohol. Whether or not rape was involved was undetermined, but because of her nudity and traces of semen in her sex organ, it was assumed the crime was sexual in nature. Police and newsmen here could think of no crime in recent years that matched this for sheer brutality. Lieutenant Paul Holmer, in charge of the case, said, "The *modus operandi*, the style of this killer, has no parallel in our active files."

New York has at least two unsolved murders that come close, though sexual union wasn't indicated in either the Jane Austen or Corinne Bain murders, as it wasn't in the "Slaughter-House Slaying" of model Judith Keel last Sunday. Veteran detectives caution against the drawing of lines between such mutilation and evisceration murders because there are a dozen or more scattered across the country in any given year.

Wayside Inn employees were shown photographs of the victim's face and couldn't identify her as a guest. The manager, Irving Watterman, said that police weren't automatically assuming she'd been killed in or near the motel, or had anything to do with the plush Wayside Inn. "She could just as well have been killed somewhere else and brought to our bin because it's so large, and because it's emptied in mid-day, giving someone a chance to get away. We've checked every room, and our maids report no sign of such a bloody crime. It's my hope that this will prove to be unconnected with the Wayside Inn."

As of now, police have no murder weapon, witnesses, or leads of any kind. And the nude-in-black-boots has no clothes and no name.

Having read the story carefully, Roersch wondered whether *he* wasn't drawing lines between unconnected murders. Evisceration, gutting a victim, was as old as humanity itself, and not the exclusive property of any one killer. And Keel was a whole different style . . .

Roersch went to the phone, got the number of the Wayside Inn, St. Louis, from Information, dialed the operator and asked her to connect him. He dropped in three quarters, and heard the phone ring at the other end. "Wayside Inn, good evening."

"Mr. Evan Bley."

"Just a moment." It was a long moment. "Do you have his room number?"

"Afraid I don't."

"He's not listed with us."

"He might have left earlier today. He was supposed to tell me where to meet him."

"I'll connect you with the message center."

"Make it the desk. Maybe I've got the wrong motel."

"A moment, please."

This time it was a few seconds: "Reservations, can I help you?"

"I asked the operator to check on whether a friend of mine, Mr. Evan Bley, was at your motel earlier today. He might have left something for me."

"Bley . . . a moment . . . yes, he was here for two nights and left us early Thursday afternoon. Was it a package . . . ?"

Roersch hung up. He rolled the *News* tightly as he

walked to his car; made it into a thin, hard cylinder and slapped it against the palm of his left hand. He wasn't drawing any lines between the murders; they were being drawn for him.

Mr. Lowenthal of the A.A.A. had also drawn lines . . . on a map, and that map was in Roersch's zipper case. It showed Bley's route as passing through St. Louis, Oklahoma City, Kingman, Albuquerque, to Flagstaff and a sidetrip to the Grand Canyon. Reservations had been made at the Bright Angel Lodge, just as indicated on Bley's yellow pad. Bley had also asked for a Triptik to Las Vegas, saying he might go there instead of directly to Los Angeles. No reservations in Las Vegas, and he still expected to be in L.A. for his reserved two-night stay at the Bel Air Hotel.

So the lines were clear. He just hoped Bley hadn't left any for some St. Louis detective to follow.

He drove home and got into pajamas; then had a last cigarette at the kitchen table, going through the material in his portfolio and in Bley's attaché case. It all added up. In fact, he wished it would *stop* adding up. *No more, Mr. Bley!* Otherwise, police from here to Los Angeles would be in on it!

He flipped through his notebook. Nothing he'd learned today had weakened his case against Bley . . . and he'd been checking out leads from the time he'd left the Auto Club and returned to the station. Mostly by phone.

Vince McKenney's mother had confirmed her son's alibi for Sunday.

Bley had no permit to own a handgun in the city; or anywhere else in New York State, according to the records in Albany.

Judith Keel's father had answered when Roersch phoned their home in Rye. He said he'd given a statement to some officer or other—"or was it a coroner's office employee?"—and it was no trouble at all to repeat it. Neither he nor his wife knew anyone who would want to hurt Judith. "We were aware that she had a few men friends, very few actually, and that among them was a man named Evan Bley whom she was fond of. But Judith wasn't involved in any serious love affairs, and she was quite content pursuing her job and career and living quietly. She was a good girl, Sergeant. I know that sounds like a foolish cliché, but in Judith's case it is . . . was . . . quite literally true. She didn't date often, and then usually someone we *all* knew and trusted. She was content with her home life, her acting and modeling training, her plans for the future. Our Judy was not one of your modern swingers."

Roersch said he would do his best, personally, to bring the news media up to date, and that meant to a clearer picture of the kind of girl Judy had been. He added that it was his opinion that someone she didn't know, a total stranger, a psychotic intruder, had committed the crime.

"Yes," Keel said. "No one who knew Judy would do such a thing. Such a terrible . . ." His voice broke and he excused himself.

Roersch had left the station again, partly to get away from Chauger's rigid back, and Hawly's too frequent and too casual strolls from his office, but mainly to check on Nick McKenney. The super told him McKenney had left "sometime last night . . . right after you were here, I think, 'cause I heard him moving around and drawers and doors and whatnot. Went into his place this morning. Some stuff still there, but most of his things're gone. You want me to call you if he shows up?" Roersch had said no; Mr. McKenney wasn't wanted for anything.

He'd returned to the station and used the portable typewriter under Jones's desk to work on his reports. He wrote up Jones's visit to Nick McKenney, just as it had taken place, but without any of the detective's speculation. Which left Judith Keel clean, and Bley with no motive for murder. He wrote up his own visit to Nick as a routine double-check, to clear up questions of Bley's attitude and Keel's activities, and ended with: "The private investigator, Nicholas McKenney, stated that his report for the Congrove Agency (Xerox copy secured by Detective Jones, attached) was correct in all details. He also stated that Mr. Bley had met with him to have personal contact with the surveillance, and that in his opinion Mr. Bley was satisfied with the accuracy of the report. Mr. Bley will be questioned on his return from vacation, but the investigation is continuing in other directions. A robbery with psycho sex offshoot by person or persons unknown to the victim . . ."

Jones had come in at that point. The lab tests hadn't taken very long, because the knives hadn't been used on living tissue, so far as residue on the blades indicated. "But in the joinings of blades to handles . . ." Jones said. He paused as Roersch leaned forward tensely. "There were elements of wood on the switchblade, and elements of bread or pastry on the kitchen knife." He smiled as Roersch leaned back. "Now do I get promoted from *Sanford and Son* to *The F.B.I.?*"

Roersch re-tagged the knives, saying he'd confirmed ownership. He was careful to speak softly because of Chauger, though Chauger had been staying as far away from him as possible, not even *looking* his way. He wrote McKenney's and Bley's names on the tags, now that the knives were harmless. He then went back to his report, adding the information on the knives, not worrying about anyone asking how he'd secured Bley's. Only if the lab tests had turned up incriminating evidence would anyone have questioned methods and legality, because only then would a defense attorney have had a chance to yell mistrial.

He looked through the other reports, to see if they contradicted anything he'd written, or led in a direction he wanted to block. Satisfied, he turned to the Jane Austen and Corinne Bain files; then realized everyone was gone except for Hawly and the desk man, and the next tour was drifting in. He put the files in his zipper case, and phoned

Jimmy Weir at Patrol Boro Manhattan North. "He's gone," a Sergeant Craig said. "This Eddy Roersch? Weir said if you called he's at Danziger's."

Roersch had driven way downtown to Erickson Place, the neighborhood of the Fourth Precinct and of the old German restaurant. Danziger's hadn't been robbed once in thirty-four years, because there was always a cop or two eating there and the station close by. The old kraut used to say it was a hell of a lot cheaper serving a few meals on the pad than being robbed, especially since he limited the freebies to the inexpensive specials.

He'd found Jimmy at a wooden booth in back. They had three beers—for which they paid—and the waiter said tonight they were overstocked on schnitzel, which was fine with Roersch. They ate schnitzel and boiled potatoes and red cabbage, and Jimmy belched and said, "What's wrong, Eddy? Why so quiet tonight?" Eddy said, "Tired," and realized he had nothing to say to his old friend. He never bulled Jimmy, and to talk his thoughts, his plans, his activities since he'd last seen Jimmy a week ago tonight, was impossible.

He led Jimmy into reminiscences of Teresa, his young ex-wife, a subject Jimmy never tired of, could go on about for hours. How she'd played his daughter in order to save money on their honeymoon flight to Jamaica. How she'd been asked for her I.D. at a bar one time, and flashed his badge, lifted from his wallet without his knowledge, saying, "Vice Squad, kiddy patrol," to a shocked waitress. Of how young, good-looking guys were always after her, because she was so pretty, so cute, so full of life, and how she always played straight with Jimmy, was always faithful . . . until she told him she'd met someone and was going to marry him and goodbye. "And even then, she was straight," Jimmy said, swishing a little beer around in the bottom of his glass, looking into it as if to find his lost joy. "Even then she didn't sneak around on me. And every Christmas there's a card, and every birthday there's a little present, but no return address. The postmark said Philadelphia, last time. I think if I'd had some money, *real* money, and been able to spend more time with her instead of with bunko artists and junkies and burglars and killers . . ."

Jimmy roused himself from the past. "Hell, I'll stand treat for a bottle of Liebfraumilch." But he'd made Eddy think of another cute young chick and how he might have her all for himself when *he* got real money.

He had left Jimmy with his memories and gone to Glen's. And was surprised at himself for thinking of Ruthie so much, of wanting her two, three nights in a row, when he'd considered himself old for that kind of action.

Roersch began clearing the kitchen table, putting everything away; then looked at the files of the two unsolved murders. They were thin enough for quick reading.

He opened the Austen folder, and was suddenly sick of psycho-murders and nude corpses and plans and cons. He wanted something sweet and simple. LaGrange was lost, and Ruthie seemed a close second tonight.

Maybe her trick hadn't stayed after all. She said that sometimes when they bought a full night, they left in the early morning hours, played out, preferring their hotels, or wives, for sleep.

But he was embarrassed to call a *third* time. Especially at two in the morning. She'd think he was nuts.

He was in bed, lights out, eyes closed, when he reached for the phone. Ruthie answered on the first ring, wide awake and irritable. "*Yes?* Who is it?"

"Eddy. Just wanted to say goodnight. Okay?"

She was silent a moment; then said, "Okay," voice very soft.

He was finally able to sleep.

14: | Friday a.m.

He had been lying on the bed, clothed, the lights off, listening to Lois breathing slow, heavy breaths, almost gasps. Now he got up and put on his shoes, and got his short leather jacket and made sure the key was in the pocket. He went out, closing the door quietly behind him. The motel was a one-story barracks in the shape of a large U, the open end facing the road, a dark road off Highway 40 and Route 66. They were in the center of the north wing, and all around was darkness and a silence made even more dense by a light, spring insect-humming. The smell was delicate; mildly sweet. No lush, heavy, Hudson Valley vegetation here. It was dryer, thinner in Oklahoma . . . strange and therefore exciting.

The silence was disturbed by sudden laughter from a room on the other side. It broke the spell. He looked, listened, heard faint music, then more loud laughter. He went next door to John's room and light showed through the drapes of the picture window. He knocked, and John opened the door. He too was dressed and wide awake. "Hey, we going someplace?"

"I'd like to look around."

Teeth illuminated the hairy face. "Been *dying* to find some action!" He went to the bed and sat down, putting on his big-heeled, multi-colored shoes. "You hear that party across the way? I walked over a while ago to see what was doing. Some business-types and girls . . . saw them when a dude came out to get cigarettes from the machine at the office. I asked if it was open house, and he said it was poker, hundred-dollar minimum. He wasn't too friendly, but I'll bet if we went over together . . . You play poker?"

"When there's nothing better to do."

"*Correct.* Let's check out the terrain. But those girls looked foxy. Hookers, maybe, latching onto a heavy-bread situation." He laced the second shoe and stood up. "One thing's sure, they weren't the salemen's wives!"

"What would Lois say?"

John was getting his denim jacket, and turned quickly to look at him. "It's your play, of course. I wouldn't want to make trouble . . ."

"No trouble, as long as she's sleeping."

John's caution evaporated on the instant. "She wouldn't have to know, would she?" He got his key and almost *ran* to the door. "We can just kick around and whatever happens, you know . . . I'd just as soon *talk*, man."

They went to the car and drove onto the road, heading away from the steak house and the highway, away from where they'd come. John was bubbling, and Evan asked if he'd been in Oklahoma before.

"Not to stay. What's in Oklahoma? There's Lawton and Oklahoma City and Fort Smith and Tulsa, and I saw them all when I wanted to see everything. If you live someplace and have family and friends and action going, then it's different, it's home, and that's where it's at for you. But only a few towns work for strangers, people in off the road. Towns like L.A. and Frisco and Chi and Boston and New York. Sure, they can *kill* you, those towns, but they still got things going, things to see and do, things to hold you."

Evan nodded slightly, driving through unbroken darkness, waiting for lights and life to appear. It was only twelve-thirty; there had to be *something* open.

John said, "Like right here, for instance. Say we're *walking* along this road, trying to find a room and then people to dig and then a job. *Scary*, correct?"

Evan couldn't conceive of it, or didn't want to. He slowed. "There doesn't seem to be anything in this direction. What do you think?"

"Turn around. At least we know the restaurant's back there, and they had a bar off the side. It might be open late. And then there's the highway, and something might be doing on the *other* side, you never know."

They turned and headed back. John said, "Is it raining?" A moment later, Evan picked up the mist on his windshield, and a moment after that it became a steady pattern of drops and rivulets. He set the wipers on low, but by the time they passed the motel he had to put them on high. Not a downpour, but a steady, heavy fall. They raised their windows, Evan leaving his open about two inches for the *smell* of it, the increasing sweetness of air. Things were soaking up that water out there; things were drinking, enjoying, growing. It made the night more beautiful.

"Goddamn rain," John muttered.

"Not so bad."

"Guess not. Guess I'm still functioning by a hitcher's standards. Rain like this keeps you crouched, huddling under a plastic or canvas or slicker if you're lucky. Then you watch for headlights and step out and thumb 'em and get water down your neck and after an hour, if no ride, you're a soaked rag. At the beginning, just out of Frisco on my way east along the northern routes, I had some good equipment, an Army poncho and flap-hat, and I didn't mind the rain so much, especially in Yellowstone." He nodded to himself. "Though I don't think I'll ever like *snow* again. Jesus, hitching out of Denver in December, and my feet turning *blue*, and the snow starting again. I was afraid I'd die and they wouldn't find me until spring; I'd be a little bump in a drift at the side of the road. And Chicago in January, with that wind and a lousy eight bucks for the first ten days. Got a good job, though, and met a nice guy who used to invite me to his folks' place for dinner where I'd load up on *real* food, not cafeteria shit, to last me until the next dinner. His cousin Meg— remembered her name!—Meg was good-looking. She was engaged, but the guy was in the Navy and we had a nice three months. Then he came back and he'd heard stories and came looking for me." He shook his head.

"Did he find you?"

"Yes," he said slowly. "He was a sailor and thought he was tough, but like most guys he didn't really know how to fight. Had a stance and threw punches, but no way. I put him down three times; then I ran because I was afraid I'd kill him if he kept getting up. And hitched out and then St. Louis and then Philly and out of there *fast* and Boston and New York the first time and down south to Florida and back up the coast with stops all along the way and then New York for the big stay, almost three years. And damned glad to get out!" He looked at Evan and quickly added, "Not that New Yorkers aren't . . ."

"Don't apologize to *me*," Evan interrupted. "I hope never to see Fun City again."

They came to the steak house. It was dark; the parking lot empty. They went on. The rain held steady; the windshield wipers slapped rhythmically; the Jaguar swished along on its radials. John said, "This car is something else!

But I'd bet my Dad would lecture you about the Mercedes being less trouble, less upkeep, less repairs. Half of Beverly Hills has Mercedes, sedans and sports coupes."

They came to the highway overpass. The rain increased. Evan slowed a little, but continued to enjoy the ride, thinking the slashing lines of rain in his headlights were beautiful; everything tonight was beautiful.

"How'd you become an advertising writer?" John asked.

Evan smiled, thinking of it. "You'll find it hard to believe." He asked for a cigarette. "I was teaching high school English and not at all happy about it. I wanted to be a writer . . . not an advertising writer. I read a lot, and had written some poetry in high school and college, and I wanted to be a writer of fiction—short stories and novels. I had several ideas . . ."

He sucked smoke, still smiling a little, the day-by-day anguish of his teaching, of his living at home with Mom, dim now, remote now . . . until he remembered how Dad had died. His smile went away and he spoke quickly to block the memory. "I registered with several employment agencies, asking for editorial jobs. I had a Master's in English Literature, and I was willing to take on anything. The employment counselor at one agency was rushed, and I wasn't a very good prospect for a big fee anyway, so he didn't consider my preference important. When he gave me an appointment card for a Tate Incorporated, I assumed it was a small publisher. It turned out to be a small advertising agency, and I figured as long as I was there I'd try for the job, as a temporary measure, expediency, just to get out of teaching. I wrote a few sample ads, was interviewed by the creative director and agency owner, and got the job. Within six months I went to a major agency, and after that it was advancement after advancement and no time to look back at publishing."

"Jesus, what a break!" John exclaimed. "That's the kind of thing you hear whenever important men, successes and big-money earners, tell about their lives. Always some little turn in the road, some funny mistake or switch in signals. Imagine if you'd *gotten* that job with a publisher? You'd probably be a small-time editor right now, or a hack writer. Or even if you'd done all right, you probably wouldn't be making seventy grand. They don't pay that kind of bread in publishing do they?"

"At my level, I doubt it."

But Evan wondered, as he always did, what might have happened if Tate Inc. had been a publisher. Not that he had any regrets, or illusions that he would have done nearly as well. But less success, less money didn't necessarily preclude more personal happiness. He might have become a less agonized person much earlier in the game. He might have escaped the insanities and agonies of living on with his mother, of Merri and Judy and the other *courvas*, of self-torture far into adulthood. Reading for a living and editing and writing *full* sentences, *full* thoughts, concepts other than BUY, might have helped him to self-awareness and maturity. He'd recognized a long time ago that copywriting was a form of *shorthand*—a frantic, inventive, clever, short-handing of reality, of universal themes, of self-analysis. A short-handing of life.

But still, no regrets . . . except for the *timing* of his switch to advertising; the argument it had precipitated with his father just hours before he'd died; the things he'd said that he'd wanted to take back, and couldn't.

It still hurt, though he no longer had that incredible, neurotic guilt; no longer felt he had killed his father.

Now he blamed his mother, insofar as he blamed anyone. His mother and cholesterol.

Lights shimmered through the rain. John said, "Well all right! There's life on the planet after all!" He bent forward, peering; then clapped his hands and bounced on the seat, a bearded infant exuding joy. "See it? The Rogues Club!"

Evan's eyes were no longer that good. It was another few seconds before he could make out the neon lettering.

"With a name like that," John said, "there's gotta be

pussy hanging around. In fact," he said, making sniffing sounds as Evan pulled into the parking lot, "I can smell it from here!"

"Few others can," Evan said, cutting lights and ignition. There were three cars and a pickup truck headed in against the square frame building. And one or two of them had to belong to the staff.

But it was the only game in town, and they ran through the rain and opened the door and stepped inside.

The room was smaller than the building; storage area or kitchen lay in back. There were five little tables and eight or nine bar stools, and it was dimly lighted in blues and reds, except for a little circular stage behind the bar. On that stage a young redhead in lacy diaphanous bottoms and sparkler pasties danced to hard rock music under a yellow-white light. She was medium-sized, except for her breasts; they were large. When she turned her back to the bar and bent and swiveled her hips, she showed a tight, round bottom. She was pretty in a small-featured, vacant-faced way, and didn't bother to smile when she faced her audience again. That audience was composed of the bald, gut-heavy bartender, a cocktail waitress in bikini and high heels, and three youngish men, two sitting together drinking beer, the third at a table talking to the waitress.

John murmured, "I didn't expect the Whiskey A-Go-Go, but this is *sad*."

Evan glanced at him, surprised. John wasn't looking at the dancer or the waitress. John was looking at the *men*.

They reached the bar and sat down, three stools removed from the beer drinkers.

"Hey," the dancer said, waving and smiling. Evan smiled back, but John was lighting a cigarette and shifting around on his stool. He looked tense.

Evan was about to ask what was wrong, when the bartender walked up. He was big, barrel-chested, thick of arm in his short-sleeved white shirt. He was also sullen. "Yes?" he asked.

"Good evening," Evan said.

The man waited.

"Scotch on the rocks," Evan said.

"Same," John said, looking at his cigarette.

The bartender said, "You paying for *both*?" to Evan.

Evan stared at him. "That's a strange question. What difference does it make which of us pays? He's of age."

John touched his arm and gave a little shake of the head.

The bartender said, "Just so long as *someone* pays." He stood there.

Evan felt himself going white. Now he understood John's tension. John had picked up on something here; something alien to Evan. "How much?" he asked.

"Two-forty."

Evan put down a five. The bartender took it and went to a register and rang up the sale. He brought back the change, and only then got glasses and scooped ice and poured the drinks. He brought them over and put them down and walked to the two men drinking beer. He leaned there, his back to John and Evan, and talked. The two men wore tan work clothes and heavy shoes. The man at the table was in a rumpled suit and skinny tie. "Stump-jumpers," John said, but he barely whispered. "Goddamn fucking stump-jumpers."

"Forget it," Evan said, and was still angry, and didn't know what to do about it.

The two men drinking beer looked their way. One laughed and turned back to the other and Evan heard, ". . . stand hippies, but an *old* freak . . ." There was general laughter from the three of them, and "Fuckin' pansies" as a closer.

John drank. He looked at the dancer. He whispered, "Nothing here. Let's try that poker game. Hick places . . ." He shook his head. "Happens sometimes."

Evan turned to look at the table. The man there looked back at him, curiously, as if at an exhibit. But the waitress looked back with interest and a tentative smile. Then she glanced at the others and the smile faded and she looked upset.

The dancer finished her number. Evan applauded and no one else did and she gave him a vulgar little bow, spreading her knees with her hands. He laughed as loud as he could, and said, "That deserves a drink."

The bartender turned to the girl. "You got another number in this set."

"No, Walt, I finished my set. Punched my four numbers and the jukebox's stopped, hasn't it? I get five minutes . . ."

The bartender said, "Another number," and walked to the end of the bar and leaned over to a lighted jukebox and punched a button. Rock music by the Jackson Five pounded into the room. The girl stood with hands on hips, staring. "Holy *cow*, Walt! What's wrong with you?"

He went back to the beer drinkers, and now all three stared at Evan and John; hard stares from hard men; laborer types, physical types. John kept looking at his drink, and Evan wanted to do the same . . . but he stared back at the three men. The bartender said something, voice low and blocked out by the music, but Evan was sure he'd read the word "Jew" on his lips. And John, whose eyes and ears were better than his, suddenly said, "Let's get out of here." He was no longer whispering. "C'mon, they ain't worth the trouble."

One of the two beer drinkers half rose. The bartender pushed him back down with a hand on his shoulder. "Long as they're leaving," he said.

Evan turned to the man at the table. "Perhaps *you* could tell me what country this is, what century this is?"

The man looked at the bartender and grinned, and Evan realized he was another one of the boys, in different dress but with the same mentality.

The waitress said, "Walt, *c'mon* now," pleading.

The bartender said, "You want to go home, Cleo, it's all right. We'll close soon anyway. Not enough business." He turned to look at the stage, where the dancer was barely moving. "Give your friends their money's worth," he said.

The girl stepped down from the stage and walked around the back, away from the bartender, toward where Evan and John were sitting. She said, "This is too much. Because someone wants to buy me a drink . . ."

"It's the clothing," Evan said. He touched his leather jacket; he looked down at his tie-dyes and suede boots. "It makes them look bad, feel bad. As does my friend's beard and mustache and long hair. And clothing. All this threatens their fragile masculinity. But only because they're idiots."

John got off the stool as the bartender took a step toward them and the two beer drinkers rose. The man at the table got up and walked out the door. The dancer said, "He didn't mean it, Walt. He got angry because you acted so *grouchy.*"

John said to Evan, "Well, that tears it. I agree with you, but I'd have liked better odds."

The dancer came around the bar, running, and stepped between John and the beer drinkers. "C'mon, now! I want the drink the gentleman promised!"

The bartender said, "Did you call me an idiot, you freaky Jew hip?"

Evan said, "I called you an idiot, you pot-bellied imbecile."

The bartender was lurching forward and the beer drinkers were up and moving and the waitress cried out. The dancer simply turned and walked to the waitress in a way that showed surrender to the inevitable. Evan admired her logic, even as he saw the massive arm reaching for his neck. Even as he grasped the thick wrist in both his hands and twisted with all his strength and let go as the man grunted and bent. He then leaned over the bar, chopping rightward with stiff left hand and leftward with stiff right hand. He caught the thick neck twice, and the bartender went down, and he turned to where John was swinging and ducking, trying to handle the two beer drinkers.

Evan came off the stool. He was happy now. The training he'd taken so seriously had paid off. He saw John land a very good blow to one man's cheek. That man stumbled to the side and was clear enough to be approached. Evan approached him, saying, *"Here!"* The man recovered and sent out a fist. Evan turned his right side and kicked and struck the rib cage. The man went *"Uuuuh!"* Evan karate-punched and struck the neck and the man sat down and Evan kicked him in the side of the head, just hard enough, he hoped, to end his part in the fight.

John was doing very well with the other beer drinker, panting and cursing and punching and driving the man back toward the jukebox. Doing well and needing no help . . . but Evan had more jukarte training in him; had what his instructor had called "fighting spirit," which was actually forty-six years, at that time, of rage and fear and hate for all mankind stored up in him, bottled tightly and waiting to explode. So he had to do *more* . . . and heard the dancer yell, "Walt, you bastard!" and saw something to his right and slightly behind him. He crouched and turned and reached up all at the same time. And caught a hammer blow on his shoulder that drove him to his knees, but didn't stop him. He grasped the white shirt and fell on his back, pulling the bartender onto him. He caught the heavy body on the soles of his shoes and pushed up and used the man's own momentum to send him and his wooden billy flying.

He rose before the bartender could, and kicked judiciously, and heard himself laughing, saying, "Now you're a *bloody* idiot, as our English cousins would say."

The bartender said, "Fuck . . . enough!" thickly, spitting teeth and blood. John came over to stand beside him and John's opponent was leaning against the far wall with hands up, angry bruises and a cornered look on his face. John panted, "Was I ever . . . goddamn lucky not to . . . try and take . . . you!"

Which was the laurel wreath, the accolade, something

that had eluded him until now. He had learned to ski and swim and trout-cast and play tennis and run four to six miles, but years too late to eradicate failure at stickball. He had worked hard at jukarte, winning praise and belts in the *randori*, the mock-combat, but it hadn't erased childhood humiliation at Seymour's hands.

Until *this!* This was the conquest he had needed. Not praise and belts, but the prize of blood. *Blood* was what counted!

He threw his arm around John's shoulder. "You're a tiger."

"Then what the hell are you, a herd of elephants?"

They laughed, and the beer drinker against the wall moved to his friend on the floor and struggled and helped him out the door. The bartender sat up.

"Would you like to call the police?" Evan asked, arm still around John.

John muttered, "Hey, man, no need . . ."

"That's all right," Evan said. "I'll be glad to make the call for him, if he says so."

The dancer came over and took each by an arm and pulled them away. "That'll only make trouble for us and we've got trouble enough in this county, what with the Ladies Temperance after us, and not only for booze." She opened the door, and whispered, "Where you staying? Keep it low."

"Gladtimes Motel," Evan said.

"Room eight," John said, and added, "Bring your friend."

They walked to the car, and John was rubbing his hands together and talking a blue streak. "I knew right off it was a bummer. I've seen those faces and clothes and *looks* in a hundred towns, mostly South but other sections too. But I figured Oklahoma . . . well, I stopped only in the cities and I never had bread enough for bars and clubs . . ." He went on and on, the words tumbling out, vocalizing the exhilaration Evan felt.

They drove to the motel and went to John's room. Only then did Evan feel the pain in his right shoulder. He took off his jacket and shirt, and saw the big red blotch. He touched it, and it hurt, but not too much. Besides, it was a badge, a medal, a souvenir of victory.

They both washed up, and John touched his lip, which was puffing. "We got off easy. Where'd you ever learn to scramble like that?"

Evan shrugged, still little-boy pleased, but beginning to recover his sense of self—*adult* self—and turned on the television. He glanced at the wall behind the bed. It was the wall between their two rooms, and he wondered if Lois would be disturbed.

Probably not. She was sleeping, and their bed was on the *other* wall.

Still, he lowered the volume; and decided to check on her, to see if she was all right.

The dancer and the waitress arrived as he was buttoning his shirt. The waitress had a pint of Scotch—"One good drink for all of us," she said. They sat around drinking and John kept looking at the redheaded dancer, Marie, who was about twenty-two, twenty-three, and who in turn kept looking at Evan. Marie said, "Walt's a dumb square. But part of the trouble tonight was he's been trying to make it with me for the last week . . . I only been working there about ten days. I can't see it, no how, not for love . . ." she gave a sharp laugh . . . "or money. He just turns me off. So when he got the idea I was angling toward you . . ."

John waited, not making a move, sitting back and letting Evan have his choice. But Evan wanted them to be equals tonight, because they'd shared the combat and the victory. Besides, the waitress was taller, plumper, bigger in the rear, not as pretty as the dancer, but more suggestive in manner, more his taste. He finished his drink and took her by the hand and said, "Shall we?"

The dancer rose, "Whyn't we *all*?"

They undressed and got into bed.

She'd awakened, having to run to the bathroom, and done the whole bit again, retching on an empty stomach. She figured Evan had decided to sleep in John's room, and she didn't blame him. But she felt alone. When she returned to bed, she heard noise from next door. She didn't know where John's room was, having conked out without asking, but she put the water glass from the bathroom against the wall and her ear to the glass. And she heard and she knew.

The bastards!

She was too weak to stand there for long, and who wanted to hear them doing their dirty tricks anyway!

Back in bed, she pulled the covers over her head . . . and imagined Evan balling and grouping and hated him. And heard him give that special kind of yell.

Damn, damn, damn! One night sick and they did this to her. She'd been wrong to trust John, to think of him as her friend. He'd be the one to suggest hunting. He had it in for her; hated her for ditching him in front of Evan.

They'd gone out and met some girls and nature had taken its course. But tomorrow they'd be back on the road; at least she hoped she'd be well enough to travel. Evan wouldn't play around if she was available. And she'd *be* available! She liked him, dug his sex, could see a long stretch with him . . . and if later, after she'd begun acting, he wanted to split, okay! But that wouldn't be for a long time; maybe years.

Nothing to sweat about, whatever was happening next door.

Sex was like food . . . you took a meal here and you took a meal there. But once you had a home, *that* was where you took your meals. She'd provide that home for Evan.

John was something else. John was a problem. He'd

want action, and he'd want it with Evan. Because Evan paid the bills. And more than that, because Evan gave him the security he needed.

John had to go. She'd forgotten that for a while. Now she knew it had to happen, and soon. John would pull Evan in other directions. John had nothing to gain and everything to lose from Evan's sticking with her.

She thought about it for a while. She made and discarded plans. She decided to play it by ear, and drifted into a half-sleep.

Men, always her problem. She remembered L.A. just after arriving from Australia, newly divorced. She remembered looking up some people from Sydney, a married couple, and the man making a pitch for her after only three days' sleeping on their couch. She remembered working as a waitress, and losing the job because some makeout guy pushed her too hard and she blew up. She remembered going to the Crazy Panther topless club on Sunset with a date, and coming back alone, and getting a job as a dancer.

And Cy, the actor who gave her lessons in passion as well as drama, and who turned out to be a sick junkie. She'd run from the memory of waking up and seeing him sticking a needle in his arm.

She ran to New York, where it didn't change. She worked first in the Garden of Allah Massage Palace and later, after meeting John and having a few good months and then getting the tights, the rages, because of his trying to *own* her, working at the Bantam Royal Club in Greenwich Village.

And the tights, the rages, had been with her forever. And they'd started back when she didn't want to remember. And they'd led to her going to hospital, like Dad, after she and Mitchel broke up and he sent her the divorce papers and Clothilde turned out to be a bitch who laughed when Lois said she would be a great actress.

Between Mitchel and Clothilde she'd gone mental, and

it had been a lost time and she wouldn't remember and it would never happen again . . .

And she was frightened.

She was awake an hour later when Evan stepped inside and took off his shoes near the door and padded to the bathroom. The shower ran, and she was glad he hadn't tried to get into bed with her still stinking of cunt. She might have screamed him out . . . might have blown it all . . .

He came back and slipped in beside her, and she murmured, "Honey? Where were you?"

"Did I wake you? I'm sorry. Are you feeling better?" He touched her face.

"A little better. Where were you?"

"John suggested a ride and we went up and down the road. We had a few drinks and talked to a few people. Better get some sleep."

"What time is it?"

He curled on his side, his back to her. "Don't know. Good night."

She came up close to him. "Evan? Hey, do you want . . . you know?"

"It wouldn't be smart," he said. "Not when you're ill."

She moved her hand along his leg, around front to where the monster seemed changed to a worm, it was that small, that limp and withdrawn. He moved her hand away and said, "Let's wait for tomorrow, all right?"

She didn't answer.

He turned and looked at her. "Is there anything wrong?"

She wanted to tell him what a fucking liar he was! She said, "No, just felt . . . lonely. See you in the morning. Ni-night."

"Ni-night," he laughed, and turned on his side again, and was out like a light.

She felt the looseness sweep through her bowels, and ran for the bathroom. After that she retched and stood leaning against the sink, head low, splashing water into her face. At least he hadn't hit her with the truth and said what-of-it. At least he'd worried about what she would think . . . like a husband in a movie or TV comedy . . . they always stuck with the wives when the chips were down. For once she was playing the wife part, the fiancée or lover part, not the cunt on the side. For once someone cared enough to lie to her, to protect her from hurt.

It made her feel better.

15: | Friday a.m and p.m.

Roersch signed in at the range in the basement of Manhattan West Homicide and was issued fifty rounds of .38-caliber ammunition and a set of "headphones" to block out the deafening blasts. It was only nine o'clock, but three of the five lanes were already taken. He took his position on the one to the far left. He fired six rounds rapid and six rounds slow, standing close in to the new targets—a paper drawing of a thug firing right-handed directly at *him*.

Roersch held his revolver with *both* hands, the left steadying the right, and crouched low, facing his target head-on. This wasn't the way pistol teams fired, nor was it the way he'd been taught back in Dutchess County as a sheriff's deputy. There they'd stood sideways, raising the pistol high for each shot, firing on the downward move of the gun. But that was a long time ago . . . and it wasn't combat training.

He reloaded for the second time and stepped back to the edge of the lane for long-range firing. He went through the rapid and slow firing procedures, and shrugged when his score showed he'd slipped a bit under his last session. His tired eyes, he figured. And his *will* to score high. Besides, his knees ached from protracted crouching.

He was reloading when the range supervisor, a young sergeant named Weinstein, came over and checked his targets. "Better than most, Eddy. We're getting a good crop of sociologists and a bad crop of marksmen. Want to try prone position now?"

Roersch lay down and went through twelve rounds. His score was better this time, mainly because he'd been resting. That made thirty-six rounds. Weinstein suggested he fire his remaining fourteen rounds at the crouch, rapid-fire, in close, "because that's the probability on the streets, right?"

Roersch said, "Right." If he'd said, "Wrong," Weinstein would have accepted it, and allowed him to fire as he wished. Because Eddy Roersch had been in four shootouts during his career, and killed a man and wounded two. The other shootout had ended in no-contest, with the criminal, a kid with a light automatic, getting away through the back of the drugstore he'd tried to rob. Eddy wondered where that kid was today . . . whether he'd taken the lesson presented by flying lead; whether he'd been as scared as Roersch and decided against risking his life again. Or had he robbed and killed, maybe *been* killed?

He finished and asked Weinstein if he could fire his own fifty rounds right away, then have his guns checked and leave before the lectures started. The sergeant looked pained. He, like most men on the force, had never fired a gun in line of duty, or had a gun fired at him. Roersch had learned it meant something. They respected the cop who'd been in combat. They deferred to him . . . even while some resented him. He didn't know *why*, since any sane man was scared shitless in a shootout.

"I'm sorry, Eddy, no can do. The Commissioner himself said all levels have to attend lectures." He paused. "Didn't any of them ever come in handy . . . I mean, when you were in a shootout?"

Eddy said, "Yeah, some," though he couldn't remember a single one. His first shootout had been over so quickly, he hadn't had time to remember anything at all, firing his gun without actually knowing it, and dropping to the pavement when a bullet fragmented the brick wall close to his ear. He'd heard a scream sometime during the exchange of shots between himself and the "armed robber leaving scene of crime on Seventh Avenue and Thirty-first Street." His partner had circled around behind a line of parked cars, hoping to get behind the gunman, and Eddy was suddenly sure that scream was Mulvaney's. But then the skinny mick had appeared, crouching, almost crawling down the dark street, and Eddy had raised himself and seen a man writhing on the pavement in a growing puddle of blood. It turned out he'd nailed him in the stomach with one of four shots.

He'd received a commendation for that. The robber was a parolee who'd failed to report for three months, using the time to pull off at least five heists. He couldn't be identified by the victim of the sixth, because that poor bastard had been shot to death in his West Side grocery for eighteen dollars and change, but the M.O. sure looked like his. The robber had recovered, and been sent back up for eight to twelve. He'd been paroled again. And had robbed again, and had killed, and been sent to the chair.

In common with most police officers, Roersch had a deep and abiding dislike for and mistrust of New York's judicial process, especially as pertained to crimes of violence. But when he heard hard-heads like Deverney offer *their* solutions, which amounted to execution or life imprisonment for anyone who fired a weapon during the course of a crime, and the elimination of the parole system for *all* crimes, he found himself backing rapidly away. He also found that think on it as he would—and he *had*, during arguments with Helen, who'd considered *him* a hard-head!—he could come up with nothing better than the system in use. Sure, he'd crack down harder on repeat robbers, and never parole a murderer at all . . . but then again, some robbers *did* go straight after a second, sometimes even a third rap, and not all killings were planned murders—some could be seen as extensions of self-defense.

It was too complex a matter for a cop. He'd hate to be around when the men who ran the department also ran the courts. And yet, that was what many cops and some politicians seemed to want.

He had his .38 checked out, and Weinstein said he could fire his off-duty automatic after the lectures. He said, "Gee, thanks," sourly, and Weinstein said, "If I could work it different, Eddy . . ." Roersch waved as he walked into the lecture room, which was really a storage room fitted out with folding chairs.

He sat there with seven other officers who had finished their initial firing procedure, waiting for a quorum of ten or more, and figured he was lucky at that. Some precincts didn't have their own ranges. And in summer, he might have had to go to the department's outdoor range at Rodman's Neck which was way the hell up in the North Bronx near Orchard Beach. That was a whole-day affair, and the goddamn racket of over a hundred fifty fire-lanes gave you a headache for a week. Not only handguns were fired there, but rifles, shotguns, machine guns, gas-grenade launchers, the whole police arsenal. It always reminded him of his third shootout.

His second shootout had been the kid that got away. His third had taken place shortly after he'd made detective and was full of ambition; the right time to come up against a madman with a shotgun holding his wife hostage in a third-floor Houston Street apartment. There'd been five radio cars and an emergency van and guys in bulletproof vests, and shotguns and tear gas and the works. But it was Roersch and his then sidekick, Jimmy Weir, who had gone up the steps, armed only with their service revolvers, clearing people out of apartments along the way, until they'd come to the right door. Sitting out in the hall was a little boy, maybe five or six, crying hysterically. Jimmy was good with kids, and held him and quieted him down and got him to talk. Seems the kid's daddy had come home from "vacation" and he'd "yelled at Mommy" and "Mommy tried to run away but Daddy had a big gun." The father had shoved the kid out and locked the door. The kid didn't know the rest, which was that the father had dragged the mother to a window and put the shotgun to her head and began screaming that he knew she was screwing around with "dozens of you dirty bums" and he was going to blow her brains out as soon as all the guilty men were there to see it. He'd been holding her for about half an hour now. He had the shotgun, a double-barreled affair as seen through binoculars, cocked and ready. The woman had screamed down to the first responding radiocar officers that they shouldn't come closer; he would kill her if they did.

Jimmy handed the kid to a patrolman. Eddy stood to one side of the door and Jimmy to the other, and Eddy put out his hand and slowly turned the knob. Locked, as the kid had said. If they tried to break it down, they would catch both barrels.

Jimmy looked at him and he looked at Jimmy and each waited for the other to suggest something. The cop who'd taken the kid downstairs came back and whispered, "The captain says not to do anything rash."

Roersch had wanted to laugh. *Rash!* He was shitting his pants! And what could they do anyway, without costing the woman her life?

They waited while a priest with a bullhorn tried to talk

the nut out of it. He shouted back that priests and nuns had ruined his life by advising his wife first to leave him and then to have him committed to a mental institution.

They waited while a doctor from Kings County tried a little psychology, saying that he knew Mr. Rinaldi—the nut's name—had been illegally committed, and he was going to have the wife arrested just as soon as Rinaldi allowed her to come down. The nut liked that, but said he'd punish her himself.

Roersch and Weir had been outside that door for more than an hour when word came from the captain that they were to try "a diversionary tactic," so that two officers could come down the fire escape from the roof. "Like what?" Roersch had whispered. "Like get him away from the window," the patrolman in bulletproof vest had answered, halfway down the stairs and crouching even there.

Roersch and Weir had exchanged a long look. It was earn-your-pay-and-pad time. Finally, Roersch motioned Jimmy further back, took a deep breath . . . and knocked on the door.

"Who is it?" the nut sang out, as if he were expecting friends.

"Western Union," Roersch answered. "Telegram for Mr. Rinaldi."

"Telegram? For *which* Mr. Rinaldi, Ricco or James?"

Weir's eyes were wide, his expression incredulous. Roersch jerked his head around to stare at the patrolman. The patrolman turned and spoke down the stairwell. The nut said, "Hey, which Rinaldi do you want?"

"The one that lives here," Roersch said, switching the service revolver to his left hand, wiping his sweaty right on his trousers, switching the gun back.

The cop on the stairs suddenly whispered, "*Ricco!*"

"Mr. Ricco Rinaldi," Roersch said. "It's addressed to Ricco Rinaldi. If he's not here, I'll take it back to the office. But it's important."

"I'm Ricco Rinaldi." Then they heard violent move-

ment, something fall, a woman crying. "Shhh!" the nut
said. "You want the telegram man to hear?" Footsteps
approached the door. "Important? What does it say?"

"We're not allowed to read the telegrams, Mr. Rinaldi."

"How about putting it under the door?"

"You've got to sign, Mr. Rinaldi. All I know is they said
it was a rush telegram and very important."

"From Kansas City?"

"I don't know where it's from. That's private. Only *you*
can know where it's from and what it says. Just sign for it,
okay? I've got others . . ." His voice cracked at that point,
and he cleared his throat and said, "You want it or not,
Mr. Rinaldi?"

"Sure." And then the door opened and the shotgun
blasted and the nut was yelling, "Sure, I want it! I
want . . ."

The cop on the stairwell had straightened to see what
was happening. His bulletproof vest didn't help much
when he caught that blast in the face. His scream seemed
to freeze Jimmy Weir, and the nut was swinging around
on Jimmy, and Eddy couldn't take the chance with his
friend's life to do anything but what he had to do. And
what he had to do wasn't all that simple. He couldn't fire
directly into the side-which-was-becoming-a-back as the
nut turned on Jimmy, because he might hit Jimmy. Even
if he hit the nut, the bullets could go through to Jimmy.
So he jumped away from the wall, and the nut heard and
tried to swing back. Jimmy fired and missed. Eddy emptied
his gun, all six shots, at the nut. The shotgun went off
again, into the wall above the stairwell, as the nut fell back
into the apartment. He moved a little, but he was dead by
the time the doctor arrived. Roersch had nailed him with
four of six slugs.

The wife had been punched in the mouth, but except for
a bad case of nerves and a loose tooth, she was fine. The
little boy had stopped crying by the time he rejoined her.
Everyone went home . . . except the patrolman and the

nut; they went to the morgue. The patrolman got an Inspector's Funeral. The nut got a lot of publicity when his brother, James Rinaldi, told reporters at graveside that "Ricco was murdered by vicious, impatient, unfeeling men. If they'd waited for Ricco's own doctor . . ."

Ricco's doctor was at some institution in Carmel. If they'd waited, the wife might have been dead.

But later, Helen had said the captain in charge of the operation should have been prepared to wait all day and all night, longer if necessary, to save not only the wife's but Rinaldi's life. "And," she'd added, "that patrolman's too. Not to say yours and Jimmy's, if things had gone wrong."

Maybe she'd been right. Certainly they thought that way nowadays. But they hadn't been that patient fifteen years ago, before airplane hijackers and Arab "patriots" and all kinds of "revolutionaries" began grabbing hostages and making deals for money and politics and whatnot.

He found himself involved again, remembering past discussions, arguments with Helen, anger at news stories. He re-experienced rage at the department's decision in the Rinaldi case not to "draw further adverse publicity" by giving him a citation. And the lecturer droned on and Roersch wondered at himself. What the hell difference did it all make now? He would soon be finished with police work. And he was already finished with the *law*, moving as he was toward his shakedown. And while he'd deliberately avoided coming to a decision, had made no definite plans, his two days off would be just right . . .

The lecturer was reading statistics on police accidents with guns, citing it as a need for increased weapons training and time on the range. He began describing "some recent mishaps," and laughter rose in the room.

There were the cops who didn't know how to uncock their pistols, or were actually afraid to do as they'd been instructed—place the left thumb between the hammer and the bullet, let the hammer down slowly, then slip the thumb out and let the hammer down *lightly* the rest of the way. Instead, one high-ranking officer, "who will remain nameless," had fired his revolver into the earth in his backyard at two in the morning, hoping to solve his problem unseen if not unheard and be innocently in bed when the neighbors reacted. Instead, he was seen by an old lady across the yard whose custom it was to sit up half the night and sleep half the day. She called the police, and the high-ranking officer had been rousted from his bed by a *higher*-ranking officer. Further promotion wasn't likely; at least not until the brass stopped laughing.

There was the officer who *taped* his hammer back until such time as he could get help in uncocking it, and found himself in a high-speed auto chase with two armed thugs. Luckily, three other radio cars joined in . . . but unluckily he drew his gun at the scene and one of the subdued thugs pointed it out.

There were cops who caught their guns on belts or furniture, cocking them without realizing it, and fired into floors and ceilings.

And the less humorous accidents, that still made cops laugh. The driver of the radio car who drew and cocked his gun with one hand and tried to steer with the other while approaching the scene of a robbery. He drove the radio car through the plate-glass window of a store which *wasn't* being robbed, and at the same time fired a bullet through his partner's right thigh.

The cop who grabbed his revolver away from his eight-year-old son, and while lecturing him on the dangers of going near Daddy's gun, demonstrating how easily it could become cocked and lethal, fired a bullet through his own foot.

The detective who answered a 10:30, "crime in progress" call while on his way home, and had his revolver knocked from his hand by a robber armed with a realistic toy pistol. The revolver was cocked and went off when it hit the floor. It shot the robber—a big, burly man much younger than the detective and until then getting the best of the fight—in the left shoulder. The detective had received a fractured jaw, a commendation for bravery, and a long overdue promotion to sergeant.

Roersch laughed aloud, along with the rest of the class, though this last incident was his personal memory and not what the lecturer was describing. This last incident was his fourth and final shootout and no one, not even the wounded robber, had known exactly how he'd been shot and subdued. Because it had been one hell of a wild fight back there in the tailor's section of the fashionable men's clothing store with sewing machines crashing down and material flying around and all the staff and customers pouring out the front door. And Roersch certainly hadn't volunteered the information!

His last promotion. Almost five years ago. And Jimmy Weir was a lieutenant and Mulvaney a night-school success and practicing attorney and the others dumb coppers who couldn't handle being brass. And Eddy Roersch, who'd never been dumb except in a scholastic way, a take-a-test way, a fuck-around-with-reports way . . . Eddy Roersch, the best detective Manhattan West Homicide had by actual record . . . Eddy Roersch was a sergeant and fifty-six and fat and screwed-blued-tattooed as they used to say in the old days.

He was glad he'd been forced to sit in this room, been forced to think back. To remember that Helen was dead. The past was dead. This was a new deal. He would go to the Grand Canyon.

He left the lecture room in a state of certainty, of tranquility, and fired his off-duty automatic and scored high. He had both his guns checked out and returned to the lecture hall for another hour. He was out by one-thirty, and had lunch at the Hungarian place three blocks east with plenty of spaetzel. And didn't mind paying for it, as he hadn't minded paying for fifty rounds of .25-caliber ammunition. Everything was settled now. He'd definitely go after the money now.

His feeling of certainty, tranquility lasted until he returned to the station . . . and saw four reporters, including that anti-police sonofabitch from the Long Island newspaper, sitting around his desk. One was talking to Chauger, but Chauger was shaking his head and concentrating on his work.

Roersch backtracked quickly, knocking at Hawly's door, and walked in without waiting for an answer. Deverney was moving around like a big, pockmarked shark, running his hand over his slicked-back gray hair, saying, ". . . too goddamn many unsolved cases!" Then he saw Roersch. "Where the hell you been!"

Roersch spoke to Hawly. "Downstairs at the range for my semi-annual qualification, Bill."

Hawly said, "That's right. I asked Chauger to mention it."

Deverney said, "Okay. Sorry. Those motherfuckers outside want updating on the Keel case. You're the man, so handle it."

He didn't sound sorry. He sounded edgy.

Roersch nodded slowly. "Anything else on your mind, Captain?"

Deverney was fifty-eight and big as a house and had the meanest ice-blue eyes when he was pissed. As he was now. "What's the beef between you and Chauger? I don't like my men fighting each other when we've got a city full of spooks and junkies."

"Did you ask Chauger, sir?"

"He said it was nothing. But Bill says there was one hell of a racket . . ."

"It was nothing."

Hawly said, "It certainly *sounded* like something, Eddy. I think it would be best to air the disagreement."

"Chauger bugged me with suggestions on how to handle the Keel case. I told him, with a little pizzazz, to butt out. Unless I'm off the case, I handle it my own way."

"Your own way," Deverney said, "seems to be getting us nowhere fast."

"Then I'd like to be taken off it, sir. There's other work for me."

"I'd do just that," Deverney said, but he didn't sound as pissed now, or as sure of himself. "Bill, however, thinks you're doing the best you can . . ."

"I'd say the best *anyone* can," Hawly interrupted quietly.

"Well, maybe," Deverney muttered. "It's just that those goddamn reporters have been making us look bad lately. They jump on the President and they jump on us. Nosy bastards."

Roersch waited a moment to see if the shit-storm was over. Then he unfroze a little. "We can definitely say we're making progress. We're eliminating suspects, which at least points us in the right direction."

"Which is?" Deverney asked.

"As I stated in my report, we'll soon begin a search for a perpetrator not known to the victim . . ."

"And that'll mean another unsolved!" Deverney shouted. "What's happening to our record here? We'll have ten unsolveds for every make!"

"Not far off the city average, Mark," Hawly said.

"Fucking black killers running all over this fucking city!"

"Jones is outside," Hawly said, pushing a smile.

Deverney waved his hands. "I don't mean *cops!* I mean *niggers!* We shouldn't include them in the statistics! How the hell can anyone be responsible for Harlem!" He stamped past Roersch to the door. "Make us look halfway decent, Eddy, for Chrissakes!" And out he went.

Hawly looked at some papers. Roersch said, "Want me off the case, Bill? It won't bother me. There's a good man on the night shift; Harry Balleau. We can trade tours."

"If I thought that would make a difference, I'd do it. But your record is better than Balleau's, better than anyone's here. The captain knows it and I know it." He hesitated. "And Chauger knows it."

Roersch wondered whether Chauger had opened up to him. Made no difference. He'd offered to leave the case, in front of both the lieutenant and the captain. He was covered.

Still, it was getting sticky. He'd have to do some more work, fatten the report, just in case anything broke in another direction . . . though he couldn't see how that could happen.

He said, "Speaking of Chauger, I asked him to do a job at Latent Prints today. I see he's still typing."

"I'm responsible for that, Eddy. We need Chauger on the typewriter. He's the only one who can handle the paperwork around here. One day we'll get a real secretary, but until then . . . Anyway, I gave the assignment to Jones, and he came back half an hour ago. I hope he left for lunch before Mark started shouting."

"I do too."

Hawly seemed to be thinking. "I know you've been passed over for promotion too many times, Eddy. I was talking about it to Deverney only last week. Cops, even good ones, get typecast by Headquarters—the perennial sergeant, and so on. I guess your P.R. was bad. Also, there are very few openings at the moment. But I want you to know I'm aware of the problem. I just hope you're not, shall we say, turning a little *sour*." Before Roersch could respond, Hawly added, "It happens. We both know how often it happens—good cops going sour and not giving their all anymore. Not that I'd blame you. And not that I'm saying that's what's happening with you on the Keel case."

Roersch waited.

"Here's the point, Eddy. Crack this case and you'll get the bars. Within a month. I'll guarantee it myself."

"How can you?" Roersch asked.

"I've got friends at the Mayor's office. Don't tell me you haven't heard the stories about how I made lieutenant?" He chuckled.

Roersch had. He'd heard similar stories about most men who'd won promotion . . . from men who hadn't.

"They wouldn't do anything for me personally, Eddy. It would lead to trouble. Besides, would you say I'm the sort of man who needs help?"

"No," Roersch said truthfully, but *didn't* say, "Not in *today's* department."

"But they *would* do something for a man I recommended, if that man was deserving. Put a collar on Judith Keel's murderer, give the D.A.'s office enough for an indictment, and you've got that promotion. My word of honor."

Roersch said, "Now if I could just wave a magic wand and turn an impossible case into an open-and-shut."

Hawly shrugged and returned to his paperwork.

Roersch went out. He had to admit he believed Hawly, and that it excited him. To be a lieutenant; to *retire* as a lieutenant; to get out of the complications, the dangers, of his squeeze play . . .

Forget cops and robbers, Eddy! The game is over . . . except for an extra day or two of work to strengthen the cover.

He went to his desk and the reporters. He handled them easily, reading sections of the reports, answering their questions, making the elimination of all possible suspects sound like a major triumph, hinting that the "robber-intruder-killer" had slipped up in leaving prints and it was possible they'd get a make.

At which point Jones returned from lunch.

Roersch excused himself and walked across the room. They talked near the entry desk.

"No local makes on any of the prints, Sergeant."

Roersch nodded, knowing that if he threw Bley's name at them—as he'd orginally intended doing—they'd get a quick make from the F.B.I. files, because Bley had been in the Air Corps, and Bley's prints were bound to be somewhere in Keel's apartment.

He took Jones over to the reporters. "This is Detective Willis Jones, my right-hand man. You might remember he helped apprehend the Michaelson killer. Jones tells me we're moving in the direction I mentioned; those prints are going to be checked all the way . . ."

He went on, and Jones kept a straight face, and the reporters finally left. Except for the prick from Long Island, who came back alone and talked to Jones. Jones had a hell of a time getting rid of him.

"Let me guess," Roersch said, when Jones came over. "He wants to do an article, or a series. Not just for his newspaper, but for top magazines, maybe a book. It'll make you famous, like Serpico. And like Serpico, you won't be a cop anymore. The subject? How tough it is to be black and beautiful on the pig-brutality force."

"That's close enough. He was upset when I wouldn't go for it. I tell you, if I wasn't a cop, I'd put one in his mouth! The *patronizing*, man!" He lowered his voice. "I'll take Deverney any day."

"Would you now?"

"Make that any *sick* day."

"That gets you onto *Flip Wilson*."

Jones grinned. "I'd rather be Kojak's sidekick."

Roersch watched him return to his desk . . . and thought it was too bad he couldn't capitalize on Hawly's offer. As a lieutenant, he could build himself the best Homicide squad in the city, starting with Balleau . . . and Jones.

He looked at his watch. A quarter to three. He leafed through his notebook, and saw areas that Roersch the cop would have checked by now. Areas he would have to handle because of Chauger; because of Deverney's edginess and Hawly's veiled pressure.

He began to feel uncomfortable; the same discomfort he'd felt before leaving Bley's apartment. Loose ends. Goddamn loose ends!

Not that it would change anything . . .

But he'd told himself that too many times, was sick of

it, picked up the phone and called Ruthie. A little pleasure, that's what he needed.

She said maybe ten, ten-thirty, but he'd have to call back. Her trick was coming up at nine; for an hour, he said, but he'd said that before and stayed all night.

Roersch sighed.

"I'd really like to see you, Eddy. I'm sorry."

"Hell, why be sorry? Business comes first, right?"

She was quiet, and he regretted his tone of voice.

He said, "Listen, you've got to take care of Jen. And yourself. I understand."

"Do you, Eddy? I'm not so sure *I* do anymore. Your call last night . . ."

"Yeah, well, I'll call at ten."

She said, "Okay," voice very small.

He couldn't leave it like that; couldn't hang up on her. "Maybe we'll go out for dinner. Do you like Chinese Mandarin cooking?"

"I like *any* cooking! Where do you think I got that big thing I sit on?"

He laughed. "So go have a snack."

He looked at the Austen and Bain folders, still waiting to be read. He left them on his desk and went outside and across the street to make another phone call. This one he couldn't risk in the station.

He called La Guardia Airport and got information on connections to Grand Canyon. He made reservations on a flight to Las Vegas late Saturday night, and on an Air West flight from Vegas to the canyon at seven Sunday morning. He was told there would be no problem getting a room at one of the several lodges this early in the season, but if he wanted to be certain . . .

He took the number and got change and made the call. He reserved a room at the Bright Angel Lodge for Sunday night, and the man said, "We're looking forward to having you here, Mr. Roersch. The weather's been unusually mild."

He had never been to the Grand Canyon. If Bley didn't

go completely crazy, it shouldn't take more than a few hours to settle things. Then he could spend part of Sunday and Monday looking around. And if Bley didn't show up, he'd figure on getting him next week in Los Angeles, and still enjoy the scenery. Either way—*some* way—he'd get to him. A man with hundreds of thousands in bank accounts and stock and property couldn't disappear.

He had a cup of coffee at the pharmacy lunch counter, and realized he hadn't had a cigarette all day. He lit up, and for the first few drags it tasted as good as before the Surgeon General's warning . . . but then he was leafing through his notebook and the smoke became harsh and discomfort returned and he jabbed the cigarette out.

All right, he'd play cops and robbers. He'd play What-If, a game that had helped him come up with some surprising solutions in the past.

What if Bley wasn't guilty?

He ordered a container of coffee to go and returned to the station and his desk. He read the Corinne Bain and Jane Austen folders. He finished them before he finished the coffee, that's how much information was there.

Corinne Bain had been black and beautiful and a few weeks past her twenty-fifth birthday when found in her new Corvette on Eighth Street in Greenwich Village, the morning of August 16th, nine months ago. Not so beautiful anymore, because her throat had been cut, her belly sliced open, the intestines pulled out and wrapped around her head and body. She was wearing a pantsuit, the pants down, the jacket open, no underwear. There were no indications of sexual activity—no semen in vagina, mouth, or anywhere on the body. She was a "dancer, singer, actress," according to her landlady, but her only professional work had been in topless and nude clubs around the city. Last place of employment—Chelsea's Coven, a topless joint with voodoo decor and stiff prices, uptown just east of Fifth. She still had her last paycheck in her purse, as well as her watch and a good ring. Corinne had family in Detroit, but no one had claimed her body.

The investigation had rambled around her dates, black and white, who seemed to number in the hundreds, and she'd been known to turn a trick every so often for a free-spending member of the audience. There were some smudged prints, not Corinne's, on her big belt buckle, but Latent hadn't gotten a make. Without a murder weapon or known motive, the case had died. It was listed as "active," but no one had done any work on it in months.

Jane Austen was a runaway who had been identified through Missing Persons three days after her death. Her real name was Berdine Wallach, and she'd been a secretary, a waitress, and finally a massage parlor "hostess." She claimed to be twenty-one, but had been fifteen when she disappeared from her home in Perth Amboy, and had been missing two years when she turned up, dead, January 25th, some five months ago. Her father said she'd written regularly, without a return address, and that her problem was "she matured too soon." She was a big-chested red-head who had moved from parlor to parlor in the past year, as many of the girls did. Her last place of employment was the Garden of Allah Massage Palace, and she'd worked for at least two other places. Roersch copied down names and addresses. She'd been discovered in her apartment on East Fifty-seventh Street when a friend came to find out why she hadn't been to work for five days, and the superintendent coupled this with a "bad smell" on the third floor. She was nude in bed, bound and gagged with towels, her right arm severed at the shoulder, her left leg severed at the hip, her stomach opened but the intestines left inside. No sign of sexual activity, despite the nudity. No other wounds, and she had obviously died hard.

The investigation had floundered among the same excess of men friends as Corinne Bain's. The murder weapon had been turned in by a sanitation man who found it wrapped in a bloody towel in a garbage can at the victim's address, appropriated it, then read about the murder. It was an electric meat-slicer with interchangeable blades. The blade used had a serrated edge. The sanitation man's wife had washed everything, so there were no prints. The victim had a roommate, who owned the electric knife, but she had been on a two-week vacation in the Bahamas. Her name was Phyllis Dayton, and she gave the police the name of a man who had tried to force Jane into prostitution. He was a known pimp with a homicide conviction as a teen-ager; a hot suspect, until he was found to be serving time for a narcotics offense.

The case was listed as "active" and an anonymous letter had been received only a month ago, naming a Negro boyfriend as the killer. The tone of the letter, its wild racist ranting, caused investigators to concentrate on the sender, who was found to be Phyllis Dayton. She insisted she was correct, but the man she accused had an airtight alibi.

Roersch drained his container of coffee, put the folders in the Out box, and leaned back in his chair. So he'd read them. So what?

After a while, he leaned forward and looked at his fingers . . . and thought. He played cops and robbers, and got up and left.

16: Friday p.m.

It had changed. John was certain of that, though not of what would happen. Glancing into the rear-view mirror, he again caught Lois's eyes on him. She smiled and nodded, but he wasn't fooled. He'd read her look—her *many* looks—in the past four hours.

It had changed, and he'd have to begin watching himself again. Before it had been Evan, and now it was Lois, and a goddamn shame too because he had really relaxed and started enjoying things. Like last night; beautiful in more ways than he could put his finger on.

Evan was dozing, head in the corner. Lois sat close beside him, wide awake, licking her lips the way she did when she was thinking. She was pale, her eyes looked sunken, she hadn't eaten anything but a bite of toast and a glass of warm chocolate milk when they'd had brunch at the small lunchroom beside the motel. But she'd insisted she could travel, so they'd left the motel at noon and taken sandwiches and two quarts of milk and decided to make heavy time.

Except for two brief stops, once for gas and once when Lois had to go, he'd been breaking speed limits in Oklahoma and Texas. They were now approaching Claude, just a hop from Amarillo, and if Lois meant what she'd said about being able to drive on through the night, they would make Flagstaff by three, four a.m. Evan said they'd sack out there before going up to the canyon, so they'd be nice and fresh on Saturday afternoon.

It was almost four-thirty when Lois leaned forward and whispered, "Let's stop soon."

"Okay. We need gas anyway. How do you feel?"

"I'm with my friends; how *should* I feel? Beaut, right?"

"Sure. Just stay cool. It's all fun and games, baby."

She leaned back. Their eyes met in the rear-view. She didn't answer, but her lips were pressed thin and hard.

She must have heard them last night. She was reading more into it than she should.

He accelerated to over eighty miles per hour, thrilling to the smooth surge of power. Energy crises and national speed limits and doing your bit . . . he'd settle for that later, after they'd reached Los Angeles. But this was a road he'd hitched and hated because of the cars *roaring* by, far too fast to consider stopping. Now *he* was doing the roaring . . . on Interstate 40, which they'd picked up after leaving 44 back around Tulsa. Interstate 40, which was the old U.S. Route 66.

Great road, U.S. 66, John thought. Something like the Way West with covered wagons and such! Well, Model T's anyway, and old trucks like in *The Grapes of Wrath* on the Late Show with Henry Fonda and that fat old broad, Darwell. It was one of the movies he'd really dug, relating as he did to being on the road. Okies, sure . . . out of Oklahoma along old 66. Coming to the promised land . . . like *they* were doing in their covered Jaguar.

He laughed aloud.

Lois murmured, "Have your kicks while you can, jack-off."

He snapped his eyes to the mirror. "What's wrong with you?"

"Now I know why they call a toilet a *john*."

He made a smile. "Don't blow it any sooner than you have to."

"Now *I'm* going to blow it?"

"That's right."

They stared at each other, and she was a goddamn douchebag with her hard eyes and tight mouth and cracks about johns. He tried to warn her with a look: *Don't fuck with me, cunt!* His hands were clenching on the wheel, his foot twitching on the gas pedal. He shook his head slightly.

And then he realized Evan's eyes were open. Lois realized it a moment later.

"Did he wake you, hon?" she said, all sweetness and love.

He!

Evan straightened and stretched. "Where are we?"

John told him. Evan said, "Beautiful! We're eating up the road!"

John grinned. Lois said, "I've asked him twice to get me to a bathroom. He just won't."

John's grin remained, but only for Evan. "No services sign since she asked me, *once*."

"And would you do me a favor, hon? Tell him to stop that sex crap, at least until I'm feeling better. I know I promised, but he's really too much. He never lets up."

Evan looked at him in the mirror. John told himself not to react, but he felt himself paling and wondered whether Evan would believe her . . . and why shouldn't he?

"The closest we got to sex," he murmured, "was to discuss toilets. Which," he just couldn't help adding, "I'll admit relates to the lady in question."

She lunged forward and slapped him across the back of the head. The car swerved as he half-turned.

Evan was holding her back, hands on both her wrists.

"You heard what he said! I won't let anyone talk that way . . ."

"And I won't let anyone get us killed," Evan said firmly. "So stop it, both of you."

"*Both* of us?" John said, and he knew he was falling into the cunt's trap, playing *her* game. "I'm just trying to drive."

She began to cry. "He said things . . . about last night. Said I wasn't *needed* anymore, as if I'm just for *that*! I couldn't stand thinking *you* thought . . . I'm sorry, hon! I'm *sorry*!" She was up against him, sobbing. And what the hell could John do but keep driving and keep building up rage against this douchebag. And remember anew how she had betrayed him in New York and betrayed him on the road; how she was now knifing him in the nuts.

He was afraid to look in the mirror again. When he finally did, Evan had his hand inside her blouse. The "sex crap" she was too sick to tolerate included her hand working over his crotch. Evan's eyes closed; that crotch became distended. And try to fight her *now*, Johnnie!

A sign announcing services finally appeared. They were all silent as he took the off-ramp. All silent, but Lois looked pleased with herself. So fucking obvious . . . and so fucking effective! She was making a big mistake, though. She couldn't know it, but he was fighting for more than a cushy hitch. She thought Evan was *her* big chance, and maybe she was right. But Evan was his *last* chance, and he was fighting for his life.

He decided to try and heal things when they stopped at the station. He walked quickly, catching up with Lois as she headed for the bathroom. He put his arm around her shoulders and said, "Baby, why can't we . . . ?"

She shrieked, "*Let me alone!*" and swung at him with both fists and kept screaming. There was another car and people looking out at them and the two attendants turning and staring. He couldn't get away from her and wanted to

smash her face and she was landing all over his bent head
and back. Evan got there and shoved *him*, sent him slamming into a big metal garbage bin, and John suddenly
straightened and said, "You fucking . . ."

Evan said, "John, *enough.*"

John went into the men's room. He'd been so sure last
night . . . and one sex pitch and one Lois Chandler fit, and
all the certainty was gone.

When he came out, the other car was just pulling away
from the gas pumps. A kid pointed at him and a woman
yanked the kid from the window and the driver, a big, red-
faced square with a buzz-cut, maybe half an inch of hair,
said something with a look that made John *hate*. Hate
Lois.

Evan was signing the tab. John said, "Want me to keep
driving?" Evan shook his head, and spoke to the attendant
about weather forecasts and road conditions. John got in
back.

Lois walked up and got in front and they drove out.

Lois spoke to Evan like John wasn't there. Evan answered her, and didn't look in the rear-view . . . at least
not at John.

John said, "Radio says rain. Looks like it too."

Evan grunted. Lois blew smoke at the ceiling.

How fast it had changed!

He lay down and closed his eyes. It would change back,
or he would do something. That was one big hole in the
ground they were going to; a mile deep and a dozen or
more miles across; a grave big enough for a *million*
douchebags.

He slept, and dreamed of someone falling lazily through
dusky canyon space, turning and gesturing and calling, but
without urgency, without fear. He wasn't sure if it was a
man or a woman . . . until huge cruel slabs of granite
thrust upward and the figure accelerated downward and
he felt terror and understood how fragile his body was and
smashed into the rock and disintegrated into bloody frag-

ments. One of his eyes survived intact, looking upward. Lois was there, a mile above, all tits, ass and cunt, a big, disembodied cock ramming into her from the rear. She was waving at him, saying, "Ni-night, darling. Ni-night."

He waited until he was sure John slept, then spoke softly. "I doubt John would tell you about last night. It's more likely you overheard us."

She began to protest. He was irritated, remembering too many ploys, plays, plots by Merri, by Judy, by other dingies . . . and always to disguise something, to protect a lie, to advance a subterfuge. He spoke on, quieting her with a look.

"You blame him, and you're giving more importance to our evening's entertainment than you should. You're over-reacting, and I won't allow you to hit and scream."

"You won't *allow* . . . ?" she began, voice rising.

"I won't allow!" he snapped, jerking his head around at her, staring for too long a moment, forgetting he was driving, forgetting everything but the need to subdue her, to make her understand he would *not* be manipulated!

"Evan, watch the road!"

He watched the road. He said, "You don't have to do anything for anyone. Not for John, and not for me. But you *do* have to act with restraint. There will be no more accusations, and no more violence either by hand or voice. Is that understood?"

She was terribly white. Her eyes seemed to bulge, and for a moment he thought she was going to attack him. He began to draw back, the feeling was so strong; his right hand left the wheel and stiffened and rose. She said, "What are you doing?"

He dropped his hand, but he remembered his mother's whiteness and rage, the last time he ever allowed her to direct it at him.

It began with his announcement that he was leaving teaching for advertising . . . followed by her shouts and attempted blows—he was able to handle her physically by then—and his father's surprising agreement with her that Evan was throwing away "a fine career." It had led to a wild scene, a bad scene, one he'd ended by telling them both they'd destroyed him, ruined him, and he would do as he wanted because it made no difference. Teacher or adman, success or failure, money or not, he'd shouted, he would always be ruined, destroyed, miserable, beyond redemption. Because of them. Because of *their* ruined lives.

He'd run from the apartment, and when he returned his father was sitting beside the window, clutching his chest, begging his mother to call the doctor. They had no phone. Calling meant going downstairs to the drug or candy store. His mother said he was a "gas factory" and the pains were the usual result of his eating *chazarei*, pig food, "trash from the cafeteria." His father had turned to him, appealing with a sick look, a frightened look, but Evan had said, "Fight it out yourselves . . . I'm finished with both of you . . . I'm leaving tomorrow!" and gone to his room.

A few minutes later, his father made a high-pitched, choking sound and fell off his chair. By the time Evan ran in, his father was dying. By the time he got back from calling an ambulance, his father was dead. And his mother shrieked and wailed and carried on . . . until he shook her and said, "You *hated* him! You *killed* him!" and didn't realize he was holding a kitchen knife until a neighbor grabbed him.

Shouts and blows, twists and confusions—they had killed his father; they would kill him, if he let them. He didn't accept such things anymore. He stopped them, dead.

As he had with Judy, when she'd shouted that she owed him nothing, had asked him for nothing, that she couldn't be bought, she belonged to no one, she would see anyone she chose, she wouldn't be *forced*, she would call for help, for police, for friends to *beat* him. And the words and the shrillness had beat him. And he'd gone to the kitchen and run the cold water and poured a Scotch and opened the silverware drawer for a spoon to mix his drink, and seen the long knife. He'd come back to the living room and she wasn't there and he'd gone to the bedroom where she lay face-down on the water bed, her pride and joy, the brass posts high and the special liner bulging over the sides and the built-in heater and vibrator and timer and the whole thing costing eight hundred dollars and along with the other gifts the best, whatever he'd bought her, the best. She had deceived him, taken him, cheated him, like Merri. But he was stronger now; he would punish her as he hadn't been able to punish Merri; he would do it himself, not use a hired hand on a lover. He came at Judy, the knife rising. She rolled over to look at him, to shout again. Her shout froze in her throat and her mouth opened and her teeth and tongue showed and he laughed at this beautiful girl who'd tormented him and was now ugly with fear. He slashed down with the knife and she made a dying sound . . . and he sliced open her treasured water bed and the heated water, the vibrating water, surged up and over her and onto the floor, a torrent, a flood, and she sobbed helplessly, looking at it, drenched in it, yet raising her hands delicately as if to prevent them from being dampened. He said, "Be grateful. It could have been you." He began to leave as the water lapped around his shoes, and she jumped up, soaking, shouting. He turned and said, "Maybe it *will* be you," his head pounding, determined that no one would shout and deceive and defy and betray and confuse him.

By the time he'd reached the lobby, he'd calmed enough to phone the water-bed emergency service and have them and their vacuum pumps rush over in the ambulance-like van. And he'd paid for the damage to the downstairs neighbor's ceiling. And had bought Judy a new liner-mattress and seen her again . . . but not for long. Because no one would twist him, use him . . .

He turned to Lois. "*No one*, including you, do you understand!"

John roused and cleared his throat. "What?"

Lois was staring at him, still with a whiteness of rage . . . but with something else, something new. Respect, he thought . . . or fear. Made no difference which, as long as it kept her quiet.

He looked at John in the rear-view. "We're to be *quiet!*"

"You got it," John said quickly.

Lois looked out the window. John lay back down. Evan drove.

It was quiet.

17: | Friday p.m.

Roersch went to Judith Keel's apartment house and spoke to the doorman, offering him a cigarette and saying the case looked pretty bad. "But have to keep doing my job, like you do yours—opening and closing a few doors."

The old man—well, about sixty-five—said, "You wouldn't believe it, but some people gave *me* funny looks afterward. Figure just 'cause I'm colored . . ."

Roersch sympathized, and noted the word "colored," and thought it must be tough on elderly Negroes to take the quick changes in style and language. Must be some, like this light-skinned old-timer, who resented being called black, and feared the skyrocketing incidence of black crime. Still, Roersch managed to get around to asking if Keel had ever entertained blacks.

"Not that one. Lots of others, sure. Woman on the fifth floor, she had *three* come visit her." He gave Roersch a level look. "Guess turn-about is fair play."

"Guess so," Roersch replied.

They stood outside the lobby in mild, humid air and discussed the possibility of rain. They watched young people walking by.

"She'd've been better off sticking to her girlfriend," Roersch said, stepping on his cigarette.

"Who's that?"

"Miss Keel. Should've stuck to her friend, Lizbeth, down the hall, you know."

"Mrs. Oron? She and Keel *that* way?"

"So I gathered."

"Well, could be. *Anything* could be now'days. But you can't tell by working this door."

Which finished today's segment of the new soap opera, Amiable Eddy, and sent him inside and upstairs to Keel's apartment with a master key procured from the super. The water bed had been drained of excess blood, but everything else had been left the same; Keel's door still hung with the "Crime Scene" placard, another propped on a cabinet just inside, making it off-limits except to police personnel. The colors in that butcher-shop bedroom were now dried browns, and the body—more correctly, the *meat*—was gone. Yet a certain smell lingered. Not a pleasant place to be, but he *needed* to be here, to *feel* what had happened.

He walked through three large rooms and ended in the bathroom. He used it, and sitting there allowed his thoughts wide range. He included Bley, but only as part of his What-If game; only as a red herring. Say someone was hiding behind Mr. Marvin Bleywitz and his surveillance and his motives and his kinky sex? Well, hard to believe . . . but necessary to this day's work.

He went down the hall to the apartment the doorman had mentioned. He rang the bell and heard, "Who is it?"

and said, "Police." He waited about five minutes for the door to open.

"Lizbeth Oron?"

She wore a long, shiny, orange wrap and fuzzy white slippers. Her hair was in curlers and her face was pale and there were wrinkles around the mouth and bags under the eyes. She was maybe sixty, but still reminded him of a baby-doll, with her wide-eyed look and sullen little mouth and squeaky, girlie-girl voice. An old dolly. An over-the-hill Shirley Temple. "I'm Mrs. Elizabeth Oron," she said, like a chorus cutie playing Queen Victoria.

He explained that he was "gathering information to close out the file on Judith Keel."

"Close out? You mean you've arrested that madman?"

"Which one?" he asked, smiling. He got no smile in return.

"The one who killed her—Evan Bley. The *only* one who would do such a thing."

He asked if he could come inside.

They sat in the kitchen and talked. She poured coffee and her mouth remained little-girl bitter and her wide eyes blinked furiously. "*Proof*? What better proof than Judy *telling* me he was going to kill her! It was just a matter of time until he found out . . ." She said, "Sugar," and went to the counter and got the bowl. She didn't complete her interrupted sentence when she sat down. "You know, of course, about his *stabbing* her water bed? Personally, I believe he wanted to stab *her*, and missed, and the insanity passed, for the moment. Judy wasn't certain."

"You said it was only a matter of time until he found out something and would kill her. What was it he found out?"

She waved a hand. It was covered with rings—four of them. She said, "The usual. Other friends. He was one of those incredible idiots who expect to *own* a woman, have her abstain totally from other relationships. When he found out she wouldn't be his slave . . ." She waved her other hand; this one had three rings.

He looked around. "You and your husband have a nice place here, Mrs. Oron."

"I'm divorced," she said, not quite as baby-doll. "I use the *Mrs.* to discourage certain kinds of contact, so persistently imposed on women in this joyous city of ours."

He rose and thanked her. On the way through the living room, he asked if he might wash his hands in her bathroom. "Sticky sugar," he said, and turned to the left without waiting for her reply, and was in her bedroom. She said, "It's *here*, off the living room!" He was looking at the radio, a big job, AM and FM, with small stereo speakers, all set on a shelf which was part of a headboard. He was looking at a framed photograph, Judith Keel in a bikini, an eight-by-twelve blowup of a snapshot. He was looking at a painting, much like the one in adman Burns's office— Wedgwood blues and creams, the figures in Grecian dress, or *un*dress. Except that these girls were lying down, and one was kissing the other's breasts. He was looking at a lamp with copper-banded, red-glass Tiffany shade, nude dancing girls spaced around it.

"I said *this* way," Elizabeth Oron snapped from the doorway.

He said sorry, and followed her into the living room. She pointed at a door. He said, "Interesting bedroom," and looked at her.

She met his look, the old-child's mouth pushing out, the ringed fingers clenching. "*I* like it."

"You also liked Judy."

"She was a nice girl."

"You like nice girls, don't you?" Before she could translate a look of anger to words, he said, "Don't misunderstand. I'm all in favor of consenting adults doing their thing."

"The modern colloquial doesn't suit you, Sergeant." But the mouth relaxed a bit. "Judy would come to me when she had problems."

"And when she had visitors, like her employer and his friends."

"You know about that, do you?"

"Ever listen to ham radio operators on your short-wave bands?"

The change of subject made her pause. "Sometimes."

"Police calls?"

"Yes. I like to remind myself of just what men do to women in this so-called civilization of ours."

He didn't point out the high incidence of what women did to *men*. "Ever listen in on car-phone conversations? I do." He chuckled. "A bit of Peeping Tom in all of us."

"Acoustic voyeurism. And this is leading to Evan Bley's car phone and whether I heard any of his calls to Judy. Yes, many. Because he would cruise around close to this address and phone as if from a distance. He'd ask if she was alone, and then come over to check on her. He never caught her with anyone, not only because she didn't really see many people, but also because I kept my radio tuned in on his band and was able to alert her. I'm here almost all the time, and I have little else to do."

"Just your radio and your friends."

"Yes, and not that many friends anymore. Judy was very sweet, very kind, perhaps a bit vulnerable to . . . lower-class types, but still a good friend. I heard that madman threaten to cut her heart out. Those exact words. And he once said that if he caught her with someone else in his bed—he bought it for her, but how *dare* he think of it as *his!*—he would murder her. His exact words: 'I'll murder you in that bed!' If it wasn't for his being so very middle-class, so very *Jewish* in his concepts of possible moral turpitude, he'd have realized he *had* caught her in that bed with someone else, at least once that I know of." She smiled a very-mean-kid's smile. "I had dropped over for a cup of coffee, and simply stayed a while."

Roersch went through the act of washing his hands. He thanked her, and walked out the door, and stopped her from closing it.

"You wouldn't happen to know anything about the murder weapon, would you?"

She laughed. "Afraid not."

"Would you come to her apartment and look through the silverware?"

"You mean the cutlery." She hesitated. "I don't exactly like the idea of being in there . . . but none of the other officers had the good sense to ask *me* to do that before, and I *do* know Judy's possessions rather well."

"The other officers didn't know you two were . . . friends." He smiled. "And you didn't volunteer the information."

In Keel's apartment, she walked straight to the kitchen, keeping her eyes from the bedroom doorway, and went through the drawers. She finished and looked around, hands clasped at her waist. "There was a large carving knife, a chrome-plated thing more for show than for use. Looked like a shiny saw. She was going to mount it on brackets above the table . . . I don't see it anywhere."

He wrote it in his notebook. He walked her back to her door, and waited until she opened it, and said, "She had another friend. A blonde girl; kind of cheap-looking, according to one description I got."

"She had several such friends. As I told you, she was vulnerable to certain lower-class types. I wasn't privy to those liaisons. She would mention she was seeing someone at a particular time and would I keep my radio on in case Bley tried his phone-and-check trick." She paused. "I did see one, running from her apartment after he phoned some weeks ago. Long blonde hair—looked like a cheap wig. But I never met her. Don't know her name or anything about her."

Roersch thanked her again, and left. No matter how hard he played What-If, it stayed Bley.

Chelsea's Coven was getting ready for its five o'clock opening. He seemed to remember the place as being a jazz joint some years ago, and mentioned it to the manager.

"That's right," the bouncer-type in tux said. "All the greats, Monk and Diz and the others, were here. So was I.

Times change." They watched two bikini-clad girls in knee-high red boots and little devil's horn hats lighting blood-red candles. "How does it look for going nude again, Sergeant?" Roersch explained he was Homicide, and asked about Corinne Bain. "You still working on that? Man, with the action these chicks get . . . not that they're *all* like that, at least not at the beginning . . . but it usually gets to them, if they stay with the business. Like I told the other cops, it's a needle in a haystack. She was one pretty jigaboo, and there were just too many guys."

"And girls," Roersch said, lighting a cigarette and watching a big-bottomed blonde bending over a stubborn wick.

"Yeah, some les action. But it wasn't the kind of killing a *woman* would do, was it?"

Roersch didn't go into the Countess Bathory. "Did she have any *special* friends, men or women?"

The manager said she'd been divorced and the cops had checked out her husband, a white musician, "sort of jealous for a drummer," but he'd been two thousand miles away. "Otherwise, she played the field."

"With women too?" Roersch persisted. "No long-term roommates?"

"Not that anyone here knew of. She played the girls the same as the men. Quickies. She was soured on what she called 'meaningful relationships.' "

Roersch refused the offer of a drink, and headed for the next club on his list, the Bantam Royal in Greenwich Village.

According to a billboard, showtime wasn't until seven, but a liquor delivery truck was out front and the door was propped open. He walked into a small place with twenty tables jammed into a space that should have held maybe ten, and a long, plush-padded bar. It must've been dim as hell during business hours, because a pole light and unshaded bulb didn't do much to dispel the gloom. And musty, even for a bar in off hours.

No one seemed to be around. He caught the delivery man on his way out of a swinging back door and asked for the manager.

"Mr. Kendricks doesn't come in till eight, but Fasty's in the john. What's the roust? You gonna close this place? They owe for two weeks' deliveries."

Roersch thumbed him out and sat down at a table. He barely had room to cross his legs.

"Hey there, what can I do for you?"

A medium-sized black man, not young and not old, not bushy-haired and not flat-topped, was striding toward him. He wore snug dark pants, a dark V-necked pullover, and a heavy silver chain around his neck. He looked slightly dated—sharp, but it suited him.

Roersch identified himself and his business, flashing the badge.

"Right. I'm Fasty, the bartender."

Roersch waited. The man leaned against the bar, elbows up and back, ankles crossed. "I'm clean. No wanteds against me. Haven't even got a record, 'cept for a pot bust back in '68. My legals read Mordechai Berry, and what would *you* do with a name like that in a racket like this? No sweet teeny-bopper's gonna go for old Mordechai. Besides, I'm fast like a bunny."

Roersch wrote down the name.

"But I went through all this fascinating stuff nine, ten months ago. As for Corinne, I think you should know I don't dig black chicks. So what's the scam now?"

"Same thing. Final run-through before we close it out. How was she with girls?"

"She *was* a girl, Sergeant. Plenty girl. If she'd been white, I'd have dug her."

Roersch sighed. "Do we have to go back to the Emancipation Proclamation? Do you want my permission to leave those old cotton fields back home? Okay, you got it."

The man nodded slowly, smiling, and went around behind the bar. "My evening constitutional. *To* the Cold

Duck and *to* the brandy and mix lightly and pour over one small ice cube. How about you?"

Roersch said yes. Fasty brought him the drink and leaned against the bar and raised his glass. "To law and order."

"I'll drink to that."

"Don't think I'm kidding. When you live where *I* live, it's important."

Roersch said, "Back to Corinne Bain. How was she with girls?"

"So the *poh*-leece finally found out it's happening. You know, not one cop out of maybe five that came here asked that. She was like most chicks in these clubs. She didn't know about it at first and then someone followed her into the crapper and she knew about it. I don't think it was where her whole head was at—she liked cock too much to go straight lezzie—but she dug it on occasion."

"Who'd she dig it with?"

"Butch types. Some with money. One or two of the other dancers. I'd like to see you people keep the case open. I'd like to see you keep *every* case open. Bad business, stopping people from breathing. Whoever did her should get done too." He drank. "You want names for your little black book? Not easy, because they'd leave separately and get together later and who's to know? But let's see. There was a fantastic looking Oriental chick, Billie Coo she called herself. Hair down to her beautiful yellow ass. And who else . . . maybe The Nun. She seemed to talk to Corinne more than necessary. I had my feelers out on The Nun . . . was singing my old September Song around her, waiting it out, thinking maybe we could leave the cotton fields together for a few rounds. It didn't work, and she split. But my type, The Nun. Blonde, at least the wigs. Built strong and could dance, *really* dance, where most of these girls just shake."

"The Nun who?"

Fasty laughed. "Can't be sure of names around here.

The girls use fake I.D.'s all the time. If you ask too many questions, they go someplace where they don't. I think her Social Security was Lita Hoff . . . something like that. You can come back when Kendricks is around. He's got the books. But it's odds on the name won't be any more real than The Nun."

Roersch finished his drink.

"Come around at showtime. I'll let you scare the pants off a girl who really fills them."

Roersch said he might just do that.

Not always unpleasant, bird-dogging.

He was beginning to get hungry, and Mario's wasn't more than a few blocks away. But checking his book, he saw that the Garden of Allah wasn't far either.

The waiting room had a desk with a high-backed chair, two couches for the customers, and a life-sized plaster Venus on a low pedestal. He sat down on one of the couches, facing a curtained-off doorway. Before he could cross his legs, the girl came through the curtain and gave him a big smile. "Hi! I'm Cindy. If you'd like, I'll be your masseuse. We accept American Express, Diners, Master . . ."

He was almost sorry to flash his badge. She wore hot-pants and klunkers and a thin white blouse with a good pair of knockers showing through it. Her smile died and she picked up the phone. "I'll get Murray."

"It's just a routine check on an old case. Jane Austen."

She dialed. "I don't know anything about that. I'll get the owner. I've only been here about a month."

She spoke into the phone, turning her back and whispering. He heard, "Hurry . . . police . . . I don't want . . ."

She hung up and sat down behind the desk. He said, "Good job?" conversationally.

She took cigarettes from a drawer and fumbled one out and flicked a lighter half a dozen times before getting flame. Her hands shook. "It's okay. They told me it's legal and all."

"If it wasn't, you couldn't operate in the open this way."

"Yes, that's so."

He lit a cigarette too. They smoked. She said, "This Jane . . ."

"Austen."

She laughed nervously. "I read a book by her in school. What do you want her for?"

"Nothing. She's dead. We're trying to find who did it."

"Oh . . . Jesus. It didn't happen *here*, did it?"

"No. But she was employed here at the time."

"We get a few strange customers—you know, kinky— but most are just, well, businessmen and straight guys."

"How old are you?"

She opened the drawer. "Got my I.D. Twenty-one last December. Straight I.D. too. Only thing, I wouldn't want my parents . . ."

He said, "Forget it," and concentrated on his cigarette. She smoked and wet her lips and tried not to look at him. He felt like a cobra with a bird.

It seemed a long time before the youngish man with long hair and bright checkered suit came in. "What's the trouble, officer?"

"No trouble. Just a routine check on the Jane Austen case. You remember that, don't you?"

"Cindy, see if there's enough lotion in the cabinet. We don't want to run short."

Cindy was glad to go back through the curtain.

"Don't like to upset the help. What can I tell you about Jane that I didn't tell the other officers?"

"She had friends among the girls, didn't she?"

"The girls knew each other, of course. But close friends . . . it's been so long . . . I don't think she had any in the Palace."

"Did she like girls? Sexually?"

"If you mean did we have a scene going here . . ."

"Nothing like that. Just covering ground not covered before. Did she go for girls?"

"She might have, occasionally. There's a lot of pressure, if a butch is around. But I couldn't be specific . . ."

"I'd like to know the names of the girls who worked with her."

"It would mean checking my books. Jane was here a long time. Almost a year, I believe. We had a lot of girls in and out in that time."

"Check your books."

"Yeah, sure." Murray wasn't happy as he went to a low wood cabinet, used a key and opened double doors. He pulled out three ledgers, went to the desk and sat down. He began turning pages.

"Here's Jane's entry—first day, third shift. We have three eight-hour shifts. Like most new girls, she was on midnight to eight a.m."

"Don't tell me you get customers at six and seven in the morning?"

Murray smiled, and began reading names. Roersch began writing them in his book. "Just don't expect them all to be legal identification," Murray said, waiting for Roersch to catch up. "We get a lot of nom de plumes. But I *try* for legitimate identification." He went back to reading names, and as Roersch hurried to keep up, said, "She was moved to the prime-time second shift, four p.m. to midnight . . ."

Roersch said, "Hold it. Repeat the last name you read."

Murray looked down at his finger in the ledger. "Lita Hoffer."

"What did she look like?"

Murray said it had been a while and he couldn't be sure, and gave a description much like Fasty's of the girl he called The Nun, right down to the long blonde wigs. The Nun, who'd used an I.D. of "Lita Hoff . . . something like that."

"Didn't she ever take off the wigs; wear her own hair?"

"Not that I could tell. She applied for the job in one,

and had a few others, and maybe I mistook her own hair for a wig, but I doubt it."

"What do you think of her name, Lita Hoffer? Real or phony?"

"Like I said, I try for legal identification. Would it help to know she had an accent? English, I think."

Roersch made a note. "Anything else you can tell me about her? Nicknames? Unusual habits? Anything at all?"

"She had a nasty temper. Maybe she had problems, but when she began hassling the customers, I gave her fair warning. I was about ready to fire her when she quit."

"Is there anyone you now employ who worked with Lita?"

Murray went back to his books. He turned pages for quite a while, then stabbed at a line with his finger. "Sheri Cage. She's at another place, a few blocks away. The Golden Cloud. I own a piece of the action."

"Get her over here."

"She's not on duty now. I can't bother the girls on their free time. If you drop around there between midnight . . ."

"It's important I speak to her *now*. I'll remember the favor, Murray. I've heard talk of a new round of massage-parlor rousts, using officers who don't look or act like officers, with special electronic devices . . ."

Murray got on the phone.

While they waited, Roersch went through his notebook. And thought of Keel's cleaning lady saying she'd seen "a blonde girl, maybe some people would say cheap-looking." That fit. Nick McKenney's description of the girl Keel had met at a Greenwich Village bar didn't . . . at least not the hair. Reddish-brown and frosted in front. On the other hand, she'd gotten "hot" and stalked away from Keel's table, which matched Lita Hoff or Hoffer's temper.

"Did Lita ever wear *brunette* wigs?" he asked Murray.

"I don't think so. But I didn't exactly spend my time watching . . ."

The door opened and a big girl in a short raincoat came

in. Her face was washed-out, and sullen. "I was *sleeping!* What sort of life-and-death crap . . ."

Murray introduced Roersch. The girl stopped complaining. Murray said, "Remember Lita Hoffer? The blonde with the wigs and temper?"

"Lita? Sure. But was she blonde? I worked the second shift with her a few weeks and she liked my shade." She touched her shoulder-length auburn hair. "She bought a wig and had the front frosted. I think she was really brunette . . ."

Roersch said, "Did she have a nickname?"

"I thought *Lita* was her nickname."

Roersch began to get up.

"Because everyone called her The Nun." She laughed at her funny, and Murray said, "Jokes we need?" and Roersch thanked them and left. He stopped at a newsstand. The *Daily News* had a follow-up story on the St. Louis murder. The victim had been identified as an Alma-Jean Radford of Manchester Avenue. Her employer, who'd made the identification after seeing head-shots of the victim on a TV news program, was giving "important information" to the police.

Roersch drove to Mario's, and was surprised at how crowded the small restaurant was. He took a table near the kitchen, and Mario finally came over, looking not too pleased to see him. Roersch said, "I'm paying today, *paisan.* How come so busy?"

"It's Friday night, Eddy! Dinner Friday night's my best time! If it could be dinner Friday night all week long I'd make a fortune!" And he was off to work the cash register.

Roersch remembered he might be taking Ruthie out later tonight for Chinese food. He'd forgotten everything in his What-If game; in the development of the "cheap blonde" who might also be Nick McKenney's frosted redhead with the hot temper who might also be Lita Hoff or Hoffer, The Nun. Damned interesting, even though it was probably not important. Probably three different girls. The Nun, who'd

worked both the topless club and the massage parlor,
where Corinne Bain and Jane Austen had worked. A coincidence, and not too strange since many of these girls
doubled . . .

All right. The Nun was interesting.

Judith Keel's blonde girlfriend was someone else.

Nick McKenney's frosted redhead was someone else.

He ate lightly, a plate of veal scaloppine with green
beans, and sipped a glass of wine. And thought, *But what
if they're all the same girl?* What then?

Why then he'd have one hell of a headache! Then he'd
have to bring The Nun right up alongside Bley as a prime
suspect.

But no way to tie her in with Keel.

He finished his wine and paid Mario at the register and
was surprised at the price . . . damned high! He grumbled
to himself, realizing he'd never paid for a meal here, and
went out to his car. And told himself to forget it. Bley was
still his pigeon, and Sunday he'd collect enough for
twenty, maybe thirty thousand ten-buck dinners!

Driving home, he began to get that headache.

18: Saturday a.m. and p.m.

It had stayed quiet, all those long hours—from about five Friday afternoon, when they had the scene in the gas station, to almost five Saturday morning, when they checked into the motel off Route 40 in Flagstaff—twelve hours of solid driving broken only by a quick meal in a diner and six stops for gas and bathroom. Twelve hours, and quiet wasn't really the word for it; fucking armed truce was more like it! She was almost sorry she'd started the action against John . . . but then again, she had no choice. One of them had to go.

John and Evan took turns driving, changing after each stop, and slept when they weren't driving. She followed Evan from front to rear and back again and sat beside him and tried to get *close*. But Jesus, it felt as if she were alone on the goddamn *moon*! No one spoke to her. No one spoke to anyone else. She couldn't wait to get to Flagstaff and a motel and a bed and some human contact!

They shared one room, John taking the fold-out couch, she and Evan a big bed. Outside, trucks roared by and the sky was getting light. She said something the black bartender at the Bantam Royal in the Village used to say: "Late to bed and late to rise, we'll soon be dead, all you guys!" John went into the bathroom without a word. Evan began unpacking his small suitcase. It was as if she wasn't there!

She said, "Evan," coming up behind him, putting her arms around his waist, pressing her head to his back. "Don't be mad at me, baby. I didn't mean . . ."

He said, "Wait until we're in bed."

She almost blew up then. She almost told him what he could do with his car and his bed and his cock and his bread. She almost got her pack and went out on the highway to hitch back to Albuquerque and the guy she'd met in L.A. who wanted her to spend a month's vacation with him.

But a month's vacation would still leave her in Albuquerque. The only way out was Hollywood and acting and contacts and someone like Evan to grease the wheels.

John walked by in his shorts and got on the couch and under the covers. He didn't look at her; not even in her direction. He said, "Goodnight, all," and turned his back to the room.

Evan went into the bathroom. She sat down at the edge of the bed and began to undress. John spoke, voice muffled by bedding. "We're not far from Albuquerque and your friend. I'll give you ten bucks if you take off now."

She said, "Fuck you!"

He said, "You'll have to do that too, if you stick around."

She got up and started for him; then stopped. Evan wanted *quiet.*

Evan came out, and she went to the bathroom and

showered and used a little of her dwindling supply of Chanel Number Five. She dried her hair and brushed it until it shone. She reached for the door, then put a dab of perfume between her legs.

The lights were out in the bedroom. She felt her way to the bed, got in beside Evan, and snuggled close. She kissed his mouth, and he said, "The agreement was all of us, together."

She got her hand on his cock, and whispered, "Maybe tomorrow, if he apologizes. But for tonight . . ."

He was stiffening in her hand, yet he turned over and said, "Goodnight. Tomorrow is fine."

All right, motherfucker! She could hold out a lot longer than anyone with a pair of balls!

But she couldn't fall asleep, and when she finally did it was fully light and sounds of traffic got right into the room and she slept uneasily, with confused dreams. The only thing she could remember about them when she awoke and they began rushing to get out by noon—Evan wanted part of today at the canyon—was the goddamn Bantam Royal Club. There was the jukebox and the combo on Saturday night and that toilet with the single booth and the door that wouldn't lock. And the dumb-chick customers going in there and Michelle always ready to follow one who was sauced high and how the chick's date would begin to wonder what the hell was taking so long and ask Lois to go in there "and see if she's all right." She was usually *fine*, a little shell-shocked but up against the wall with panties down and legs spread and Michelle giving her a fast intro into the les scene. In the dream, the club and bathroom and Michelle and Lois were all mixed up, and it was dark and it was ugly and it was wild and it was exciting. Above all, it was dangerous, terribly dangerous, and she knew she had to get the hell out and stay the hell out or she would be damned for all eternity.

So she was glad to leave nightmares and *quiet* and start

for the canyon. Things were bound to get better. They
certainly couldn't get worse!

They were on a climbing road and not much doing on
either side. "What about breakfast?" she asked.

"We decided to wait until we could eat at the canyon,"
John said, from the back seat.

We? No one had consulted *her!*

"Great floor show," Evan said.

"Really?" she said. "I didn't know they had entertainment at a place like . . ." And then John laughed and she
realized she'd been sandbagged. He meant the scenery.

She had a time making herself chuckle. It was like laying eggs with her throat!

John asked Evan about the kind of country they were
passing through. Evan said they were entering "some of
the most beautiful forest in America . . . not the heaviest,
by any means, but as we climb you'll get trees in hilly
settings—piñon, juniper, ponderosa pine, some Gambel
oak with entwined roots . . ." John talked about a trip he'd
taken to Yosemite National Park, and Evan talked about
redwoods and black bears . . . and she wanted to join their
conversation. But she didn't know anything about parks
and nature and such. She knew about men and women . . .
and felt Evan was *tired* of men and women.

John had an edge. Maybe he knew it and maybe he only
acted as if he knew it, but he had a definite edge now. She
was in trouble. She'd done the wrong things and he'd done
the right things, and with a character like Evan that could
be dangerous.

John said, "How'd you learn so much about nature, a
city boy like you?"

"I always used the outdoors as an escape, though not in
an *actual* sense, not by getting out into the wilderness. I've
been to the Grand Canyon once, years ago, a one-day
stopover on the way back from a West Coast client meeting. I did the same in Yosemite and Yellowstone and
Glacier; brief hours; mere glimpses. But all my life I've

read. I joined the Sierra Club and read everything they published. And watched the National Geographic television specials, and paid more than casual attention to details . . ." He paused. "If I could control my appetites, my inbred ideas about success, my subconscious drives, I'd make a happy forest ranger."

She wanted to laugh, but didn't dare.

John did laugh, and said, "Yeah, wouldn't we all."

Evan nodded, smiling.

Lois realized how boxed in she was. She kept her face to the window, and thought it through.

Evan would turn back to her. He couldn't fuck a pine tree, now could he? He was bound to come her way . . . unless John moved him toward pickup chicks like in Oklahoma.

She said, "Hey, you guys, can I apologize for what a bitch I was yesterday?"

John quickly said, "It's okay with me, Lois." Then he stole her line. "You were sick, we know that."

Evan said, "You're recovered now, I presume?"

She nodded, smiling at him and smiling at sweet Saint John the Baptist . . . who smiled back, forgiving all and loving all because he had his game under tight control.

How surprised he'd be when she wiped him out. She kept smiling.

"Yes, you *are* recovered," Evan said, and patted her knee.

She beckoned John to lean forward. His smile faded a bit, but he obeyed. She said, "Kiss and make up, Johnnie?" and put her hand behind his head. He stiffened. She pulled him forward a little more and kissed his lips. And watched as he leaned back.

Their eyes locked. No doubt about it, it was war. She looked out the window and began asking questions about trees, flowers, anything that would get her into Evan's nature bag. He answered, and told them about Bright Angel Trail and the hike they would take along its twists and turns into the mile-deep canyon. He said there were mule trips, but he much preferred to hike. She said, "Me too. Sneakers and a canteen are all I need." She looked back at John. "What do you think, Johnnie?" He said hiking was great, just as long as it wasn't cross-country. "I've had more than enough of *that*."

She laughed for him, and for Evan . . . but most of all for herself. Whenever they thought they had little Lo-lo boxed in, she gave them a *big* surprise! Now it was Johnnie's turn.

John finished eating before Evan and Lois, and excused himself. He said he was going to the bathroom, but he'd seen the canteen-souvenir shop across the parking lot from the old hotel, and *ran* there. As expected, they had sporting goods, and among them were Bowie-type hunting knives. He chose quickly, taking one that wasn't as big as he'd have liked, but that could be concealed a lot more easily. Besides, a four-inch blade could do the job, if you knew how to handle it.

He knew how to handle it.

He was back at the restaurant, the knife under his shirt and jacket, in time for coffee and a cigarette. Evan was staring out the window, murmuring, "Incredible."

A fucking big hole, yeah! He smoked and watched Lois put on the big interest act. And was on full alert . . . because he knew her; knew it wasn't like her to kiss and make up when she was losing. And Evan; telling him to be quiet, putting him down . . .

They walked out and over to the railing. And the big hole became the Grand Canyon; took over; made him step back, suddenly frightened. Because it was enormous and old and so . . . so *scary*. Because it was like looking up at the sky that night near the pool when he was a kid and Dad was bombed from the party going on inside and Dad pointed out Orion and the Big Dipper and other constellations and stars and said, "Trillions and billions of light-years away, Johnnie. Vast, vast, and every star huge, huge, and what are we but bacteria floating around and trying to make believe we're important?" And if *Dad* felt that way, then what was *he*, Johnnie had thought . . . and his stomach had lurched and his head had swum and he'd trembled and run inside to bed, to things as small as he was and as unimportant as he was, and had tried to feel he *mattered* again.

Now the Grand Canyon, vast, vast, and somehow even more unnerving than the stars because it was right *here*, right at his feet, right in front of his eyes and hands. And nose . . . he could *smell* the vastness, a cool and empty smell rising up out of the canyon, making him weak and giddy.

And again he felt a loss of self; of size and perspective.

He disengaged from the big hole. He looked at Lois. She was staring across the miles and miles of bottomless space, but she wasn't looking *down*. And down was where it was at.

Evan said, "It's just a short walk to the trail. We can go down a few hundred yards, get an idea of what we'll do tomorrow. Come on!" He rushed ahead like a kid, stepping to the edge every so often, leaning over the railing . . . and John felt a choking fear, and looked at Lois. She was pale; she looked *surprised* at the canyon. He spoke softly. "Bet you never saw anything like this before, did you?"

She said, "No," and looked around at the sides, at the rock ledges and cliffs, at the formations. And at the colors, mostly reds and purples this time of day. But she still didn't look down. "Takes some getting used to."

He agreed. He had been here before, hitching a ride in with a college girl, and had concentrated on shacking up in her camper. He'd avoided feelings about the canyon, barely going near it. But he'd known it was there. It was like the ocean, waiting over a hill. You knew it was there. The girl had split to camp along the Colorado with a group, and he'd hitched out. Not his bag.

They reached the trail. It had a sign warning about sufficient water and steep cliffs and pacing yourself for the trip back up. It looked okay, a normal touristy thing, not Orion and the Big Dipper and being a bacteria. But about thirty, forty feet down, it began to change, began to feel like a rope bridge hanging in the sky. There were no railings here. He slowed his pace, hugging the rock wall to his left. They went around a turn.

Suddenly, the lodge and cars and other people—the world and what was important—were *gone*. Just like that, they were alone like he'd never been alone, somewhere ancient and frightening, even though it was also beautiful. A terrible beauty for anyone not used to it. And who could get used to a thing this *big*, this . . . *unmanageable?* This place . . . it just couldn't *be!*

Evan was in front. John was following, with Lois behind him. Evan went right to the edge, staring straight down. "Isn't that the river? Look . . ."

John waited for Lois. She stopped behind him, also against the rock. He said, "Where?" to Evan, and turned and took Lois's hand. She yanked it free, backing up, staring at him. He waited. He took a little step forward; she did the same. Then, together, they walked over to Evan. Lois went to his right and John to his left. Only then did John look down, to the tiny, narrow world at the bottom with its pencil-line river. "Jesus Christ Almighty," he said, and he wasn't swearing, he was praying. He stepped back, because one look was enough, at least for now.

Lois was also looking down. And tilting forward. He glanced at Evan. Evan didn't notice anything or anyone. Lois was still tilting; seemed about to fall. He wanted to shout at her . . . and didn't.

Then she shook her head and shuffled back. She was pale, like when she'd been sick, and she whispered, "Let's go to the hotel."

Evan didn't hear. Evan kept staring down, his head moving, his lips moving. John said, "Aren't you afraid?"

"What?" Evan muttered, and he was inching forward, his shoe-tops crossing the edge of eternity.

"To stand there like that . . . you can't be afraid of *anything.*"

Lois said, "Evan! Don't lean . . ."

Evan backed up, looking like he'd just gotten out of bed, his eyes misty, cloudy. "Maybe flying the old Air Corps trainers—Stearman Nineteens with wide-open cockpits; felt like you were *hanging* in the sky—maybe that prepared me. I don't know."

"*Nothing* prepares you for this," John said, with utter conviction.

Evan looked at the canyon again. "I'm glad we're together. I've never been anywhere with friends. And *here* . . ." He faced them. "Don't spoil it, *please.*"

Lois said, "Why would we spoil . . . ?" and John said, "Think we're crazy?" and Evan walked by them up the trail.

They reached the rim. It was like coming back through time . . . so much easier to *breathe* on top, with the railings and the hotels and the parking lots and the people.

Evan said they would go to the Bright Angel Lodge and check in; put their things away before driving to various view spots. Afterward, they'd pick up some camping equipment for tomorrow. And maybe they'd stay overnight at the bottom and explore the older, narrower trails. And wasn't the air magnificent and the weather just perfect and he could hardly wait for morning!

Lois said, "Me too, hon."

John said, "Hey, yeah," and wondered at himself, at his fear, his *dread* of what could happen.

Evan felt delight; and felt oppression. The Grand Canyon was a catalyst, it seemed, changing everything. There was less need for Lois and John; a re-examination of Lois and John. They seemed . . . unimportant. They seemed part of what had been cheap and dangerous in his life.

He took them shopping, and wanted to be alone.

He bought them and himself canteens and camping equipment and proper shoes, and wanted to sit somewhere and decide what his life could be . . . if it could be anything.

He bought a gallon of California chablis and food and they drove to several lookout points. It grew dark and they returned to the lodge and their room.

He showered and took a long time at it, trying for a return to joy, to hope for Los Angeles and the future. This enormous space in the earth, this place where time itself was buried . . . it was for strong people, balanced people.

It wasn't for him, no matter how he was drawn to looking at it . . . looking *down* into it.

What the hell was he thinking of?

He opened the bathroom door. John was lying on the nearest of the twin beds, shoes and trousers off, eyes closed. Lois was on the other bed—the one he and she would share—fully clothed, her back to John. John turned his head and looked at her, a long moment . . . then put his hands between his legs, and rubbed. Evan watched.

That was the answer to utter and confusing nonsense. He said, "John."

The man jerked his hand away. "Yeah . . . what?" His face reddened—the cheeks and forehead, the rest being masked by hair.

"Roll some joints. And open the wine."

John swung his feet over the edge of the bed. Lois rolled to face them both. Evan had a bath towel wrapped around his middle. He removed it, and said, "Let's get comfortable."

She said, "You mean . . . ?"

"Turn up the thermostat." He closed the door again, and splashed on cologne and combed his hair. He examined himself in the mirror. Some ugliness was returning.

Nonsense!

But he *felt* it as he had when he'd been a child and his

mother looked at him and he looked at himself after masturbation. Felt it as he had all his life.

He turned from the mirror and wondered if *they* would
see it when he came out.

He combed his hair once again. He smoothed his eyebrows. He told himself he had good color in his cheeks.

The ugliness seemed more pronounced, and he left the
bathroom to escape it.

Lois was hanging her jeans over the back of a chair.
Her panties and blouse lay on the seat. John was nude,
sitting on his bed, rolling a joint and looking at her. His
penis was turgid.

Evan sucked in his gut as he came to Lois. He put his
hand on her bottom, slid it between her legs, fingered her
cleft. She was startled, then smiled back at him. It was a
false smile; she was dry down there. He fingered her more
actively. She turned, disengaging his finger, and said, "I'll
get the wine."

He went to their bed and sat down. His own penis was
distending.

She brought him the stack of plastic glasses from the
dresser, and the bottle, and he poured himself some wine.
He drank without waiting for her or John, without waiting
for toasts or smiles or raised glasses. She poured herself a
glass, and put the bottle and glasses on the floor. He said,
"What about John?"

She said, "Sure, hon," and gave that lying smile again
and went to John. She poured, standing beside him, and
the bearded face tilted up and then dipped slowly, to her
breasts, her stomach, her cunt, her full thighs. As she held
out the glass, John stroked her backside. She froze, and
said, "Your wine, Johnnie."

He took the wine. She took the two joints he handed her
and returned to sit beside Evan.

They drank. They smoked. His ugliness receded. There
was no television in the room, but a radio stood on the
table between the beds. Evan put it on. He found music,

soft music. Lois reached past him and changed stations. She found rock music, wild music, and began to shake her shoulders, her breasts, shift her bottom, smoking the joint and sipping the wine and looking at him without false smiles.

They finished the joints. They drank more wine. Lois went to John and refilled his glass once, twice, three times. The third time he reached for her, pressed his mouth between her legs. She laughed and turned away and bent her ass for his lips. He didn't hesitate. His face went there, pressed there, and she looked at Evan across the four or five feet of space, lips parted and eyes half-closed, and moaned, "Up the hole, Johnnie-boy, where you belong." John didn't stop and Evan felt his penis stiffening and wanted her and John together, all together.

He began to rise, to come to them and help John subjugate her. He had a flaming need to slam her, to shove his cock down her throat and do the choking and hurting . . . and she spun out of John's clutching hands and said, "Sweat for it, Johnnie-boy!" and jumped onto the bed beside Evan. John rose, his penis out and slightly up, short and reddish-purple and full of *need*, the testicles hanging low and heavy.

Evan tore his eyes away. Lois pulled him down to her lips, and he said, "Wait," and drained his glass and dropped it to the floor. He kissed her wet and open mouth, and murmured, "John too," and from the corner of his eye saw that short penis beside him and saw John's knee press the bed.

She was looking past him at John. "First you, Evan," she said. "Then him. Then the three of us. But please baby first you alone. I need that, I do."

It was salve for the ego, and he spoke to that reddish-purple penis. "Go back to your bed. For a while."

The rigid penis stayed there. So close. Never before had a rigid penis been that close to him; to his eyes, to his face, to his mouth. He stared at it, hypnotized.

But that was the wine and the pot and the whirling of his head and the pounding rock music.

He began to lift himself. "Back to your bed, I said."

The penis withdrew, but just a little. Evan got up. John was swaying and John was looking at *his* penis, and he looked too. It was huge. It was something to be proud of. It was manhood and power . . .

He remembered his mother and the neighbor woman laughing, and he remembered Judy saying it *hurt*, and he was ashamed and began to cringe. He shoved John away. "Go on!"

"What's with the fucking *commands!*" John said, fists clenching. "What's with the shoves and the master-and-slave bit! I'm nobody's goddamn . . ."

Evan came toward him. His erection remained, actually strengthened. John's erection dipped and John turned and stumbled around his bed and toward the closet.

Something in that closet?

Evan lunged after him. John had the closet door open and was bending to reach to the floor. Evan was on him, trying to spin him away. His penis was huge, and stiff, and it pressed John's flesh and the contact burned him and it was *he* who spun away.

John turned, and he had a knife.

Evan didn't hesitate. He slapped the bearded face with his left hand, and chopped down on the knife-wrist with his right. The knife fell to the carpet. He stepped forward . . . and John stepped back. He picked up the knife and looked at it and looked at John. John huddled against the door. "I bought it for the trail . . . cutting kindling . . . everyone carries . . ." Evan raised the knife. John cringed against the door. Evan looked at John and at John's penis, which cringed too, which was shriveled and dead. Evan smiled. *His* erection was powerful. He wasn't affected enough by this foolish act of defiance to lose even a particle of lust for Lois.

But was it lust? And for Lois?

John's body cringed and John's voice cringed. "Hey, man, I wasn't really . . . just all this wine and pot . . . I'm sorry . . . Lois, tell him!"

Evan glanced at her. She said nothing. She stared at them, lips parted and smiling at the corners. Her eyes flicked back and forth . . . and he felt them touch his erection and felt it throb. He turned from John and went to the window. He slid it open and threw the knife into the darkness.

Lois was stretching out when he turned. Lois was raising her legs and grasping her ankles. Lois was opening her cunt to him and saying, "C'mon, baby! Show him how! C'mon . . ."

He was on her, feeling a lion, a tiger, a thing with teeth and claws. He was in her, slamming, making her grunt, making her moan. And he was aware of the huddled shape slinking to the other bed, the beaten thing watching in desire and envy.

He fucked wildly, abandonedly, turning Lois so that his ass was to John; shaking that ass at him and feeling it and turning on to it. He was as attuned to his ass as he was to Lois's. He was as attuned to what he looked like to John as he was to the flesh turning damp under his pounding body. The basic act of contempt—kiss my ass! The basic act of subjugation—watch me fuck your woman! The ultimate male triumph . . . and yet orgasm eluded him. He worked for it, *strained* for it, and felt something was missing. Something to get by the wine and pot and pounding music and whirling in his brain.

He waited for that something.

John spat into his hand and rubbed his cock. He rose and spat again and rubbed again. He stepped forward and his legs were almost touching Evan's legs. He spat a third time, copiously, and made the head of his cock slippery wet. He crouched a little and aimed and leaned forward, toppling, coming to rest with his hands on either side of

Lois's shoulders. He could see nothing but their heads now, but he could *smell* them—the rank, randy smell of aroused genitals; male or female, all alike; orifices, holes, sheaths for his cock. He still hadn't *touched* Evan, keeping his groin up and away, but Lois looked at him and said, "Hey!" and Evan stopped moving, began turning his head.

John brought his groin forward in hatred and fear and urgency and revenge and lust and love and felt his penis slide between the hot, sweaty cheeks and shoved and felt it press against the hairy hole and felt that hole expand. Lois's eyes widened and flashed to Evan, and Evan had his head half-turned, frozen it seemed, and Evan's body was also frozen in mid-stroke, half up and half down.

He came down on Evan's body now, had to as he leaned to the left, withdrawing his right hand from beside Lois's shoulder to grasp his cock, to steady it. The contact was warm, leg to leg and groin to ass and belly to curved back; warm and not unlike mounting a woman; warm and of increasing excitement. He shoved hard, a jolting snap of his loins, and felt his glans enter and heard Evan gasp, and felt the sweaty cheeks jerk down and away from him, but only inches since they had nowhere to go. Because of Lois. Because he was lying on both of them. Because Evan was joined to Lois and he was joined to Evan and he was entering both of them, shoving harder and dropping his right hand back beside Lois's shoulder and ramming all the way in. God, up to the nuts and sheathed tightly . . . and everything stopped.

The room was filled with pounding breath, his and Evan's and Lois's. He was suddenly afraid to move, and yet *had* to move before the world exploded into madness and death; *had* to move because he was sheathed in flesh and his body demanded movement.

He drew back an inch and shoved forward an inch. And it was suddenly slippery and it was suddenly smooth and it was flesh, ass, love, *good!*

He wrapped his arms around Evan's body, shoving them

between Evan's flesh and Lois's flesh, feeling the softness of two bellies. Then he began the act of love, jabbing in and out. And it all came together, what had been done to him and what he was doing to them, and he jabbed *furiously*.

Evan *cried*, a wail, a terrible sound, but it was John's triumph and it was John's turn-on and seeing Lois's shocked face and gaping mouth and feeling they were both helpless beneath him, he went on.

And Evan's ass *moved*.

As his had moved, against his will, in the Miami lockup.

Evan dropped his head all the way down beside Lois's, and fucked Lois. And in fucking Lois, he helped John fuck him. And John shut his eyes and worked that tight hole and forgot everything but pleasure.

19: | Sunday a.m.

He reached the Bright Angel Lodge, the one on Bley's notepad, somewhat later Sunday morning than he'd expected. It was ten after eight, and he was tired after all that flying.

The desk clerk, who looked like a refined woodsman, found his reservation, talking all the while in a soft drawl.

"We'll have you settled straight away, Mr. Roersch. You'll want to change into something casual . . ." Roersch told himself the man's eyes hadn't really *blinked* at his baggy brown suit . . . "and walk over to the canyon. This time of day is my personal favorite. The light is perfect for seeing sparrows and juncos going from rock formation to rock formation. They work their way across, rather than try it in one jump. And then there are hawks, circling . . ."

Roersch signed his name twice and waited for his receipt and key; and thought *he* was the hawk, circling his sparrow. "I'll do that," he said, "but first I want to see if my friend, Evan Bley, is up. Now what was his room number?"

The clerk checked. "Mr. and Mrs. Bley and nephew . . ." He gave Roersch the room.

Mrs. Bley? And nephew?

He went up one flight of stairs, carrying his overnight case. His room had a view of the canyon, and that long window filled with what looked like a *sky* in the earth almost stopped him.

He opened his bag, dug under the windbreaker and took out his off-duty automatic. He got his toilet kit, opened the zipper, unwrapped the handkerchief and took out the full clip of .25-caliber bullets. He snapped it into the handle of the gun, jacked a round into the chamber, and made sure the safety was on.

Not legal, shipping it this way, but the only alternative to having a warrant and traveling as a cop-on-assignment.

He shoved the gun into the waistband of his trousers, far back on the left hip, where it would be well hidden. He tightened his belt, buttoned his jacket, and checked himself in the dresser mirror. He was satisfied; his jacket was as baggy as his trousers.

He took another look out the window, and said, "Hey, Ruthie, would you get a kick out of *this!*" And didn't question himself on it as he would have a week ago.

Friday night had been something special—dinner and then driving all the way to Queens and back so she could have Jen, even though it meant waking the kid. She'd wanted her daughter with them, and somehow he hadn't minded; had actually enjoyed it. The kid had gone to sleep on the couch, and he and Ruthie had gone to bed. They'd kept it quiet, and still it had been wild and fine and somehow *better* with a child in the next room; somehow all the whore part was gone. And then the three of them breakfasting together . . .

Money could end the whore part for good. He'd think on that. And not on doubts and Lita Hoff-Hoffer-Nun. Money was the name of his game. *That's* what he would think on.

He left the room, and walked down the wide hall, and returned a "Mornin' " from an old guy and a nod from his old lady. They were hand-in-hand, like kids.

He smiled, but then he was at the right door and warned himself this was the way to get killed and to forget sky-in-the-ground like pie-in-the-sky.

He had that shootout feeling; that dry-mouthed, hammer-in-the-head feeling. Because he was here, at last, and what he *thought* he knew about how Bley would react and what Bley might actually do could be two different things.

He knocked, feeling as he had when he and Jimmy had braced the nut on Houston Street.

"Someone's at the door," a woman's voice said, and Roersch thought he heard an English accent and laughed at himself and knocked again.

"Who the hell . . . ?" a man's voice said.

The door opened. A knockout blonde in jeans, sweat-shirt and sneakers said, "Yes?"

He tried not to stare at her. He moved a half-step in and to the side. "Evan Bley?"

A freaky-looking guy, more hair than Wolfman, was sitting on the bed, lacing up sneakers.

The girl backed up a step. "He's in the bathroom."

That's when Roersch's headache returned. That's when he admitted he heard an accent—more Australian than English, but what many would classify as English—and looked at her hard and thought, *But how could it be?* And besides, there were *thousands* of English and Australian and other such accented people in the States.

"Great!" he said. "I thought he said he'd be stopping here. Some timing, huh?"

The bearded man rose. He was big, rawboned, and he didn't look happy. Neither did the girl. The room was a mess with clothes and bedding and plastic glasses tossed around and the feeling, the atmosphere, was tense and down. Maybe that was because of *him*. They looked as if they knew he was a cop. Maybe they'd had occasion to know a cop or two in their day. Roersch didn't kid himself he looked like a doctor.

A door opened in back, and out came Bley . . . bigger than his pictures, but otherwise the same. Grimmer, grayer of face than his pictures, but that would fit a man who'd killed. Roersch said, "Mr. Bley?"

"I thought he *knew* you!" the girl said to Bley, and stepped all the way back into the room.

Bley shook his head slowly. "Not that I can remember."

"If I can have a minute of your time, alone, I'll explain."

"Why alone?" Bley asked, his voice also grim and gray.

Roersch hesitated, warning himself to be careful, that shootout feeling growing.

Bley turned to a closet, and Roersch felt his dryness of mouth increase and put his hand closer to the opening of his jacket.

Bley took out a tan windbreaker and slipped into it. "If this is some kind of sales pitch, I'm not interested in anything but hiking today."

"It's about Judith Keel."

Bley froze in the act of pulling up the zipper. The whole room seemed to freeze. Roersch said, "You heard about her, didn't you, Mr. Bley?"

"Heard what? And who are you?"

Roersch looked at the others. "Why don't you two step outside a moment? This is private."

The girl started for the door. The bearded man looked at Bley. Bley said, "Are you going to tell me who you are?"

Roersch couldn't do that; not with unknown quantities present; not with that girl . . .

Bley stepped toward a phone on a night stand. "I'm calling the management."

Roersch moved forward, saying, "Wait . . ." The bearded man was on his left, and went into a crouch. Roersch said, "Don't do it. I'm just going to show Mr. Bley something." He went by the bearded man, cautiously, and approached Bley. He reached into his breast pocket, and the bearded man said, "Evan, watch it!"

Bley swung around fast, much faster than Roersch thought he would, and a hand was flashing at him, a chopping blow aimed at his neck. He got his own hand up just in time, felt it grow numb at the wrist, grunted and whispered, "Police, you dumb bastard!"

Bley didn't seem impressed. He had both hands up and moving now, his body coiled tight, his face white and tense. And the bearded man was sliding around behind Roersch. And the girl was pressed up against the wall near the door. And these were no quiet citizens, no easy marks, no patsies . . . and he might need his gun . . . and Jesus what a mess if he did! "My identification," he whispered, and took out his wallet and flipped it open. And rubbed his other hand against his thigh, chasing the numbness, thinking if Bley had caught his neck, he'd be down and maybe dead. "Tell them to go. It won't take long."

Bley reached out with his left hand, the right going further back, further up, and took the wallet. He looked at it maybe ten times, quick looks, not taking his attention off Roersch. Then he gave it back and dropped his hand. "Wait for me outside," he told the others.

The girl was gone, in a flash. She'd been busted before, for sure . . . and Roersch pushed back the impulse to follow and question. His plan was working now. Bley was the one and it would soon be over.

The bearded man said, "Are you *sure?*"

Bley didn't look at him. "Yes. It's all right. He's a . . ."

Roersch said, "Mr. Bley," and told himself it made no difference that a guilty man would have more sense of self-preservation, because *this* guilty man was insane; had to be insane after Keel and that girl in St. Louis.

Or were the *three* of them in it together . . . in on

Corinne Bain and Jane Austen . . . and how the hell could *that* be?

The bearded man left. They were finally alone. Roersch stepped back, out of reach of those quick hands, and felt sweat trickling down his sides and decided he was too old for this kind of thing. "You're Evan Bley. You work at Grayson & Burns. You had problems with Judith Keel, put her under surveillance, paid an investigator, Nick McKenney, a thousand dollars to hand in a false report. Last Sunday you went to her apartment and killed her. You can do one of two things—come back to New York in my custody to stand trial for murder, or we can talk about it."

Bley stared at him, his face a study in incredulity.

"C'mon now. Do I have to go through *everything*? Your buying her expensive gifts? Your suspicions, confirmed by the surveillance? Your calls on the car-phone, overheard by a neighbor of Keel's, Elizabeth Oron, on her short-wave set? Threats she heard? Threats Keel told others about, including your boss, Morgan Burns, and your assistant, Vince McKenney? Your belting her around? Your cutting her water bed? Your writing a threatening letter, which you didn't mail? Your writing her name into a porno-sadism book? Your Polaroid pictures, acting out that book? Your taking her earrings, with blood on them, and a picture off her dresser, maybe blood on that too? Nick McKenney continuing the surveillance on *you*, hoping for more blackmail? Your being *seen* entering Keel's apartment house the night of the murder?" As he spoke, he grew sure again, because there was enough evidence to convict a *dozen* men! "How much more do you want?"

Bley's face was red. "You were in my home?"

"Yes. And visited your mother. And after talking to her, I can almost understand why you would want to kill . . ."

Bley's hand shot up. Roersch jumped back, drawing his gun. But it wasn't another attack. Bley waved that hand, palm out, telling him to stop. Bley said, voice choked, "No one should intrude in another man's home, in another man's life. It's . . . indecent." He sank to the edge of the bed. "No one should judge a man . . ." He groaned and touched his face, all over, as if examining it; then dropped his head. "Ugly," he whispered. "Oh, God, ugly!"

"I understand, Mr. Bley. Now what we have to do is find an alternative to your standing trial."

Bley's head was still down. He stayed that way a moment, then slowly looked up. "Does my mother know?"

"No one knows but me." He put the gun away, warning himself not to relax too much.

"How did Judy die?"

Roersch sighed. "Do I have to talk about that girl in St. Louis? The one found in the garbage at the Wayside Inn Motel?"

"Wayside Inn? You don't mean Alma-Jean?"

He'd practically confessed! And yet that goddamn *look* —stunned, shocked, unbelieving.

"Yes, Alma-Jean Radford. Naked and her belly cut open. You don't like women very much, do you?"

"Naked . . . cut open . . . *Alma-Jean?*" His acting was Academy Awards stuff, if it *was* acting.

"Naked in black boots," Roersch said heavily, "and her guts wrapped around her neck and your come in her cunt and if you don't talk sense to me you'll rot in prison the rest of your life. Or in a hospital for the criminally insane, and that's not too much better, take my word for it."

"Black boots," Bley muttered. "I remember . . ."

"That's the boy," Roersch said, hoping. "What you have to do is keep traveling, because the St. Louis police have someone who's giving information on the Alma-Jean murder. A clothing store owner . . ."

"Her employer," Bley interrupted. "He knows my name. I used my credit card."

"So time is short. You've got to head for the hills. One of the smaller South American countries. But first you have to do something else." Bley looked at him. "You know what that is, don't you . . . Evan? I can't see any point in putting an intelligent man, a confused man, away for the rest of his life. You can get help wherever you go . . ."

"I remember Alma-Jean didn't take off her boots," Bley said, "but she must have dressed before she left the room."

Roersch wanted to get him back on the road to the payoff, but Bley's face was changing, clearing, firming. "And what's that got to do with *me?*" And before Roersch could speak, he stood up. "And what has Judy's death got to do with me? I don't care what you think about the surveillance . . . I may have made some wild plans . . . but I never carried them out! I don't care what McKenney or anyone else says, I didn't kill her and I didn't kill Alma-Jean and I didn't kill anyone! I grabbed those earrings and she may have bled a little . . . but she was alive when I left."

"I guess you'll stand trial then."

"It's all circumstantial . . ."

"People have gone to the chair on less circumstantial evidence than this."

Bley shook his head. "You're not serious?"

Roersch hadn't heard a thing that refuted the facts; just the usual I-didn't-do-it crap. "Don't try me, Evan."

Bley smiled, unbelievingly. "What's the alternative?"

"Come up with three hundred thousand in cash, and you're out of it. You'll still have enough left to start over again. Just don't try to beat the system, once the system has you cold."

Bley said, "So *that's* the story?"

Roersch felt himself flushing, turning as red as Bley had when caught with his pornography down. He snapped, "That's the story. And if I were you, with this much evidence stacked against me, I'd pay and run."

Bley said, "Humor me. How did Judy die?"

"That proves you're lying! You'd be bound to have seen it in the papers, or heard it on radio or television. By

Monday noon the story was all over New York. And by evening it hit the rest of the country."

"I slept late Monday, and then packed. I didn't read a paper or listen to radio or television. Then I was on my way. I've gone a week or more without knowing a thing about *important* news, when working on a big campaign. As for sports and crime . . ." He shrugged. "Are you going to tell me?"

Roersch told him, with all the bloody details. "No hope for parole there, Evan. Or release from an institution."

Bley said, "Incredible! Who would do such a thing?" And then, as Roersch gave him the cynical smile, "I won't pay you any money . . . Edmund. I assure you I would, if I'd killed anyone. I'd pay *anything*, if I'd killed anyone. But I didn't kill anyone."

"In my suitcase, I've got hard evidence . . ."

"Not hard enough. You have no witnesses to my killing Judy or Alma-Jean or a murder weapon that relates to me. You *can't* have, because I didn't do it." He smiled, and now it was a normal smile, a pleased smile. "I don't feel any particular sense of loss, or grief, for either girl, but I had no part in their deaths." He paused. "Alma-Jean puzzles me. Are the two murders connected?"

Roersch said, "Come off it," watching him, studying him, thinking he had to be a pure psycho . . . tough and bright, but psycho. There were nuts who could beat lie detectors and psychiatrists . . . and juries. They wiped out the past; *believed* in their innocence.

But it could still be an act. Only one way to find out. "Then you're ready to come with me?"

"If you've got a warrant."

"A matter of time . . ."

Bley stood up. "Until that time, I'm not going anywhere with you. I'm going hiking." He stepped forward. Roersch reached for his gun, blocking the way. Bley turned to the phone. Roersch said, "All right," and moved aside. "We'll find you, Evan, no matter where you go."

"Not necessarily, Edmund. And if you do, think of explaining this blackmail attempt." Bley walked by him, *strolled* by him contemptuously.

Roersch allowed him to get to the door. "That Valentine's Day photograph of your mother. That lovely heart you drew . . ."

Bley turned, face draining of blood.

"If you want to accuse me of blackmail . . ." Roersch shrugged. "It *might* cause me some embarrassment, if anyone'll believe you. But not nearly the embarrassment that picture will cause *you*. Because I'll see that it's made public. Well, at least to your friends . . . and your mother."

Bley stepped to the bed and sat down. He wet his lips. "How much?"

Roersch didn't have an immediate answer. He'd have taken all he could get for the results of his investigation; for trapping Bley in a murder, then releasing him from the prospect of a lifetime in prison. But this . . .

"I'd pay perhaps twenty, twenty-five thousand. Is that all right?"

Roersch felt a terrible taste in his mouth; a taste of shit.

"I'll make it fifty thousand," Bley said. "That's certainly a record for one photograph! You'll give me the picture, and any copies you made. I'll take your word . . ."

He was shaking, *begging*. He was a pitiful kid, a brutalized kid, *terrified* of his mother. He was more afraid of her than of prison!

Roersch couldn't stand that taste. He wanted the money, sure. Goddamn it, how he wanted that fifty grand to offset the bare years, the lean years, the years of being overlooked and shoved aside despite his record! It would mean some luxury for him and Ruthie and Jen, if not the lifetime of security, leisure and travel he'd dreamed of. But his mouth actually twisted as the taste grew thicker, fouler.

"How much can you expect for one picture?" Bley

whispered. "One crazy moment? Be reasonable. Set a figure . . ."

All he had to do was keep quiet, and the price would go
up. Bley would pay as much to keep that picture from his
mother as he'd pay for *anything* . . . as he'd pay for his
life! Looking at him, Roersch knew he had him by the
balls. He still could get that lifetime of security, of leisure
and travel, if he played his cards right.

But he swallowed dryly, that taste killing him. This was
straight-out blackmail. He wasn't trading the results of his
skill, his craft, for a payoff. He was peddling a dirty picture . . . one he'd stolen from a man's home.

And he couldn't live with it. "Forget it," he said. "You
can have the picture."

Bley stood up. "What sort of game *is* this!" He wasn't
relieved. He was angry.

Roersch didn't blame him.

"Just between us, Evan . . . *did* you kill Judith Keel?"

Bley took a deep breath. "Recorders and similar devices,
Edmund. Is *that* the game you're playing? Crush me, and
let up, and then try to trap me?"

Roersch said nothing.

Bley went to the door; then stopped with his hand on
the knob. "I still can't understand Alma-Jean. If the murders are connected, how . . . ?"

"They're not connected, except through you. If you
didn't do Keel, then there's no connection. So you *had* to
have done Keel."

"And I didn't. So it's *coincidence?* Two girls I knew—
though Alma-Jean only for a night—brutally murdered?"
He shrugged and opened the door. "Goodbye, Edmund.
Maybe it's all a figment of your imagination."

Roersch walked slowly toward him. It was time to play
What-If with a vengeance. "Close the door," he said.

Bley said, "Get out! I could have been a good distance
down the trail by now. I could have begun forgetting
everything unpleasant, especially my own life."

Roersch *kicked* the door shut. Bley whitened. "You're hard to take, Edmund. But of course, you're a police officer with a gun and stolen photographs."

"We'll fight it out in the schoolyard some other time," Roersch said, and was surprised at the color which flamed into Bley's cheeks. "But we'll play a kids' game anyway. We'll play make-believe—make believe you didn't kill Judith Keel or Alma-Jean Radford. Coincidence is too much to accept. You don't accept it yourself. So how long have you known these friends of yours—the blonde and the bearded man? Are they from New York? Were they with you in St. Louis?"

Bley's color was down. "Lois and John? They're hitchhikers, and I gave them a ride from Manhattan. They're not from New York originally, but they've been living there for some time, I gather. Why?"

"So they were with you in St. Louis when you met this Alma-Jean?"

"Obviously."

"Not so obviously," Roersch snapped. "You could have left them somewhere. You could have balled the girl yourself."

"We were together," Bley said.

"Their full names?"

"Lois Chandler and John Fredericks."

"Are you sure those're their *real* names?"

"If you mean have I seen birth or baptismal certificates, no."

"How about driver's licenses or any other kind of I.D.?"

"No."

"Is Lois English?"

"Australian. But what . . . ?"

"Does she ever go by the name Lita Hoffer? Or a nickname, The Nun?"

Bley shook his head.

Roersch looked at the door. "They're waiting outside, aren't they?"

"I presume so."

"Didn't you see them when you opened the door a minute ago?"

"No, but I didn't look."

"If they listened," Roersch muttered, "they might have heard us." He looked around the room. "Does Lois have luggage?"

"Just a bedroll-pack combination. But I don't think you should touch it without her permission."

Roersch didn't have time for that, or for explanations. "Where is it?"

Bley was silent.

Roersch walked to the open closet. When he heard movement at the door, he turned and drew his gun.

Bley dropped his hand from the knob. "You're not really a detective sergeant, are you?"

"Yes, just that. Sit on the bed, please."

Bley went to the nearest bed and sat down. Roersch kept an eye on him as he dragged two bedrolls from the closet floor. Both were unstrapped, and he unrolled the one that had a pink styling brush stuck in a fold. He pulled jeans and a blouse and panties out. He unsnapped a flap-pocket and reached in and said, "Hello, Lita." He held up a dark-red wig with a splash of silver-gray across the front—what they called frosting.

Bley said, "I never saw that before."

"Keel did. So did at least one other girl." The taste of shit was gone from his mouth and the What-If game was now How-To—how to figure out the answer to one big question. "You *must* have known her in New York."

"I didn't. Does that wig mean anything?"

"You say you picked them up in Manhattan. Was that last year, or the year before?"

"Your humor eludes me, Edmund. It was Monday evening, about eight o'clock, at a club called the Bantam Royal. I'd stopped for a drink . . ."

"And you'd never seen either one of them before?"

"I've known them five days."

Roersch stared at him. Bley met his look. *How could*

these two have gotten together? Roersch asked himself. *Bley and The Nun . . . how?*

He could figure every answer but that one. That one would have to come from Bley, if he knew the answer. Or Lois-Lita-Nun, if *she* did.

And she *had* to know the answer.

If he was right.

He had to make her *give* him the answer, because on that hinged the case. First Keel's murder. Then Keel and Alma-Jean Radford. Then Keel and Radford and Bain and Austen. Four murders, and no matter what Hawly and Deverney might say about his trip here, no matter what they might suspect because of Chauger, he'd hand them four solutions. They'd do *anything* for that kind of score. He'd get his promotion and he'd get his lieutenant's pension and he'd lose the taste of shit forever.

He tossed the wig into the closet, put his gun back in the waistband of his trousers and buttoned his jacket. He went to the door, opened it and stepped outside. The hall was empty. He went to the stairwell. No one.

He went down to the lobby and looked around, and Bley joined him. "You were going hiking," Roersch said. "Maybe they went on without you?"

"But they didn't take their canteens, their packs with food . . ."

Roersch went to the lobby doors and looked around. No blonde and no bearded man. He stepped outside and thought through his options and he hadn't too many. He could wait for them here, or he could look around the canyon.

Alerting the local police was out. He had no business being here, and couldn't present a case anyway. Not legally. And returning to New York and running name and print checks on Lois-Lita-Nun and coming up with a justifiable solution would give the blonde too much time to disappear.

Bley stood beside him. "Which way to the trail?" Roersch asked.

They walked it in five minutes. They left buildings, cars, people . . . and approached that sky in the ground. Roersch looked ahead as he walked, and everything ended in space—a vista of emptiness beyond a certain point. They reached that point, and Roersch sucked in his breath. Bley said, "You're not dressed for hiking. And we've got to have water."

Roersch glanced at the warning sign. The Bright Angel Trail was nothing to be taken lightly. He looked past the railing, across and into the canyon. That was *definitely* not to be taken lightly! But he said, "I'll make do," and, "They haven't got water either," and turned the corner past railing and sign.

The trail dropped steeply. He stayed close to the rock wall, feeling stones through his thin-soled city shoes. They turned from black to reddish-brown as dust kicked up with each step. He was uncomfortable, and early as it was began to feel the sun burning his bare head.

After the first hairpin turn, he glanced back and saw Bley following. He looked at the edge, at the mile-deep chasm, and decided to glance back *often*. Bley might not have killed Keel, or anyone else . . . but he was still a Grade-A nut. And he might have some sort of stake in Lois; some sort of tie-in . . .

He came around a second turn, and saw the bearded man, John, ahead of him. John was sitting on the ground, back pressed to the rock wall, looking at the canyon. He heard Roersch, and scrambled erect. Roersch came closer, but stopped some five or six feet away. "Where's the girl?"

The bearded man waved his hand, down-trail. He looked past Roersch, and Roersch turned and moved to stand against the rock wall as Bley came up to him. Bley was the only one who stood to the right, near the chasm. Bley asked, "Why did you leave?"

The bearded man looked at Roersch. Bley said, "He's a police officer. From New York. Did you know Judith Keel?"

"I didn't really *know* her. I heard about her on the news

Monday afternoon, and I . . ." He interrupted himself to say, "Jesus, I only *phoned* her! I wanted her to stop seeing Lois!"

Bley was staring, and seemed about to say something, and Roersch wanted John to keep talking. "How did you meet Keel?"

"I followed her and Lois one night to Keel's place and got Keel's name from the doorman and checked the phone book and called and said I'd tell her friends, her family, what she was. If she didn't stop seeing Lois. But it was just a scare. I didn't *know* her friends or family. I only saw her that one time."

"You and Lois knew about me and Judy?" Bley said, and he was stunned, or still the greatest actor alive.

"You and Judy? You mean *you* knew her too? I thought this cop told you . . ."

"Why did you decide to leave New York after you heard about Keel's death?" Roersch asked.

"I was scared! What if that doorman remembered me and told the cops? What if Miss Keel told her friends and they were looking for me? What if they thought *I* did it? Jesus, how could I know *what* they would think! Lois was pushing for a hitch to Albuquerque, so I made up my mind and we left Monday about seven-thirty. We went to a club where Lois thought she could borrow some money . . ."

"*What* were you going to tell Judy's friends?" Bley asked.

"I wasn't *really*. I was just throwing a scare into her."

"That she was a lesbian," Roersch said.

Bley said, "That can't be!"

John said, "Maybe not all the way," trying to placate Bley. "But yeah, that's what I was scaring her with. Honest, Evan, I didn't know about you! Maybe Lois knew . . . but she never said anything . . . and how could she know we'd meet you? It was just a break, a coincidence, running into you at the Bantam Royal. And I never hurt Keel, honest." He looked at Roersch. "You're not going to take me back, are you? I'm going to L.A. with Evan . . ."

Roersch said, "Tell me about Lois. Did she call herself Lita Hoff, or Hoffer?"

John shook his head.

"The Nun?"

"I think so. Once, at the club where she worked, I think the bartender called her that. But it was noisy and I was bombed . . ."

"You visited her at the Bantam Royal? How about the Garden of Allah Massage Palace?"

"The Royal, yeah. The other place . . . I didn't know she worked at a massage parlor. Must have been before my time. We were together maybe five, six months, that's all."

Bley was touching his face again. He looked gray and sick, and spoke to John. "What about Alma-Jean? Do you know how she died?"

The bearded man said, "Oh God oh Jesus," and huddled into himself. "She's dead too? I chased her out after you and Lois left the room. We had a beef, but I couldn't find her in the parking lot. Those cops the next morning . . . that ambulance . . . oh Jesus, I never . . ." He looked at the canyon and sat down, quickly, as if his legs had folded. He mumbled something too low for Roersch to hear.

Roersch saw the man's fresh fear, and said, "Did Lois do anything just now, before we arrived?"

"She said she tripped," John mumbled. "She almost knocked me over the edge, but I was lucky. I just dropped and she went past me and said she was going ahead and I sat here, shaking, because I thought maybe she was out to get me. But I wasn't sure. Now I'm sure."

So was Roersch.

"Why did you leave?" Bley asked. "I asked you to wait and you didn't take your canteens . . ."

"Lois just took off," John said, still staring at the canyon. "I told her to wait but she said you'd meet us on the trail. She was scared but I swear I didn't know why. I was scared too, so I figured I'd go along and we'd wait and you'd find us." He looked at Bley. "Did she kill Keel? Did she kill Alma-Jean? Why?"

Bley looked at Roersch. Roersch said, "I don't know why," but he did, in a general way. The amputations and the eviscerations and the Countess Bathory and the Texas horrors—hatred of the thing which attracted her. Insanity and hatred and explosion and death. And she was on this trail and the chasm waited below and he had to get to her before his case dissolved in still another death; hers.

He began to walk. He went past the bearded man and walked faster. His feet hurt and he wanted to take off his jacket and couldn't because of his gun.

He heard footsteps behind him. Bley was following. The bearded man was following Bley.

Roersch lowered his head and concentrated on staying ahead of them. He didn't trust them. He *couldn't* trust them. The truth was coming out and he was adding it up and they knew it and The Nun feared it. The Nun somewhere in front of him and those two behind him and that chasm just a few feet away and a gun might not be enough —especially a pop-gun like his off-duty .25 automatic— with the three of them and death just one little shove to his right. Oh yes, much too old for this kind of thing, and a chance he wouldn't get much older.

The sun burned and his feet ached. He *poured* perspiration, and it wasn't all from exertion; far from it. And what if she kept going to the bottom? He'd never make it . . . and he had to make it . . . and why weren't there any other people on this fucking trail?

He kept going, faster and faster, and when he glanced back they were right there with him, maybe a little closer than before. They didn't talk to each other and they didn't talk to him. And what the hell was there to say anyway? He was out to nail their friend, their girl, whatever she was to them. And maybe she would say something that would implicate *them*. And he'd never sweated as much in all his life.

When the two girls in hiking gear came around the turn, struggling up the trail toward him with heavy packs on their backs, tanned, pretty faces straining, sweating, it didn't improve matters. He had to move to the right, to the outside of the trail, to the chasm side, and said, "Sweaty work," and took their surprised looks at his suit and shoes and fat and age. One said, "Wait'll you go *up*," and they were past him and he was able to hug the stone wall again. He glanced back, to see Bley step *far* to the outside, to the chasm side, and *look* down there. John refused to give way, flattening himself against the wall and earning cold looks from both hikers.

They were alone again, and Bley was coming on. Roersch hurried to the next turn and around it, and there was another turn ahead, always another turn ahead; this trail was a million hairpin turns and endless and getting dustier and hotter by the second.

He almost ran into her.

She was standing in the middle of the trail, just around the turn, looking out at the canyon. He came to a stop, stumbling a little, and she walked away from him and over to the edge. "There was no place to go," she said.

He said, "Easy now. You'll go to a hospital."

She said, "What for? I'm not sick," standing there with her left side to the canyon, her feet inches from space, facing him, looking at him. Then she said, "Fucking fathers. The old ones are the worst. They ask for the worst and they smell the worst. You want a massage, father?"

Her hatred and contempt and loathing were clear, and he flushed as he moved to stand against the wall. Bley came around the turn, and stopped. Roersch said, "Watch it," as John bumped Bley from behind. Bley swung around, shouting, "Scum!" and it was terrifying, on that trail, his twisting body, his flailing arms. And if it was terrifying to Roersch, it was a world-shaker for the bearded man . . . who ducked and cringed and then *ran* around Bley, risking the eternity side, and between Roersch and Lois-Lita-Nun to come to a stop a few feet beyond her, flat against the wall. He stared at Bley, and Bley looked away, at the girl, and said, voice shaking, "Why did you kill Judy? And Alma-Jean? How did you know about me?" He began to move toward her, face crazy white . . . and Roersch said, "Mr. Bley," as calmly as he could. "Don't rush her. See where she is. Let her alone. She'll come back with us and explain everything."

"Explain what?" she said, but her voice was different now, dull and quiet, and her face was different now, dull and despairing. She looked at Bley. "Explain that I've lost my chance because you're a goddamn closet queen?"

Bley was going to go for her. Roersch had to stop it and drew his gun. Bley didn't see and Roersch had to *make* him see; had to snap him out of his white-faced frenzy. He fired once, into the dust. The sound wasn't much. It hadn't been much even on the enclosed range; here it was a pop in eternity.

But the dust exploded and Bley jerked and stopped and looked at his feet and then at Roersch.

"Fucking fathers," the girl muttered. "Fucking guns and do this and do that. I was better off with Clothilde. If she hadn't laughed when I asked her to represent me. If she hadn't said those things about my never making it. If she hadn't *made* me do it."

Roersch put his gun away. "Who's Clothilde?" he asked quietly, conversationally.

"Who're *you?*" she said, contemptuously.

"He's a detective," Bley said, and his face remained white and he said it with definite satisfaction. "He's here to . . ."

"I'm here to help you get well," Roersch said, cursing the man and his private war, and the bearded hip and his private war. Here he was stuck in the middle and they'd blow it for him. "Tell me about Clothilde."

She smiled. "You tell *me*, Mr. Pig."

"All right. Correct me when I'm wrong, Lita. Fill in the missing parts, won't you, Nun?"

She *blinked.*

He said, "I don't know why you always wore wigs at the Garden of Allah and the Bantam Royal . . . that frosted wig, the blonde wigs, when your own hair is so nice."

She smiled, and touched her hair. Then her smile was wiped away as if by a hand, and she whispered, leaning toward Roersch, "Don't tell them about the massage palace, *please!*" as if they couldn't hear.

"All right. If you'll tell me about the wigs and the Bantam Royal."

She nodded.

"And about the girls."

"What girls?"

"Judy and Alma-Jean."

She said, "Oh," and chewed her lip a moment. "I was a winner. No one knew. How did you find out?"

He went on. "And Corinne Bain and Jane Austen."

"You found out about *all* of them?"

"I didn't know about Clothilde. She was your first, right?"

"In Australia. But that doesn't count, because it's too far away. Tell me about the others. How did you find out?"

"You promised to tell *me.*"

"Only about the wigs. I wore them so people wouldn't know me outside the clubs, in L.A. and New York. And outside the massage . . ." She shook her head; put her finger to her lips.

Roersch nodded. He flashed a glance at Bley and then at the bearded man. Bley was about three feet from Lois, in the center of the trail, much too close to her. But Roersch didn't want to do anything to break the momentum, the spell. John was down the trail, had edged even further from Lois, was now some seven or eight feet from her and still against the wall. Roersch himself was almost directly opposite her, she at the cliff's edge and he at the wall—perhaps four feet apart.

"At the clubs, it's real dark and the spotlights are colored and heavy because the law . . . they try to keep from getting busted. I wore the wigs and only the regulars could recognize me outside and even *they* didn't, sometimes, because I always dressed different." She looked at Bley. "You didn't know me, did you?"

"I never saw you before Monday night," Bley said, touching his face. "You're a liar if you say I did."

She laughed. "How do you think I met Judy? Don't you remember once before at the Bantam Royal?"

Bley said, "We did go there, some months ago. But *you* weren't there and Judy didn't like it and we left . . ."

"Sure, she *made* you take her home. After she went to the bathroom. Because I followed her there. Because the bitch sent me signals, *made* me follow her, the way they all did. The dirty bitches always made me . . ."

Roersch said, "And then you dated her," to stop her building rage, to stop her rocking body, so close to the edge. He needed her alive. "And Sunday night you killed her, because she made you do what you didn't want to do."

She said, "I only have to tell about the wigs. That's the deal." She spoke to Evan. "I was dancing on stage that time you and Judy came in. I was already on for three numbers and did two more, one while you were being seated and only one while you were watching. I was wearing my long blonde wig and panties and no top. They have heavy red-blue lighting at the Bantam. You looked right at me, and I looked right at Judy." She clapped her hands and laughed and rocked back and forth in glee. Roersch wanted to grab her and pull her from that edge, but didn't dare.

Bley said, "I don't believe it."

She said, "I don't *lie*, Evan!"

Roersch said, "You must have been shocked when you

saw Bley Monday night at the club," to end her anger, to end their private war, to get the one answer he didn't have.

"Was I ever! Here we're scrounging to get a little more bread to hitch out of town and I try the Bantam Royal and outside I see that green Jag with the big bent-back aerial for special radios or that phone you used to bug Judy with." She was looking at Bley. "I saw it once, when Judy made me split after one of your dumb calls, but I wasn't sure. And then you walked to the trunk and it was *you*, just like your picture on Judy's dresser!"

She turned back to Roersch. "What a wild card, right? I pushed John ahead of me into the club, hoping Evan wouldn't see him. And even if he did, I'd be alone inside. I told John to go to the crapper and let *me* handle the hitch and I'd work him into it one way or the other."

She was looking at Bley again. "When I saw your luggage, I figured maybe *you* were running. Maybe the cops were going to pin it on *you*. I mean, after all those things Judy said about you Sunday. Anyway, I had nothing to lose.

"You watched me when I was at the bar, and I watched you in the mirror. Then I pitched you, and you didn't bite. So I walked back to the bar for my pack, and posed a little, the leg and bending and all. That did it. And I'd already got Fasty to say he'd load your drinks, first to help with the pitch, and then to make you easier to handle when I sprung John on you. I didn't know you'd bomb out like you did, but that was even better and we were on our way.

"If John went for a rip-off like he'd been saying he might, okay. And if he didn't, still okay. It was a toss-up and we'd see. But then I got to like you and I'd never have let John try anything again . . . until last night. Why, Evan? How come you let . . . ?"

John and Bley were both talking at once, John saying, "I never tried anything!" and Bley asking how she happened to be at Keel's place Sunday . . . and whatever they were trying to drown out, to smother with words, wasn't as important as the answer to Bley's question. Roersch repeated it, when she continued to stare at Bley, chewing her lip, blinking her eyes as if about to cry.

"How did you happen to be at Judy's Sunday?"

"I'd been calling her. She'd said she wouldn't see me anymore, but I knew she was sending me signals. I *felt* it, and so I called almost every night and I called that night and she said you had just left and she was scared you'd come back again and hurt her and would I stay with her. I went there about twelve, maybe a little later, and she was *rude*, saying it was a mistake and I had to leave and that was after we'd done it and she was still tied up with those ropes you'd left there and she'd wanted to try it freaky and now she was yelling untie me and get out and I couldn't stand it and I shoved my bandana in her mouth and punished her." She was crying, swiping at her eyes. "It always comes to yelling and then I can't stand it because they *make* me do it and I never get to start the first day of the rest of my life. Jesus, so many bitches . . ." She shook her head wildly. She rocked in agony.

Roersch said, "What did you do with the telephone books, the knife?" to get her talking; to stop her from rocking so close to eternity.

She shrugged. "Down a sewer a few blocks away. I took the books 'cause they had my name. But I didn't *steal* anything like the radio said. I *never* stole anything." She was looking at Bley. "Judy wasn't worth a damn, hon. She was *rude*, even with her fancy talk, and if you'd bought *me* such nice things I'd've been your girl and never bothered with girls or anyone else. You know that, don't you? We can still be that way, can't we?"

Bley mumbled, "Yes."

Roersch said, "Why don't you and Evan walk back . . ."

She jerked her head around to Roersch. "I wasn't supposed to talk about anything but wigs! You didn't play fair! Goddamn it, you were supposed to talk about the other . . ."

"I'll do it now," Roersch said. "Alma-Jean. You met her in the parking lot, after she left the room." He waited for her nod. "You had a knife and you talked her into a sex scene near the garbage bin and then punished her."

She laughed. "You're not as smart as I thought. You're about as smart as you look. I didn't *have* a knife. I got one off the trays they leave outside the doors after room-service dinners; a steak knife. I watched for her, but not to make love. I was going to pay her back, the hillbilly cunt! But I figured one more time, why not, and it was in the back of a truck parked near the bin. It had branches and grass and gunny sacks, enough to cover her clothes, but not her. Some job getting her from there to the bin! Bet *you'd* have had trouble hauling that load of meat." She laughed and laughed, then cried and cried. "You're cheating again," she wept.

Roersch had enough now. The rest could come later. Her prints would be matched against prints on all four cases. She would be identified by the doorman and by others, witnesses who would come forward once her picture was printed, her story was out. He wanted her back in the lodge, and he wanted to call Hawly, and he wanted the legalities begun.

He said, "Well, that's not important now. That's over now. What's important is what you said . . . the first day of the rest of your life. A good doctor . . ."

"I've *been* that route!" she shouted. "I'm *not* mental anymore!"

And a couple appeared around the turn below them, starting toward them. Roersch stepped away from the wall and waved at them. They didn't seem to see him. He called, "Hold it a moment, please! We've got a situation here!"

The couple stopped. Lois said, "Why are you stopping them? You think I'm going to hurt someone? Why should

I? It doesn't matter what you know because Evan won't let you . . ." She stopped and raised both hands to her head and whispered, "Wait. Did I blow it? What did I say?" She looked at Evan. "Can he do anything to me, hon?"

Bley looked almost as scattered, almost as confused as she did. He said, "No, of course not. Let's go back to our room." He held out his hand, and for a moment it looked as if she'd take it . . . but then she jerked back and was swaying over emptiness. She steadied herself, and said, "You're lying, Evan! He knows *things* about me!" She looked at Roersch. "You know about Corinne and Jane. You said so."

"I was lying," Roersch said.

"Just knowing their *names*," she said . . . and she was right.

"C'mon now," Roersch said, moving his hand out a little.

She swayed back, and he dropped the hand.

"Tell me about Corinne and Jane," she said. "I want to know!"

"You killed Corinne in her car and you killed Jane in her room. They sent you signals and then they changed. You couldn't help it."

"That's right," she mumbled. "Corinne said I was *rough* and she didn't like long relationships, and Jane said her roommate was coming back and I couldn't see her anymore. After they *made* me do it. What else do you know?"

"That's all. Judy and Alma-Jean and Corinne and Jane made you do it. I'll say so and so will a doctor. You won't go to prison, Lois." That, at least, was the truth.

But it *would* go to the D.A.'s office; it *would* be four solveds; and Christ he had to get her off this trail!

The couple below was moving up again. He tried to wave them back while standing against the wall. The man seemed angry, and pulled the woman along by the hand. Roersch stepped out to block them, but the man said, "We've got our own *situation,* mister!" and kept to the right, and Roersch was forced toward the edge, toward Lois, and froze there, making himself small as the woman, towed along behind, murmured, "Sorry," and glared at the man.

They went past Bley and around the turn. Roersch was almost touching Lois, and put his hand on her arm, gently. She looked at it. He tightened his grip and stepped back a little, tugging her.

And she lunged away and toward the cliff ana he was caught off balance and she was strong, Jesus, he was going with her and to hell with makes and collars and promotions, he had to let go! And she had *his* arm and he couldn't believe it and screamed . . .

Evan listened to Lois and listened to Roersch and felt the rawness of his rectum, and the rawness of his thoughts. He was ugly now, uglier than he'd *ever* been.

It was worse than the other times. In the Air Corps when that captain gave him a lift to town and put a hand on his leg and he froze and he couldn't do anything because he was a cadet and this was a *captain* and all the way to town the hand moved and stopped, moved and stopped.

And at N.Y.U. with that strange guy Lormer who invited him to a party and there was only one girl and she was serving and he left early because he saw what it was and feared becoming part of it.

And last night, when he *was* part of it. When he should have gotten off Lois and *killed* John for the filthy act and he couldn't move and told himself it was the wine and pot and being inside Lois and besides he didn't really feel it. But God how he'd felt it! Hated it . . . the pain and degradation! Hated it . . . *and loved it.* The pulsing flesh inside him. The acceptance of pain and the acceptance of pleasure. The incredible moment when that tube of flesh had spasmed inside him, turning him female, flooding him with sperm.

What if he tried it again, and became *that?*

Too late to become that.

Too late to become anything new.

And what he already was, was total ugliness. Ugly life and ugly thoughts and ugly face. Too late to live with that.

And Lois talking and the impossible revelations and the ugliness he'd mated, the ugliness multiplying his own.

The people going past them and Roersch close to Lois and grasping her arm and she'd be in the newspapers and she'd tell about him and John and Roersch might tell about the Valentine's Day photograph and his mother would know . . .

Then Lois's hand curving up and she had Roersch's arm now and Roersch had let go but was still moving after her as she hung out into space.

That was what he wanted! For both of them!

But Marvin Bleywitz would be left.

He moved as if in a dream . . . slowly, trying to accelerate. He was holding Roersch, grasping the thick arm with his left hand. He was reaching around the man's chest, grasping Lois's wrist with his right, pulling at it, twisting it to make her let go of Roersch. He was digging in his heels and lunging back with all his strength. He was playing man again, and he wouldn't give in, and he had them both moving toward the trail and solid ground. Suddenly, Roersch was free of her and fell past him and against the wall. And Evan was alone with Lois.

He held that wrist, and wrapped the other arm around her. He held her steady, and moved her slightly toward him. She looked at him, and stopped pulling. She hung there and he could handle her and he caught movement from the corner of his eye where Roersch was struggling to his feet. She said, "Evan . . ." and in another minute Roersch would come to help and it would be out of his hands.

He began to go with Lois's body weight. Her eyes

widened, and now she tried to stop and couldn't, was tilting out over the canyon.

No, she couldn't stop, but *he* could . . . could release his arm from around her waist and let go of her wrist and she'd be gone.

Her left arm flailed in space. Her right wrist jerked in his grasp, fingers clawing up to clutch at him, to clutch at life. He held it down, *bent* it down. He could let her fall and say he'd saved the detective and couldn't save her and no one would blame him. She was a killer and he'd done his best and he'd be blameless.

But he had died last night and it only remained for him to be buried.

The slow motion ended. He simply leaned forward and giddiness seized him and they fell over the edge together.

She screamed, screamed, and he wanted *quiet*.

He let her go. She fell away, faster than he, and off to the side. He saw her bounce there and splatter there. He spread his arms and *flew*. He flew faster and faster, the world blurring, the breath torn from his mouth.

When the time came to scream, he couldn't.

20: | Sunday a.m.

At first he just stared at where Bley and the girl had been. Then he turned to the bearded man, wanting to say something. Because this *demanded* comment. Two people were gone, and one of them had saved his life just seconds ago, and it had all happened too fast, too damned fast and he had to make sense of it . . .

He didn't get the chance to say a word. John was on his hands and knees, crying, shaking, and already in motion. He scurried up the trail, a frantic animal in a cloud of dust, staying low until he was past Roersch. Then he straightened and disappeared around the turn.

Roersch also went into action. He ran after the bearded man. He ran hard, fast, around the turn and up the trail, holding his own, holding the distance between himself and his quarry . . . for a few seconds. Then his body failed him; his knees buckled. He hadn't been in any sort of condition to begin with, and the hike to find Lois hadn't helped, and the shock, the bone-chilling shock of sudden death, had put the final touches to his exhaustion.

He came to an abrupt halt, and crouched, drawing his gun at the same time. Exhausted or not, he did it smoothly, professionally. And brought up his left hand to steady the right, aiming at the flashing blue-jeaned legs which pumped up the trail toward the sanctuary of the next turn.

The trail climbed too steeply. It was no place to run. John was slowing, and Roersch knew he had time to squeeze off three or four shots, to move the gun in a slight arc, left to right, and send a curtain of bullets at John's knees. The odds were excellent he'd bring him down.

Then he'd have at least one of the three.

Then he'd have a witness to a confession of four murders.

He tightened his finger on the trigger . . . yet didn't fire. The running man was almost at the turn, and still Roersch didn't fire.

How could he justify putting bullets into a man's legs when that man had done nothing, and could insist he'd *heard* nothing? And when Roersch *and* his gun were here illegally?

How could he prove the murders without the murderer's confession?

How could he even report on his trip here without revealing his lies, his misdirection?

He lowered the gun. He realized he'd covered his tracks too well—doing everything himself; in his reports and talks with Deverney and Hawly. He'd been too clever and he'd been too dumb and his solution would come out of the blue and reveal him as a crooked cop.

He watched John turn the corner and disappear.

He put the gun back in his belt and buttoned his jacket over it.

He looked at the edge, and thought maybe he should go down and find Lois's body. There might be enough left to raise a set of prints. Those prints might match some in Keel's apartment; in other victims' homes. And her wig . . .

But what was the use? What good to try and convict the dead? He'd only convict himself.

Besides, she was already punished.

And what the hell good was it to keep remembering that the man he'd hunted down, the man he'd tried to squeeze, had saved his life?

That made him wince, and he stood there, confused, sweating, exhausted, head aching from sun and the terrible image of Bley and Lois going over the edge.

He had to find them! He couldn't think anymore, be logical anymore! Look what logic had brought him to! He had to bring them up; had to repay Marvin Bleywitz . . .

He'd actually begun walking back down the trail when footsteps pounded toward him. He got to the right, though he dreaded that edge, and two young men burst around the turn, almost together. He backed up. One panted, "Someone went over the edge! Arms spread, like a sky-diver!"

The other said, "There were two, maybe three! I *saw* them!"

"We gotta get help!" the first said, turning up the trail.

The other waved his arm disgustedly. *"Nothing'll* help. The girl broke like a rotten egg! The guy went a *mile* before he hit! The other, if there was . . . what could be left?" They both ran.

Roersch turned slowly and followed them, slogging up the trail in the heat and dust. He no longer felt exhaustion. He no longer felt the sun burning his head and the sweat streaking his face. He was numb.

There was nothing to be done.

21: | Tuesday p.m.

It was a hell of a day. Jones asked him what he'd done with his time off, and he said, "Hiked." Jones laughed at what he thought was a joke, and Roersch felt the charley horses of both legs that hadn't loosened yet. And a charley horse of the brain that would *never* loosen.

He'd solved four murders, and couldn't tell a soul.

Hawly called him in and discussed the information Roersch had added to the reports on Saturday. "This Lita Hoffer looks promising. Any chance of tying her into Keel?"

Roersch said he'd follow it up.

Hawly said not to forget that promotion. Roersch said he wouldn't.

How could he? He'd earned it, and would never get it.

He cut out at four, saying he had some legwork, and went home. All he wanted to do was sleep. Not only because he was tired. Because it was either that or booze to stop the goddamn thoughts. And he didn't feel like drinking. And he didn't think *anything* would erase the picture of those two falling into the canyon.

He sat in the kitchen and rubbed his face and wondered whether to take one of Helen's sleeping pills. They were still in the medicine chest.

He was on his way to the bathroom, when he suddenly went out the door and down the hall to Ruthie's. He rang the bell and she opened up.

"Hey, fuzz, what happened to you since Friday? Find another freebie?"

"Can I come in?" he asked.

"Not really. Got a trick in half an hour and have to shower and make up."

He came in anyway, pushing by her and going to the kitchen table. She stared at him a moment, then closed the door and went to the stove for the coffee pot. She poured him a cup. He stirred sugar into it and examined the spoon and sipped.

"What's wrong, Eddy?"

"What if I said cancel the trick? What would you do?"

She was about to sit down. She remained standing. She didn't look as pretty as usual, because he'd caught her by surprise. She wore an old housecoat and flat, worn slippers and her hair wasn't as clean and shiny as he remembered. Her face was pale and there were lines around her eyes. She looked kind of heavy without high heels.

Strangely, it comforted him. He liked it. She was a person, a woman, not a plastic sexpot. And maybe it comforted him because he thought there was a chance she'd settle for what Lois Chandler had called a "fucking father."

"I don't know what you mean, Eddy. You saying I should cancel a client because you want to take his place? You saying I *have* to?"

He shook his head. He drank coffee.

"That time you called to say goodnight. I . . . wondered."

He reached for his cigarettes. He'd bought a pack of Luckies, his old brand back when no one knew they could kill you. He lit one and cleared his throat. "Sit down," he muttered.

She sat down.

"How's Jen?"

"Fine. She loved our picking her up Friday. She asked . . ." She laughed. "She asked if you were her daddy."

"Too fucking old, right?" He was angry at her laughter.

"No, Jesus, I didn't mean that! It tickled me. What's wrong with you, Eddy? You don't look at me and . . . what'd I do?"

He looked at her. "I'm a detective sergeant. It's not much. Not much pay and not much retirement. Certainly not as much as *you* make. And it's all I'll ever have. But I was married and got along okay."

Her face showed shock. He quickly added, "Of course, the buck's not worth as much . . ."

The bell rang. She jumped up, spreading her hands. "Must be the trick. He came early the last time too."

He put down his cup and ground out his cigarette. He rose and went to the door. She said, "I'm sorry. Maybe later . . ."

He opened the door. The man was tall, slim, gray-haired, and dressed like an *Esquire* ad. He was smiling, but that changed when Roersch said, "Police," and pulled out his wallet and flashed his badge.

"Uh . . . is this the Kleinman residence?"

Roersch said, "No," and shut the door. He returned to the table and sat down. "He looked pretty good."

"Good for a hundred."

"I'll make it up," he muttered.

"You were saying something, Eddy. About being a sergeant and a sergeant's pay."

"Yeah, well." He fiddled with his cigarettes.

"Were you talking marriage to a *whore?*" Her voice trembled.

"Well, marriage, living together, whatever. I guess marriage, because of Jen." He dropped his eyes again. He wasn't worried about her saying no. He'd understand. Maybe he'd be relieved. Maybe not. He didn't know. But he was glad she'd dragged it out of him. "I like the kid," he said, when she said nothing.

"She likes you," Ruthie murmured.

"I think we'd get along. You'd have the same kind of apartment you have now, but my furniture is better."

"I know. I've seen it, remember?"

"Yeah. You wouldn't have much money, but you'd have Jen with you all the time."

"I'd want to move, because some people here wonder . . . hell, they *know.*"

He nodded. "We'd need an extra bedroom anyway . . ." Then he realized what she'd said. He looked up. She was pale, solemn. He said, "I'm fifty-six. You won't get the action . . ."

"I've *had* the action. Let's not worry about that until you're in a wheelchair. I'll settle for five good years."

"Hey, lady, make that ten, at least!"

She was coming around the table to him. She was bending and kissing his face. "I like you, Eddy. Is that enough?"

"Is it enough? It's all there is, Ruthie. The rest is bullshit."

They went into the bedroom, the cop and the whore, because the ten years weren't up yet; not even the five.

But Jesus, he was tired afterward! And when he said so and began dragging himself off the bed, she said he didn't have to. "Or have you forgotten we're going to be together from now on?"

He laughed. He *had* forgotten. He held her in his arms,

thinking he might tell her about solving four murders, maybe five . . . and knew he wouldn't and fell asleep.

Later, he got up to go to the bathroom. Walking through the kitchen, he took his cigarettes from the table and lit one, then looked at it. He kept walking and dropped the cigarette in the toilet. He crumpled the pack in his fist and tossed it into the waste basket.

He had a future again.

Such as it was.